www.sevenstonesofpower.com

THE
OPAL
CROWN

ANDY STONE

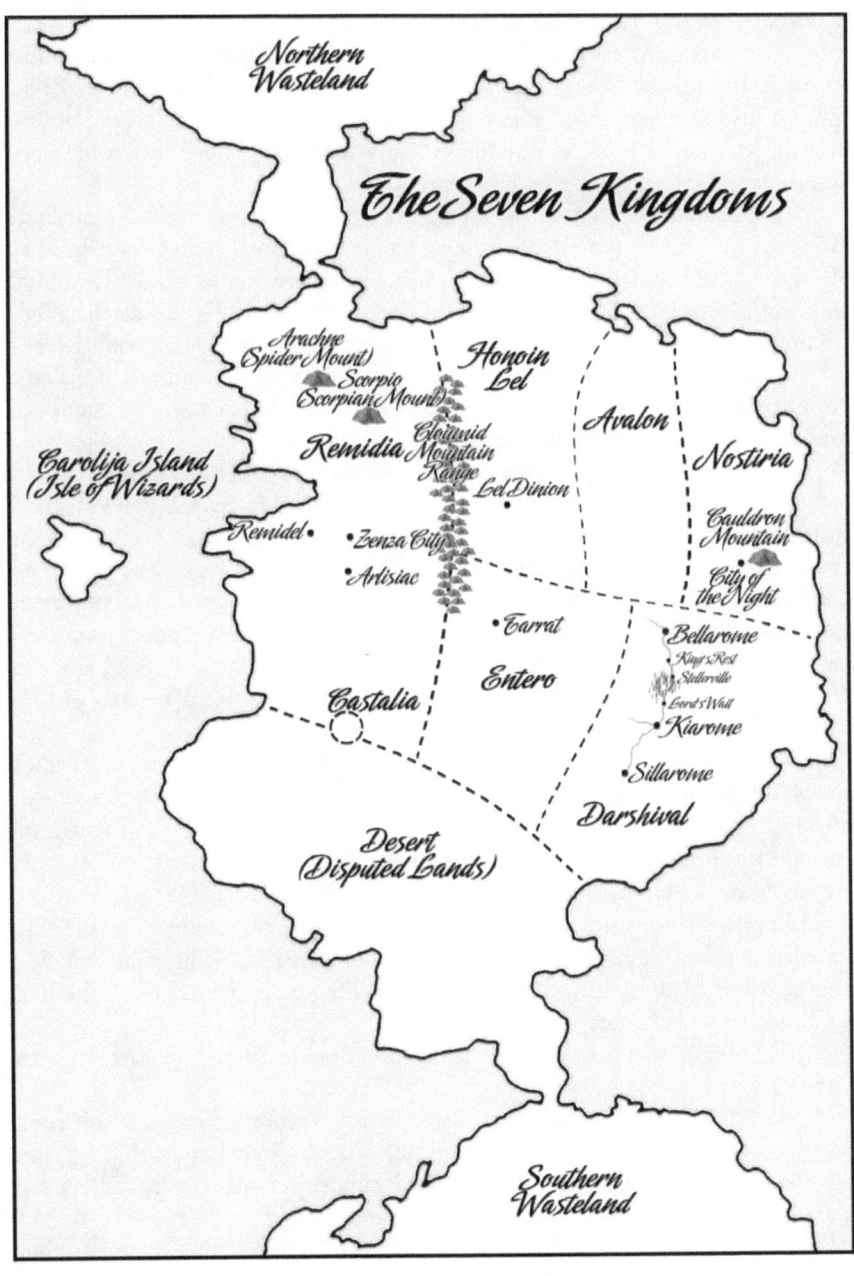

Prologue: A Need to Escape

The constant sound of iron chipping away at stone had almost become soothing. In the beginning it was rare for Augustus to have lucid moments, but he knew the Dark Knight had taken his mantle and left him to rot in the mines. It was almost poetic. He knew the diamonds that had funded his extravagant lifestyle had come from an unsavoury place, but he had no idea what he had put his citizens through. The conditions were less than what he would give to a street cur.

He had long given up trying to explain himself to the guards in his lucid moments, which were becoming closer and longer than before. He did not know if that was a good thing or a bad thing. With his mental state returning so too were the memories of his previous life as the High Chancellor. He doubted he would ever return to that life. No one except for the Dark Knight knew who or where he was. He doubted the Dark Knight would grow a conscience and let him out. At least when Augustus' mind was clouded he did not realise his grim fate.

"Hurry up slave," a gruff voice barked from behind him.

Augustus, the once great and powerful High Chancellor, had stopped working as he pondered his fate. That was a big mistake, one that could easily have him beaten. He had learnt that the hard way when he tried to protest his position and his true identity. The guards had not even given him a warning. They simply took him away and whipped him until he could no longer stand. Then he was dragged back to work. They did not even give him a chance to recover. It was at that point he thought he was going to die and he slipped back into his foggy existence.

Now that his mind had almost completely returned to its former glory the thought of escape was foremost. Although his body had been broken his mind was strong again. If he could remain unhurt for a long enough period of time then he would have the strength to try and escape. He knew he would only have one chance. If he was caught trying then he would certainly be put to death. That was a risk he was willing to take. He could not stand being confined underground, and knowing that evil was in control of his kingdom did not make his life any easier. The fact he had let himself be tricked made it even worse.

"Sorry boss," he slurred as to not draw any further attention to himself.

When he spoke his pick was already swinging towards the rock wall. It was the only way he could avoid a beating and even that was an off chance. He was not sure if he could last another session with the slave master. He did not think his body was strong enough.

"Don't let me catch you slacking off again," the slave watcher barked.

There was no real chance of the slave watcher remembering who he was. It was a throwaway line. Augustus was just fortunate that the slave watcher did not wish to attract attention to himself. If it had been a slave master who had caught him then it would have been an entirely different outcome.

If he ever escaped from the mines and returned to his position as High Chancellor then things would change. He would not let things continue the way they were and those who had misled him would also suffer. He could not believe that such a place existed under his rule. He had been blinded by the riches he had received. He had buried his head in the sand and believed the lies he had been told.

He did not have long to formulate a plan. The average life expectancy of someone in the mines was no more than a year, two at best. At least, as close to a year as they could estimate. The sun did not reach the depths of the mines and it was therefore impossible to tell the time of day. Augustus did not believe that they worked a standard day. They worked a lot harder and a lot longer. It was that treatment that vastly reduced their lives. Not only that, but also the meagre food and drink they were given. Even the strongest, healthiest of bodies would eventually succumb to the rigours of the mines.

It was not long before his arms started to ache again. He had been trapped in the mines for what he assumed to be about six months. The best way he could tell the time was by the length of his beard and hair. The guards didn't care for appearances. When the mines first opened and were used as a punishment for the most hardened of criminals they were allowed scissors to cut their hair, but soon enough the prisoners were using them to kill both others and themselves.

When he first arrived he thought he was going to die within the week. Being the High Chancellor he had never done any manual labour in his life. Even as a child he was protected from menial tasks. Now his body was being put through a test that would make the strongest man suffer. He felt as thought his arms would come off at the sockets each time his lifted the pick.

The longer he worked in the mines the stronger his body became. He was growing muscles where there had been few before, but it still did not make his life any easier. If he had a decent rest, then he would have been fine, but that was not the case. He was expected to work until he was told otherwise. If he was no longer able to work then he would be beaten. That, unfortunately, he had no control over.

Once the pain kicked in there was little chance for him to think about anything important. There was no chance for him to formulate a plan to escape. If he did not use all his mental capacity on his physical state then he was afraid he would lose control. That would mean another beating or maybe worse. He did not know how many more beatings he would be able to withstand until his body gave out.

As he chipped away at the stone he was sure there was something he could do to be able to do to escape. A new hope filled his body. He hoped that it would remain there for a least the rest of the day. It was the only thing that could keep him going.

Even when he was finally allowed to return to his cell to rest there was little satisfaction. The cells, which he was sure were originally designed for one person, housed at least half a dozen slaves. There was one bed and that always seemed to be taken whenever Augustus wanted to rest. He had made the mistake of asking for the bed, or really demanding the bed, when he first arrived. The result was a severe beating by his fellow inmates.

At least there were a number of dirty blankets and pillows to give him some warmth and comfort, but it didn't take long for the sweat and heat of the day's, or maybe night's, work to wear off and the chill of the mines to set in. Without the blankets he knew they would all soon die of exposure. Even with them it was far from comfortable. All they had to wear were the dirty rags they were either wearing when they arrived or those of the slaves who had died before them.

None of the slaves wanted to speak with each other and Augustus was grateful for the time to himself. If he was ever going to work out a plan to escape it was the only time he had. Just as the thoughts entered his mind his consciousness started to fade. At first he thought it was the effects of his hard labour, but he knew it was something different. Slowly he faded into the haze that had dogged his ability to think for as long as he could remember.

***

It had taken Minerva just over four weeks to reach the Isle of Wizards. She had not run into any major trouble, but she did have a small skirmish with a group of bandits on the highway to Remidel. They did not really stand a chance. Minerva sensed their attack before they started and she was able to create a spell to knock the bandits off their feet. At first they did not know what was happening and continued trying to attack, so Minerva made them suffer for their ignorance. A few blows around the head and they soon understood that things were not going to plan. Eventually they gave up and went running back into the forest. Minerva had to laugh as they fled from her. She did enjoy turning the tables on such people. They would think twice the next time they decided to attack a lone woman on the road.

She did not get to savour her victory for long. She new what she was riding towards. Her brethren would not be happy with the news she had for them. They had disagreed with her decision to leave the island. She knew how they had reacted to Eldred leaving and as much as they could never disown one of the council they had certainly tried their best. No matter the text they read, and they all loved reading text, they all came back to the same conclusion. To remove a member of the Council of Wizards required a unanimous vote, including the vote of the member being dismissed.

As much as she always knew it was going to happen it was still something she wished she did not have to do. She was ingrained in the prophecy and she would have to pull the other five in with her and Eldred. Even though she had not been away for long it seemed like a lifetime.

During her travels she had changed her facade into her usual appearance she had on the island. The young woman turned into a woman of middle age with shoulder length blonde hair. As much as she had enjoyed the younger woman it was something she wore only in Castalia. It helped to keep those she didn't want to know from knowing who she was. Although the other wizards would recognise her regardless of how she looked she had to admit her old facade felt much more comfortable. The light blue dress she wore fit tightly around her lithe figure.

Once she took her first step off the boat onto the white sandy beach she instantly felt as though she was home. Although she had been born in Castalia, Carolija Island had been her home for more years than she could remember. She took a deep breath and sucked in the salty air. She thought there was no better scent in the world.

The oarsmen seemed happy to have their boat back on the water. Although it was considered an honour to be able to sail the Isle of Wizards being so close to it wasn't as appealing. Very few sailors were allowed to sail there and those that did had been told stories of the mysterious island and they were never pleasant.

Minerva took her shoes off and let he toes play with the soft sand. There was little time for her to savour the moment, but she would take all she could. Although she had not sent a message of her arrival she knew the other wizards would be waiting for her. As much as they tried, they could not ignore the prophecy forever.

The small village they had created was a short walk from the beach through a scattering of coconut palms. Minerva took her time. It wasn't because she enjoyed the feeling of the sand and soft grass under her feet, it was because she was trying to work out what she was going to tell the others. Although she had been having the conversation over and over in her head on the journey from Castalia she had still not come up with a solution. In the end she would just have to work it out as the conversation progressed.

The wizards would be gathered at the meeting hall in the middle of their little village. If no one knew any better they would think it was the focal point of the island. The seven wizards had their buildings, houses, studies and libraries fanned out around the hall. They only met in the meeting hall on very rare occasions when they would all need to be gathered together. Despite Eldred's absence Minerva knew that's where they would all be.

The hall was simple in design. A log building constructed from the island's palm trees. It was completely different from the other buildings around the island that were constructed from materials from the owner's home kingdoms. Inside there was a large round table suitable for the seven wizards to comfortably sit. There was no head at the table as there was no true leader of the wizards. Seven chairs of the same highbacked design were placed evenly around the table.

"What news have you brought us?" Brielle asked as soon as she entered the room.

Minerva had never really liked the wizard from Entero. She did not know what it was, but there was something about her that just didn't sit right. Minerva did nothing to show her true feelings, that was not the way things were done. Maybe it was the fact that there were never any pleasantries from Brielle. She was always straight down to business.

Brielle always kept her dark brown hair in a bun at the back of her head. Although she was in fact younger than Minerva her facade said otherwise. Minerva didn't know why she wore the subtle wrinkles of age on her face. She reminded Minerva of a school teacher she had when she was younger. Maybe that's why she never liked her. Brielle wore a simple robe of green and a silver ring with an emerald on her right index finger. Although her clothes changed, Minerva could never recall seeing her without the ring on one of her fingers.

"It is good to see you too," she couldn't resist the little dig.

"We are glad you are back," Drake Auger added before Brielle had a chance to speak. "But I think you can understand our need for abruptness."

There was something about Drake that Minerva liked. He could always change her mood from angry to happy. It might have been the fact that he was the youngest of the seven wizards. He liked to play on the fact. He always kept a young facade and for those who didn't know him they would have guessed he was in his mid-twenties. His true age, like all the wizards, was unknown, but he was well into his hundreds. He had a soft demeanour. His face was always clean shaven and his dark hair was always brushed to shoulder length. His blue eyes sparkled whenever any light fell on them. If Minerva was ever going to fall in love again she could see herself doing it with Drake.

"Of course my dear, I understand completely," she spoke to Drake as if he were her child. She liked to play the mother figure to his youth-like appearance. "I would not have come here unless the situation was dire."

"We appreciate that fact. Now if you would please continue," Brielle could not let it go.

Minerva wanted to walk around the table and smack her across the face. The thought crossed her mind that Brielle could possibly be jealous of the ease in which she spoke with Drake. It was quite possible that Brielle herself was in love with him. That thought made a lot of sense.

"Please, Minerva," Gwydion 'r Brudiwr spoke calmly.

The wizard from Nostiria, and possibly the last of his kind from the west of the border, was the eldest of the seven and the father figure of the group. Although they were all treated as equals they all treated him as their unofficial leader. His hair was wispy white which matched his beard. It had been a long time since he had cut his facial hair or the hair on his head for that matter. He did nothing to reduce the signs of aging that didn't come naturally to a wizard. Although he looked aged there was nothing but strength in his demeanour. He was not only the eldest, but also the strongest of the seven. That also added to the aura of respect that followed him.

"If you could explain to us your reason for being here that would be greatly appreciated," Gwydion continued.

There was no way Minerva could say anything to Gwydion. She respected the wizard more than anyone else. His words commanded respect. She had not planned on having a combative attitude, but that was just the way Brielle had made her feel. She wished any of the others had spoken first.

"There is now a Dark Knight in command of Castalia," Minerva didn't waste anymore time.

No one could believe what they were hearing. She knew Brielle would blame her and she couldn't really argue with the fact. They had known the High Chancellor was in trouble, that was why Minerva had gone there. They had no idea when the danger would come, but that was not the point. If anything had happened to the High Chancellor then it would be her fault.

She continued to explain everything that had happened once Alaric had reached the city. With each word she hoped they would understand her point of view. She could see in Brielle's face that she did not approve of what she had done. Minerva had expected such a response. She could only hope that no one else felt the same way. As much as no one had agreed with her decision to leave the island they would have to agree it was worthwhile.

"That is indeed a disturbing story," Gwydion spoke calmly.

"This is unforgivable," Brielle snapped as it seemed that Gwydion was not going to berate her.

"Enough Brielle," Ulman Zauber spoke for the first time.

The Wizard from Darshival and brother of Eldred sat with his legs crossed and his feet on the table. He was the least likely person to be a wizard in the room. He preferred to be physically fit rather than mentally fit. A trait that was not suited to a wizard. His broad shoulders looked more like those of a Darshivallian soldier. He kept his head shaved almost to the skin and he also liked to keep his appearance as that of a man of much younger years. There was no real reason to look in his forties, besides the fact it made him feel better about himself.

He was the only one who had carried a weapon into the meeting room. His large claymore was leaning against his chair. He normally wore it strapped to his back, but that was not conducive to sitting. There was no real reason to carry a weapon on the island. There was no one else there except for the six wizards and their small retinue of retainers. Any traders who visited the island would only travel as far as the beach and then leave again.

"This is no one's fault," Ulman continued in his gruff voice.

"Remember we all disagreed with the decision Minerva made to leave and no one was more vocal on the point than you Brielle. It seems as though she knows more than we do," Gwydion replied.

Brielle did not like being rebuked by the two wizards. Although they had not said as much she knew what they meant. Abruptly she stood and walked out of the room. She was not going to sit around whilst they were behaving like that.

"What is wrong with her?" Minerva had to do her best not to smile as she asked the question.

The four remaining wizards looked at each other with concern. It was obvious they were not sure if they wanted to tell Minerva what was wrong with Brielle. They all knew the two rarely saw eye to eye and this was not going to make it any better.

"She had a vision recently," Althea spoke for the first time. It had been agreed that she would break the news as she had the most information. Of all the seven she was closest to Brielle. In the right light the two could have been mistaken for twins. Althea had short brown hair and a motherly look about her. Although she didn't really need them she wore a thin rimmed pair of glasses. It was rumoured that before she became a wizard she really did need the glasses and she wore them as a matter of habit. "We do not know the full extent yet, but it seems as though she believes that you will do something to betray us." Althea knew more, but she didn't feel it was her place to divulge any further information.

"That is impossible," Minerva raised her voice and was about to stand, but she resisted the urge. "You know that she has always had it in for me. She has never liked me."

"I think this is the reason why," Althea continued to explain. "We are yet to know anymore information, but we have all agreed that you should stay on the island until we know more."

"So you are imprisoning me?" Minerva did not like what she was hearing. It had never been done before, but it was certainly something the five could achieve if they wanted to.

"No, it is nothing like that," Ulman's voice was not good for diplomacy. It was great for barking orders, but not for calming situations. "We just think it would be better until we know more about her vision." He shot Althea a look, but there was no response.

It was not at all what Minerva had expected when she returned home. She was wondering if her urge to return had been natural, but now she was starting to doubt it. They must have been calling to her. It had been a trap. She could not believe that they had done such a thing.

"I have things to do. I have to get back to Castalia. The High Chancellor needs me," there was panic starting to come into her voice.

"There is time. For now you have to stay here," Gwydion spoke again. "I know this is hard to understand, but you must trust us. You need to speak with Brielle. She will explain things to you."

"I am sure she *will* explain things to me." It was all Minerva could do to remain seated. She knew the other four had drawn in some energy. It was not much, but it would be enough to contain her. She was quickly running out of ideas. "It looks as though I do not have a choice."

"I am sorry Minerva. We all believe this is for the best." Gwydion didn't know what else he to say.

The old wizard led Minerva from the meeting room. There was no need for further discussion. She was under house arrest, there was no better word for it. She could not believe what was happening. She had always known that Brielle had it in for her, but she never believed she would go so far. There was nothing else she could do for the moment, but she would stay alert. If the chance came then she would break free.

***

Nyrra could feel that he was getting close. He had to be getting close. He had travelled all around the cursed land, but just when he thought he was close the feeling disappeared. He wished he had the Jade stone. With the help of that stone it would only be a matter of days before he had the Ruby stone again. Once that happened there would be no stopping him.

His Dark Knights had been disappointing. There were only a few left and they did not look as though they were going to last long, but that was not the point. If they had done what he had asked then things would be over much sooner, but it didn't seem that was going to happen. They were serving their purpose and it would all come to bear when the time mattered. All he had to do was find the Ruby stone. That was the most important thing to him.

He sat on top of the mountain again. It was where he felt most at home, at least when he was away. He could not return to his fortress until he had the stone. Then he would be able to return and then he would be able to rule. The snow fell around him, but didn't fall on him. He would never let the cold, wet snow touch him. He liked fire and heat. That was where he really wanted to be, but not until he was done. It would be too easy to become complacent and that was when he would fail.

Again he could feel the great creature sleeping in the bowels of the mountain. He could feel the pure evil radiating from below. That was the reason he liked being on the mountain. He thought of waking the sleeping beast, but he knew it was not the right time. He had to let it sleep. When the time was right the great monster would cause its own kind of mayhem. He would just have to wait for that day to come.

Now it was time to be off again. He could sense something in the back of his mind. Again he had purpose and if this was the right time then he would be victorious. He knew the Cursed One was behind time. His Dark Knight's had successfully stalled him to the point that he could not recover. He was happy to sacrifice his Dark Knights if it caused the Cursed One heartache. There was a surprise he would have waiting, but that was a thought for another time. There was still much to be done before he could do anything with his Dark Knights.

It was the location of the Ruby stone that was thick in his mind as he blinked off the mountain.

***

Za'aroz had remained hidden in his room ever since Alaric had disappeared from the chapel. He had thought he had trapped the Cursed One. He half expected to see the Great Lord appear and punish him. That is why he remained in his private apartment. He liked the life of the High Chancellor and he didn't want anything to ruin it.

Everyone else just assumed his mood was due to losing the people who had tried to steal from him. They did not know what was really happening and that's the way Za'aroz wanted to keep it. They were as good as his slaves and they did not need to know anything else.

It would be time for him to make a decision soon. Castalia had a large army and he needed to use it to fight the Alliance. The only problem was that he didn't know if he should move it or wait for the Alliance to come to him. He was protected behind his walls, but he did not know if that was the best thing for the Great Lord. He knew that Ra'naroz had failed. He knew that he would be punished. That would give him a good opportunity to come into the Great Lord's favour.

Za'aroz could not believe the Topaz stone had been in the Great Cathedral all along. He could not believe that his brother had so easily given it to the Cursed One. He was losing touch with the prophecy. He should have known the stone was there and he should have known that Alaric was coming to get it. He had to spend more time retuning himself to the world around him. It would be the only way he would remain alive long enough to see the Great Lord victorious.

He pulled on the rope next to his chair and a bell rang somewhere below him. He had suddenly had an idea and he needed to put it into place. He hoped it was the right one.

"Yes, High Chancellor." A young man entered the room. He prostrated a number of times.

"Have the army mobilised inside the inner city," his attitude had perked up.

"Yes, High Chancellor, but are we under attack?" the serving man asked, a little confused with the command.

"No, but I believe that it will not be long. We need to be prepared," he looked out of the window as he spoke. He almost expected to see an army coming over the horizon.

"Yes, sir," he seemed happy enough with the answer.

Za'aroz spent the rest of the day staring out of the window. There was something about his meeting with Alaric that had disturbed him. He didn't want to admit that Alaric had been too strong for him. There was nothing he could do to stop the Cursed One from leaving. That was a disturbing thought. He didn't know what he could do if Alaric returned. He could not use his position as High Chancellor as a defence forever. There was no doubt that Alaric would kill him given half a chance. He had a lot to ponder on and not much time to come up with a solution.

Chapter 1: Return to Jarrat

The throne room was nearly full when Alaric suddenly appeared. His appearance caused the room to break into chaos. No one was as surprised as Duke Xarles who was sitting on the throne. Alaric and Linus suddenly appeared to his right without any warning and Xarles nearly jumped out of his skin. His heart was racing and he started breathing heavily. He quickly ran his hands through his short blonde hair.

Alaric had not planned to arrive in the throne room. He thought it would be better to arrive in the courtyard, but his timing was a little off. It was a long leap from Castalia and it was not an exact science. He had hoped for a more secret arrival, but all hope of that had gone.

"What are you doing here?" Xarles asked when he regained his breath.

"I am sorry. I did not mean to land here," there was a strange look on Alaric's face. His bronzed skin, even more tanned from his time in Castalia, looked out of place in the throne room. The nobles watching the scene had no idea what was happening. "I need to find Alena." Alaric didn't want to wait on normal pleasantries. He knew time was precious and there was none to waste. Deep down he knew Alena needed to be with him in the end and if she was dead then it would all be for nothing.

There was only one thing on his mind and that was saving her. He had no idea if she was still alive. His trip to Castalia had taken longer than it should, he knew that. He had to believe she was still alive. He could not believe the prophecy would let him fail at something so important.

Xarles did not know what to say. He was still in shock. Everyone in the room had stopped talking. They all wanted to hear what the newcomers had to say. Those at the front of the room were able to recognise Alaric, but they did not know who the other man was. All they could tell was that he did not look comfortable. His face was deathly pale. They thought he was about to lose consciousness, but he remained on his feet.

Linus was dressed in his white priest robes. The old man was clearly shaken from the experience of Alaric transporting them from Castalia to Jarrat. His soft white hair, which was normally closely brushed to his scalp, looked windblown. A drop of sweat had also appeared on his forehead. Nausea had set in from the journey and as much as he wanted to ask questions he had to concentrate on keeping the contents of his stomach inside.

"Please Xarles. I need to find Alena," Alaric should have been able to find her room on his own, but he couldn't.

There was a great roar inside his head and there was nothing he could do to silence it. It had caused his mind to become clouded and he could not remember the simplest things. All he knew was that he had one task that he had to achieve. No other thoughts could enter his mind, including the location of Alena's room.

Xarles looked at Alaric and shrunk back slightly. There was definitely something different about him. At first he didn't realise what it was, but suddenly it dawned on him. His eyes, which he was sure were naturally green, were bright yellow. There was no white and only the pupil was breaking the colour.

He could only look Alaric in the eyes for a moment before he had to look away. When he looked down he saw Alaric was holding a golden sceptre in his right hand. Inset at the top was a yellow gem. The most shocking thing was that the stone was pulsating with light. It was not at all something Xarles was expecting.

"She is in the same place as when you left." Xarles was still coming to terms with the sudden arrival of the pair. Of all the questions he wanted to ask all he could do was answer Alaric's.

"I will need someone to escort us." Alaric's was becoming annoyed. Things were taking longer than he wanted. The noise inside his head was almost overpowering. He knew it was the Topaz stone trying to control him.

Xarles didn't know how to respond. He looked out at the crowd for answers, but all they did was stare back expectantly. The morning meeting had ended up so much better than expected. They were sure the information they could gather would be very important to them later. Those who had not turned up to the meeting or had left early would be at a great disadvantage.

"Of course." Xarles shook his head. He did not know what he was thinking. "I will escort you myself." it was more out of curiosity than anything else. "My council is over for the day. Go about your own business now." He addressed the crowd of nobles with the most commanding voice he could muster.

It was not going to be easy to escape the prying eyes of the nobles. They had the advantage of exiting out of the door from behind the thrones, but the nobles would be quick to find them if they did not hurry. Xarles thought about forbidding them from following, but he didn't want to have to dish out punishments for those who disobeyed.

The duke led them out through the back door. Even though he had recovered from the initial shock he still felt as though something was not right with Alaric. Although he had only met the man briefly in the past he still noticed the difference. The yellow eyes were the most disturbing change, but there was also something in his voice that made Xarles nervous.

Alaric didn't bother knocking on the door once they reached the apartment where Alena was resting. He simply pushed it open and walked into the room. He looked around quickly until his eyes locked on the bed where Alena was unconscious. He ignored the fact that Eldred was lying on a bed next to her in a similar condition. He also didn't notice that his old friend Bern had risen when he entered.

"No, no, no. This is not right. Kill them. Kill them all," the voice barked orders inside his head. As much as he didn't like the voice he was grateful the yelling and screaming had stopped. At least he would be able to concentrate at the job at hand. He needed to overpower the Topaz stone and save Alena's life.

"I have to save Alena." That was the only thought in his head and it was fading quickly. He could feel himself slipping away.

"Quickly Alaric!" Bern spoke when he realised who it was. He was so excited that he didn't notice the change in his old friend. "Alena does not have much time left. It has been three hours since Eldred lost consciousness."

Alaric had not moved since he had entered the apartment. Bern looked at him for the first time and the first thing he noticed was the yellow ring around Alaric's irises. He took a step back when he saw it. He instantly knew that something was wrong and it wasn't until his eyes settled on the yellow stone did he realise what it was. The stone was glowing softly as it had in the throne room.

"You can't do this Alaric," the voice screamed inside his mind. "You have to kill them before they kill you. You cannot trust them. They will betray you. You know this is true."

Alaric could not move. His mind was filled with the ranting of the Topaz stone. All other thoughts had left him. He could not even remember what he was doing in the room. He could feel his very essence slipping away. He had to be strong, but there was no will left in his body.

"Alaric!" Bern grabbed Alaric's arm as he spoke.

Alaric struck out at Bern when he felt his touch knocking his old friend across the room. Bern could not believe the strength it took to do so. There was no doubt that the Topaz stone was taking control.

He wished Eldred had not lost consciousness. With the sudden movement the voice started screaming inside his mind again and Alaric forgot what he was trying to do.

"You have to be strong Alaric," Bern called out as he picked himself off the floor. "Do not let the stone take control of you."

"What is he talking about?" Xarles asked the old man standing next to him.

"I have no idea," Linus was just as clueless. "I am sure we are about to find out."

Bern's words just broke through the incessant screaming in Alaric's mind. It was as soft as a whisper, but it gave Alaric something else to concentrate on. For a moment he thought he could remember something, but it quickly disappeared.

"That's right Alaric. It is time to take control. It is time to destroy them all," the voice was almost gloating.

"I... I..." Alaric didn't know how to respond. He could do nothing to fight against the stone.

"You have to fight it Alaric. You are stronger than you think. You have been able to fight off the other stones." Bern was not going to give up.

"Kill them all," the voice continued over and over again.

Alaric grasped the sceptre and held it in front of him. The Topaz stone glowed even brighter. The entire room had a yellow tinge to it and Alaric could feel the power rippling through his body. The feeling was both terrifying and exhilarating at the same time. Alaric wanted to hold onto to it for the rest of his life.

"That's right," the voice sounded pleased with itself. "Do what I command."

The stone started to glow even brighter as the battle within his mind continued.

"Alaric!" Bern shouted. He wished that either Eldred or the entity residing in his body would awaken. "You must fight the stone. You have to take control."

The words rattled Alaric. They were only soft, but they were enough to break through the screaming. He recognised the voice, but he could not place from where. He knew the words made sense, but he did not know why. There was a struggle happening, but he did not know who he was fighting with.

"Come on Alaric," Bern continued to yell. He thought he could see some recognition on Alaric's face, but he could not be completely sure. "Don't give up. We have come too far."

"What am I doing?" Alaric spoke with his mind's voice. His words were clearly heard over the screaming.

"You are doing what you are supposed to do. You are going to kill those who mean to do you harm," the voice was becoming less cocky.

"No, that is not right." Alaric placed his free hand up to his head. He wanted to drop the sceptre, but he knew that would be impossible. "I am in control." Alaric strained.

"I have been kind to you so far. If you go against me I can be just as cruel," the voice laughed.

Alaric suddenly dropped to his knees. A wave of pain ripped through his body. All he could do was stay motionless and suffer the pain. He wanted to drop the sceptre, but his hand would not release its grip. He was beginning to understand the severity of the situation. He had let the Topaz stone take control of his body, something he knew he should not have done. It was going to be even harder for him to regain control, but he knew he had the strength.

"I will not let you do this," Alaric clenched his teeth and almost spoke verbally.

"What is happening?" Xarles asked Bern as he thought his life may be in danger.

"Alaric is wrestling with a great power inside himself. We can only hope that he wins," Bern's voice was a lot calmer than it should have been.

"You cannot defeat me. Just do what I say and I will make you feel good again," there was a slight strain in its voice.

It was a tempting deal. All Alaric felt was pain. His entire body hurt and the memory of the intense feeling of pleasure remained in his mind. It would be easy to except the offer, but he knew there was something he had to do. He needed to take control.

"I have beaten all the others and I will beat you," his mind's strength returned.

The stone glowed even brighter as Alaric tried to regain control. Bern was the only one who really knew what was happening and that was only a vague idea. Linus and Xarles only remained in the room because they wanted to find out what was happening. If they really knew they would have left a long time ago.

"I will see you dead before I help you heal one of them," if the voice could spit then Alaric thought that it did.

"You are not as strong as you think," Alaric strained, but he was already starting to see results.

At the mention of healing Alaric suddenly remembered what he was supposed to do. A vision of Alena popped into his mind. It pushed back the fog the stone had created. Her face was aglow. She wore a white silk dress that hung tightly to her body and her blonde hair swished gently behind her back. Alaric thought she was the most beautiful sight in the world. It was because of her he had returned to Jarrat. It was Alena he needed to heal. He could not let her die. He could not live with himself if he let her die.

"This is my body. You have no place being here," Alaric's voice roared in his head.

When he finished speaking to the stone he returned to his feet. His willpower had increased and he was starting to regain control of his body. The stone's glow started to lose its intensity. It was a clear sign to all in the room that Alaric was winning the battle.

"Now, you cannot make me do it. Please, you cannot make me do this," the voice had suddenly changed. It was now begging Alaric to do its will.

"You work for me. You will do what I command you to do and there is going to be no further debate." Alaric's body suddenly became pain free.

Alaric had defeated the stone. The memory of Alena was just what he needed to overcome the temptation to lie down. He could still hear the voice, but it had changed to a whimper in the back of his mind. He was willing to allow the stone that much for the moment. He would deal with it completely later.

Slowly Alaric looked around the room, as if he was seeing it for the first time. Bern noticed there was still a yellow tinge to his eyes, but it was nowhere near as strong as it had been. He wasn't sure if it was a good sign or a bad sign. Alaric ignored the look on his face and he focused his full attention on Alena. He could not believe she looked closer to death than the last time he had seen her. Her skin was completely pale and looked cold. There looked to be no life left in her and for a moment Alaric thought he had wasted too much time.

"There is no time to waste," Bern wasn't sure if he should have spoken, but he couldn't contain himself.

Alaric didn't shift his attention, but Bern's words gave him hope. He needed to concentrate on Alena if he was going to help her. He couldn't believe she was dead. It was no simple disease that had caused her illness. Ra'naroz did something to her and he had to work out what it was before he could heal her. It was not going to be as easy as everyone had hoped.

The stone started to glow again as Alaric concentrated on its healing power. Again the voice started to roar, but Alaric quickly silenced it. He was not going to give the stone another chance to take control.

"I need your help." Alaric had no idea what he was doing.

"Now you ask for my assistance," the voice sounded superior.

"I do not ask for it, I demand it," Alaric's mind-voice boomed.

The stone's voice started to whimper again. Alaric had finally taken control. The stone would do what it was told. Alaric did not think he had the strength to overcome it, but he was not about to submit.

"Now tell me how to find the disease," Alaric commanded.

"Touch me to her chest and concentrate on her body. It shouldn't take you too long to find the sickness," the voice had become subservient.

Alaric did as he was instructed. He had no doubt the stone was trying to help. He commanded the stone and there was nothing it could do about it, at least not for the moment. His love for Alena had given him strength and the Topaz stone knew it could not overpower him. There was still a risk Alaric's mind could split, but that was always going to be a risk.

Once the stone touched Alena's chest his reality suddenly shifted. The room spun once and he felt like he was going to fall over. Before he lost his balance everything disappeared. Everything around him was black. Even though there was no light he could still see himself. At first he thought the stone had betrayed him, but then he felt something. There was another presence nearby. He looked around, at least as best he could in the nothingness, and at first there was nothing there. As he did another turn he thought he saw a shimmer of yellow light in the distance, at least what he assumed was the distance, it was impossible to gauge anything in his current state.

It did not take long for the light to come closer. Alaric could see a silhouette. He thought it looked as though it was a man, but he could not be completely sure.

"What do you want?" the words were Alaric's, but they did not come from his mouth. The words echoed around the space around them.

"I am here to help," this time the words originated from inside the yellow light.

Suddenly Alaric remembered why he was there. It was not easy staying in control in such a place. There was no telling how long they had been there. Alaric had to concentrate to keep his sanity. The nothingness had an overpowering presence and it threatened to swallow him whole.

"Let's get moving," Alaric's voice echoed again.

The light started moving away from him. Alaric wanted to start walking, but he had no idea how to move. He had been in the void before, but that was a distant memory. The light moved around at the edge of his vision. It did not completely disappear, but it did not get any closer. Not being able to move was frustrating. He knew he had to be closer to the light. He also knew he had the ability to move, but he just couldn't remember.

"You need to be over here. I think I have found something," the voice called out to him.

Alaric tried his best to move, but nothing happened. The thought consumed him. All he wanted to do was to take a step forward. Things worked a lot differently in the void. Alaric had to change his perception if he was going to get anywhere. That thought consumed him. Nothing else mattered.

"What are you doing?" the voice sounded confused. "What are you waiting for? There is not much time left," the voice urged.

Alaric didn't want to explain that he could not move. He could not give the Topaz stone any advantage. He could not remember why he needed to move, it was just the compulsion to do so. He concentrated again, but still nothing happened. He wanted to close his eyes, but he did not think he had any eyelids to close.

"I can't move," Alaric finally said when he couldn't do anything to change his situation.

Although there were no words from the light Alaric could sense it was annoyed. It stopped moving for a moment and then started moving back towards Alaric. He felt suddenly like a child again, having to learn such a simple thing as walking. He could feel the scolding eyes of the figure in the light staring at him.

"What is the problem?" the light asked.

"I can't move," Alaric sounded ashamed as he spoke.

"Don't think of it as moving in the traditional sense. This place does not follow the same rules as your world. Your form is a mental image of yourself. It is not real, as in the sense that you would understand. You have to move yourself mentally not physically. Now I really think you should see this," when it finished speaking the light was suddenly in the distance again.

Alaric had to admit that the words made sense to him, but that did not make it any easier. He had to forget everything he had learnt and figure out how to move again. All along he had been trying to walk with his legs, but now he knew that was not going to work. He pictured himself gliding across the blackness and suddenly he found himself moving, albeit very slowly. Another thought suddenly entered his mind. He had watched the light suddenly appear in another place and figured that he could do the same himself. As soon as the thought entered his mind he was standing next to the yellow light. The movement was so sudden he thought he was going to be sick, but he had no stomach to lose its contents.

"Look at that!" Although he could not see any movement he thought the figure was pointing downwards..

Alaric looked in the direction he thought he was supposed to. It wasn't actually down, as there was no down and no up, but it helped Alaric to think that way. If he looked too closely into the void then his mind would fracture and he would lose control. It was safer to believe he was looking down.

At first he couldn't see what he was supposed to, but slowly an image came into view. There was a collage of colour swirling below him. Alaric was not sure what he was looking at, but he was getting a bad feeling from it. He knew it was not supposed to be there, not that he knew where there was. He hoped the Topaz stone was going to give him some more information.

"What am I looking at?" Alaric asked the question when there was no response.

"That is the essence of the disease that Ra'naroz left behind." the Topaz stone was being very helpful. "That is what you have to destroy."

"How do I do that?" There was silence. Alaric hoped it was because the Topaz stone was thinking about the question, although he did not know if that was a good sign. He was starting to lose control of his thoughts. It was hard for him to contain himself in the void. A moment of panic washed over him, but it was gone in a second. It was not a pleasant feeling.

"I will make the colours coalesce into something more tangible for you. It will be up to you to destroy it," Topaz continued with his explanation.

Alaric did not like the sound of that. It had taken him a long time to simply move. He did not know how he was going to fight something. As he watched the colours he realised that Topaz was not going to wait. Suddenly the thought of Alena, sick and helpless, came into his mind. He thought he could see her beyond the swirling colours, but he could not be sure. He couldn't shake the feeling she was going to die. The feeling was almost overwhelming.

"You have to defeat it," the voice was urging Alaric to succeed.

Alaric did not know what the stone meant. There was nothing for him to defeat. The feeling kept pulling him down and he did not think there was any chance. He had failed. He knew that to be true. As those thoughts ran through his mind he saw something appear in the swirling colours. At first it was just a black blob, but soon it started to take shape. It was not long before a man, or at least something that was shaped like a man, stood before him. The figure radiated pure evil, Alaric figured out that much. It was robed and doing its best to remain hidden.

"I was wondering when you were going to arrive," the voice was familiar, yet different. It didn't take Alaric long to realise that it was Ra'naroz.

"What are you doing here?" Alaric sounded scared and confused.

"It looks like I have overestimated your ability. It seems as though I might survive after all." Alaric thought he heard laughter in Ra'naroz's voice.

"This is not the Dark Knight Ra'naroz. This is a shadow of his essence. This is the disease that is killing Alena," Topaz explained. There was a strained tone to its voice. Alaric was not sure what it meant.

"I think it is about time you shut your mouth, or whatever it is you are speaking with," the disease almost spat the words. It was a big mistake.

"Use my energy Alaric," the yellow light glowed more intensely and suddenly the morose feeling left him.

Now Alaric was ready to fight. The Topaz stone it would have loved to destroy the disease, but there was a good chance he would also destroy Alaric. That was something he could not risk. If the stone destroyed Alaric then he would be trapped in the void for eternity. That was a fate worse than death.

The fog that had clouded his mind had suddenly dispersed and he remembered the reason he was there. He now knew what he was facing. If he destroyed the disease then Alena would survive. That was all that mattered. It was that thought that gave him strength. He suddenly felt a great pain in his stomach, or at least where he thought his stomach would be. The disease was starting its attack. It had given up on Alena and moved onto attacking Alaric. When it was done with Alaric it would return to finishing off the elf. That was its only real purpose, but something had changed and like a lot of pathogens it had to adjust to survive.

There was nothing that Alaric could do to stop the pain. He searched for the power to sever it, but he couldn't find anything. Just when he thought the pain was going to overpower him it disappeared. He noticed the yellow light had also increased. The stone was doing its best to assist. That was a promising sign.

Alaric needed to stop thinking and start acting. It was not a regular fight. He could not strike out with his fists or a sword, he had to summon a power far greater and from far deeper inside him. The nothingness started to swirl around him, if that was even possible. Alaric didn't know if he was doing it or if it was the disease. He concentrated on the figure in front of him. He had to kill the disease. He had to find a way.

"No!" the sound came from the figure.

Alaric was concentrating all his energy on the fight and it seemed to be working. The harder he pushed the greater the affect. Slowly the figure started to shrink. When the disease tried to fight back the yellow light intensified. Topaz would not let Ra'naroz gain the upper hand. His disease was going to die. Alaric continued to put all his energy into destroying it. He didn't really know what he was doing, but he knew that it was working.

Soon the figure started to shrink before it disappeared completely. Only the swirling colours remained. Alaric knew the swirling colours also had to go. They were the remnants of the disease. If he didn't finish the job then there was good chance she could be reinfected. He could not allow that. His strength was starting to waver. Destroying the image of Ra'naroz took more out of him than he thought and the battle was not over.

Whilst Alaric was trying to gather his strength the disease had another chance to attack. This time the pain struck his head causing Alaric to cry out. The yellow light intensified again, but the pain remained. There was laughter coming from somewhere in the distance. It did not originate from the swirling colours, but Alaric knew who had made the sound. The disease had finally gained the advantage.

"What is happening?" Alaric asked.

"Shut up! I need to concentrate," Topaz's voice was strained.

Alaric wanted to grab at his head to subdue the pain, but he neither had hands nor a head. Even his image had disappeared. It seemed as though he would have to overcome the pain himself. The Topaz stone was doing all it could to help. That was not a promising thought. The thought made the pain worse. The disease was starting to win.

There was nothing Alaric could do to regain his normal reality. He had to come to terms with the conditions of the void. That was the only way he could defeat the disease. Slowly he started to push the pain away. The pain in his head did not make sense and therefore could not exist. That was the thought that Alaric put in his mind. That was the thought that he focused all his energy on and sure enough the pain started to dissipate. He was finally on the right track.

Once the pain was gone Alaric was able to focus on his attack. This time he concentrated on the figure in the yellow light. It was the Topaz stone that needed his support to defeat the disease and not the other way around. Alaric used all his energy to help the stone.

"Finally," the voice sounded tired.

The coloured lights started to bubble. The brightness of the colour turned dull. It was obvious the stone was starting to win. He could feel the angst coming from the disease as it tried to overpower the stone. There was nothing it could do. By Alaric adding his strength to the stone's there was no chance of it destroying him. He was protected by his own efforts.

With a great cry of anguish the sickened mass of colour disappeared. If Alaric had his body he thought that he would collapse. He did not have a drop of energy left in him. At least he had been able to save Alena, even if he was to die in the void.

"Don't give up yet," the stone also sounded exhausted. "It is time we return to reality. I don't know about you, but I have had enough of this place."

Alaric wanted to reply, but no words came out. There was something very rewarding about working together with the Topaz stone.

He had to agree that he wanted to be out of the void. He would not care if he never came back to the place, but he knew that would not be the case. He did not know why, but he figured he would need to master the void before his job was done.

As the thoughts raced through his mind the nothingness started to ripple. It was not an easy concept to grasp and Alaric felt himself becoming dizzy. Again, if he had a body he would have fallen over, but instead he just had to endure it. The reality, or more so non-reality, started to break apart. Alaric could only hope it was Topaz stone bringing them back to reality and not the void collapsing in on itself.

Suddenly a flash of white light blinded Alaric. He could not see anything. When his sight returned he was back in the apartment standing over Alena. The memory of the void was now distant and vague; he could not remember any specific details. Instantly he looked down to where Alena was still unconscious. He still had the Topaz stone pressed against her chest. It was glowing softly and almost unnoticeable to the others in the room. His right hand gripped the sceptre as hard as he could. His knuckles had turned white with the strain.

"What are you going to do?" Linus asked the question from the doorway.

The sudden noise brought Alaric's attention back to the room. He let his grip soften before lifting the sceptre and the stone instantly stopped glowing. Alena suddenly sat up and sucked in air like it was the first breath she had ever taken. She looked straight into Alaric's eyes before her eyelids shut and she collapsed back on the bed.

Chapter 2: Recovery

The room was completely silent when Alena fell back on her bed. No one could believe what they just had seen. They all waited for Alaric's reaction before they spoke, but he was in no hurry to speak. He looked down at Alena. The colour had returned to her face and there was no longer perspiration on her body. He breathing had returned to normal and although she was still unconscious Alaric was sure she was going to get better.

"What did you do?" Linus could no longer restrain himself. The priest was dying to find out what had happened. "I thought it would have taken much longer."

It was the last comment that made Alaric turn around. Although time was different in the void it had felt like he had been gone for at least an hour. The struggle could not have been that quick.

"What do you mean? How long did it take?" Alaric spoke softly.

Linus wasn't sure about the question, but he thought he would answer it as it was asked. "You placed the stone on her chest and then a second or two later you brought it back up again. After that it was all over."

Alaric's perception suddenly shifted for a split second before returning to normal. He wasn't sure if he heard Linus correctly and re-asked the question. Linus was starting to think Alaric's mind had cracked, but he answered again anyway. Alaric knew that strange things happened in the void, but he had no idea that time could stand still.

"Is she going to be alright?" Bern asked from the other side of the room.

"I believe so," Alaric faced him as he replied.

Bern could see that there was still a yellow tinge to Alaric's eyes. That was something that was still disturbing. He did not know for sure, but he thought that the Topaz stone was taking control of him.

"Then I think you should cover the Topaz stone now," Bern tried to sound casual with his suggestion.

"I have one more thing to do before I can do that," Alaric's voice sounded distant.

"What is that?" Linus asked.

"I have to heal Tancred," Alaric replied, but remained seated.

"Tancred died a few hours before you arrived," Xarles was the one to break the bad news.

"Then I will need somewhere to sleep," Alaric replied as he stood.

"Of course," Xarles was quick to respond.

Alaric was almost out the door when Bern spoke. "I think Eldred might need some healing."

"Why? What is wrong with him?" Alaric sounded surprised. When he had left for Castalia, Eldred was confident that he would be fine.

"The spell was harder than he thought. I think it has drained him of all his energy. I don't know if he has the strength to recover," Bern sounded concerned.

Alaric moved to where Eldred was sleeping. The old wizard looked more aged than he could remember. He had always carried his age well and although he had the wrinkles of time they contained wisdom more than age. His looks had always commanded strength and not frailty. Now Alaric thought he just looked old. That in itself was a disturbing thought. He knew he had to help the old wizard.

Slowly Alaric moved the Topaz stone over Eldred's chest. Healing the wizard was not going to be such an arduous task as healing Alena. He could feel a tug at the back of his mind as he concentrated, but he quickly pushed it aside. There was nothing good in that tug. It didn't take long for the Topaz stone to start glowing, only gently, but still glowing nonetheless.

Alaric waved the stone over Eldred's chest and face once and then drew it back. Almost instantly Eldred sat bolt upright and sucked in a great gasp of air. It was very similar to the reaction Alena had had. It took him a moment to realise where he was, but when he saw Alaric he instantly knew what had happened.

"You should not have done that," Eldred did not sound grateful.

"A simple thank you would be nice," Alaric replied.

Eldred looked down at the sceptre in Alaric's hand. Suddenly he put his hand over his ears and cried out as the stone started to glow more intensely. At first Alaric didn't realise what was happening. Normally such a reaction brought the voices to his mind, but it was different this time. There were just his own thoughts in his head. He concentrated on the stone until the light slowly dampened, but it did not completely disappear.

"You need to cover that thing," Eldred removed his hand as he spoke. "And not use it for such a frivolous act."

"Easier said than done," Alaric replied, his voice strained.

Eldred did not like what he was hearing. He was afraid such a thing would happen. "The stone is trying to take control of you."

"Yes and no," Alaric replied before Eldred could continue. "I am drawing my strength from its energy. Once I cover it then I will collapse. Yes it is trying to take control of me, but it is not winning the battle. You don't have to worry. I just need a place to crash."

"I know there is an apartment nearby that is vacant," Xarles explained.

"I will go with you," Bern added.

There three of them left Eldred and Alena in the room. The wizard wanted to stay and watch over her. He was sure that Alaric had done the job, but he wanted to make sure. Keeping her alive had almost cost him his life and he wanted to make sure she survived. He was sure that Alaric was able to take care of himself, at least he sounded as though he could.

The men walked in silence until they reached the apartment. Xarles opened the door and offered the other two to enter. Alaric did not have to be asked twice. Even though the stone was keeping him awake his energy levels were starting to wane. He knew he could not rely any further on the Topaz stone. It was now time for him to recover on his own. He could not think of anything better. It had been too long since he had been able to sleep well and he could not remember the last time he had slept soundly.

Alaric did not waste any time in finding the bed. Once he was in he produced the velvet cover and placed it over the Topaz stone. As soon as the stone was covered Alaric collapsed. His body was completely drained of energy. His eyes remained open, but Bern was not sure if there was any awareness in them.

"Are you alright?" it seemed like a silly question, but Bern asked it anyway.

"I will be fine," Alaric's voice was extremely weak. Bern was surprised to hear the words come out of his mouth. "You can leave me now. I will call if I need anything."

Xarles wanted to speak, but Bern ushered him out of the room. "I don't think we should linger. He needs rest."

The duke was not happy, but he had to accept what Bern said. "I think it would be a good chance for us to speak."

Bern was not in the mood for a chat, but he knew that he could not avoid the duke forever. For the moment he wanted to speak with Eldred. He was dying to find out what had happened.

"I will check on Eldred and Alena and then I will meet you in your offices," Bern spoke firmly. He did not want to give the duke a chance to refute him.

"Very well," Xarles did not sound happy. "I will be waiting."

Bern was happy to be walking through the hallway by himself. It was so rare that he was able to have time alone that he almost felt like returning to his room. He knew he did not have time for indulgences now that Alaric had returned. It would soon be time for the army to be on the move again, so he needed to make sure that everything in Jarrat had been completed.

He found Eldred standing over the Alena. There was still concern written on his face, but it was obvious she was starting to recover. At first Bern did not want to disturb him, but he needed information. There was much to be discussed and very little time to do so.

"Is she going to be alright?" he asked.

"I think she will be fine," Eldred did not look up as he spoke. "I don't know what Alaric did, but it seems to have done the job." Eldred paused as he thought on his words. "That is very interesting indeed," Eldred mused. "I have heard of people entering the void, but I never knew it was true. I thought they were just stories from people who believed in their own self worth."

"I am afraid I don't know what you are talking about," Bern seemed a little confused.

Eldred sighed before he spoke again. "The void is a place, in theory, that is not in this world. It is a place between words, yes, that is the best way to describe it. I don't know why Alaric was taken there, but obviously it was something he had to do. It actually makes sense now that I think about it. If it had been anything else then I would have been able to cure her. It seems as though I have underestimated the power of the enemy yet again."

Bern still had no idea what Eldred was talking about. All he really wanted to know was that she was going to be alright. At least the more Eldred spoke the less time he had to worry about his other tasks. It was nice to be able to listen and not be expected to come up with an answer.

"So I guess that means that she is going to recover?" Bern asked when Eldred did not continue.

"Yes. She will recover in time, although I do not know how long that will take," Eldred looked back down at Alena.

The colour had almost completely returned to her skin. Her lips were still dry, but they were not as bad as they had been. Eldred dripped water into her mouth. It had not been necessary whilst his spell was working, but now she would need nourishment. For the moment a little water was all that he could give her. He smiled as he looked at her. Bern could not remember the last time he had seen the wizard smile.

"There is still much to be done," Eldred's words sounded grave.

"Yes. You are right. Do you have any idea where we are supposed to go from here?" Bern thought it was worth the question.

Eldred laughed an ironical laugh. "Normally that is something I would know, but I have no idea. It seems as though things have slipped away from me. I guess we are not going anywhere until Alaric recovers."

That was the answer Bern was expecting. He had hoped that the answer would come to him, like it had so many times before, when Alaric returned. It was disappointing when that was not the case. There was no other option, but to wait.

It was now time for him to speak with Xarles. It was something he was not looking forward to, but something he had to do. He had to admit that the duke was doing a good job under the circumstances. The queen was still not fit to rule. He could only imagine that pain she had gone through and the memory would be even worse, if that was possible. He could understand why the duke would need some assistance, but that did not make it any easier. Bern was having a hard enough time organising the army, a job which he didn't want to do. He had no idea how to run a city, let alone a kingdom, and yet Xarles kept pushing him.

"Thank the Gods you're here," Xarles sounded relieved when Bern entered the Royal office.

There was a pile of paperwork on his desk that was in a shambled mess. It did not look like he was getting on top of his workload. Bern had to feel sorry for the man. As much as he didn't want to help, he felt as though he should.

"What's happening?" Bern asked the obvious question.

"The paperwork keeps piling up. I am in court all day and have little time for anything else. I fear that there is much going undone."

Bern didn't like where he was going. "Shouldn't you have staff to help with this?"

"I should, but when we cleaned out all the traitors it seemed as though I lost a lot of the queen's functionaries," Xarles didn't sound happy.

"Surely you could employ someone new?" Bern couldn't fathom the problem.

"That is not as easy as it sounds. I know there are a lot of people keen for the promotion, but I need to make sure that they are the right people for the job. With what has happened recently that is not as easy as it sounds. If we missed just one of the Evil One's followers then we could be in just as much trouble." He sounded a little paranoid, but Bern thought it made sense.

"How is the queen?" Bern thought he would change the subject.

Xarles looked back down at the mess in front of him. It was clearly written on his face that the queen was still not well. He looked as though he was deep in thought and Bern wanted to press him.

"She has still yet to come out of her apartment. She has not spoken a word since the prince has left. All she does is stare out the window or into the room, depending on which way she is facing. She has to be fed and bathed. It is heartbreaking to watch her," Xarles explained.

"That is indeed disturbing. I wonder if we should have Alaric talk to her. No one has more experience with Dark Knight's than him," Bern suggested.

"Do you think that would work?" Xarles sounded hopeful.

Bern was not so sure of his own words, but he did not want the duke to know. Any hope at this point was better than none. He would fall harder if it didn't work, but he could deal with that later. "I am sure he will be able to help.'

Bern wished he could do more to help, but there were other issues that he had to concentrate on. The army would soon be ready to march and he needed to make sure that all the traitors had been caught. He was sure they were close, but the conversation was worth having nonetheless. From there he would need to convince Xarles into letting him take the bulk of his army. That was not going to be an easy conversation and would have to wait for another time.

"How is the round-up going?" Bern blurted out before Xarles could slip back into his malaise.

"I believe that we are almost done," Xarles changed his tone. "All being well we should have them all by nightfall."

"What have you decided to do with them?" Bern asked.

"They will stand trial," Xarles did not sound happy with his decision. "I had hoped Queen Oriana would be able to sit in judgement, but that doesn't look like it will happen."

"Do you have the authority to stand in judgement?"

"Unfortunately, yes," Xarles sighed. "I have seen so much suffering to my kinsman and now I will be forced to cause more. Many of the traitors will have to be sentenced to death. Some of them I do not believe will deserve such a sentence."

Bern looked confused. "I don't understand. If they do not deserve death then why would you pass down such a sentence?"

"The answer is both simple and more complicated than you could ever know. We simply do not have the room to imprison so many people. There are two choices. The first is to let them go and the second is the execute them. As we cannot risk freeing them there is only one other choice," there was no joy in his words.

"I see your point, but I don't think this is something that the queen needs to be burdened with at the moment. I am sure that you are the right man for the job," Bern tried to reassure him.

"I know you are right, but that still doesn't make it any easier."

It was not the right time, but Bern did not want to stay any longer. He had all the information that he required and the longer he stayed the more Xarles would want his assistance. He had a bad feeling that the duke would ask him to sit in judgment of the traitors. That was something he definitely did not want to do. It wasn't that he didn't want the responsibility, but he knew that he did not have the time. He would be very surprised if they were to remain in Jarrat for more than a day. Once Alaric had recovered they would be on the move again.

"I think that I should keep moving. I have a lot to do today," Bern was about to walk out of the room, but Xarles coughed. He knew that it was more than just a dry throat.

"I need your assistance," Xarles spoke.

Bern paused before his hand reached the handle. He thought about making a run for it, but he knew that was not the right option. Xarles had done a lot to make sure that Jarrat, and all of Entero for that matter, was safe from the Evil One. Without his help Bern did not know if they would succeed. He did not want to help, but he had little choice.

"Of course, what is it?" he hid his true feelings from his voice.

"I need your help with Queen Oriana," Xarles had not been sure if he would be able to ask the question. Now he knew that it was something he had to do. "I saw what Alaric did for Alena and Eldred. I was hoping that he would be able to do the same for her. I thought that she would recover on her own, but now I don't think that will be the case. I don't know what else I can do," there was deep regret in his voice.

"Of course, I will see what I can do," Bern was sure that Alaric would be happy to help. Now was his chance to ask a favour of Xarles. "There has been something that I have been meaning to ask you," Bern walked back into the room. "We need most of your army to join the Alliance. We still have a long way to go and we lost a lot of soldiers in the recent battle. If we are going to succeed then we need more men."

"I wish I could help you," Xarles had known that the question would eventually come and had his speech prepared. "It is beyond my power to release the soldiers to your command. Only Queen Oriana has the power to do that."

Bern didn't like the answer. He knew that if he really wanted to the duke could command the army. It was an easy way out for a decision that he didn't want to make. It also made it more imperative that Alaric healed the queen. He had a very bad feeling that he was being played. He wanted to push harder, but he didn't see the point. He would save that in case Alaric could not heal Queen Oriana.

"I understand," he lied. "We can only hope that she recovers quickly," that was all Bern was going to say on the matter.

Before Xarles was able to speak Bern had turned his back and left the room. He did not want to give the duke as chance to change the subject. There were still plenty of problems that Xarles would want him to fix. It was time that he visited the army. Again it was not something that he wanted to do, but he had to give them an update.

It was like running the gauntlet as he travelled through the corridors. The nobles could not get it through their heads that he did not want to speak with them. It was the duke they needed to pester, not him. He tried his best to remain polite when he brushed them off, but when they persisted he had to become harsher. More so than before, he had no time to deal with their petty concerns.

Bern sent word on ahead for the army command group to assemble for his arrival. He did not expect everyone to be there and to his surprise he found the command tent was full. There was only one seat left at the table for him. Around the room a number of servants waited for orders. It was not at all what he was expecting.

"It is good to see you could all make it," Bern spoke after he was seated. "I don't know if you have heard, but Alaric has returned."

"It did not take long for the news to reach us. It was not the most subtle of ways for him to enter the castle," General Jarwe spoke.

"It is disturbing what we have heard," Orric spoke. The elf did not sound impressed. "I think a little subtlety should have been in order."

"What do you mean?" Bern asked. It was obvious that the group had been discussing the matter before he arrived.

"His powers are growing, there can be no doubt about that," Orric continued. "But some are saying he is starting to grow evil. They say there is a madness about him."

"And do you believe that this is true?" Bern could not believe what he was hearing.

"Of course we don't," Captain Sorrell spoke before anyone else had a chance. "But the rumours are disturbing nevertheless."

Bern had to admit that they weren't completely unfounded. Something had changed in Alaric, Bern knew that was true, but he refused to believe that he was going crazy.

"Good, because the last thing we need is anyone from this group encouraging such reckless conversation," Bern glared at each member in turn. His hard gaze brought him some surprising results. Although he could not be completely sure he now had a fair indication of who believed the rumours.

"I am sure that no one would be that stupid," Jarwe's comment was pointed at those who believed.

Bern hoped that would be the case. The army needed to believe that Alaric was their saviour. He had no doubt that they would still follow his orders, but he really wanted to pass the touch to his old friend. It was now Alaric's time to lead the army and the transition needed to be smooth.

"We need to mobilize the army. We need to be ready to move any day now," Bern explained, changing the subject.

"Finally!" Sorrell's words were echoed around the table.

"Where are we moving to?" Jarwe asked.

"We don't know yet," this was the part that Bern did not want to explain. "Alaric is resting now. We have to wait for him to wake. He will tell us where we need to be."

"I thought *you* would be able to tell us when Alaric returned," Orric sounded concerned. It was never a good sign when the old elf sounded concerned.

"I thought that would be the case as well, but it seems as though it is not," Bern replied. "Now am I sure that it will be Alaric who gives us direction. I think that my time as general of this army is over," Bern revealed his revelation.

There was a lot of muttered conversation around the table. It was not something that they were prepared to hear. They had all become accustomed to Bern being their leader. They were not happy with that fact it was changing. They all knew that Alaric was the Chosen One, but he had not proven himself to the Alliance. That was something Bern had done over and over again.

"I don't think that this is a good idea," Jarwe was the first one to speak with Bern. "I don't think that the soldiers will accept Alaric as their general."

"I am sure that they will be fine," Orric did not agree with Jarwe's opinion. He was the one who completely believed in Alaric's abilities.

"With all due respect I don't think that you know our soldiers as well as we do. Your elves might believe in him, but they only make up a small component of this army," Jarwe continued.

The arguments fired across the table. Bern knew better than to try and talk over them, at least he would have if he had anything to say. The arguing gave him a chance to think. He had not thought they would have taken the news in such a manner. Now he had to think of a way to appease them. It did not seem as though it was going to be an easy task.

"I don't think that you have a choice," Bern finally spoke, even though the arguing had not died down. He had to repeat himself to get everyone to listen. "Alaric will lead this army. You know that is what he is destined to do."

"That is where I must step in." Orric spoke again.

"I thought you would be the first one to agree," Bern replied.

"I have my doubts if Alaric is meant to lead this army," Orric explained.

"What are you talking about? He is the Chosen One. He is meant to lead this army into battle with the Evil One," Bern interrupted before Orric had a chance to continue.

"It is true that eventually he will have to fight with the Evil One, but I don't think it will be at the head of the army. I think his destiny lies on a different road to the Alliance," there was mystery in his voice.

"Be that as if may, we will see what happens when Alaric wakes. At the moment we are just guessing," Bern was hoping that would end the conversation.

"So what do we do now?" Jarwe asked after a moment of silence.

"We clean up all the loose ends and then get ready to move," Bern replied. "That is all we can do."

"We believe that we have captured all the traitors. The last of them have been moved into the detention centre. I don't think we can hold any more. The conditions are quite bad," Captain Tyson explained.

"I don't suppose they are getting anywhere near what they deserve. Let's not forget that these people were trying to bring this word into darkness," Bern didn't like what Tyson was suggesting. "Anyway, it is a moot point now," he thought it was better to continue before anyone had a chance to speak. "Xarles is going to start the trials tomorrow. I believe that most of them will be executed."

"Surely he does not have the power to do that?" Tyson did not like what he was hearing.

"The queen is still sick. He had the power to command until she recovers," Bern was very firm with his point. "It is a tough decision, but I believe it is the right one to make."

That brought another round of discussions to the table. Bern was again happy for them to speak for a while. He ignored the conversation, which he knew was going around in circles. There was little more he could discuss with the others. He needed to make his way back to the castle. As much as he doubted Alaric would be up again he needed to check. That was now the most important thing. There was nothing more he could do until Alaric recovered.

Chapter 3: More Recovery Time

It took Alaric two more days to recover. He slept for the entire time. A serving girl brought him food and drink, but took it away again when it became cold and untouched. Bern checked on his friend regularly to see if he had awakened. The gentle breathing showed he was still alive, but that was all. On the morning of the second day Bern was concerned he was not going to wake. He was sure there was more to it than just sleep.

Eldred stood next to Bern and looked over Alaric as he lay motionless in his bed. It was the first time he had left Alena's side since they had left the dungeons. He could sense the tension, but there was little he could do to ease his mind.

"I am sure that he will be alright." Eldred said, knowing his words were weak.

"He has been sleeping for a long time. By all accounts he has not woken at all." Bern was not so sure. "I know he has been through a lot, but surely it's not natural to sleep so long."

"We have no idea what he has been through. No one has ever experienced anything like it before." For all intents and purposes that was true. "I don't think he is in any danger. I think it will do him good to get some natural sleep. It is hard to say what sort of hold the Topaz stone had over him and how long it will take for him to recover from it."

Bern was still not satisfied, but he had to accept the response. There did not seem to be anything wrong with Alaric, so there was little he could do. He could call for a physician, but he doubted that would do any good. Instead he left to return to the trials. Xarles had started the trials the previous afternoon. The duke had put it off for as long as he could, but the conditions inside the makeshift detention centre were becoming too cruel. There was not enough room for all the traitors and it seemed as though the trials were the fairest option.

Before nightfall on the first day the duke had already sentenced twelve people to their deaths. That was as many people as he could see. No one had survived his judgement. Those he had sentenced to death were to be hung at first light. They would spend their last night in the death cells. In the current circumstances it was the best option for them. There was more room than the detention centre and it was more comfortable than the dungeons. Xarles thought it was the least he could do for them as there would be no last meal. There were too many potential cases to waste the food. To add to that Xarles knew the Alliance would require most of their stores and he couldn't waste anything on traitors.

Bern left Eldred alone with Alaric. There was nothing else he could do to help and there was so such much he had yet to achieve. When Alaric had recovered, which he hoped was sooner rather than later, they would have their next destination. The Alliance needed to be on the move again. The army had been stationary for too long and it was only a matter of time before the soldiers got themselves into trouble. The city of Jarrat had suffered enough under the yolk of the Dark Knight and it didn't need to suffer bored soldiers on the rampage.

The soldiers had stayed out of the city when it was under lockdown and even after the lockdown had been lifted the soldiers had been instructed not to enter. Bern knew that wouldn't last long. When some soldiers eventually broke the rules and entered the city only trouble would ensue.

The soldiers were the last thing on his mind as Bern made his way to the courtyard. He hoped the hangings had been completed. As much as he knew it was a vital service it was still one he did not want to witness. Normally trials took place in the throne room, but Xarles had decided it would be better in the courtyard. There were too many to accommodate within the castle and the risk of someone escaping was too great.

Bern stood beside Xarles and ruffled his shirt. As much as he wanted to wear his army leathers he had been told he needed to wear his noble finery. Although he had grown used to the fine material the silk of his shirt seemed to irritate him. He didn't really want to be there, but as the general of the Alliance he had to show his support. The duke had just finished sentencing a small group of men to death. He had decided instead of one by one, as he had done the day before, he would try the traitors in groups. It was not a truly fair system, but it would speed the process. If he kept trying them individually it would take months to finish the task. It was not something he wanted to draw out.

"How is everything going?" Bern asked sardonically.

"Don't ask, I don't think you would like the answer." Xarles didn't really know how to respond. It was not a pleasant task, but it was a necessary one. "I would quite happily give the job to someone else if I thought they would do what is required."

There was no amusement in the conversation. Bern felt for the duke. It was never an easy task to sentence someone to death, but to do it to so many was even worse. Bern could only imagine what he was going through. He wished he could help, but he knew the decision to execute had to come from an Enteroite.

"Has Alaric woken yet?" there was a sense of urgency in his voice.

"I am afraid not. Eldred thinks he will wake when he is ready, but I am not so sure," Bern spoke as another group of traitors was brought out before them.

Bern stood in support for most of the morning, before he had to return inside the castle. It was a sad state of affairs. There were some sorrowful stories that almost broke his heart, but he also had to doubt the validity of such words. He was glad it was Xarles who had to make the decisions. He did not sentence everyone to death. There were a small number that he sentenced to a lifetime in the dungeons. Although it was only slim, there was still a chance they could be released.

Bern was eager to see if Alaric had awoken. He did not believe it would be the case, but he had to check. Until Alaric had recovered there was nothing he could do with the army and he would do everything he could to avoid the nobles stalking him around the castle.

He was pleasantly surprised to see his old friend sitting at the table eating a plate of food when he arrived. He didn't bother to look up when Bern entered. He was too engrossed in what he was doing. Bern doubted Alaric had even noticed his arrival.

"Don't just stand there staring, come and join me," Alaric didn't look up when he spoke, but he knew he had caught Bern by surprise.

Bern did as he was offered. There was an extra plate of food on the table and although he doubted it was meant for him he started eating it anyway. Alaric could always order more if he was still hungry. The empty plate on the side table showed that he had already eaten one meal.

"It is good to see you up again," Bern started after he had taken a mouthful. He had not realised how hungry he was.

"You are telling me," Alaric stuffed more food in his mouth before he continued. "I am just grateful that I have my memory still intact."

Bern was not sure what that meant. He wanted to ask, but he thought he would let it go. There were more important things to discuss. In addition he was too busy filling his mouth. Once they started talking seriously he did not want to be distracted by food.

"Do you know if Alena is up yet?" Alaric asked when it was clear Bern was not going to respond.

"Eldred told me that she woke up briefly, but she is sleeping again. She was able to eat and drink something before she returned to sleep." Bern thought that was a positive sign. The look on Alaric's face made him think otherwise.

"That is good news," Bern was not expecting the words to come out of Alaric's mouth. "I thought I would have woken before she did."

"You have been asleep for two days now," Bern wasn't sure if Alaric realised.

Alaric started laughing. "I guess that is starting to make sense then." Alaric thought for a moment before he spoke again. "It seems as though the Topaz stone had a greater hold on me than I originally thought."

"What does that mean?" Bern was keen for information.

"I had not slept for over a day, and before that I had not had a good night sleep for a long time. I was still suffering the effects from when I fought Ra'naroz to make matters worse. The Topaz stone cured me of all my pains, but it seems as though it was only a short term fix," Alaric explained. "It cured me of my pain, but it could only stave off the exhaustion whilst I held it. The temptation to overuse its power is great, but it would eventually destroy me. If I kept it out much longer then I don't think I would have been able to hide it again," Alaric sounded as though he was as much explaining things to himself as he was to Bern.

Bern was not completely sure what Alaric was telling him, but it made more sense than before. He knew the stones were dangerous, but it was the first time he had seen it first hand. Now Alaric held three *Stones of Power*. The risk of damaging himself was even greater. Bern hoped that he knew what he was doing.

For the first time Bern noticed that the yellow tinge had gone from Alaric's eyes. In his sleep they had returned to their natural green colour. Bern thought it was a good sign that he had completely recovered from the Topaz stone's affect. There was a good chance they could be on the move again soon.

"Don't worry. I am not about to attempt to use all three at once any time soon. It has taken me too long to recover from the Topaz stone," it was as if Alaric had read his mind. "I still have a long way to go."

Bern was glad to hear Alaric's words. They had come a long way since they had left Arsiliac. If anyone had told him when he was working on the farm that this would be his destiny then he would have laughed them out of his house. Now he could not imagine his life any other way. He missed his family, but the thought of them was becoming less and less. He thought the entity that inhabited his body had a part to play in that. He didn't mind so much. Some nights the thoughts of his wife and children brought terror to his heart. He missed them so much that he thought his heart was going to break. The detachment made life a lot easier for him.

"Speaking of having a long way to go," Bern thought it was a good chance to change the subject. "Do you have any idea on where we have to go next?"

Alaric knew exactly where they had to go. Castalia was under the control of a Dark Knight and that was something he would have to change. If Za'aroz was able to control the Castalial army then they would be in great danger. It was an army that Alaric would have to assimilate into the Alliance if they were going to succeed.

"The army must move to Castalia. Za'aroz is masquerading as the High Chancellor." Alaric paused and let the information sink in. "We can no longer let him have the run of the place."

Bern could hardly believe what he was hearing. There was something very disturbing in his words. It was not only the fact that the High Chancellor was a Dark Knight, but also the fact that he was planing on taking the army there. He did not think that was the right decision.

"Surely you don't expect us to attack Castalia. No army has ever been able to breech the inner wall," Bern sounded shocked. "There has to be another way."

"I'm afraid there is no other way," Alaric continued. "The High Chancellor is being held prisoner in the mines. You need to rescue him before you can destroy the Dark Knight. If not he will succeed in turning the most powerful kingdom against us."

Bern picked up on something in Alaric words. He was not sure at first, but the more he thought about it the more it made sense. When he came to the realisation he was very disturbed.

"You said that I have to free the High Chancellor and I have to destroy the Dark Knight. Does that mean you are not coming with us?" Bern asked.

"I don't think our paths are on the same route." Alaric was being a little vague.

"Where are you planning on going?"

"I do not know that yet. I just have a feeling that I have to go somewhere else. I am hoping the prophecy will give me some idea."

It had been a long time since Alaric had been able to refer to the prophecy. He was looking forward to flicking through its pages.

Bern was not happy with what he was hearing, but at least it would put the command group's minds at rest. It seemed as though Bern would be in control of the Alliance for a little longer. He had to digress to the original plan, which he was not overly happy with.

"How do you think we are going to take Castalia if you are not coming with us?" Bern asked.

"There will be time for that later." Alaric was not yet ready to reveal his plan. "It would be better if I explained it to everyone at once."

As much as Bern wanted to know what Alaric had planned he was happy with the result. At least he could not be blamed for it if Alaric explained it to everyone. At least now he could get the army on the move. It would take a day to start packing down and moving towards Castalia. It would take two or three days more before the entire army would have left Jarrat. It gave him a little more time to gather information.

"I suppose I should go and inform the army that we shall be moving west." Bern stood and turned to leave the room. Just before he reached the door a thought crossed his mind. The memory had been locked away and only just returned to him. "There is one more thing." Bern returned to the table.

"What is it Bern?"

"There is another serpentant in the picture," Bern was not really sure how to start the conversation. "Adder was in Jarrat and he gave me a message to pass on to you." Alaric was very interested to hear what he had to say. "He wants you to meet him on the summit of Mount Scorpio. He has given you until the 'waning of the next full moon' as he liked to call it."

"Did he give you an indication of what he wanted?" Alaric asked.

"No, but he said if you didn't meet him then he would destroy Arsiliac. From what I have seen him do in Jarrat I would believe him." Bern added for effect.

"I see," was Alaric response. He had no ties to Arsiliac, except for Bern's family. He was not sure what he should do. There could be no good reason for Adder to call a meeting. His only experience with Serpentants was with Viper and he did not trust him. "What do you think I should do?"

Bern knew what he wanted to say, but he didn't know if that was the right thing. The thought of his wife and children being slaughtered by the evil creature made knots in his stomach. A few months ago that would have been the only point in his mind, but now he knew there was more at stake.

"I do not know. I feel as though you should meet the snake, but that could just be the thoughts of my family." Bern had to be honest.

Alaric had to admit he was expecting such a response. He just wanted the extra time to think, but the answer still did not come to him. He knew he would have to decide, but now was not the time. There was something more important for him to do. He had to see Alena. The thought of her made his heart skip. A lot had happened since they had last spoken, but as soon as he saw her lying in bed a world of feelings came rushing back to him.

"I think you should go and get the army on the move. Make sure the command group remains in camp. I will explain what needs to be done tomorrow." Alaric had a lot to think about, but firstly he wanted to see Alena.

Bern was not overly happy with being dismissed, but he knew what he had to do. He wished Alaric had given him more information, but that was not going to happen. The command group might question him, but in the end they would follow his orders. There was plenty more they needed to discuss, but it would have to wait for another time.

Alaric remained seated until Bern left the room. He suddenly felt very nervous. He hoped that Alena was better. That was what he wished for more than anything else. There was no reason why he should remain in the room and yet he could not bring himself to leave. There was something that was holding him back. Slowly he shook the feeling off and left the apartment.

The nobles, who would have normally looked to gain advantage by speaking with Alaric, gave him a wide berth as he walked through the corridors. There was no doubting who was wearing the black leather jerkins, trousers and long jacket. No one from Jarrat would wear such clothing in the castle and the rumours had already spread of his arrival. No one knew where he had found the clothes as they were not what he had been wearing when he arrived. Little did they know that Alaric had magically created them. He felt more comfortable wearing them than what the servants had brought for him. Like Bern he didn't want to wear court finery if he could avoid it.

Normally Alaric would have pushed the door open and entered without permission, but he paused. Taking a deep breath Alaric knocked and waited. It was not long before he heard Eldred call out from inside. He had half expected it to be Alena's voice. Without waiting he twisted the handle and pushed the door open.

"It is good to see you are up," Eldred spoke first.

Alaric ignored the comment and looked around for Alena. He didn't seem to even notice that Eldred had seemingly fully recovered from the ordeal of keeping her alive. His long, soft grey hair and beard were no longer wet and matted. Although he always had the lines of age on his face they were no longer the thick wrinkles of the elderly. He wore a new white robe and he held his staff in his right hand. He looked the epitome of wizardry.

"She is getting dressed." Eldred knew what he wanted. "She will be out here in a moment. Until then I think it is time we had a conversation."

Alaric was not happy, but he knew Eldred was right. He had to plan his next move. There would be little time for him to sit back and relax, especially with the deadline ticking on Adder's threat. He had hoped he would have felt a tug in the direction of the Scorpion Mountain, but he didn't. It seemed as though the prophecy had another plan for him.

"What is it that you wish to discuss?" Alaric did not sound comfortable.

"It seems as though you are beginning to master the stones." Eldred cut straight to the point. "It also seems as though you are not completely in control when you use one of them."

"It is nice of you to state the obvious, but is there a point to this." Alaric started to pace up and down.

Eldred was taken aback by Alaric's attitude. At first he was offended, but then he came to a realisation. Alaric had changed considerably since Eldred had been captured. He had missed a lot of Alaric's development. That was both exciting and disturbing. He doubted anyone had been training him, which meant he had learnt the information on his own.

"Tell me what you have been doing since we last saw each other." Eldred spoke warmly. He offered Alaric a seat. The man's pacing was starting to make him nervous.

The last thing Alaric wanted to do was to recall the past few months. There were still gaps in his memory that had not fully returned with his health. He looked towards the bedroom door as he took a seat. If Alena surfaced then it would give him the distraction that he needed. Alaric started his story.

He only got as far as his fight with Fenaroz and gaining the Jade dagger before the door finally opened. Alaric's eyes moved quickly towards the bedroom, anticipation clearly written on his face. It was the moment he had been waiting for and he could hardly believe it was true.

Alena stepped out of the bedroom and paused when she saw Alaric sitting before her. A beaming smile appeared on her face. The colour had returned to her skin, although Alaric had a suspicion she wore makeup. Her blonde hair fell down in ringlets around her shoulders. She wore a gentle, white, silk dress. It was not quite a formal gown, but it was still nicer than regular day-to-day clothes. Alaric could not believe what he was seeing.

"It is good to see you again." Alena giggled when she finished speaking before rushing into his arms. At first Alaric didn't know what to do, but he quickly wrapped his arms around her.

Alaric took a deep breath. Her hair smelt like roses. His heart skipped a beat as he held her. He did not want to let her go, but he knew the embrace would eventually end. There was no time for such pleasures, but he would make the most of every second he had with her. The moment lasted and then was lost forever as Alena stood.

"I am sorry to interrupt." The smile remained on her face. "I believe my father is with the army." Alaric thought her voice sounded like beautiful music. "I would like to go and see him now." She knew the two men were discussing something important and didn't want to get in their way.

"I don't think that is the best idea." Alaric was glad when he heard Eldred's words. "You have been through a great ordeal and I don't believe you are up to such a journey."

"Don't be silly. I feel fine." Alena didn't think Eldred knew what he was talking about.

"It is the effect of the Topaz stone. We don't know how long that will keep you going. For the moment I would prefer it if you stayed in the castle grounds." Eldred would not be dissuaded.

"I think she will be fine now." Alaric couldn't believe the words had come out of his mouth. "The stone won't have the same affect on Alena as it had on me. If she feels fine then she is alright."

Alena shot Eldred a look as he spoke under his breath. He quickly recovered and attempted a smile. He was not sure if what Alaric was saying was in fact true, but there was no way for him to refute it. He still didn't think that it was a good idea for her to leave the castle.

"Be that as it may I would still prefer it if you stayed within the castle walls." Eldred was going to be stubborn.

"Okay Eldred, either way I need to get some fresh air. I will leave you boys to it." She smiled an even warmer smile at Alaric before she left the room.

Eldred had a very bad feeling that Alena was not going to do as she was told. He wanted to go after her, but there were more important things for him to do. There had been some interesting pieces to Alaric's story, but he knew there was more to come. In the end he remained seated and no one knew the turmoil inside him.

"Please continue." Eldred spoke when Alaric didn't.

It took Eldred's words to bring his attention back to the room. His mind had wandered out of the door with Alena. He wished he had also left. He didn't want to continue, but he felt compelled. He was sure there was something better he could be doing. It took most of the day for Alaric to tell his story. Eldred did his best not to ask too many questions, but he couldn't help himself. There were holes in the story, mostly because Alaric's memory wasn't right. He tried his best to explain, but Eldred was left feeling unsatisfied.

"This gives me much to think about." Eldred spoke when Alaric was finished.

"I am not sure of my next direction. I feel as though I should be going after Marina and the Sapphire stone, but I can't bring myself to leave. I guess it will just come to me when the time is right." Alaric sounded defeated, although it was more from the extended story telling than anything else.

"I think I might know of our next move." It was not lost on Alaric that Eldred included himself. "I think it would be better if I consult the prophecy before I continue."

It was the first time that Alaric had thought about the whereabouts of the *Prophecy of the Stone* since he regained consciousness. He had left the great tome in the castle for safe keeping. He did not want to lose it again and he did not trust Ra'naroz. He had gambled that it would be safer in Jarrat. He had not checked for it since his return and hoped it was still in his room. He was not sure if he wanted Eldred to have it as he would also need to consult its wisdom.

"I think it is in my room. I will go and check for you." Alaric realised he had paused for too long.

"Very good, I will come with you. My old legs need a little exercise."

Alaric didn't know if the wizard was telling the truth or that he didn't trust him. Either way he could not be bothered arguing. The two left the apartment in silence. Recounting his journey had left Alaric feeling uninspired. He needed to concentrate on the future.

Once Eldred had the *Prophecy of the Stone* he left the apartment. He was keen to start reading. Alaric was glad to be alone again, although that did not last long. Soon there came a knock on the door. He remained silent and hoped that whoever it was on the outside would leave. That was not the case. When the knock came again he knew he had to answer.

"Enter." He called out.

The door opened and Duke Xarles entered. Alaric did not think it was a good sign. The duke had a sorrowful expression on his face. Alaric knew he had spent the day sentencing his kinsfolk to death. That would not be an easy task for anyone.

"What is it I can do for you?" Alaric asked before he had a chance to speak.

"Has Bern spoken with you?"

"I saw him this morning." There seemed to be something else in the question, but Alaric didn't know what it was.

Xarles looked at Alaric as if he should know what he was talking about. When it was clear he didn't the duke spoke again. "Did he speak to you about Queen Oriana?"

Alaric thought for a moment. A lot had happened since his discussion with Bern, but he could not recall the queen being mentioned. "I don't believe so."

The duke suddenly looked upset. He quickly wiped the expression from his face before he spoke again. "She has not recovered from what the prince, err, I mean the Dark Knight did to her." He paused as he thought for the right words. "I know you were able to heal Alena with the Topaz stone. I was hoping that you might be able to do the same with Queen Oriana."

Alaric did not like what he was hearing. It had been a great strain for him to relinquish the Topaz stone once it was free. He was not sure if he was ready to fight that battle again so soon. The look on Xarles' face showed that he was in dire need. From what Bern had told him the duke was true to their cause, so he could not deny the man.

"I will have a look at her and see what I can do." Alaric spoke slowly, as if he was still unsure.

"Thank you." Xarles turned to leave the room, but he noticed Alaric didn't move. "Are you coming?"

Alaric shook his head. "I will see her tomorrow. At the moment I have a lot to think about."

The comment was true, but it was only an excuse to give himself another day before he had to fight the stone. As much as Xarles didn't like it there was nothing he could do. He could not risk upsetting Alaric, so he simply thanked him and left.

Alaric was happy to be on his own. There was still much he needed to do, but for the moment he was happy to sit in silence. He knew soon enough there would be noise again in his life and he was happy to sit in silence.

Chapter 4: Starting to Move

The command tent was in an uproar again. Bern had just finished explaining Alaric's plan for them, or at least as much as he knew, and no one was happy. Even Orric seemed disturbed. The old elf was normally the first to agree with what they were doing and Bern was not pleased with this result.

"He cannot be serious," Jarwe spoke with a raised voice. "We have already suffered great loses. This is a suicide mission. No army has ever been able to break the walls of Castalia. He may as well take us out and kill us himself."

The general from Remidia had once been the Commander of the Alliance, but after the battle in Avalon that job had been given to Bern. He had shaved his head in anticipation for the morning's meeting. He always felt more in control with a clean pate, which accentuated his already strong jaw line. He wore a green tunic with his family crest, a white dove over a wreath of maple leaves, which everyone thought was an odd choice, but no one said anything. There were more important matters to be discussed than the general's choice of clothing.

Bern had been expecting the comments from the others and to be honest he believed them himself. He had no feeling drawing him towards Castalia. He thought once he had been told where he was going he would feel the prophecy again. It was not a good sign, but he could not go against Alaric's word. If he wanted them to travel to Castalia then that is what they had to do.

"Under no circumstances can we leave a Dark Knight in control of Castalia. If he moves the army out to join Nyrra's then we have already lost. Alaric has told us that we need to rescue the High Chancellor and that is what we must do." Bern tried to remain calm.

Although his words made sense they did nothing to calm the mood inside the tent. No one wanted to move to Castalia and they didn't mind letting him know. Bern wished they would stop talking. The decision was out of his hands, although they still believed it was his to make. When it was said and done the army would start moving before nightfall. There was nothing that could change his mind.

"I still don't understand. It is impossible for us to take Castalia. There is nothing we can do. We will all be killed and the Dark Knight will still be in control of Castalia's army. This is folly." Sorrell added his thoughts.

"I hate to disagree with Alaric, but I think these men are right," Orric spoke for the first time.

Bern listened to the arguments for not taking the army to Castalia. They all made sense and he had to admit that his doubts were starting to take over. Again he had to believe that Alaric knew what he was doing. He wished his old friend had explained his plan to him. It would have made life so much easier.

"There is no point in discussing this further." Bern had finally had enough. "We can talk about this all day, but nothing is going to change. We need to get the army moving and we need to do it now."

Bern's words brought silence to the tent. No one expected him to be so firm in disagreeing with them. They had made him the general of the Alliance and they had to do what he said. The command group did have a certain amount of power, but they all had to defer to Bern.

"Are you sure that is what you want us to do?" Jarwe thought he would still give him a chance to change his mind.

"It is not something I want to do. I agree with all your reasoning, but this is what Alaric wants us to do. He said he would explain his reasoning to us, so until then we just have to trust that he is doing the right thing." Bern hoped they accepted his answer.

"That is all well and good for you to say. You have known Alaric for a long time. I, on the other hand, do not quite have the same amount of faith. I for one would like some more information before we rush off to war." Jarwe was still not convinced.

"I for one have seen Alaric at work first hand and I have to agree with Bern. I am sure that it will all be made clear when he speaks to us, but in the meantime we need to have a little faith." Hulkan had changed his mind.

"They are both right," Orric added. If we do not then we may as well just quit now."

A smile crossed Bern's face. He was glad they were starting to come around. It made his life a lot easier. He did not want to fight with the command group all the way to Castalia, especially since Alaric was not coming with them. All he could do was wait for Alaric to inform them on what they had to do.

"Start the army moving. It will take a good five days for the entire army to be on the move. It is almost noon now, so we need to get started."

Jarwe and a few of the others were still not happy with the result, but they were not willing to argue any further. It seemed as though Bern had made his decision and he had enough support from others. Any confrontation would be a waste of time.

Bern was happy to be out of the tent and on his way back to the castle. It had been a stressful meeting. He had expected as much of a response, but he had hoped they would have come around in the end. Now he could only hope that Alaric would be able to appease them.

As he made his way back to the castle he hoped he would not need to speak with Xarles. He had already had enough of intrigues for one day. Those of the court were even more tedious than those of the army. He had to wonder how he ever got himself into such a situation.

***

Alaric woke the next day to a loud banging on the door. The sun had only just risen and he could only wonder at who could be in such a hurry to see him. He should not have been surprised when he saw Xarles on the other side door. The duke had a concerned expression on his face. Alaric had hoped he would be able to avoid the impending meeting with the queen.

"I'm sorry to disturb you so early in the morning, but I have to start the trials again soon. I was hoping you would be able to see the queen now?" there was more than a little hope in his voice.

"I don't see any reason why not." Alaric had been desperately thinking of a reason. "Let's get going."

He would have liked to have eaten before he left, but that would just be another distraction. If he was going to help Oriana then there was no time to waste. He grabbed the Topaz sceptre before following Xarles out of the room. He would keep the stone covered until he needed to use it.

"How is everything moving along?" Alaric asked as they walked towards the royal apartments.

"I am sure you have heard that the trials have started." He paused, but when there was no response he continued. "It is the hardest thing I have had to do in my life. I was so concerned about restoring control to Entero that I didn't think of the cost. I feel that a lot of people have been led astray and didn't really know what they were getting themselves into. I fear I have sent some people to hang that were only guilty of being ignorant."

"Unfortunately in these times that is all that it takes. I think you are making the right decision. The enemy is very wily. Just because they seem ignorant doesn't mean that they are. I don't think you can trust anyone." Alaric offered his support. He was glad he was not the one sitting in judgement.

They continued on in silence. Xarles was consoled by Alaric's words, but he didn't want to continue the conversation. It was the only chance he had to escape from the trials and he really didn't want to waste it discussing them. The images of the men and women hanging in the castle courtyard had kept him up during the night. He only had a short sleep and he was keen to get out of bed. The longer he remained the more the disturbing images came to him. He needed the distraction of helping the queen.

The duke paused when he reached the door to the royal apartment, his heart was pounding. He wasn't sure he was doing the right thing. If Alaric could not help the queen then he was not sure she could be saved. That was something that he really didn't want to think about, and it was keeping him from opening the door. Alaric, was also in no hurry to enter.

Taking a deep breath and closing his eyes was the only way Xarles could bring himself to enter to the room.

Once they were inside they found the queen in her bedroom sitting on the end of her bed. All she was doing was staring at the door. Nothing registered on her face when the two men entered. Xarles was relieved to see that she was wearing clothes. It had happened all too often that he would walk into the apartment and find Oriana completely naked.

It was obvious that her servants had been in and she had not dressed herself on her own. Her long brown hair had been brushed and tied in a single plait. Her young skin was starting to show the sign of age, but had been hidden with makeup.

"Hello, your Majesty." Xarles liked to speak to her, although he was sure she didn't hear his words. "This is Alaric. He is here to help you."

Alaric stood behind the duke. He had a bad feeling when he entered the room. He could instantly tell that something was not right. He was not sure if it was evil, but whatever was causing her condition made Alaric wait in the doorway.

"Are you going to come in?" Xarles asked.

"I think we should do this in her sitting room." Alaric would not enter the bedroom.

"What are you talking about?" Xarles did not sound happy.

"There is something wrong with her bedroom. I am not comfortable entering." Alaric tried to keep strength in his voice.

Xarles looked around the room. He had no idea what Alaric was talking about. There didn't seem to be anything wrong with the room. He was concerned that Alaric didn't know what he was talking about. In the end he had to trust Alaric and he helped Oriana to her feet and led her out of the room. That movement was about all that the queen was capable of.

Alaric felt a lot better when they were in the sitting room. He would need to return to the bedroom, but that could wait until later. He needed to concentrate his energy on the queen. At first glance there didn't seem to be anything wrong with her. That could either be a good sign or a really bad one. It would be a lot easier to help her if there was no inlying spell. On the other hand if there was a spell it was not so apparent.

Xarles watched nervously as Alaric examined the queen. He knew he should be getting ready for the trials, but he couldn't leave. He had to know that Oriana was going to be alright. If she wasn't then he didn't know if he could continue.

Alaric had to concentrate to try and find a spell. He drew in a small amount of energy before scanning her body. He delved into places a normal person would not be able to find. He didn't really know what he was looking for, but he believed he would know when he found it. If there was anything magical then he would be able to locate it and hopeful destroy it without having to use the Topaz stone.

"I am afraid there is nothing I can do." He spoke when he finished searching. "There is no spell causing her malaise. There doesn't seem to be any disease or physical illness causing it."

"That is a good thing. You should be able to use the stone to heal her?" Xarles sounded confused.

"The Topaz stone works on physical ailments. The queen's affliction is of the mind. I don't believe the Topaz stone will be any good." Alaric explained.

"Surely you could try." Xarles was not going to be dissuaded so easily.

"It's not worth the risk. I could do more damage if I tried. The only way I can help her is with the Opal stone." Alaric did not sound confident.

"Then find the stone!" There was new hope in his voice.

Alaric looked at the queen. She stared at the wall in front of her, not realising they were there. He could feel for the duke, but that did not excuse him. There was more at stake than one queen, one woman, one kingdom. He calmed himself before he spoke again.

"It is not that easy."

"What do you mean?" the duke raised his voice. His feelings for Oriana were starting to show. Alaric would have to tread lightly. "You have found stones before. It can't be that hard to find the Opal stone!"

"It is not that easy. I do not decide which stone I find. I do not decide which path I follow." It was as much a realisation to himself as it was for Xarles. He walked to the window and stared outside. The queen's apartment faced out over the Eastern forest and the field were the battle had taken place. The makeshift detention centre stood out like a sore thumb. The field was a hive of activity as the army broke down the camp. Alaric took a deep breath and calmed himself before he spoke again. "There is still much I have to do. I can't stray from my path no matter what the cause." Xarles wanted to speak, but he didn't have the heart.

Alaric turned back to face him. "There is one thing I can promise you. When I find the Opal stone I will return and help Oriana."

Xarles relaxed with Alaric's words. There was light at the end of the tunnel. He wanted to jump and cheer, but refrained. He knew it would not be appropriate.

"I think you should continue with the trials." Alaric spoke when Xarles didn't. "There is still much to be done."

The duke had to agree. He was already late, not that he thought the prisoners would be in any rush. As much as he wanted to stay with the queen he knew the trials were more important. Sadly they would be a welcome distraction, at least for a short time.

Alaric was glad to be out of the queen's apartment. There was something not right with the place. He thought about suggesting to Xarles to move her to a different apartment to aid her recovery. He hoped it was only the residue of evil that Ra'naroz had left behind that was preventing her from getting better. If it was anything more then there was little chance for the queen. As much as it worried him there were more important matters for him to attend to. He knew Bern would have a hard time explaining to the others why they were to move to Castalia, especially with the limited information he had supplied. It was important that he set their minds at ease before they left Jarrat.

The next problem Alaric had was finding the priest Linus. He had almost forgotten about him when he had recovered. The priest was a pivotal part of his plan for the army. He was the only one who could direct them to the secret entrance to the mines. Alaric had planted the memory inside Linus' mind before they had left Castalia. It would only come back to him once he started looking and would disappear once he had achieved his goal. That was the only way they would be able to rescue the High Chancellor.

It took Alaric almost an hour before he found the priest. Linus was praying in a small chapel on the other side of the courtyard, the same courtyard that Xarles was conducting the trials. Alaric had tried to avoid the scene, but it had become an impossible task.

When he left the castle he could see the chapel on the far side of the courtyard. It was only a short distance, but the gathered crowd made it almost impossible to reach. The duke stood on a large dais presiding over those being tried.

Slowly Alaric tried to push his way through the crowd. He knew that Xarles would make them part for him, but he didn't want his presence known. He had managed to stay out of view so far and that was the way he wanted to keep it. The crowd, however, was not so accommodating. They all wanted to be in the front row to see the accused. Those at the back didn't have such a great view and as Alaric tried to move through the crowd he was blocked and pushed backwards. He really felt like creating a spell to move them all aside, but that would defeat the purpose of remaining anonymous. It wasn't until the duke had sentenced the prisoners to death did the crowd start to disperse. On the previous days Xarles had been doing one trial straight after another, followed by the executions later in the day. It did not take long before the constant string of trials broke his spirit. As of that morning he had decided to take a half hour break between trials. In the meantime those who had been sentenced to death would be executed. It was the perfect time for Alaric to make his way to the chapel.

"Good morning priest." Alaric gave a warm greeting when he found Linus.

"Huh!" Linus looked up from where he was praying. He was somewhat surprised to see Alaric. "I didn't think I would be seeing you today."

"I need you to come with me to the army. I need to explain my plan to them."

Linus didn't look like he was ready to move, but eventually he stood. "I guess I don't have a choice. I somehow think that this has always been my fate."

Alaric didn't know what to say. He was surprised by Linus' tone. He had not explained anything to him, but it seemed as though the priest was happy to go along with whatever he wanted. Linus waited for Alaric to make the first move. He was in no hurry to leave the chapel. As a priest it was where he felt most at home. If Alaric wanted him to leave then he would have to lead the way.

"If you are done, then I think we should get moving." It seemed the most appropriate response.

Linus nodded his head and Alaric simply turned and led the way out of the chapel. The courtyard was starting to fill again as the first of the executions were about to start. This was something that neither Alaric nor Linus wanted to witness. The priest had been praying for the souls of those who had been sentenced to death all morning, as he had done the previous days. He had heard the screams of all those about to die.

Luckily for the two of them there was a clear path between the chapel and the main gate. Alaric quickly made his way through the crowd. Once the executions had started he was sure the crowd would gather a lot closer. Once that happened he did not want to do was get stuck watching people die. He had seen enough death in his life and there was still more to come.

Once they were at the main gate they were stopped. "I am sorry, but no one is allowed to leave the castle." The captain-of-the-guard spoke in a firm voice.

Alaric had known the entrance in and out of the castle had been restricted, but he didn't think he would have any issues. He should have realised that if no one knew who he was then no one was going to help him. He didn't think he would have too many problems talking his way out, but that would involve revealing his identity.

"I have a meeting with the Alliance." It wasn't much of a start, but at least it would start the dialogue.

"I am sure that you do, but as I said, no one is allowed through and that is not going to change." The captain would not be deterred.

"I am sure if General Bern was thinking about it he would have told you to let me through. I don't think you want to get on his bad side." There was an underlying threat in his words.

"That is all well and good, but I take my orders from queen Oriana, or Duke Xarles in her stead."

"That is true, but it is General Bern who gives Xarles his commands." That was only partly true. "I don't think you should delay us any longer."

It was Alaric's confidence and his strange attire that had the captain somewhat unsure of himself. At first he had just been prepared to brush the two aside and not really taken any notice of them, but on closer inspection he knew there was something different about them. There was something in the back of his mind telling him that he should be letting them through. Regardless of that feeling he knew he could not. He needed some more information before he made his decision.

"I am sure that if you tell me your name it might recall something."

That was something that Alaric was expecting, although he was hoping he would not be asked. He still wanted to keep his identity a secret, but he now doubted he would be able to. He noticed that the other guards were listening intently to the discussion. If it had just been the captain, Alaric wouldn't have cared about using his name, but letting everyone know was a completely different story.

"This is Priest Linus from Castalia." He thought it would be a better idea to use Linus' name. He could only hope that it worked. "He has some important information about the upcoming trial for the army."

It was well known that the army was moving west. Alaric hoped that the captain would know what he was talking about. It was his only chance to escape with his identity intact. The captain was taking an even closer look at Linus. There was no doubt that the man was a priest. His white robes were clearly of a religious cut, but it was debatable that the man was from Castalia. Linus' skin didn't reflect the darkness that Castalials were famous for.

"Unfortunately that name does not ring any bells. Tell me your name, that might sway my decision."

Alaric sighed. It was clear to all that he wanted to remain anonymous. It was also clear that the captain was not going to let him pass without his name. Alaric should really have known better. His experience with guards and soldiers was advanced, but he no longer had the time to waste. The command group needed information before they could leave. He could not let the army get too far ahead of them.

"I am Alaric." the captain looked as though he had heard the name. "Or you may know me as the Chosen One." Alaric added to help his memory.

It took the captain a moment to realise what Alaric had told him. It was clear the other guards realised sooner as they started to go about their business. They had been warned that Alaric was in the castle and he was, under no circumstances, to be delayed. The captain wanted to run and hide, but there was no where for him to go. All he could do was apologise and let the pair through.

"Is it often like this?" Linus asked when they were on their way to the campsite.

"More than I would like to mention, but it's not always the same result. Sometimes I get passed through and other times I get sent back." Alaric spoke mindlessly. His thoughts were on the upcoming meeting.

Linus was about to speak, but decided against it. He could tell from Alaric's tone that he was not interested in conversation. Linus was old enough to know not to push. He was happy to take the rest of the journey in silence, there were plenty of things he had to think about.

The command tent was almost empty when they arrived. One thing Alaric had forgotten to do was to send word of his arrival. Orric was the only one from the command group in the tent, the rest were functionaries preparing to pack the tent down. He stood when Alaric entered, a look of surprise on his face.

"Alaric! It is good to see you. We were not expecting you so soon." Orric didn't really know what to say. "You have just missed Alena, if you were looking for her."

Alaric smiled and was only just able to control himself from laughing. He had thought Alena would disobey Eldred's order not to leave the castle. He wondered if she had as much trouble leaving as he did. He highly doubted it. She was too beautiful for any man to block her path.

"How long do you think it will take to assemble the council?" Alaric ignored the question and came straight to the point.

"It might take a while. We are mobilising the army at the moment. It is hard to say where everyone is." Orric replied.

"You have half an hour to get everyone here. If they are not here then they will miss out." The words did not sound right coming from his mouth. He shouldn't have been capable of ordering Orric to do anything.

The elderly elf was quick to move, regardless of whether it was proper or not. He knew that Alaric had some information for them. The sooner he was able to gather the command group the sooner he would learn what Alaric had to say. That was something more important than ceremony.

Bern was the first one to enter the tent. No one had told him Alaric was there. He had been walking throughout the camp with no real direction until he ended up at the command tent. When he saw Alaric he was drawn there.

"I wasn't sure if you were going to make it." Bern smiled as he spoke.

"I nearly didn't." Alaric was not going to bring it up, but since Bern mentioned it. "It would have been nice if you had informed the guards that I would be passing through today. They nearly didn't let me out."

"Where is the fun in that?" there was a smirk on Bern's face. "I can't make life too easy for you. Anyway, I thought you wanted to keep your identity a secret."

There was nothing Alaric could say about that. He did want to remain anonymous, but when the words came out of Bern's mouth he realised how stupid it sounded. He could not ask for special treatment and not expect people to ask questions. In the end he would have to accept that his arrival to Jarrat would soon be known by all. At least he would not be staying long enough for things to get annoying.

"Point taken," Alaric also smiled. "I guess that is the least of our problems."

They both had to laugh. There really was no point in arguing over such matters. There were much more important things to discuss.

"I don't understand the joke." The two had forgotten about the priest.

"Never mind, it's not that funny," Alaric said as General Jarwe entered the tent. He was glad for the distraction.

It wasn't long before the command tent was almost full. The only ones missing were Dorn and Wojtek. Alaric was happy to begin without them. He didn't want to wait around all day. Once he was finished with the command group he needed to speak with Eldred. He hoped the wizard had realised their next move.

"Thank you for meeting me here." It seemed like the most appropriate way to start the meeting. "I understand you have concerns with travelling to Castalia."

"You could say that." Jarwe almost forgot himself when he spoke.

"I know, I know, but I can assure you that there is a good reason. The Dark Knight Za'aroz is masquerading as the High Chancellor and he has everyone fooled. The real High Chancellor is now trapped working in the diamond mines. Some of you may or may not know of these mines. It is my understanding they are somewhat of a dirty little secret."

"The mines don't exist." Alaric was surprised to hear Hulkan speak.

The dwarf had an angry expression on his face. He had worked most of his life in the sand mines. For a long time he was the President of the Western Federation until he was betrayed by his brother. Even so he was still passionate about the integrity of his homeland.

"I have worked in Castalia for most of my life." He continued when no one else spoke. "I have never seen anything that makes me believe there is a secret mine."

Alaric waited from him to finish before he continued. "I can understand your concern Hulkan, but this is not up for debate. I have been in the mines and I have seen what is happening." It was clear that Hulkan wanted to argue some more, but Alaric did not give him the chance. "Whether you want to believe it is not going to change the fact." Alaric's words were starting to get heated. Hulkan stopped what he was about to say.

"I hate to admit it, but Alaric is right. I have lived most of my life in the Grand Cathedral and I had no idea about the mines underneath." Linus felt it was appropriate to speak.

"And who might you be?" Hulkan asked.

"This is Priest Linus." Alaric introduced him before Linus had a chance to. "I think his words shed some light on the situation. There is no point in having a secret diamond mine if you let everyone know it is there." Hulkan had to admit that Alaric made sense.

"So what is it you want us to do?" Jarwe was confused. "I don't think they are just going to let us wander in."

"That is where Linus comes into play." There was a wry smile on Alaric's face and a confused expression on Linus'. "There is a secret shaft into the mine. The wizard Minerva took me there when we were trying to get into the Inner Circle." Alaric continued to tell the story.

"So you are going to show us how to get into this shaft?" Sorrell spoke when Alaric had finished.

"Unfortunately I will not be going with you." Alaric's words brought an uproar from around the tent.

"You want us to besiege Castalia. You want us to attack a Dark Knight and you want us to do this without you?" Sorrell could not believe what he was hearing. "You are sending us to our deaths and you are simply going to walk away."

"Enough Sorrell!" Bern's voice boomed. "You will listen to Alaric in silence. There will be time to ask questions when he is done."

"Thank you Bern." Alaric's voice remained calm. "Linus will lead a small group to the entrance to the mines." Linus opened his mouth to speak, but then decided against it. He had no idea how Alaric was expecting him to find the secret entrance, but he assumed it would all come to light soon enough. It wasn't the time for him to question the Chosen One. "In the mines you will need to find the real High Chancellor. That is the only way you will be able to wrest power from the Dark Knight."

"I still can't see that helping us. How are we going to destroy a Dark Knight?" Sorrell still couldn't see the plan working.

"True the Dark Knight's are strong, but they can not stand up against the might of two armies. Za'aroz will have to surrender." Alaric sounded sure of his words

"It sounds all a little too easy. Where's the catch?" Jarwe asked.

"You will still need to create a distraction for those to enter the mines." Alaric had hoped he wouldn't have to explain that part. He wanted to tell Bern in private. "You will have to attack the city."

The room went completely silent as everyone let Alaric's words sink in. For a moment there had been a chance they would survive. In just one sentence Alaric had taken that away from them.

"What you ask of us is impossible." Hulkan spoke again. "We will waste many lives if we try to breach the walls of the city."

There were murmured agreements throughout the tent. Alaric sat patiently, waiting for the noise to die down. He had known that was going to be the response. He knew they would not understand what he was saying. There was more to the plan, but he wanted to wait for their complete attention before he explained it.

"You are to be a distraction, not the main event. All you need to do is pester the Dark Knight enough to keep his thoughts away from the High Chancellor. If he gains word of what we are doing then the High Chancellor is as good as dead."

The plan was a little better, but it was still flawed.

"And that's exactly what you wanted us to do here and we ended up losing many lives," Jarwe replied. "What is to stop the Dark Knight from sending out his soldiers like Ra'naroz did?"

Alaric knew that was true. There was nothing stopping Za'aroz from unleashing the Castalial army on the Alliance, but then he would lose the advantage of their high walls.

"As much as we don't want to fight the soldiers from Castalial, it will hold to our advantage. If the soldiers come out from behind their walls they will lose their protection. From there you will have to do your best to try and avoid any conflict."

That was all the time Alaric had for the discussion. He knew, given a chance, the command group would keep him there all day. Alaric raised his hand as a number of the command group opened their mouths to speak.

"Good, now that we know what we are up against we should get moving. The front of the army is already a day ahead of us." Bern stood as he spoke.

Alaric nodded to rest of the commanders as he stood and left with Linus. The priest would need some clothes and supplies before he was ready to travel.

"How am I supposed to get into the mines? I have no idea where this secret entrance is," Linus asked when they we out of the camp.

"I have implanted the memory in your mind. You will be able to draw on it only when the time is right." It was all Alaric was going to tell him.

Chapter 5: A New Direction

Alaric was glad to be back in the castle. The talk with the command group had been a lot harder than expected. There was much to be said for being the Chosen One, but having people blindly take directions was not one of them. In the end he was sure they were going to do the right thing. If nothing else Bern had faith in him and that was all that mattered. The army would do as Bern instructed.

The duke was in-between hangings and trials when he walked through the castle gate. The crowd in the courtyard was a lot smaller and he managed to pick his way through without too much trouble. He kept his head down so Xarles would not see him. The last thing he wanted to do was get involved.

Once he was back inside the castle Alaric made his way straight to Alena and Eldred's apartment. He hoped the wizard had managed to work out their next move. He still felt no compulsion to leave Jarrat, but he knew Eldred and Alena would be travelling with him. There was nothing left for him to do in Jarrat, however, it was time to move on.

Eldred was sitting by himself in the front room of their apartment. Alaric looked around for Alena, but she was not there. Although he was glad to see Eldred, he had really hoped to see her. They had only briefly spoken the day before and he wanted nothing else in the world than to hold her in his arms. He could almost smell the scent of her hair. Before he spoke he had to compose himself.

"Hello Eldred!" Alaric spoke warmly.

Eldred looked up from what he was doing. Alaric knew the great book in front of him was the prophecy. There was a slight flutter in his chest when he saw it. He felt as though he should be the one reading it.

"Good afternoon Alaric. It is good to see you today." It was obvious he had something else on his mind.

"Have you managed to find the passage you were looking for?" Alaric cut straight to the point.

"I believe so." Eldred seemed to focus. "I think I have worked out where we need to go."

Finally it seemed as though they were getting somewhere. As much as he thought the prophecy would be telling him where to go he was glad someone had finally found the answer. He had to admit it was a relief to have Eldred back. He needed someone to help make the decisions that were so critical for the Seven Kingdoms.

"I believe we have to travel to Čarolija Island. It is time the other wizards join the battle." Eldred seemed pleased with himself.

"Minerva has gone to speak with the others." Alaric explained, he was not so sure that Eldred's motives were true. "We need to focus on Adder and what we are going to do about him."

Alaric had his own agenda. The Serpentant's threat was still strong in his memory. He couldn't imagine his home town being destroyed by the evil creature. He needed to work out what Adder had in mind. It was very strange that he had demanded a meeting. It was then that he recognised the look of concern on Eldred's face.

"What is it?" he asked.

"There is a passage from the prophecy that really didn't make much sense.

One will return
From far away
She will be taken in
And made to stay
It doesn't matter what she wants
The other five will hold her there
It isn't right
But none do care

"It goes on, but that is the crux of it. It seems as though the others have taken Minerva prisoner."

"Are you sure that is what it means? We know the prophecy is not that straight forward. Is there anything that would lead you to believe the other five would betray her?"

"It is not something I would have thought, but she didn't leave on the greatest of terms. Many believed she should have remained on the island. The two of us knew the importance of keeping an eye on the High Chancellor and it seems as though she didn't do such a great job anyway." Eldred explained.

"I don't think that you should blame her. Za'aroz was very sneaky. No one knew he was the High Chancellor. The Gods only know how long he has been there."

"Be that as it may we knew that Castalia was a pivotal kingdom in all of this. She should have been paying more attention." Eldred was not as forgiving. "But you are right, there is no point in blaming her. What we have to worry about is what is happening on the island. This doesn't sound like something the other wizards would do. I would hate to think that another Dark Knight was causing trouble."

That was indeed a troubling idea. Alaric hoped it was not the case. He had to admit the words of the prophecy were disturbing, if they were indeed related to the Isle of Wizards. There was nothing that suggested a Dark Knight had infiltrated the island and there was nothing to suggest that Minerva was in danger, but he had a bad feeling something was not right.

"There is more," Eldred continued.

> Take the light off shore
> There is much to see
> And much to share
> But that is not all to be
> A plan be hatched
> An end in sight
> To meet the end
> Before the night.

"The rest of the passage seems to drift away into obscurity, but that seems pretty obvious to me."

Alaric knew that Eldred was reaching for an excuse to travel to Čarolija Island. He had to admit he was beginning to see his point of view. There was nothing in the prophecy to make him believe that was his destiny, although he could see the vague reference. He was starting to believe it was about time for the other five on the council to join the battle. The idea was starting to make sense to him.

"If we go to the island then what about Adder?" Alaric couldn't get the serpentant out of his mind.

Eldred had to think. He had to admit he had not been looking for answers to that riddle in the prophecy. Even so he had not read anything that he thought would be pertinent to the situation. As he remained quiet Alaric knew what the answer was going to be.

"I have read nothing about the Serpentant." Eldred made a sign of returning to the prophecy, but then looked up again.

"How long will it take us to reach Čarolija Island?" Alaric didn't sound enthused.

Eldred knew the question was coming. He also knew that Alaric would realise the discrepancy. A lie would be the only way to get around it, but that was out of the question.

"It will take at least six weeks for us to reach the island." Eldred paused and waited for Alaric to realise what he was saying.

That only allowed Alaric another two weeks to reach Scorpion Mountain. There was a chance that would work. Eldred didn't realise that Alaric could jump through the fabric of reality, but it was something Alaric had wanted to avoid. The effort it took to perform such a spell drained a lot of energy. He had only just recovered from one ordeal and he was going to have to start another. However, he was not going to go on Eldred's word completely.

"I think it would be a good idea if I read through the prophecy," Alaric kept his voice level. He didn't want to upset Eldred. "I need to make sure before I make my decision."

"That is all well and good, but don't wait too long. We need to be on the road very soon." Eldred warned.

Alaric didn't need to be told. He knew that time was of the essence. He wished he had more time, but that was not the case. He needed to find an answer and he needed to find it soon. Alaric moved to take the prophecy, but stopped before he was within reaching distance.

"I really believe that we need to travel to Čarolija Island. It is time that the other wizards get involved." Eldred said.

Before he could go any further the door opened behind him. The scent that followed the slight breeze indicated who it was before he could see. His heart skipped a beat. It was the moment he had been waiting for. All thoughts of the prophecy completely left his mind.

"Alena, it is good to see you again." Alaric stood as he spoke, a large smile appearing on his face. There was no sign of the seriousness of the previous conversation.

Alena returned his smile before she spoke. "It is good to see you too Alaric."

"How are you feeling today?" Eldred asked.

"I am feeling much better. I think I am ready to travel again." there was strength in her voice.

"I still think that it would be best for you to join your father and the other elves." Eldred returned. "It will be less dangerous for you."

"When has that ever been a concern?" Alaric wasn't sure if she was upset or just being playful. "It is my mission to stay with you and Alaric. When you leave I will leave."

Alaric's heart lifted with joy. As much as he had always been expecting Alena to be travelling with them he wasn't completely sure. As much as Alaric wanted to spend time with Alena he knew there were more important matters for him to deal with. At least he could spend time with her when they left the city.

"I should get back to business." Alaric said. "I think we will be on the move tomorrow." He picked up the prophecy before turning to leave the room.

"We will be ready to go." It seemed like the most appropriate response from Eldred.

As much as Alaric wanted to stay with Alena he was glad to be out of the apartment. The large tome felt light under his right arm. There was something homely about the book and he had a spring in his step as he made his way back to his apartment.

He ignored everyone else around him. Rumours had reached the castle of his arrival, but unlike Bern no one was prepared to speak to him. There was an air of mystery about him and the stories that had circulated the castle were of a man who was not to be disturbed.

There was a plate of food waiting for Alaric when he arrived back at his apartment. He had almost forgotten that he had not eaten since the morning meal. It was mid-afternoon and his stomach rumbled at the sight before him. Placing the prophecy on the table next to his plate he took a seat. He ignored the book until he had completely finished his meal.

Once he had eaten he opened the prophecy to a random page. He knew there was no particular order to the way it was written. He also remembered that the passages could change at any time. He needed to concentrate. He only had until morning to find the answers that he needed. There was no way the prophecy was going to make life easy for him.

It was late in the night when Alaric finally snuffed out the candle and went to bed. He thought he might have found a passage or two to explain what he had to do, but the references were extremely vague. More to the point the feeling that it was time to leave grew ever stronger throughout the afternoon. The direction gave him no real answers. It was a general tug towards the North-West. It could have been either the Scorpion Mountain or the Isle of Wizards.

There was one thing he did gauge from his reading and that was there was a fourth to join his group. At first he was unsure, but the more he read the more apparent it came. The only problem was that he was not sure if the man was ready to leave. Lord Richmond had taken the death of his advisor very hard. He had yet to leave his apartment and Alaric knew he would have his work cut out for him in the morning. For the moment he would just enjoy the comfort of the castle for one more night.

His dreams were disturbed during the night. It was not the restful sleep he had hoped for. At first he dreamt of Adder, sitting, by himself on the peak of Mount Scorpio. He sat there with the moon high in the sky. Alaric wanted to reach out to him, but he could not move. All he could do was watch as the moon slowly set. When morning came the serpentant had disappeared from the mountain.

The dream suddenly shifted to a familiar place. Alaric recognised his home town of Arsiliac, the town where he had spent most of his life, but something was different. There was an air of panic. At first Alaric didn't know what it was, but then it became all too apparent. Black smoke was thick in the air. People were running through the streets in pure terror. Alaric didn't need to see who it was to know who was causing the chaos. He had missed his meeting on top of the mountain and now Adder was taking his revenge. His heart sunk when he saw Bern's wife Mary and their two children running.

Adder was slowly stalking his prey. There were very few left alive, as if he had been saving Mary for when Alaric arrived. He wanted to help her, but there was nothing he could do. Although she was running and Adder was walking she didn't seem to be getting away from her predator. Adder seemed to be in no hurry. Alaric tried to look away. If he could not help then he didn't want to watch, but that was not going to happen. He couldn't control himself to look away.

What Alaric saw next made him scream in anguish. The serpentant had caught Mary. The two children had managed to escape, although that was a small mercy. Mary tried to struggle, but Adder's grip was too strong. He seemed to revel in her discomfort and fear, but that did not last long. For a moment he looked up, as if he was looking directly at Alaric. An unnatural smile crossed his face. When the smile passed he ripped Mary to shreds. Alaric couldn't look away whilst the serpentant bathed in her blood. Adder looked up one more time. Alaric tried to scream, but nothing came out, and then suddenly everything went black.

Alaric woke suddenly. His body was drenched in sweat. The ordeal of his dream was not lost on him. He could still see Mary as she was being torn apart. There was nothing he could do to wipe the image from his mind. The last thing he wanted to do was to fall asleep again, but he was exhausted and it was not long before his mind drifted away.

The rest of his dreams were not as violent or as memorable. When he woke in the morning the vision of Adder was still thick in his mind. He knew he had to meet the Serpentant on top of the mountain. The only problem was that he still didn't know if he had to go to the island. He would have to wait and see where the feeling led him. That was all he could do.

There were more immediate matters for him to deal with,he needed to convince Richmond that he had to travel with them. He knew that the lord was still grieving for his friend and he could only hope that Richmond could feel his own destiny drawing him away from the city.

He found Richmond sitting in his apartment staring out the window. The Lord of Bellarome didn't look up when Alaric entered. That was not a good sign. Alaric could hardly bring himself to speak, but he didn't have time to waste. They had to be out of Jarrat by midday.

"I am sorry to hear about Tancred. If I could have gotten here sooner I would have." He didn't know what else to say. He still felt somewhat responsible for Tancred's death.

"It was not your fault." There didn't seem to be much truth in Richmond's words. "We knew what we were getting into when we joined this folly. It was only a matter of time before one of us ended up dead." His words were cold.

Alaric knew he had his work cut out for him. "We need to talk."

"I know. I know what you want, but I don't know if I can help you. I think that my part in this story is over." Richmond sounded defeated.

"What would Tancred say?" It was too soon to bring up Tancred by name, but Alaric had no choice. He waited for the question to sink in before he continued. "He would tell you to keep going. He would tell you not to waste his death by giving up."

Alaric's words made sense, but that still didn't bring Richmond out of his malaise. He felt for the lord. It can't have been easy losing his best friend. He couldn't imagine what he would do if Bern was to die. The thought almost made him want to give up himself, but that wasn't an option. He had to convince Richmond that his life was not over. There was still more for him to do.

"I have consulted the *Prophecy of the Stone*." It seemed to be his last option. "Your path lies on the same a mine. You need to come with me if I am going to succeed."

The words hit a nerve with Richmond. He had always been a slave to the prophecy and Alaric knew it would gain his attention. He could only hope that it would do more than that. He didn't think he would be able to leave without Richmond. It was what the prophecy wanted. It was what he had to do.

"That is a cheap trick. I thought you would have more guile than that." Richmond didn't sound happy.

"I do what I can. I'm sorry to do this, but we need to be leaving very soon. I know you are still grieving, but unfortunately there is no time." Alaric hated to push.

"I guess I don't have any choice." Richmond knew it would be the case. He could feel the tug of the prophecy and it was only matter of time before he conceded to it. "I will be ready to go tomorrow morning. There are a few things I need to organise before I leave."

"I am sorry to do this to you, but we will be living at midday. There is no more time for us to remain here." Alaric explained.

Richmond didn't look happy. There had been something he had been putting off that he needed to do and now he doubted he was going to have time. At the very least he needed to make sure that Tancred was transported back to Bellarome. That was one thing he had promised his old friend. If either of them died on the journey then the other would make sure they made it home. That was also something that Richmond had been postponing.

"Okay. You will have to make sure that someone has my bags ready. I have to see to something before we leave." Richmond didn't sound impressed.

It was a small trade off, but one Alaric was willing to accept. Getting Richmond to come along was easier than he thought. When the lord agreed Alaric felt like a weight had been lifted from his shoulders.

Alaric knew he was ready to leave. The only problem was that he still didn't know where he was headed. His dream had put a new light on the situation, one that was none too pleasant. He needed to speak with Eldred before he went any further.

Both Eldred and Alena already had their bags packed and ready to go. Their supplies were being packed by Xarles personal staff and would be loaded onto a number of pack animals. Alaric's bags were also being organised for him, although he didn't think we would need anything. The clothes he wore were magically created and would not need washing or changing. Despite that he did think it would be nice to have some different clothes just in case.

"That is indeed a disturbing vision." Eldred agreed when Alaric had finished telling him about his dream.

"I don't think that it changes anything though. We need to travel to Čarolija Island. I am sure of it." Eldred continued.

Alaric wasn't sure if he should mention his feelings to Eldred. There was still plenty of time for him to make his decision. The problem he had with no true direction was that he couldn't jump through reality; he would need to follow the regular path. In the end he couldn't keep his concerns to himself.

"I don't know if the Isle of Wizards is the right direction. I can feel the tug of the prophecy, but it is not precise." Alaric blurted out.

Eldred was about to speak, but Alena cut in. "I think that is fair enough. I am also unsure of the true direction."

"Then where do you suppose we go?" Eldred was not happy.

"We can still head in the general direction. At this point in time I know that much. There is still plenty of time to decide on our final destination." Alaric explained as best he could.

Eldred wanted to continue the conversation, but again Alena spoke. "That sounds like a reasonable request. We are in no hurry to make a decision."

It was time for Alaric to leave. He had achieved what he came for. However, there was still one more call he had to make. He needed to speak once more with Duke Xarles. He had not committed the Enteroite army to the Alliance. It was something he was hoping to change.

"It is disappointing that you are leaving, but I am keen to see you return with the Opal stone." Alaric had met Xarles in the Royal offices.

He was taking a day off from the trials to attend to the piles of paper work on his desk. That was only half the excuse. Xarles really needed a day away from sentencing his countrymen to death.

"Of course, but that is not the reason I came here. You need to give the Alliance the bulk of your army. They are embarking on a dangerous mission and they need all the men they can get." Alaric kept his voice firm.

"As I said before, 'that is not something that I can't authorise. It is something that the queen has to do." Xarles stood his ground.

Alaric didn't believe his excuse. He had the run of Entero and the authority to move the army. Alaric could understand why he didn't want to, but he had to keep pushing. It was vital that they bolstered the Alliance's numbers. Although his plan meant minimal deaths he knew they didn't always work out. More men increased the chances of it succeeding.

"I know that you can order the army. You were the one who assumed control when the queen was unable to rule. You have taken the responsibility. Now that you have a tough decision to make you can't hide."

For the next five minutes Alaric had to listen to all the hard decisions that Xarles had made since he had assumed control. He really didn't have time, but he had to accept it. When he finished his rant Alaric brushed it off and continued.

"We need the soldiers."

"There is only so much I can do. I know that you need the extra men, but so do we. We lost a lot of soldiers in the war with both the Alliance and the Orglin. I can't risk another attack to the city. It is not a decision that I am going to make." Xarles was adamant.

There was one argument that Alaric had left, but he was not sure that he wanted to use it. The queen's life rested on him and the Opal stone. He could always threaten Xarles with her death if he didn't commit the soldiers. The thought passed through his mind, but in the end he decided against it. He had to admit that Xarles' argument was strong.

"I am disappointed that you have made that decision." Alaric didn't know what else to say. "Bear in mind if it wasn't for the Alliance then Jarrat would still be under the rule of a Dark Knight."

Alaric didn't wait for a response. He knew his statement would have more impact the longer the words stayed in the duke's mind. He wished he wasn't in such a hurry to leave because he knew he would be able to convince Xarles. He could only hope the duke would come to the realisation on his own.

When he returned to his apartment he found four bags packed and ready to go. He had only asked for two changes of clothes, but it seemed the servers got a little carried away. There was no time to waste as he heard a knock on the door. Four pageboys entered to carry his bags to the stables where Adelanta would be waiting for him.

Chapter 6: Hatching a Plan

It took longer than Bern had expected for the army to completely pack up camp. It seemed their extended stay in Jarrat had made them somewhat lazy. It wasn't until the morning of the fifth day that they had completely left the field. Bern remained behind with Sorrell, Pernian and Hadar to make sure everyone was gone, while the rest of the command group led the army. Bern was sure that once word now reached the Alliance that they were heading toward Castalia, some of his men disappeared into the forest. It was a frustrating fact, but he could hardly blame them. What they were being asked to do was at best frightening. Without the relevant information it would seem like a suicide mission.

Bern wanted to tell everyone of their plan. It was the only way to set the men's minds at ease. Although none of the soldiers would say anything whilst their general was around he knew what they were thinking. Deep down he also knew the reasons why he couldn't reveal anything. The fewer amount of people who knew about the diamond mine the better.

For the first time since the battle with the orglin Bern wore his dress armour. Lighter than his battle armour it was still more uncomfortable than his riding leathers, but he needed to look the part. He was the General of the Alliance and he needed to look like it. His presence in itself was enough to lift the spirits of the soldiers and he would have to suffer in his armour all the way to Castalia.

The next problem Bern had was navigating the Western Woods. The forest to the west of Jarrat was denser than that to the east. The army moved slowly in and out of the trees. Making camp for the night was even worse. The army stretched out for miles, pitching their tents wherever they could find free space. There was no room for the command tent or any of the other larger tents.

Trying to travel from the back of the line to the front was not as easy as Bern had hoped. Between the soldiers and the trees there was little room for anything else. Bern didn't mind though. It meant he didn't have to meet with rest of the command group. Most of the commanders were still upset they were going to Castalia. Bern was able to hide amongst the trees and gain some kind of anonymity. Even though the soldiers knew who he was they acted as though they didn't. That was true for at least the first two days. On the morning of the third day he ran into an old friend.

"Ho there, Bern." The voice sounded familiar, but he had to turn around before he recognised who it was.

The face that met him was not as carefree as the greeting. Bern recognised the man as the bandit Delbert. Despite his black hair being cut short against his scalp there was no denying who it was. Bern suddenly felt very bad, he had not thought about the small group of bandits since they had left Kiarome. As much as they had assimilated themselves into the Darshivallian army they still held their own identity. Bern was glad to see him.

"Wonders will never cease. I am surprised to see that you still have your head."

"Is Alaric travelling with us?" Delbert sounded excited at the question.

"I'm afraid not." Bern wasn't sure where he was going with his question.

Delbert's face dropped. Bern was not really in the mood for conversation, but he couldn't brush the man aside.

"I had heard rumours, but I did not believe that they were true. I can't believe that Alaric would send us to attack Castalia and then leave us." There was a confused expression on his face.

Bern should have realised that was coming. "There is more to this than meets the eye," He said. It was vague, but Bern hoped it would be enough.

"That doesn't really answer anything." Delbert would not be so easily dissuaded.

Bern nearly walked into a tree as he tried to come up with an excuse. It was not a good place for such a discussion. There were other soldiers moving around them and they couldn't stop to talk. If they did then they would be pushed forward from those behind. There was little opportunity for privacy, even if Bern could tell Delbert the truth.

"I'm afraid not, but it is the best that I can do."

Then Bern had an idea. He needed men to go into the mines with him. At first he thought he would need to find some trusted soldiers, but he felt as though he had found his men. There was more than a little luck with their meeting. Although they had been bandits in another life Delbert and his men were part of the Alliance. Even though he felt it was the right decision it was neither the time nor the place for such a discussion.

"There will be time to explain things further, but this is not a good place." Bern made a sign of looking at the soldiers around them. He hoped Delbert would understand.

"Of course general. I didn't mean to suggest anything." Delbert accentuated his speech so more soldiers could hear. "I was just interested to know more on what is happening."

Bern wanted to tell him to keep his voice down. He was attracting more attention to them than was necessary. He armour gave away who he was if anyone took the time to look at him, but he knew the soldiers would not dare to look around aimlessly. At the mention of his name he knew the soldiers would try and listen in to their conversation and it wouldn't be long before the gossip was throughout the army. At least he could hope that most of the soldiers wouldn't know who Delbert was and he would not say anything too revealing.

"I will speak with you once we are outside the forest. There are things that need to be discussed." Bern kept his voice low. "How is Rolanda?"

"I would imagine she has calmed down by now." Delbert smiled as he spoke.

"That sounds ominous."

"Not really. The women from our small group were told to return home once we were finished at Kiarome. Rolanda was not overly happy that idea."

That didn't sound right to Bern. He didn't authorise anyone to make such a command. As far as he was concerned Rolanda was still the leader of the small group of bandits, but he had to admit he had not really thought about it much.

"That doesn't sound right to me. Do you know who it was who made such a command?"

"No, but I don't think that it really matters." Delbert didn't sound too upset.

"Why is that?"

"Women and an army don't really mix." He winked as he spoke.

Bern hadn't thought about that. He had to admit Delbert made a good point and that thought was clearly written on his face.

"Oh, that's not what I mean." Delbert continued. "It is the men I was concerned for. If they became too frisky with one of the girls they would more than likely end up losing an appendage or two."

Bern couldn't help himself and laughed out loudly. The thought of the looks on the soldiers' faces was too funny to resist. It was probably for the best that the women weren't around. He was not sure if he would be comfortable sending them into the mines.

"I think you should go back to the others." Bern suggested. "I need to make my way to the front of the line."

Delbert simply nodded his head before attempting to make his way back to the other bandits. One plus was that the Darshival Army had allowed the bandits to remain as one unit. That would make life easier for Bern.

Bern had to laugh to himself as he continued through the forest. He had no idea how, out of so many people, Delbert was able to find him. The more he thought about his idea the more he realised it was the right thing to do. The prophecy knew no bounds. It could pull people through the most impossible situations. That was made even more evident as Delbert struggled to move through the mass of soldiers.

He chanced himself one more look at Delbert and wondered at how the man had come to such a fate. Alaric had told him the story of how they met in Stellerville. One day he was drunk and in despair and not long after he was leading a small band of bandits. In truth it was his wife who led the band, but now that she had left he was in command.

Bern quickly pushed that idea out of his mind. There were more important matters for him to deal with. The closer they came to Castalia the more nervous the army would become. He would need to figure out what he was going to tell them. That was still at least two weeks away, but at the rate they were travelling through the forest Bern wouldn't be surprised if was four.

No one seemed to notice that Bern was the leader of the army as he tried to make his way through the crowd of soldiers. Even wearing his ceremonial armour didn't seem to help. Once they were out of the forest he would again ride on horseback at the front of the army, but for the moment that was just not possible. The anonymity was nice, but it didn't help his situation.

The days in the forest passed much the same as each other. The soldiers would march from dawn to dusk. They were each given a sandwich and a pouch of water to have throughout the day. When night fell the soldiers would sleep where they stopped. The cooks and their helpers came around with the evening meal, but on more than one occasion some of the soldiers went hungry. The situation was not pleasant, but they knew it was only going to last for a short period of time.

It took the army almost two weeks to be completely out of the forest. Once the vanguard was far enough ahead for the rest of the army to emerge Bern called for a halt. He knew it had been a tough march and the soldiers needed a day to rest. He also wanted to make sure they didn't leave anyone behind. Their numbers were already dangerously thin. They couldn't afford to lose any more. He was more willing to lose time than lose men.

As they had continued through the forest Bern had a feeling they were travelling too quickly. He couldn't explain why, but that was another reason why he called the army to a stop. The break finally gave him the chance to rejoin the other commanders. He wanted to meet with them before he spoke with Delbert again.

"I don't understand why we have stopped." Jarwe was in a particularly foul mood. "We have already lost enough time traipsing through the forest."

Bern couldn't understand why he was in such a hurry. There was no real reason why they needed to rush towards Castalia. It was as if he was in a hurry to die.

"We have time. I have a feeling we need to wait for something. Before you ask I don't know what it is." Bern knew that was not going to appease anyone.

"This just gets better and better." Hadar didn't sound pleased. He had always backed Bern's judgement, but even the large duke from Hondin Lel couldn't believe what he was hearing. "The longer we wait the more chance the Dark Knight will hear of our arrival. Our only chance of success is to take him by surprise. Once they are inside their walls the Castalial Army will be impossible to defeat."

The conversation continued for a few minutes with everyone agreeing with Hadar. Bern should have expected such a response and been ready with his rebuttal. It did, however, give him a chance to think. Even after all the time in the forest he had still not formulated a plan. He had hoped the command group would be of some use, but it seemed as though they just wanted to complain.

"There are things we need to plan before we reach Castalia. Remember we are not going to there to storm the city. We need to formulate a plan to make the attack purely a distraction." Bern tried to explain as best he could.

"I think it would be best if you explained what you are planning a little better." Orric replied.

That was not as easy as it sounded. Bern didn't really know what he was planning, but he was sure that he was going to take the bandits with him to the mines. He didn't know who, if anyone, he was going to take from the command group. That was not going to go down well. But Orric was right, he needed to explain things better if he was going to get the advice he needed.

"I will take a small group with me to the mines." He was interrupted before he had a chance to continue.

"And where do you suppose you are going to get this small group from?" Jarwe was still aggravated.

"I have a few ideas, but I don't want to say anything until I am sure. You can all be sure that I will handle that side of things." Bern was not yet ready to explain that side of his plan, it was the distraction he needed help with. "You need to make sure no one comes looking for us. If they realise what we are doing then the High Chancellor will be dead. If he dies then we have no proof that the Dark Knight is in charge."

"So what is the distraction that you want from us?" Jarwe asked, a little less hostile than before.

"That is what I was hoping you could help me with." Bern looked at everyone around the table.

"Assaulting the city walls would keep them distracted, but I doubt we would survive to see the result of your little espionage trip." Sorrell stated the obvious.

"That's good. One thing we don't want to do is unnecessarily waste lives. There will be deaths, but we need to keep it to a minimum." Bern was starting to relax.

"We could build catapults." Wojtek spoke for the first time that day. The old man was Sorrell's advisor and although he wasn't shy about speaking in the group he liked to listen. Only when he felt it absolutely necessary would he speak. "I am sure that would keep them distracted for a while. They would be too busy dodging rocks to notice you."

"That would be great, but there is one flaw to that plan." Hulkan spoke. "There are no rocks for you to fling. A long time ago the High Chancellor made sure there was nothing for a hundred leagues to use in a siege engine. If we're going to do that then we would have to have brought the ammunition with us."

That was true.

"What about the outer buildings?" Hadar asked. "I know it has been a long time since I have been to Castalia, but I am sure it hasn't changed too much. If the outer wall is not completely constructed then they will abandon the outer city once they are under attack. Once they are inside the inner city then we can break down the buildings of the outer city and use that against them."

"Now that is not a bad idea. We want to give them enough time to enter the inner city. What we don't want to do is cause any unnecessary deaths. If that works then we should have no problems entering the desert." Bern sounded more confident. "Anything else you can come up with?"

"We could build our own fortifications. It might not have the same impact as the bombardment, but it should get their attention," Sorrell suggested.

"What about using the archers?" Pernian added.

"I don't think that would work," Bern disagreed. "It would bring our men too close to the walls. Men would die on both sides. That is something we want to avoid."

The ideas kept flowing. Some were worth thinking about, some were laughed at and some were just passed over. In the end Bern was happy with their discussion. He felt as though the first two ideas were the best. The building of the fortification would give the Castalials a chance to move to safety and the bombardment should give him enough cover to leave the army unnoticed.

The first part of his plan was starting to come to fruition and that was a load off his mind. That was, however, the easy part. The army was not going to attack and was therefore somewhat out of danger. What he and the group of bandits had to achieve was a lot more dangerous. He could only hope that the priest was able to find the mysterious shaft into the mine. It would have been better if he had been there before. The fact that Linus had never seen this mine shaft did nothing to ease his concerns. He wasn't confident he could find it.

The army was on the move again at first light. Bern travelled as if a weight had been lifted from his shoulders. The prophecy was telling him that he had done the right thing. That thought in itself was enough to bring a smile to his face. It was the first time he had smiled in a long time. It felt good as he rode at the front of the line.

When they camped for the night Bern searched for Delbert. Once he found the man he would then need to go somewhere private to talk. The command tent was out of the question. He didn't want the others to know anything until he was sure what he was going to do.

It was not as easy to find Delbert as Bern thought. That only increased his belief that the prophecy had a hand in the two men running into each other in the forest. The bandits were not well known in the army. At first Bern asked for Private Delbert, when no one knew who he was he asked for the group of bandits, when no one knew who they were he was not sure what he could do. It took him a while but then he realised the bandits were part of the Darshivallian army. Hopefully Sorrell might have an idea where they would be stationed.

"Ah yes." Sorrell thought for a moment after Bern had asked the question. "I do remember the bandits that joined us just before we reached Kiarome. I must admit I thought it was a strange decision when they were asked to join the Alliance, but they have been quite handy."

That really didn't answer Bern's question at all. At least Sorrell knew who they were, that was a start. He wanted to ask the question again, but it was clear that the Darshivallian General had more to say.

"Why is it you are looking for them? As far as I know they are just part of the army now. I would doubt very much if they are still together."

Bern knew differently, but he didn't think Sorrell needed to know. "For argument's sake if they were still together who would I need to speak with to find them?"

"That would be Captain Coen. He keeps track of the regiments. If anyone would know it would be him." Sorrell was quick to answer.

It would be too obvious if Bern left straight away. Even though he was sure that Sorrell didn't know what he was up to he didn't want to take the chance. It still didn't feel right to tell the others what he was planning, so he made small talk for the next fifteen minutes before making an excuse to leave. He was sure when he left that Sorrell had no idea what he was planning to do.

It didn't take too long for Bern to find the captain once he started looking. Although the Alliance was considered to be one big army the separate armies that made it up liked to keep to themselves. Of course they mixed together, but when it came to sleeping and marching they remained separate. It was something that Bern wasn't overly happy about, but it kept the peace. He only hoped that it didn't cause problems when the true war started.

The Darshivallian army was camped not too far from the command tent. He found Captain Coen searching over his soldiers' tents. He was making sure they were all doing the right thing. It was important that the soldiers didn't become lax with their day-to-day duties.

"Captain Coen!" Bern kept his voice firm.

"Yes, Sir!" Coen saluted when he saw Bern. He recognised the General of the Alliance straight away. As much as he still believed Sorrell was his general, as did the rest of the Darshivallian army, he knew that Bern was in command.

"I am looking for Private Delbert. Do you know where he is?" Bern asked.

"Delbert? Ah, yes, the bandit." There was a mixture of respect and disgust in his voice. Bern wasn't sure what that meant. "They are camped at the back of our site. Go down there and you should see them."

Bern thanked Coen, saluted once and then walked away. He could feel the prophecy tugging at him again. The feeling had grown since mid-afternoon. At first it was not more than an itch, but when they stopped for the night it was a throbbing in the back of his mind. He knew it wouldn't leave until he had spoken with Delbert. At least the prophecy was helping again, even if it was being annoying.

To Bern's surprise he found that the Bandits were extremely regimented. Their tents were in perfect rows making a hollow square. In the middle of the square was a small fire. The bandits were sitting around quietly speaking with one another. Once Bern had walked into the firelight all eyes turned to him. It was well known that no one from outside the group entered their campsite. It was not that they were disliked or that they disliked others, it was just that they preferred to be left on their own.

"Bern! It is good to see you again." Delbert sounded genuinely pleased to see him. He stood and offered Bern a seat by the fire. "Come and sit. I am sure we could get some wine or ale to pass the time." It was clear by the reaction of the others that it was not something they did regularly. Alcohol was in short supply to the soldiers and Bern was surprised he made the suggestion.

"No, thank you," Bern replied. "I need to speak with you in private."

"There is nothing that you can say that I won't tell the others."

The rest of the group looked concerned at Bern's comments. When their leader replied their minds were set at ease. One thing Rolanda had said to Delbert before she had left was not to keep secrets from the others. She knew it was the way of the army that the leaders kept things from the troops, but that was not the way she wanted things.

"That is fine, but I still need to speak with you in privacy. What you tell the rest of your group is of no consequence to me." Bern didn't mean to sound condescending.

"Very well." Bern was the general and Delbert had to do as he was commanded. "Men, go to your tents."

That was not what Bern had in mind, but he was grateful for it. There was less chance of prying ears hearing what they were talking about where they were. He had expected to take a walk amongst the tents, but this was a much better situation.

Once they were alone Bern started to explain his plan. He brushed over what the main army was going to do and went straight to the infiltration of the mines. He found it hard to completely explain what his plan was, as he was not sure what was going to happen. He did his best and Delbert listened to his every word.

"It sounds like something we can help you with," Delbert didn't sound overly confident.

Bern noticed the edge in his voice and he was expecting it. He was not sure if he could trust the man if he was to follow blindly. The promising sign was that Delbert didn't instantly dismiss the idea.

"This will not be easy. If we survive the mines and reach the Grand Cathedral then we have to face the Dark Knight Za'aroz. That will potentially be a death sentence to us all." Bern wanted to make sure he knew all the risks.

"Of course, I'm not stupid." Delbert almost sounded offended. "There are risks in everything we do. One thing Rolanda said to me before she left was that I have to do anything that you ask me and that is exactly what I am doing." He sounded somewhat sure of himself.

"That is not at all what I am saying. You have a choice to say no if you think it is too dangerous. I am sure when Rolanda gave you that command she didn't realise what it meant." Bern didn't like what he was hearing.

"I think this is exactly what she meant. You know as well, if not more so, that we are all slaves to the prophecy. This feels right to me. I don't think that we have any other choice. I am sure the rest of my group will feel the same."

Bern knew exactly what he was talking about. It seemed as though the prophecy had already sunk its teeth into Delbert. He was glad in a way. He was sure the bandits needed to come with him into the mines. The prophecy had made things all too easy for him and he was not complaining. He only hoped they were doing the right thing.

"Is there anything else that you wish to discuss with me tonight?" Delbert asked when Bern didn't reply.

"No, I think that is about it." It all happened so quickly and smoothly he was not sure if it had happened at all.

"I think I should let the others know. We will need to prepare ourselves for such a mission."

"Just remember, that no one else is to know about this. There is no telling where the Evil One has spies. If Za'aroz finds out about this then we are as good as dead already. Make sure that your men know this." Bern reiterated the fact.

"Of course, my lord, I understand the situation." Bern didn't like being called a lord, but he let it slide. "We want to keep our necks as much as you do."

Bern left the firelight happy with what he had achieved. The plan was starting to take shape, although it still had a long way to go. He had not expected Delbert to accept his decision so easily. The risks of their mission were great and there was a slim chance they would survive.

***

The fire was starting to die down when they had finished talking. Delbert's gang of bandits had taken the news well. They all felt the same as their leader. The prophecy was taking hold of their lives and there was nothing they could do about it. Instead of feeling depression with their impending doom there was a feeling of purpose.

Delbert thought of his wife as he walked towards his tent. She would be proud of what he was doing. That was something that was very important to him. He was also glad she was back in Darshival. He knew all too well that if she was still with them then she would want to come. That was something he couldn't allow.

He had to chuckle to himself. It was not that long ago he was a drunk in the tavern in Stellerville. Now he was about to embark on a mission to save the Seven Kingdoms. That was something he was very proud of.

Chapter 7: Castalia

Bern had lost count of the days since they had left Jarrat. His mind was filled with the different scenarios as they came closer to Castalia. When they reached the great city Bern was still no closer to knowing the right path. All he knew was that he was to enter the mines with Delbert and the other bandits. No one else from the command group came to mind to join him. He knew it was not going to go down well. He had a feeling at least one of them was supposed to go with him, but he had no idea who and it was a frustrating thought. Each night in the command tent the other leaders pressed him for more information and each night Bern told them that once he knew they would know. Until then they would just have to wait, like Bern did himself.

Bern had hoped that the answer would have come to him once they arrived, but it didn't. He had at least a couple of days to think before he had to make a decision. They were not going to leave for the mines before everyone from Castalia was safely behind the city walls. Once that was done the army would start the bombardment giving him the distraction he needed to sneak into the desert. The thought played out in his mind over and over again.

"What do we do now?" Sorrell asked the question that was on all their minds.

The army had stopped clearly within sight of the city, but outside of firing distance. At first no one took any notice of them. They made no attempt to attack and no one made any move to run for safety. It was as if they weren't there at all.

Bern had left the front of the line once the city came into view. He didn't tell anyone where he was going or what he was doing. That put everyone on edge. They didn't want to make a decision without him, but nothing was going to plan.

"I guess we're going to have to do something to get their attention," Jarwe said as they waited for Bern to return.

"What do you propose we do?" Hadar said as he was playing with the hilt of his sword.

"I guess if we started to attack that would cause them to flee in panic. I doubt they would have enough soldiers stationed in and around the outer city to stop us," Jarwe suggested.

"Bern didn't want us to attack anyone," Pernian argued.

"Bern also said that the citizens would rush inside the city walls once they saw us arrive, and they haven't," Jarwe continued.

"Let's not do anything rash just yet. We have only been here for a couple of hours. I am sure when they realise we are not friendly they will do as we expected." Sorrell wanted to defuse the situation.

"In Bern's absence I am the highest ranking officer here. I think we should send some soldiers in to stir up trouble." Jarwe was getting upset. He didn't like the way the others were ganging up on him.

"I really don't think that is a good idea," Pernian started before Sorrell interrupted him.

"You were once the general of the Alliance, but you stepped down from that position. Now you are just the general of the Remidian army, the same rank I hold with the Darshivallian army. You don't outrank me anymore." There was a certain amount of venom in Sorrell's voice.

"This is not the place for such a conversation," Orric barked at the two men. "If you want to squabble like children then take it to the back of the line. If the soldiers knew what you were saying then they would lose all confidence with your ability to lead."

"We can't risk attacking," Hadar spoke before anyone else could. "If we do then we risk stirring up a hornets' nest. The last thing we want to do is provoke the Castalial army to attack. If that happens then we are all as good as dead."

Jarwe wanted to speak again, but stopped short. He had to admit that Hadar was right. They couldn't attack, but they still needed to show some kind of aggression. The longer they remained as they were the less frightened the people of Castalia would be.

"That still doesn't help us." Sorrell looked around when he spoke. There was still no sign of Bern. "Where is our general when we need him?"

There was an air of frustration about the group. They were sure that no one would come up with an answer before Bern returned. The most frustrating part was that they had no idea where he had gone and there was no telling when he would be back.

"Look at us!" Jarwe almost started laughing. "A few months ago and we were making all the decisions. Now, it seems as though we crumble whenever Bern is not around."

It took the others a moment for his words to sink in. At first it seemed like an offence, but when they realised the humour they all started to laugh. It was good to break the tension if it was only for a moment. It was not long before the severity of the situation took over again.

"Why is everyone looking so glum?" the sound of Bern's voice took everyone by surprise.

"No one is taking any notice of us." Jarwe was the first to recover. "We were just wondering how to get their attention."

"I wouldn't worry about that. I am sure that someone will be coming over to say hello very soon." Bern was a little too relaxed for their liking.

"That is a big risk." Hadar was the first to answer. "We could be here for a long time waiting for an emissary."

Bern looked around at the other commanders. They all sat on their horses with concerned expressions on their faces. He was surprised they didn't realise what he was thinking. It seemed so obvious to him, but it looked as though he was going to have to explain.

"What would you do if an army, not necessarily a hostile one, randomly turned up in your territory?" The question hung in the air for a moment. No one answered. "I am sure that you would send someone to speak with them before you attacked. I don't think anyone wants unnecessary violence. Even though the Dark Knight is in control it will be a while before he knows we are here. I am sure whoever is in command of the outer forces will come to treat with us."

It made sense, but the others found it highly dubious. There was so much riding on what they had planned. If it didn't work exactly how they had planned then there was a good chance they would all die and the Evil One would eventually rule the Seven Kingdoms. That thought wasn't worth thinking about and yet it played on all their minds. If anyone else had a better idea, or even any idea, they would have continued the discussion. Instead they just sat on their horses and waited.

They waited for almost an hour before they could see a small group of soldiers approach. One carried a white flag, which he was furiously waving above his head. He didn't want any doubts of their attentions as they rode towards the opposing army. It was not long before they could see the black armour and the crest of the High Chancellor's Elite guard. The looks on the soldiers' faces showed they were not happy with the situation.

"I am Captain Cassius, who should I be addressing?" Cassius looked up and down at the group of leaders.

Captain Cassius was an imposing figure on horseback as he would have been standing. On the ground he stood over six and a half feet tall and on horseback he looked down on everyone. A scar across his left cheek indicated he had seen action in the past and was not just a large man on show. His blonde hair was cut short, but not shaven like the men behind him. A short sword hung by his waist, but it was the massive claymore strapped to his back that caught everyone's attention. The expression on his face showed that he wasn't happy with the new arrivals and the white flag was certainly not his idea.

"You can speak with me," Bern spoke calmly, a slight smile on his face.

Cassius looked at him and was not sure if he was the right person to speak to. Bern had decided to forgo his armour that morning and wore a simple linen shirt and corded pants. The others soldiers wore armour with their respective crests. If anything Cassius thought he looked like a page, albeit a large one.

"And what might your name be?" Cassius was not going to take his word on face value.

"Captain Cassius, this is General Bern," Jarwe spoke before Bern had a chance. "His word is final."

Cassius still didn't look happy. Jarwe definitely looked like a soldier, but Bern did not. He would have to take their word on Bern's position, but he would watch them all very carefully. If they were lying it wouldn't be long before he would realise. He had been in the army for a long time and knew the body language of true leader.

"Why is it that you have brought your army to our borders?" Cassius cut straight to the point.

"We have some disturbing news about the High Chancellor. We believe there are traitors trying to usurp his power. We are here to offer our aid." No one really knew where Bern was going with his comments.

"I can assure you as one of the High Chancellor's Elite Guard there is no one trying to usurp his power." Cassius couldn't believe what he was hearing.

Bern knew the Castalial emissary wouldn't just believe his word and he was counting on it. He needed to goad the captain just enough to get him to do what the Alliance wanted.

"Well that is good to hear, but that doesn't change the fact that we will be moving into the city." Things were starting to make sense to the others. "We have not come all this way to turn around on your word. We will enter and conduct our own investigation. If there are any traitors then we will find them. I would think that is in the best interest of everyone." Bern kept his voice calm and level. That annoyed the captain even more.

"That is not your choice to make. Only the High Chancellor himself can authorise a foreign army to gain entrance into the city." Cassius let his hand grip the hilt of his short sword.

"Unfortunately we don't have time. Once the traitors know we are here they will go to ground. We need to act now. We have only waited for your arrival as a courtesy." Bern didn't miss a beat.

"If you come any closer to our border then it will be considered an act of war. No one has ever breached our walls. You will waste many lives trying to get into the inner city." There was a hint of pride in Cassius' voice.

Bern had achieved what he wanted. The captain knew they were planning on moving into the city. He would have to evacuate the outer city and move everyone inside the wall. The outer wall was still a few months away from being completed. The only ones who would need to be evacuated were the dwarves working in the sand mines. They would, of course, return to the city once the sun had sent.

"I am sorry that you feel that way, but there is nothing I can do about it. What we do, we do for the good of all. We have to root out the enemy. You should understand that as well as anyone."

The further the conversation continued the more irate Cassius became. He had woken up that morning thinking it was just going to be another day, but things had changed. The most frustrating thing was that the opposing commander would not see sense. He couldn't believe that an invading army would ever reach his doorstep in his lifetime.

"Very well. But I don't think you are going get very far here. I can only assume you have a death wish." Cassius resigned himself to the fact that things were not going to change.

"You should go and speak with your superiors. I am sure they will see things same as I." It was all Bern could do to stop himself from laughing. Things were working out better than expected.

"This is an act of war. I will give you until nightfall to change your mind. If by morning you have not left then I will know you all wish to die." Cassius didn't wait for a response.

The worst part was that his men had seen him lose control. Throughout the last ten years there had been no one above him. There had been no one to tell him what to do. The High Chancellor was the only one in a position to give him orders. And that hadn't happened in a long time. He was experiencing something he had never expected to see. Someone was standing up to his authority, not only that they were defying him as well. His next problem was trying to get the rest of the army to understand. He was in command of the High Chancellor's Elite Guard and no one could tell him what to do, but that didn't give him power over the regular army. He had never liked the general and the feeling was mutual and now it seemed as though they were going to have to work together. There was a lot that he had to think about before he made his next move. He wished he had given the opposing army more time.

"What was that all about?" Jarwe asked when the Elite Guard had left.

"I just wanted to give them something to think about. I think that they will be thinking about it for a while now." Bern let the smile reach his face. It had been hard holding it inside for so long.

"You know that was only the Captain of the Elite Guard." Linus took the opportunity to speak. "He doesn't speak for the bulk of the army. I think you managed to upset the wrong person."

Bern laughed out loudly. "I don't think it matters who I upset. The information will get back to the right people. They will start moving back inside the city walls. I think I have upset just the right person. I know about the differences between Captain Cassius and General Kato." He didn't know why he knew, but there was nothing more that he was sure of. "If I upset Kato then he might be inclined to attack. That is not what we want. By upsetting Cassius he will have to go to Kato. In the meantime I am sure he will do the right thing and move the citizens inside the walls. He might be arrogant and he might be self-important, but he still has the best interests of the city at heart."

Everyone looked at Bern strangely. It was not so much the words, but the tone of his voice. Even Linus, who had known Bern the least of all of them, recognised the change. The entity had come to the surface again. It seemed as though Bern was the only one who didn't realise. He knew something was not right, but he didn't know what it was. Regardless of how they felt they couldn't disagree with his logic.

"It seems as though you have everything worked out." Jarwe spoke again.

"I hope so, but then again I can only do so much. I am sure that Cassius will do the right thing," Bern replied.

His voice had returned to normal. The change was so sudden that no one knew what had happened. They couldn't be sure it was not Bern who had played the game with Cassius. The thought was very discerning and no one wanted to ponder it any further.

"What do we do now?" Hadar asked.

"Now we wait. The men can start building the catapults. Until all the citizens are inside the walls there is nothing we can do. Hopefully that will be achieved during the night. I would like to be leaving at first light," Bern explained.

Although Bern's words ended the conversation no one left. They watched the city as if something was going to happen. No one wanted to move in case they missed something important. They all stared at the city waiting for the answer to come to them. It wasn't until Bern spoke again did they move.

"You know what they say? A watched pot will never boil. I think we should make ourselves busy." It was more than a suggestion.

"How will we know when the city is clear?" Sorrell asked before they started to move.

"We will have to send some soldiers into the outer city after nightfall. I am sure it won't take them long to work out if it is empty or not." Bern explained.

"I doubt Cassius will start moving the citizens after nightfall," Linus said. "After nightfall it doesn't take long for the temperature to become deathly cold. If I was to hazard a guess I would say he will start evacuating the outer city as soon as possible. He only said he would give us until nightfall to give himself time to do what he needed to do."

Linus' words made sense and only made things better for them, but Bern would still have to send soldiers into the city to be sure.

"That being the case we should ready ourselves for a cold night. Have the soldiers prepare campfires with enough wood to last throughout the night. We don't want anyone freezing to death," Bern said, ending the meeting.

Bern sat on his horse long after the others had left. He stared at the city hoping to get a sign. As much as Linus' words made sense he couldn't be completely sure. He could see people, occasionally, moving around the buildings. From the distance he couldn't tell what they were doing. With a little luck Cassius would have ordered them inside the walls.

The sun was at the top of its arc when Bern finally turned his horse around. There was still much he had to do before he was ready to leave. With a little luck he would be able to sneak out of the camp before first light. He wanted to be at the edge of the dessert when the sun rose. There were two reasons for his plan. The first was to be able to sneak out of the camp without the army knowing where they were going and the second was to leave without the city watch being able tack him. His mission relied on stealth for the first part. That was the key to its success.

He wove his way through the camp until he found Delbert. The bandit turned corporal was inspecting his small battalion. Bern felt bad calling them bandits now that they were fully assimilated into the army. He had to get that terminology out of his head.

"I wouldn't worry too much about it," Delbert said. "I myself was only a bandit for a short period, but most of these men have been all of their lives. We are proud of our heritage and take no offence. Truth be told we are more offended at being called soldiers. It is a funny world."

Bern was glad with the candour. It had been a long time since he had been able to speak openly. It seemed that every conversation he had held such importance. He had almost forgotten what it was like to have a casual chat. He wanted to continue, but he knew he could not. Again he needed to have another serious conversation.

"I need you to have your men ready to leave before dawn. You need to choose twenty of your best and most trusted men." Bern explained.

"I thought we would all be coming?" Delbert sounded upset. "The men are all ready for your command."

"I am sorry, I also thought I would need all of you, but that is not the case. I am afraid if there are too many of us and we will be seen by the tower watch." Bern continued.

"What am I going to tell those who miss out? They will not be happy."

"I have another job for them." Bern smiled. "After nightfall I need them to enter the outer city to see if there is anyone left. We cannot start this mission until the outer city is completely empty."

Delbert thought for a moment. "Yes, that is an honourable task. I am sure that everyone will understand."

Bern was hoping that would be the result. "Now you must reiterate to your men that they must not be seen. I cannot stress this enough."

"I understand general. No one will let you down."

That was the end of the conversation. Now it was time to let the last member of his crew know what he had planned. He hoped that the man would already know. If he did then there could be no doubt. Bern was not sure he was making the right decision and that worried him. He didn't like making moves without being totally sure.

"How goes it Bern?" Hadar boomed when he saw Bern approach.

"It is all coming together nicely. How are the siege weapons coming along?" Bern returned.

"If we work through the night then we should have some ready by morning. Not sure how we will go with the cold, but I guess we can try our best. If this was a serious siege then I would suggest waiting another few days, but as it is, these things should suffice. All in all I think it will work out nicely. The attack won't be strong enough to cause any real problems, but it will be enough not to be considered a diversion. I am sure that our little ruse will work." Hadar sounded confident.

Bern was relieved to hear that. If the weapons weren't ready by morning then they would have to wait another day. He had a bad feeling they were running out of time. There was no telling what the Dark Knight would do once he realised the Alliance was on his doorstep. That was one thing that Bern cringed to think about. The sooner he was able to depose Za'aroz the safer everyone would be.

"That is good to hear."

"I will stay with the army until we have the first half dozen weapons completed. I have built a few in my time and I want to make sure they are built correctly."

"I have another task for you," Bern spoke slowly, unsure he was making the right decision.

"That sounds ominous." Hadar didn't lose his good humour.

"I need you to come with me and the small group of bandits into the mines." The words blurted out.

"I see." Hadar looked off towards the desert, although he couldn't see anything over the multitude of tents. "I must admit that I didn't think you would be choosing me to come along."

That was not what Bern wanted to hear. He really was unsure that he was making the right decision. All day he had been looking for the answer, but nothing had come to him. Each time his thoughts returned to Hadar.

"Now that you mention it though, I think I can help you," Hadar continued. "It does feel like the right thing to do."

"I am glad you feel that way." Bern felt better. "I wasn't sure if this was the right decision."

Hadar had to laugh out loud. "I know we all put a lot of faith in the prophecy, but sometimes you have to just rely on your own judgement."

Bern had to admit that he was right. The prophecy and the spirit of Heryion had got him so far, but eventually he would have to use the skills he had learnt. Everything was falling into place. His group was ready to go and the army was almost ready to start their bombardment. There wasn't much in the way of ammunition, but that was not a major concern. They only had to keep up the attack for one day until they were inside the mine. Once that was accomplished they could stop.

Now that everyone knew they were coming he had to finalise everything with the priest. The first stage of his plan lay on the memory of Linus. Bern could only hope it was good.

"So you are sure that you are going to be able to find the entrance to the mine?" it was not the first time that Bern had asked the question.

"As I told you before. I have been assured by Alaric that I will be able to find it. I don't know what else you want from me." Linus didn't sound happy with the questioning.

"I know. I would just be happier if you could explain to me how we are going to get there."

"I know you would, but there is nothing that I can do. I have told you that the information is in my head, but I won't be able to remember it until I reach the desert. I don't know how it works. I can only trust that Alaric knew what he was doing. Either way there is no way to find out until we get there."

Bern knew it was the only answer he was going to get, but he had to ask anyway. It was more something for him to pass the time. It was just a matter of waiting. The rest of the army was doing what it was supposed to do. There was nothing for him to do except wait.

Chapter 8: Into the Desert

Everything did not go to plan. The catapults had been completed early into the night, but that was insignificant. The small group of bandits that entered the outer city didn't come back with good news. As soon as the sun had set they made their way into the outer city. At first they thought everyone had left, but it wasn't until they came closer to the wall did they realise that was not the case.

Cassius had given the order for the outer city to be emptied, but word had not reached everyone. After the sun went down it was too late for everyone to evacuate. To be caught in the chilly night air for too long meant death. To hide what they were doing the bandits managed to find a friendly tavern where they could gather information and stay out of the cold. They didn't return to the camp until an hour before dawn and were a little worse for wear when they did. Bern and the others were already were getting ready to leave, despite not hearing anything from them. The news that the city had not been cleared stopped them in their tracks. Bern swore loudly when he received the news.

"What do we do now?" Delbert asked.

"We wait." Was the only response from Bern.

It was going to be a frustrating wait. There was no way to tell if and when the city would be completely vacated. The delay was not a good sign. The longer they waited the more chance the Castalial army would leave the city. It wouldn't take that long to mobilise enough soldiers to create a skirmish.

The morning passed and the siege engines were moved into place. If there had been any doubts of the Alliance's intentions before it was clear to all what they planning. It was early afternoon when Bern finally gave the order to start the bombardment.

"Are you sure it is something you want to risk?" Jarwe asked. He had thought he would be in command again, but that was not the case.

Bern looked around nervously. Again he had no idea if what he was doing was right. He wished the prophecy would help him, or at least the entity would return. It was not a decision he wanted to make, but it seemed to make sense to him. If there was anyone left in the outer city they would soon get the idea that it wasn't safe.

"No I am not sure, but I think it is the right thing to do. We can ill-afford to run the risk of the army coming out to fight. The longer we hold off our attack the greater the chance of that happening." Bern explained.

"I guess there are pros and cons for both sides of the argument." Hadar interjected before Jarwe could voice his objection. "There will be a greater loss of life if we go to war. I think Bern is making the right decision."

Bern was happy for the support. Ever since he had started to doubt himself he had been reluctant to make any decisions. If Jarwe had been given the chance to object then he would have backed down. The extra support boosted his confidence. He had a feeling that was going to be very important very soon.

The screams could be heard from the city as the first of the catapults was fired, clearly indicating that the outer city had not been completely evacuated. Bern was quick to stop the attacks. He would wait until dusk before he sent another volley. If the outer city had not been completely evacuated by then it was their own fault.

The bombardment started and hour before nightfall and stopped as soon as the sun had set. It had become eerily quiet with the only sound coming from the crackle of the many campfires. After the previous night's cold the soldiers knew what to expect and would not let their fires die down.

"We are now going to need more ammunition if we are going to keep up the attacks all day tomorrow," Jarwe didn't sound happy.

"We can always break down the half built wall. There is plenty of ammunition in the stonework," Sorrell suggested.

"I really don't want to break up the city. We need the support of the High Chancellor. I don't know how he will take it if we start destroying his city," Bern explained.

"It didn't stop you from attacking Kiarome." Sorrell wasn't impressed with his words.

"I know, I am sorry, but that doesn't change the fact. I don't want you breaking the wall. You will just have to use what we have left. Remember that we are not trying to break into the city. It is just a distraction. I am sure you will be able to do quite as well with the remaining ammunition. Just keep the attacks as slow as you can."

The discussion did not finish there. Just because Bern made the command it didn't mean the other commanders had to agree with it. Bern was leaving for the mines and was not going to be around if things changed. There was no doubt amongst the other commanders that they would need more ammunition if they were going to keep up their ruse. They had to keep the Castalial soldiers within the city walls. They couldn't risk open combat. If that happened there was a very good chance they would lose. The argument went back and forth until the commanders finally left Hadar and Bern alone.

"You have to leave the decision to them," Hadar spoke once the tent was empty.

Bern had to admit Hadar was right. He had held firm throughout the meeting. He had made it clear that he didn't like the idea, but it was not his decision to make. He had to trust that the others knew what they were doing. When it was said and done they had a lot more experience in warfare than him. He just didn't want to resign to the fact that he didn't know what he was doing.

"You are right, but I will let them stew on it for a little longer." Bern sighed.

"Good. Now I think I will get an early night. Tomorrow is going to be a tough day." Hadar turned and left the tent.

Bern remained where he was. He had to admit he was exhausted, but he couldn't bring himself to leave. The prospect of the morning's adventure would keep him awake.

Eventually sleep got the better of him and he wandered back to his tent.

As soon as his head hit the pillow Bern was asleep. His dreams were not as peaceful as he wanted. At first all was dark. He thought he was locked in a small room. When he turned around he couldn't see anything, but it felt as though the walls were closing in on him. A feeling of panic came over him and there was nothing he could do about it.

Just when he thought he was going to explode the world around him changed. The memory of the claustrophobic space quickly disappeared. Now he could only concentrate on the scene before him. When he recognised what he saw his heart started to race. Before him was a snow capped mountain. Snow fell down, but for some strange reason it wasn't touching the mountain top. A full moon was high in the sky, shining on a solitary figure. Bern wanted to cry out, but no words came from his mouth. There was nothing he could do, but watch the events unfold.

The moon sped through sky, quicker than it should have. It was something that should have worried Bern, but he didn't seem to notice. He could see the hooded figure waiting impatiently for someone. Bern knew someone was supposed to be there, but he couldn't remember who it was. All he had was a feeling of pure dread that time was running out. He wanted to do something, but he couldn't move.

As the sun started to rise the feeling piqued inside of him. As he looked out he could no longer see anyone on the mountain. The snow continued to cover its peak. Bern knew something was not right, but the memory was already gone.

The scenery suddenly changed again and he was now on an island. It was an odd place for him to be, but he didn't know why. He could see Alaric sitting inside a large building with seven other people. He recognised Eldred, but had no idea who the others where. There were serious expressions on their faces. He could see their lips moving, but no sound reached him. Although he couldn't hear what they were saying he knew the conversation was grave. The feeling of dread returned to him.

Suddenly Alaric stood and it looked as though he was ready to leave. That brought a feeling of hope to Bern. Before he could leave the group he sat down again. The motion didn't look voluntary, but Bern couldn't work out any other reason how that could happen. Eldred didn't look happy with what had happened, but there was nothing he could do about it. The feeling of hope Bern had suddenly left him.

It didn't look as though anyone was in any hurry to move. Bern wanted to call out for them to leave. He knew that Alaric should be somewhere else, he didn't know where, but he knew nevertheless. There was nothing he could do to get their attention. He felt that if only they knew he was there they would move. As he watched, the scene slowly started to fade. It was as if a fog was rolling in off the sea.

When the image became clear again he was no longer looking at the island. He instantly recognised the vision before him. He thought he would never see his home town again. The sight brought joy to his heart. The sun was shining down and he could tell it was going to be a beautiful day. He wondered what his family was doing. He had missed them more than he ever thought he could. As he walked through the streets he knew they were close.

Before he knew it he was looking down at the town from above. His heart was suddenly filled with concern. He could sense the panic from the townsfolk before he could see them. People were running everywhere in a wild state. He couldn't recognise anyone's face but he knew that he knew them. There were only three faces that he really cared about and he looked desperately for them. When he found them he wished that he hadn't.

Mary was half dragging his children as they raced through the streets. There was a look of pure horror on her face and tears ran down the stricken children's faces. Every now and then Mary would look behind her to see if there was anyone still following. Each time she looked she quickened her pace.

Bern tried to see who or what was their angst. At first he couldn't see anything. But as his eyes focused he finally saw what he was after. A lone figure walked through the streets, dressed in a black robe with the hood down. He stalked through the streets as a predator stalks its prey. Although he was not moving quickly, it still looked as though he was going to catch Mary and the children. Bern tried to move to protect them, but he couldn't. No matter what he tried there was nothing he could do, and then he realised who it was.

For the first time he was able to put a name to the fear he was feeling. Adder. He was now able to piece together the rest of his dreams. Alaric was supposed to meet the serpentant at the summit of Mount Scorpio. For whatever reason he was on an island with Eldred and six other people he still didn't recognise. Now Arsiliac was paying for his mistake.

The realisation only distracted him momentarily before his attention quickly returned to scene below. Instantly he wished he hadn't. He didn't know how it had happened, but Adder had caught up to Mary. The serpentant looked up into the sky, as if he was looking at Bern and laughed loudly. Bern screamed out in agony…

The sound of his own scream woke him from his nightmare. His body was covered in sweat and his heart was racing. At first he was confused, but it didn't take long for the memories of his dream to return.

"Are you alright?" A young voice came from outside the tent. "I heard you scream."

"I'm fine." Bern was not so sure that he believed his own words. "What time is it?"

"It is time for you to leave. I was sent to wake you." The voice came again.

"I will be up in a moment."

There was no chance Bern would be able to fall asleep again even if he wanted to. He had a job to do, but that was furthest from his mind. His family was in trouble and he had to help them. He couldn't let them become victims of a vengeful serpentant. He had to return to Arsiliac to save them.

Dressing quickly Bern rushed out of the tent. The night was still thick and only a few torches lit the campsite. If he was going to leave it was the perfect time. No one would notice him sneaking out of the camp.

Bern only managed to get a few metres before he ran into someone. He tried to get past, but a strong set of hands restrained him. It took Bern a moment in the dull light to realise it was Duke Hadar. The duke was only slightly larger than Bern himself. He tried to push his way past, but Hadar held his grip.

"Where are you going in such a hurry?" Hadar asked when Bern relaxed.

"I have to go. My family is in trouble. I have to go and save them." The words blurted out of his mouth.

"Everyone's family is in trouble. That is why we are doing what we are doing." Hadar didn't understand.

Bern sighed. He was going to have to explain his dreams. He briefly told Hadar what he had dreamt, excluding the fact that Alaric was supposed to meet Adder. He didn't think Hadar needed to know that information.

"I can see your concern, but it is only a dream. You can't go running off just because you had a bad dream," Hadar said. "We have important business to take care of here."

Bern knew it was more than a dream. He couldn't explain it, but he knew nevertheless. No matter what responsibilities he had to the Alliance he had a greater responsibility to his family. He couldn't leave them to suffer for Alaric's mistakes. He took a step forward, waiting for Hadar to respond. The large duke moved out of his way. He knew there was nothing he could do to stop Bern. If he really wanted to leave then that was what he should do.

Bern took another step forward and then stopped. He wanted to keep moving, but he couldn't. It was as if his body had a mind of its own. No matter what his mind wanted his body wouldn't respond. It suddenly hit him what was happening. The entity that shared his body was taking control. It was not letting him get away. He knew then that he had to stay and complete his task. He had no choice.

"The future is not set. Don't be fooled by premonitions." The voice was like a whisper on the wind. Only Bern was able to hear it.

"It doesn't look like I am going anywhere." Bern resigned himself.

Hadar gave him a questioning look, but quickly changed his expression. It seemed as though the general was going to stay and that was all that he needed. It was time they got moving. The rest of their group was assembled at the edge of the campsite. Hadar quickly ushered Bern towards them.

"Good to see you this morning general." Delbert greeted him. "It is going to be an interesting day."

The spirit of the man was a little too excited for Bern. He had come to terms with the fact that he had to continue, but he was still not happy about it. The voice in his head did little to reassure him. The memory of his dream was still thick in his mind and he couldn't get the image of fear out of his head. The look on Mary's and the children's faces would haunt him for a long time to come.

"Are we all ready?" was all he could bring himself to say.

"Ready and waiting, Sir!" the words echoed throughout the group.

"Good, but I think we should keep the noise down." The response was a little loud for his liking. Bern knew their words would carry in the dark.

There were murmured apologises that Bern ignored. If they were going to succeed then he needed to concentrate. There was little he could do until they reached the mines, but he would still need to be aware.

"Let's get moving."

They would travel on foot with a small group of pack animals to carry their supplies. The animals would be left to survive on their own once they entered the mines. Bern was not happy about that idea, but there was nothing he could do about it. The men would need to save their energy and anything to help was acceptable.

They moved cautiously in the dark. To aid with their secrecy they didn't use lanterns. The light would be a telltale sign of their little group. The light from the moon was obscured by clouds giving little help. Although it hindered their movement, remaining hidden was vital to the plan.

It was nearly an hour before dawn when they reached the edge of the desert. It was earlier than they had planned, but Bern had allowed for extra time. He would rather be waiting than rushing to arrive.

"Do you know where we go now?" Bern asked Linus.

"No. I need to wait until the sun rises."

"Then I suggest we eat and get some rest. I don't know if we will have another chance once we enter the desert." Bern moved away from the group when he finished speaking. He wanted time to think.

As soon as the grey of dawn was upon them, Linus spoke again. "We need to get moving. I know where we have to go."

"Would you mind explaining?" Bern asked before they left.

"I would love to, if I could. I just have a feeling, a sense of direction."

Bern had to accept the fact. He didn't completely understand, but it was not the first time he had to go on faith. Sometimes it seemed as though that was the only thing that kept him alive. The thought was more annoying than it was comforting. He was about to wander into the desert on pure faith. If they became lost then they would all die.

The sun was rising in the sky when Linus led them to large sand mine, the first of the markers. The mine was completely deserted. It seemed as though their plan was starting to work. If there had still been dwarves working the mine then Bern would not have been happy, but it seemed as though they were all safely tucked away in the city.

"So this is the first landmark that you were looking for?" Bern asked when they came to a stop.

"I guess so." Linus replied as he looked around the landscape. "As you know I don't really know what I am looking for. All I know is that once we arrived the feeling that I had disappeared."

That didn't sound like a good thing. It was good that they had arrived, but Bern had hoped they would already be on the move. All they could do was wait for Linus to receive his next feeling. The entire plan was starting to seem ridiculous. Bern could hardly believe he had agreed to it.

"We can't stand around here all day," Bern spoke out of frustration.

"It's alright. I know where we have to go now, or to say that I know in which direction I am being led." There was no humour in his voice.

Linus led them away from the quarry without really knowing where he was going. All he could do was follow the feeling that was leading him. He knew that he was not heading straight for the mine shaft, he was being led towards the next marker.

The sun was increasing its intensity as they trekked through the desert. Bern couldn't believe that a place so hot could exist. The sweat poured down his body. He wanted to take off the heavy robes they wore, but he knew that would be worse. He looked at the others. They didn't seem to be suffering as much as he was. That was enough to strengthen his resolve.

They found the next marker close to noon. The heart-shaped pair of cacti was a sight. Linus stopped them directly in front of it and as soon as he did the feeling of direction left him again. It was time for them to wait again. Bern was not so keen to keep moving and he revelled in the chance to rest. He only wished that there was somewhere he could hide in the shade. It was too difficult to relax in the heat, but they all tried their best.

It was about fifteen minutes later when Linus felt the gentle tug again. It was more subtle this time, but there could be no doubt what it was. He started moving towards the west without thought. It was as if his body was working on its own accord. As much as it was disturbing, Linus didn't really mind. He had no idea where he was going but the movement was reassuring.

The sun didn't let up as they trudged through the desert. The pack animals were sweating as much as the men. Bern didn't know how long he could keep moving. Each step was a strain and harder than the last. He looked at the others, but in the heavy robes he couldn't tell how they were travelling.

To Bern's relief they came across the next marker before he collapsed. They were all amazed to see the pattern of the outcrop. They didn't have to wait for Linus to have his next feeling to know which direction they had to travel. The rocks made a perfect arrow.

"Are you sure we shouldn't wait for Linus to give us direction?" Delbert asked after they had a short rest.

"I don't think so. I'm confident this is pointing us in the right direction," Bern replied.

"It just seems a little too easy. What if it's a trap for those who don't know what they're looking for?" Delbert was not happy.

"What are the chances of somebody wandering out here for no reason? I can't see it happening myself. I don't want to be waiting around in the desert any longer than we have to. I have no doubt this is the right direction."

Bern's words were final. He had been re-energised by having a short break and he didn't want to waste it. He knew they were close to their goal. He had to power through the heat if they were going to survive. Once they were inside the mine they would be able to have a decent rest. They continued without any further conversation. Wasted words were a waste of energy.

It didn't take long before Linus regained his sense of direction. It was a relief that they knew they were travelling in the right direction. If they had to turn around and back track Bern thought he would die. There was no way he could last in the desert.

The sun was almost half way on its downward arch when Linus brought them to a stop. They stood on top of a dune that looked like the one they had previously crested, and the one before that. He couldn't see anything that looked like a landmark. He wondered if Linus was still taking them in the right direction.

"There is nothing here," Bern finally spoke. "Are you sure this is where we are supposed to stop?"

"I have no idea. You know that I am not controlling where I'm leading us. All I am going on is the feelings that Alaric has put in me. This is where the feeling stopped, so I have to believe that the fourth marker is around here somewhere."

Bern was not happy with what he was hearing. There was nothing around him that looked like a landmark. Something had gone wrong and there was nothing he could do about it. He had a sinking feeling they had been duped. There was nothing that could distinguish their location. He had no idea how far they had travelled into the desert, but he didn't think he had the energy to make it back to the city. He was sure he was going to die.

"I think I have found what we are looking for." Delbert said.

He pointed to the valley below them. At first no one saw what he was pointing at and Bern thought he must be suffering from heat delusions. Then slowly he saw what looked to be two small dunes. He thought he was having delusions himself, but as his eyes focused he knew that they were there.

"Well, it seems as though you are better than all of us." Bern would have laughed if his mouth wasn't so dry. "I doubt I would have seen that unless I walked over them."

"Where do we go now?" Delbert asked before anyone else could praise Linus. It was too hot for congratulations.

Everyone's eyes went to Linus. Again there was no shade, so no one really wanted to be waiting. The sooner they reached the shaft the better. Linus didn't look like he was in any hurry to leave. It seemed as though the sensation had left him again.

"I'm sorry," he said after a minute had passed. "I'm not sure where we need to go."

Bern thought about making a judgement call like he had done at the last marker, but he also had no idea where to go. Last time was easy, but this time it was much harder. If he made the wrong decision then they would surely die in the desert sun. On the other hand if they didn't start moving soon then they would die where they stood.

Five minutes passed before Linus finally felt the tug again. The relief passed through his body and he felt as though he was going to collapse. He steadied himself before he started to move. He didn't have to energy to speak. He figured the others would follow suit soon enough. The tug was subtle, but there could be no doubt it was leading him towards the west. He could only hope it was leading them towards the shaft. If there were too many other landmarks they had to find he didn't know if he could keep going. Little did he know that he was, in fact, leading them straight towards the shaft.

The spire of the Grand Cathedral was in view on the horizon giving them something to follow. Bern couldn't help thinking it was a sign. He suddenly felt uplifted as a new wave of energy rushed into his body. He wanted to increase the pace, but his legs had a different idea. Just because he could no longer feel his pain didn't mean that it had left his body. He soon realised it was a sense of false security. Either way he was happy that he no longer felt like death.

It was not long before Linus brought them to a stop. Like the last time no one could see the reason why. There were no obvious landmarks, but they knew things were not always what they seemed. Once Linus had confirmed he had no idea what they were looking for Bern ordered them all check for anything that could be considered a landmark.

Their movements were slow. No wanted to be out, moving in the sun. They all trudged through the sand hoping that they could find what they were looking for. The main problem was that they had no idea what they were looking for. Again it was Delbert who finally came across the small crack in the ground. His excited words brought everyone to his side. One of the bandits was so keen that he nearly stepped into the hole.

"Thank the Gods!" Bern exclaimed when he saw the shaft.

"I wouldn't be thanking them just yet." There was something ominous in Delbert's voice. "I don't know about you, but I don't see anything to tie our ropes to."

Delbert was right. Bern looked around the shaft, but there was only sand. Bern thought about tying off to the pack animals, but it didn't look as though they would be able to handle the extra weight. He wished that Delbert had waited before he mentioned the fact. He was enjoying the hope, even if it had only been for a moment.

"What do we do now?" one of the bandits asked.

All eyes returned to the priest. They hoped he would have an answer to their dilemma. He was standing over the hole looking down. He made no response to the question, which was obviously directed at him. He stood there for almost a full minute before he turned to face the others.

"What do we do now?" Bern re-asked the question. "There is no way for us to enter the shaft." Bern held a length of rope he had unpacked to prove his point.

"It seems that we don't need any rope," Linus replied. Bern didn't know why, but he knew there was a smile on his face.

"What are you talking about?" Delbert burst out laughing.

Linus didn't reply. He simply stepped over the shaft and dropped inside. There was a simultaneous gasp throughout the group. They had expected to hear the sounds of Linus' screaming as he fell, but there was nothing. They waited for the inevitable thud when he hit the bottom, but that didn't come either.

"What do you think that was all about?" Delbert asked.

"I don't know, but there is only one way to find out. Make sure that you bring all our supplies." With that Bern jumped into the crack in the ground.

Chapter 9: Into the Mine

"That was not at all what I was expecting." Bern spoke softly when they were all grouped at the bottom of the shaft.

"I don't care how we got here. I am just glad that we're out of the sun," Delbert spoke jovially. He pulled his cloak off to accentuate his point. "The cool air is very refreshing."

The cavern they were in was just enough to accommodate all of them, but only just. There was little room for them to stretch out, but it was better than being in the sun. It was not long before they had a small fire built in the middle of the cavern. It was not because they were cold, but they needed it for light and to cook with. Soon enough they were eating and speaking casually together.

"I think we should get the men to keep their voices down," Bern spoke quietly with Delbert and Hadar. "There is no telling how far our voices will carry through these tunnels. The last thing we want is for anyone to know we're here."

"I agree," Hadar added before Delbert had a chance to speak.

Delbert knew that, but he didn't want to ruin the bandits merriment. They had slogged through the desert and deserved a good rest. He didn't think it would really matter if the guards heard them. They wouldn't know what they were doing there until it was too late. He didn't want to have an argument with Bern so he asked the others to keep their voices down.

Once they had eaten Bern suggested it would be a good idea if they had some sleep. The sun was almost set when they entered the mine and he was sure it would be dark outside. Although it was still early no one argued with him. There was no telling how far they would have to travel before they reached the diamond mine. Once they arrived there was no telling how long it would take for them to find the High Chancellor. The day's march trudging through the desert had exhausted them and although it was still early no one had any problems in falling asleep.

Bern was the only one who remained awake. He made an excuse to the others that someone had to keep guard, although there was no chance that anyone would find them. It was just that he didn't want to sleep. The trek through the desert had taken his mind from his family, but the thought of sleep brought them rushing back. The last thing he wanted to do was have another similar dream.

The men woke a couple of hours later. Bern was glad he didn't have to wake them. As much as he wanted to keep moving he didn't want to disturb them.

"Where do we go now?" Hadar asked, once they were packed and ready to move.

Everyone quickly pulled their robes back on. The thick Castalial robes served two purposes. Out in the heat of the day they kept the sun from burning their skin. In the depths of the mines they would prove to keep them warm. Even with the fire burning, the cavern had turned deathly cold.

"There is only one exit that I can see?" Surprisingly it was Delbert who responded, not Linus. "I am sure that is the way to go."

There could be no denying his logic.

Bern led the way out of the cavern. At the front of the line he held a small lantern and every third man behind him also had one. They kept the shutters almost shut, just letting enough light to see where they were walking.

As they travelled, the tunnel steadily grew shorter and narrower. It was not long before they all had to duck their heads to stop them from scraping them across the rocks. They had not travelled much further before they had to walk sideways to fit through and then crawl on their stomachs as the roof continued to lower. There was only just enough room for them to fit with their packs on their backs. Bern was not sure if they had made the right decision. He was worried they would soon be stuck with nowhere left to travel.

Slowly a feeling of panic rose in Bern's chest as the roof didn't rise. It was a struggle to carry a pack and a lantern and still be able to crawl. He wanted to turn around and go back, but that would be nearly impossible. There was no room in the tunnel for them to turn around. If they were to retreat then they would have to do so in reverse.

Just when Bern thought he was going to suffocate the tunnel opened out. He was so relieved that he didn't notice the short drop at the end. He fell to the ground with a thud and a slight cry of pain, but he wasn't too worried, he was just happy there was room to move again. He was so preoccupied that he forgot to tell the others about the drop. Hadar thudded into him causing more pain. Luckily for Hadar Bern was there to break his fall. That gave Bern the perfect reason to warn the others. He didn't think he could handle another ten or twenty bodies piling up on top of him.

Hadar had to roll off Bern before he could stand. Except for a couple of grazes he had come out unscathed. Either way there would be no lasting injuries. He was grateful that he had not smashed the lantern when he fell. Instead he was able to pick it up and open the shutter to have a good look around.

They were in another small cavern. The roof was six feet above his head. At that point Bern realised he was breathing normally again. The relief of being out of the tight tunnel was clear. He was not sure if he wanted to leave the cavern and risk travelling into another tight space, but he couldn't stay where he was, no matter how much he wanted to.

"I have a feeling we're getting close to our destination." Bern spoke when they were all together. "We need to be very careful. I doubt we will be able to find the High Chancellor without starting a fight or two, but we want to delay that for as long as possible.'

The speech was not entirely necessary. They all felt as though they were getting closer to the diamond mines and none of them wanted to cause any unnecessary trouble. What Bern said brought it to the forefront of their minds and that made it worthwhile.

"Let's keep moving and keep our wits about us." Hadar added.

There was nothing else to stay. Again there was only one tunnel leading out of the cavern. Bern looked back at the tunnel they had arrived in and was grateful they were not going back in. The tunnel they entered was large enough for them to walk two abreast, although they still walked in single file. It made the travelling much easier and kept the conversation to a minimum.

It was only a short walk before Bern came out onto a small platform that overlooked the diamond mine. He placed his lantern on the ground. The mine was lit by a multitude of torches. The platform was only large enough for Hadar, Linus and Delbert to join him. They looked out onto the many levels of the mine in shock. There could be no doubt of the validity of the stories they had heard. There were many slaves moving slowly throughout the mine. Every so often they could see one of the many slave masters. They all held evil looking whips, which they used whenever they felt one of the slaves was moving too slowly.

"This is an abomination." Linus couldn't believe what he was seeing. "I can't believe that this place exists. I have lived in the Grand Cathedral for most of my life and could never believe this was happening underneath me."

"It's alright Linus. We will make sure that things are set right," Hadar clenched his teeth as he spoke.

"How are we going to find the High Chancellor?" Delbert looked around the mine. It was larger than he could ever have imagined.

"We will have to check one level at a time." Bern couldn't take his eyes from the sight before him. "We will make those pay who get in our way."

There was confidence in his voice. He was not going to let anyone get away with what they had done. This place was a disgrace and Bern was going to make them accountable. Although they were there to save the High Chancellor, Bern made himself a promise that he would save everyone who had been enslaved. No matter what their crimes no one deserved such a fate.

"Now it is time to get serious." To accentuate his point Bern threw aside his robe. Although it was still cold inside the mine Bern knew it was only going to be a matter of time before he needed the extra movement. Instantly he shivered, but he wasn't going to let that dissuade him.

The others followed suit. The adrenaline that was starting to pump through their bodies would be enough to keep them warm. They would need that adrenaline if they were going to succeed. Once they left the platform they needed to be fully aware of their surroundings. One lapse in concentration could result in their death.

"Should be separate?" Hadar suggested. "We could cover more ground that way."

"Does everyone know what the High Chancellor looks like?" Linus asked.

"The priest has a point." There was something icy in the way Bern spoke. "We need to rescue the High Chancellor as soon as we can." As much as Bern wanted to save everyone he knew that would have to wait. They needed to restore order inside the Grand Cathedral before it was too late. "We have to stick together. There is too great a chance of us getting lost and I don't plan on losing anyone on this mission."

There was no doubt in Bern's voice. His strength reassured the others. They didn't know if it was Bern himself or the entity returning to help them but it didn't matter. They had a good feeling they were going to achieve their goal.

"Let's get moving!" Bern's voice was firm again.

"How do we get down from this ledge?" Hadar asked as he turned to move. "There doesn't seem to be any way down."

Bern's heart sank. He had been concentrating so hard on the scene before him that he didn't notice there was no way off the ledge. They had come so far, just to be thwarted at the last moment.

"We could repel down to the next level," Delbert suggested.

Hadar walked to the edge of the platform and looked down. "I am afraid not. There is nothing underneath this ledge. We would have to climb out across the mine wall and it doesn't look like that is much of an option."

"There has to be a way down. There is no way Alaric would have sent us here without a solution."

Slowly Linus started to walk towards the edge. He didn't know why, but he felt compelled. As he walked he suddenly knew he was not going to stop. The panic on his face was clear to the others, but it was too late. Before anyone could move to stop him Linus stepped off. To the shock of everyone he just took another step, but he didn't fall to his death. It was as that point that Linus regained control of his body.

"It seems as though there is a path leading down," there was a waver in his voice, but he also sounded relieved.

Bern let out a deep breath, which he had been holding ever since Linus had stepped off the ledge. Things were starting to make sense, but he was sure they didn't have to be so intense. Regardless of that, it was well past time they needed to be moving. Bern was the first to follow Linus out onto the invisible path. It was bizarre standing on the open air. As he looked down he felt as though he was going to topple over the edge. It wasn't until he looked up again before he regained his balance.

The journey down into the mine was painfully slow. Without Linus being controlled by the mysterious force he had no idea where the path led. Each step he had to take tentatively slowly. One wrong move and he would go tumbling to his death.

Bern couldn't wait to step onto solid ground again. Every step he took on the invisible path was nerve-racking. He couldn't believe he had not plummeted to the bottom. He hoped that he would never have to experience anything like that again in his life.

Once they were on the top level of the mine they could see it was not as open as they had originally thought. Many tunnels spread off from the outer walls. That was going make their task even harder. There was no telling where the High Chancellor would be. Bern didn't think that anyone would know where he was. He was sure that the guards wouldn't even know that the High Chancellor was working in the mines. It would be a perfect time for the entity to return and show him the way.

"Where are we going to start?" Hadar asked, making a point to keep his voice low.

That was the obvious question, but one Bern had no idea how to answer. If they started wandering down random tunnels then there was a good chance they would get lost. There was also a strong chance they would run into guards. On the other hand there was a chance that the High Chancellor would be down one of the tunnels.

"For the moment we stick to the outside." Bern wasn't sure why he said that, but he felt it was the right plan. There was a good chance that the entity was starting to become involved and that was a promising sign.

Bern felt as though he was doing the right thing as he started to move. If the entity was going to show him where to go then they would save a lot of time. All he could do was continue and hope they were travelling in the right direction. It didn't take him long before he walked past a tunnel that piqued his attention. He didn't get far before he turned the group around.

"Be on your guard. I have a strange feeling that we are about to hit some trouble soon," Bern spoke softly.

"Then shouldn't we try another tunnel?" Linus didn't like the sound of what he was hearing.

"Unfortunately I go where I am led these days and I am being led down here." Bern took a moment to explain.

Linus could understand what he was saying, but it didn't make it any easier. He was beginning to wonder how he ever got tied up in such matters. He was a simple priest, that was all he had ever wanted to be and all of a sudden his life had taken a strange twist. It was quite possible he was going to have to take a life. That was something he had never imagined he would have to contemplate. As much as he had received training in combat when he was young it was never something he had put into practise.

Bern led the way into the tunnel. As soon as they stepped in they could see the marks on the walls where the slaves had been forced to dig out the precious stones. Bern had to wonder how long it had taken for the tunnel to be dug out. It didn't look like the stone would be easy to break up. He couldn't believe that such a place could exist with no one knowing about it. The thought added to the rage building up inside him.

The tunnel was not very long and at the end of it was a small alcove. In the alcove there were six large men sitting around a table. At first they didn't notice Bern and the others. Bern's initial reaction was to go back down the tunnel. There was no room for them all to fight in such a confined place. Hadar, who stood by his side, would be the only other one able to fight. Before he could move one of the guards looked up.

"What are you doing here?" The guard spoke with a guttural tone.

"We have been sent from the Grand Cathedral to find a slave." Bern spoke quickly. "We require your assistance."

The guards all looked at each other. They knew there was something not right with the situation, but they couldn't work it out. They were not the brightest of men. They were employed for their strength, not their minds.

"There is no one down here. This is one of the guard houses." The same guard spoke again.

"I am sorry. I must have taken a wrong turn. We will leave you with it."

Bern was about to turn around when he saw some recognition on the guards face. At that point he knew he was not simply going to be able to leave. The guard he had been speaking with stood and the others followed quickly after. They made no movement towards the group, but they didn't look happy.

"I don't think you are who you say you are. We are always told if we are expecting people."

Occasionally there were inspections done by some high officials from the Cathedral. The guards were always told well in advance to be on their best behaviour. It also meant that no one was mistaken for a slave. It took them a moment, but eventually they all clued onto the fact.

"Then I don't suppose you are going to help us find who we are looking for?" Bern said.

Bern drew his short sword in preparation for the fight. He would have preferred to use the larger claymore, but he had chosen to leave it behind. In close quarters the sword was a much better option. Hadar quickly followed suit even though he had his broadsword strapped his back.

"Get 'em." The guard shouted as he pushed one of his companions forward.

His eagerness to start the fight did nothing for the other guard. Before he could regain his balance the guard stumbled onto Hadar's sword. The duke only just had enough time to brace himself or he would have been knocked over. He quickly pushed the limp body from his blade and readied himself for the next attack.

The confined space worked against both sides. There was little room inside the alcove for them to fight. Two more guards, brandishing mean looking cudgels, stepped forward. They were not going to wait for the same fate as their companion. Although the cudgels would do serious damage if they struck their intended target, they were not a suitable weapon for the situation. Bern and Hadar were confident, but they also knew that they had to be careful. A simple mistake and their heads could easily be cracked open.

Bern moved as far into the alcove as he could leaving Hadar enough room to manoeuvre. The extra room was handy, but not at all necessary. The guards were all used to beating unarmed, weak and tired men. They had no idea what to do against armed, experienced soldiers. Bern was surprised at how easy it was to kill the first of the guards. The guard didn't even get a chance to swing his cudgel before Bern had cut him down. Hadar also had similar success with his guard. The large man swung his cudgel with all his might. Even in the small space Hadar was able to side-step the attack and then strike out with his own. His blade passed through the guard's ribs and into his heart.

The two remaining guards looked around for a place to retreat, but one guard had already left through the only door out the back of the alcove. One of the guards tried to open it, but it was clearly bolted shut on the other side. There was nothing they could do, but fight. There was no chance Bern could accept their surrender, even if the thought had crossed their minds.

The second stage of the battle was over just as quickly as the first. The two remaining guards simply charged at the two men before them and died just the same as the others. If it wasn't for the severity of the situation Bern would have laughed at their ridiculous attempt at an attack.

"What should we do about the other one?" Hadar asked.

"I don't think he will be coming out any time soon. We don't have time to waste."

"But if he tells someone we are here we could be in a lot of trouble."

Bern knew that Hadar was right, but he also knew that there was no way they were going to get through the door. To prove his point he tried to open it and then tried to break it open.

"I don't think this door is going to open. Unless we wait here there is nothing we can do. Turn around, we go back the way we came."

Bern had no idea why he had been led down that tunnel. There was nothing there of any substance. He was sure there was a reason and that he was never going to know what it was. If nothing else they had killed four men who didn't deserve to live. They had spent their lives causing unnecessary pain to people who didn't deserve it.

Once they were back at the outer mine Bern led them away from the tunnel. He had no feeling of which direction he should take, so he just had to guess. He figured that there was no right or wrong way to go. It was not going to be easy to find the High Chancellor. He likened it to a needle in a hay stack and in many ways he thought that might be an easier task. He needed the prophecy or the entity to give assistance.

"This is ridiculous," Hadar said when Bern called them to a stop. They had checked another tunnel and ended up at a dead end. Bern had again left the main tracks on a feeling that had led them nowhere. It should have been an indication when there were no torches, but Bern would not stop until he reached the end or the feeling dissipated. "We could be here for days and still not find anything. There has to be a better way to locate the High Chancellor."

"I am happy to hear any of your suggestions," Bern snapped.

There was silence in the tunnel. No one wanted to say anything. They all thought the same as Bern, but they also didn't have any ideas themselves. They all wished they had the answer. It was only going to be so long before they ran into trouble again. They also had the concern of the guards alerting the others of their presence.

"I didn't think so," Bern sighed. As much as it was the answer he was expecting, it was not the answer he was hoping for. "I agree with you that we are getting nowhere fast, but I just don't know what else to do." He turned to Linus. "Alaric didn't give you any indication where we can find the High Chancellor did he?"

"I haven't felt a thing since we entered the mines. If she knows where we can find him then she hasn't passed on the information. I am sorry, but there is nothing I can do to help you at this point."

That brought the mood of the group even lower. They couldn't remain where they were, but Bern was lost for ideas. They couldn't keep wandering through the mines in hope of finding one man. He doubted even the guards would know where he was. He couldn't imagine they would knowingly enslave the High Chancellor and if they did he doubted they would be helpful.

***

The guard huddled in the corner of his bedroom. The room was small, but it did offer some safety. He heard one bang on the door before everything went silent. He thought for a moment they were going to break the door down and kill him. His heart raced. When he woke that morning he didn't think his day would turn out like this. Now his friends were dead and his own life was at risk. He started rocking back and forth as the thoughts of his own mortality raced through his head.

He stayed where he was for over an hour before he finally stood. He was sure they had left. There didn't seem to be any reason why they would still be waiting outside his door. Whatever they had come for he was sure that it wasn't him. He was insignificant compared to the other guards. With that thought in his mind he decided that he needed to warn someone about the intruders. It was more for his own safety than anything else. If they didn't find what they were looking for there was no reason why they wouldn't come back for him.

To his relief he found the small alcove was bereft of life. He looked down at the five dead bodies and felt nothing. He had been close to the five men, but he wouldn't necessarily call them friends. He was their commander and he was sure they were jealous of his success. He had no doubt that they would betray him if they had the chance.

The guard walked cautiously through the mines. He didn't know which way the group had gone. The last thing he wanted to do was to run into them again. He had been lucky enough to survive the first time, but he didn't think he would survive a second meeting.

"What are you doing here?" the head of the guards, a man by the name of Orson, barked at him. "You should be in your chambers."

The rules were strict about the guards wandering through the mines when they were not working. It was a crime punishable by flogging. The guard had known this when he left, but it was better than the alternative. He thought if the Head-of-the-Guards heard his reason then everything would be alright. With a little luck he might even be able to gain a promotion.

"I see…" Orson pondered after he heard the information. "This is indeed disturbing news." He knew more than he was letting on, but he couldn't let the guard know. "You can go about your way now. Go on!"

The guard thought it was odd that he didn't get in trouble. There was something strange about the Head-of-the-Guards' reaction. There was more to what was happening than he had been told. On the plus side he had not been punished and he was sure that the intruders would soon be captured. He could then return to his normal life.

Orson didn't notice that the guard had left his office. His mind was racing with the information he had been given. When he had been given the task of looking after their 'special guest' he had not thought that anyone would ever come for him. All he had to do was keep him in the mines and then he would be given many rewards. Now it didn't look as though that was going to happen. He needed to speak with the only other man who knew that the High Chancellor was in the mines.

"Find Dacey, and don't be slow," Orson called out to one of his servants.

"I think he is sleeping Sir!" came a timid reply.

Orson felt like striking the servant for speaking back, but that would just waste more time. "I don't care what he's doing. He will only be resting in the bunks. Tell him that this is more important than sleep."

Being the Head-of-the-Guards had its benefits. Orson and Dacey were both heads along with half a dozen other guards. They were the only guards who were allowed to leave the mines and for good reason. If the other guards knew what was in the outside world then they wouldn't return. They were really no better off than the slaves they guarded. Soon enough Orson would have saved enough coin to retire and with the riches promised to him that would be sooner rather than later. All he had to do was make sure that the intruders didn't spoil it.

"What is it that you felt you needed to wake me?" Dacey didn't sound impressed.

"There is a group of mercenaries in the mines looking for you-know-who." He looked around as he spoke, seeing who was listening.

Dacey's demeanour instantly changed. He couldn't believe what he was hearing. He thought that it must have been a joke.

"This cannot be true. No one has entered during my watch. The soldiers keep a close guard on the entrance. Surely this is a mistake."

"A guard came and told me. I am sure that he wouldn't risk a beating to tell false stories. You should have seen the look on his face. There was fear in his eyes, not lies. I don't know how they have gotten in, but they are here. We were warned that this day would come." Orson could hardly believe his words himself.

"Get out of here!" Dacey screamed at a servant. "Can't you see that we are having a private conversation?"

"Was that really necessary?" Orson asked when they were alone.

"Not really, but it proved the point. We are alone now and can speak freely."

"Do you know where the High Chancellor has been placed?" Even though there was no one in the room Orson still kept his voice low.

"He is somewhere on the third level. I am not sure exactly where. I doubt he will be too hard to find." Dacey smiled.

"Then I think that we should get him. If he is under our watch then the group will have to come to us. We can make sure that we have a strong contingent of soldiers and guards with us."

"Are you sure that is a good idea?" Dacey wasn't convinced. "It might be better if we send him down to the lowest level. That way he will be harder to find."

The two men argued back and forth with each other. With each idea the other came up with one he felt was better. There was no easy solution to their problem. If they had believed what they had been told then they would have been ready. Instead they had to scramble for ideas. What they did with the High Chancellor didn't change the fact that they would have to battle with the small group of mercenaries. He wasn't sure if they were up to the challenge. He would need to see their benefactor and ask for assistance.

"I wouldn't advise that," Dacey spoke when Orson suggested it. "Remember what he said? 'Under no circumstances are you to seek me out. I will come to you.' I am pretty sure that he meant what he said. I definitely wouldn't risk my life like that."

Orson had to admit that Dacey was right, but that still didn't help their problem. They needed more soldiers, he was sure of that. There was no other way to keep the High Chancellor hidden, unless...

Chapter 10: Bombardment

The bombardment started at dawn. The first stone hit the city walls with a thunderous crash, followed by a cheer from the Alliance. The next one followed shortly after. Jarwe hoped they would have enough ammunition for the ruse to work. Bern had instructed him not to destroy any of the outer city, but now it was his call. It was a decision he was hoping he didn't have to make.

"Tell the men to slow the attack. At this rate we will run out of ammunition before midday," Jarwe spoke the order as he stared at the city.

Although they did not expect to see any battle the commanders all wore their battle armour. The ruse was not known throughout the army and if they didn't look the part the rumours would start.

It didn't take long before they all wished they had decided to wear something more suited to the temperature. Although they were north of the desert and out of the extreme heat it was still hot. Jarwe wiped the sweat from his brow as he considered changing into something more comfortable.

He stood on a small hill with the Sorrell, Hulkan, Wojtek and Pernian. They all watched the bombardment in silence. The effort was futile and it was lucky that they weren't really trying to break into the city. The rock and stone they hurled against the walls simply smashed to rubble. From the distance it was impossible to tell, but Jarwe doubted they were even making a scratch.

"What are we going to do when we run out of ammunition?" Sorrell asked.

"There isn't much we can do." Jarwe didn't want to continue the assault, but then he didn't want to face Bern afterwards. "Hopefully Bern will be far enough into the desert that no one will notice. Then our job here is done."

"Do you really think that the Dark Knight will leave it at that?" Wojtek didn't sound confident. "I am sure it won't be too long before he unleashes the Castalial army."

"I know, I have already thought about that consequence, but I don't see how we have any choice. Bern doesn't want us to break down any of the buildings or the outer wall."

That was something that had crossed all their minds. There had to be a good reason why Bern had instructed them, but they had no idea what it was. It didn't make sense to stop the bombardment. In the end it wouldn't take the Castalials long to rebuild.

"What do you think Hulkan? You have lived here for most of your life," Sorrel asked.

The dwarf had remained quiet for the conversation. He couldn't take his eyes from the city. Once his home, now he was an outcast. He wanted nothing more than to join his parents at the Eastern Dwarves Guild, but that wasn't an option.

"I don't know. I can't say that I am happy with the idea of pulling the outer city apart, but I think the alternative will be worse. I guess in the end we have to do what Bern said, regardless of the outcome."

That seemed to be the consensus, even though no one liked it. When it was said and done it was their lives on the line. No one could imagine that Bern would deliberately put their lives at risk, but the thought was still deep in their minds.

Another crash brought the attention back to the bombardment. There was still no sign of their attack, except for a small pile of rubble at the base of the wall. Jarwe thought that they could throw half the outer city at the wall and it wouldn't break. He was amazed at its durability. He had read the histories of the city, but he couldn't believe they were totally true.

The bombardment continued into the afternoon before they finally ran out of ammunition. It was finally time for them to make a decision. It was the time that they were all dreading.

"What do we do now?" Pernian asked. Now that Bern was gone Jarwe was in command again.

"Now we wait." Jarwe had made the decision to stick with Bern's instructions. "We can only hope that Bern is successful sooner rather than later."

It was a nervous wait throughout the afternoon. The entire command group stood on the hill and watched the city. A makeshift canopy had been erected over the commanders to give them some relief from the sun. The army remained in regiments, waiting for a call to action. As much as Jarwe wanted them to return to the forest and out of the sun there was nothing he could do. There was no conversation as they stood there. No one could bring themselves to break the silence in case it caused something to happen.

As night fell there was no action from the city. The only movement came from the many pennants on the turrets. It almost looked as though the city was abandoned. That in itself was very disturbing. Even when the light had completely faded no one left the hill. They all remained until finally a soldier walked up with a torch in his left hand.

"Your evening meals are ready for you in the command tent." The soldiers spoke after he saluted.

It was only with the distraction did the commanders realise the temperature had started to drop. It wouldn't take too long before they would need the comfort of a fire.

"Thank you. We will be along shortly," Jarwe replied.

The soldier saluted again, handed Jarwe the torch and then returned to the campsite. The bulk of the army had returned to the campsite when the sun had set. A few battalions remained in case there was some action, not that they expected any. Eventually they too would return to camp when it became too cold and there was no further threat of attack.

Jarwe led the way towards the command tent in silence. There was plenty that needed discussing, but no one knew what to say. They had hoped there would have been sign from Bern, but that was not the case. They could only hope that he had found the High Chancellor and was on his way to defeat the Dark Knight.

"What are we going to do if Bern doesn't succeed?" Dorn asked during the meal.

The reply was silence as everyone pondered the question. It had been in the back of everyone's mind, but no one really wanted to talk about it. If Bern failed then there was a good chance that everything would fail. The worst part was that they wouldn't know until it was too late.

"We will have to retreat. There is no way we can stand up against the Castalial army." Sorrell was the first to speak.

"I don't know if we will have the chance. How will we know that he has failed until it is too late? How long do we give them before we give up?" Jarwe was not convinced.

"I don't see how we can wait. If the army comes out we have to leave." Wojtek agreed with his general.

"There's no chance we will survive an attack. We have no option, but to retreat." Hulkan added his thoughts.

"We must give Bern the support he needs. We can't leave whilst he's still in the city." Pernian didn't agree. "We *have* to give him the support he needs."

"But what good are we going to be if we are completely annihilated. There is no point in all of us dying." Sorrell argued.

The conversation when back and forth for the next hour without a solution. No one knew what to expect or what they were going to do. The one thing they did know, in case of attack they would be completely destroyed. The Dark Knight would give them no chance to surrender and there would be little hope of retreat. They wished that Bern had told them what to do and when to do it. That would have made their lives a lot easier.

"Do we pack up and leave in the morning?" Sorrel finally asked the question when the arguing died down.

His words brought another round of arguing. There were those who were for the retreat and those who were against. The discussion was threatening to rip the Alliance apart.

"We have to stay!" It was the first time that Orric had spoken since the conversation had started. Suddenly the tent went completely silent. "I am sure there is more to this situation than we can see. The prophecy would not have led us here if it just wanted us to turn and run. I have to believe that and so do you."

"Belief in the prophecy won't save us if we are attacked." Sorrell barked.

"We won't succeed if we falter at the first sign of trouble..."

"This isn't the first sign of trouble." Sorrell wouldn't let Orric finish.

"Please, Sorrell, calm yourself!" Pernian stood as he spoke. "I want to hear what Orric has to say."

"I lost my home and a lot of my kin for the good of the prophecy. If we didn't then we wouldn't have been in a position to help you at Jarrat." He paused for the information to register. "You see now? There are many twists and turn to this adventure. If we stray from our cause then we are all as good as dead. We can't leave the Dark Knight in command of Castalia. I know for a fact that it will only be a matter of time before Za'aroz moves his army against us. It is a matter of dying here fighting or dying in a few months time running. I know what I would prefer to do."

There was silence again as everyone thought on Orric's words. They had to admit that the elderly elf made sense. He was more in tune with the prophecy than anyone else and they had to respect his judgment. Sorrell also had to admit that he made sense. As much as he didn't want to stay and die, the alternative was just as bad, if not more so. Either way it seemed as though all their hopes relied on Bern succeeding.

"Then I guess in the morning we prepare for battle." Jarwe sounded surprisingly confident. "It will only be a matter of time before the Dark Knight unleashes his army. If we are going to die then we are going to do it fighting."

There was no response to his words. They all knew it was true, but they didn't want to dwell on it. For the moment they were safe and that was enough. None of them would sleep easy once they retired for the night. The worst part was informing the soldiers that they would be preparing for battle. They could only hope that the men understood.

In the morning the command group assembled in the tent at first light. They had left with the knowledge they were preparing for battle, but no one had the strength to plan anything. They had all agreed that it would be much better to sleep on the idea and come back with fresh heads in the morning.

"How do you plan the impossible attack?" Dorn asked.

"With great skill, and a little luck." Hulkan's response brought a little laughter around the table.

"Our main advantage is the high ground. Our archers and our catapults will have a far greater range. The battlefield should be far enough away from the walls to negate their archers." Sorrell suggested.

"But we don't have any ammunition for the catapults." Hulkan replied.

"I know, but I think we are going to have to go against Bern's wishes. He told us not to break down any of the outer city to hurl against the walls and that is exactly what we're going to do. The ammunition we need is for battle." There was a wry tone to Sorrell's voice.

"You're splitting hairs," Hulkan said.

"Yes he is, but I think it might just work." Jarwe liked what was hearing.

The morning conversation started on a positive note, unlike the night before. It was a promising sign. Orric watched and smiled. He was concerned they would continue their bickering and that would have solved nothing. He had hoped that his words would spark some action and it seemed as though they had.

"We have another advantage," Wojtek spoke next. General Sorrell had been involved in the planning of many battles. Most were just to control minor nobles or capture some pesky bandits, but it was all experience. "At the moment we have the greater area of land. There is not a lot a space between us and the outer city. That will decrease the amount of soldiers that can attack us at any one time. That will sway the numbers to our favour. With a little luck we might be able to create a bottleneck. If we control where the soldiers can attack us then we can control the fight."

"We don't have the material to build decent fortifications, but if we can collect enough stones from the outer walls we could make life difficult for an advancing army. Our main key is to protect the flanks. They will be the most vulnerable to attack. If we can keep the fighting to the front then we might actually have a chance to win," Jarwe added.

They were finally acting like commanders. Orric was glad that was the result. There was finally passion in the tent and not the morose veil that had been hanging over them. Orric thought it might just work. There was one problem, however, that they hadn't thought about, but he wasn't about to rain on their parade. He had his doubts whether it would actually happen, but it still played on his mind. If Za'aroz came down from on high to attack then they would lose any advantage. He kept his secret because there was really nothing they could do about it. No one would be able to stand up against him, so there was no point in mentioning it. The burden would be his and his alone to bear.

"I think we are starting to get a plan together. One thing we need to do is be quick. I am sure it won't be long before he sends his soldiers out to get us." Jarwe stood. "Let's go to work!"

The Alliance was abuzz with activity when the soldiers were given the orders. There was a feeling of purpose again. The fake bombardment had been confusing to the men. They couldn't understand what the commanders were doing. Now there was a strong sense of purpose, which overrode their impending doom. The positive attitude of the leaders filtered down through the ranks.

By midday their makeshift fortifications were starting to take shape. Barricades were being built around the flanks of the Alliance, their most vulnerable position. There had still been no movements from the city. At stages during their scavenging missions they came within range of the archers if they had been posted on the city walls.

"What do you think he's planning?" Sorrell asked from atop the small hill.

"I have no idea. The longer he waits the better it is for us," Jarwe replied.

It was as if his words marked their doom and he instantly wished he had not spoken. Slowly they saw both the eastern and southern gates being opened and soldiers start to pour out. It was a sight that brought fear into his heart. Things had been going so well that he actually thought they were going to succeed.

"I think it's time we move to the front of the line. Let's hope we have done enough." Jarwe couldn't take his eye from the swarm of soldiers.

"The men have worked hard. A few extra days would have been nice, but I think the fortifications should hold." Sorrell was trying to remain positive, more so for himself than anyone else.

The orders were quick to be distributed to the men. They were to stop work on the fortifications and prepare for battle. A pre-emptive strike would have given them an advantage, but Jarwe had decided against it. It was against his better judgement, but he had a feeling it was the right thing to do.

It took an hour for the Castalial solders to reach the edge of the outer city. They continued until they were just out of range of the archers. The catapults could easily hit them, but that didn't seem to worry their leaders. They didn't look as though they were going to make any further movement.

"What do you think they're planning?" Pernian asked.

"It doesn't make any sense. Why would they leave the protection of the city and not attack?" Jarwe mused.

"Remember they are not our enemy. They are being manipulated but Za'aroz. I'm sure they don't want to attack us as much as we don't want to attack them," Orric explained.

"Then you think there is a chance they won't attack?" Hulkan sounded hopeful.

"Very doubtful."

***

"High Chancellor!" High Priest Tybalt rushed into the High Chancellor's private chambers.

"What have I told you about entering my private chambers?" Za'aroz looked and sounded exactly like the High Chancellor. "This better be good or you will be joining my predecessor in the mines."

"Of course my lord, I didn't mean to offend." Tybalt quickly prostrated. He didn't want to gain the wrath of one of The Chosen. "The Alliance is here. They are outside the city."

Za'aroz dropped what he was doing. At first he stared out the window, as if that was going to give him some divine answer. When none was forthcoming he quickly returned his attention to the priest. The man was young for a High Priest. Za'aroz estimated that he could be no more than fifty years of age. He was a wiry looking man and Za'aroz wasn't sure if he would be any use in a fight. The Dark Knight couldn't remember which God the priest claimed to worship, but in the end that really didn't matter. He was a servant of the Great Lord and would do the bidding of one of the Chosen without question. He was a devout follower, Za'aroz was sure of that.

"What are you talking about?" He wanted to make sure he had heard correctly.

"Captain Cassius has brought word to the Grand Cathedral that the Alliance army is outside our walls. They have started bombarding the walls to the inner city," Tybalt explained.

"I see and who is leading this army?" there was a hint of concern in his voice. If Alaric had returned with an army then he was not sure he should stay. There was too great a risk to his life.

"A general by the name of Bern. I have never heard of him and neither has Cassius."

That was good news. He had not heard of Bern either, but that wasn't necessarily a bad thing. In fact he thought it was promising. Things must be starting to fall apart for the Alliance if there was an unknown general in command. It was clear if they were trying to break into the city that he was inexperienced. It was well known that the walls couldn't be breeched.

"That's promising." Za'aroz mused.

"What is it you wish to do?" Tybalt asked.

"Prepare the army. I want a full attack!" there was menace in his voice.

"But we are safe within our walls. No army has ever managed to break through. Are you sure that it wouldn't be better if we just waited them out?" Tybalt didn't like the idea.

"Are you questioning my judgement?" Za'aroz started to rise, but waited for a response before he completed it.

"No, my lord, of course not." The High Priest prostrated again. He hoped he had not enraged the Dark Knight or his fate would be terrible.

"Good, then do as I command. I want the Alliance eliminated by nightfall."

"I'm sorry, but it will take longer than that to get the army ready." Tybalt cringed.

Za'aroz thought for a moment. The High Priest was right. It would take much longer to rally the entire Castalial army, but he also didn't want to give the Alliance a free run.

"Gather as many soldiers as you can. By mid-afternoon I want them ready to march. Tell them not to attack until the rest of the army has been mobilised. I would say you should accomplish this by morning." There was an evil look in his eye, as if he was daring Tybalt to disagree.

"Yes, my lord, I will make sure it is done. All those who are not ready by morning will be whipped in the square as an example." Tybalt bowed on one knee as he spoke. He rose when he finished.

"Good, see that is done." Za'aroz dismissed him with a wave of his hand.

Za'aroz smiled when his underling had left. Things were better than he had thought. Alaric was not with the army and the general didn't really seem to know what he was doing. With a little luck by the evening of the following day the Alliance would be completely annihilated. Without an army behind him the Cursed One would have no chance against the Great Lord when it came time for the final battle. He started to drool at the thought. Soon he would be sitting on the Great Lord's right hand side.

Before he returned to what he was doing Za'aroz wiped his chin. He needed to stay focused. He held the advantage, but that could easily change. What he didn't like was the fact that he didn't know where Alaric was. That could easily be his downfall. The Cursed One had a number of stones now and if he had learnt how to use them then he doubted he would be able to defeat him. That was a thought that didn't really bear thinking about.

There was something more important that he had to decide on. He had regretted the decision to keep the High Chancellor alive ever since he had made it. It was not something he would normally do, but it had been an impulse that he couldn't resist. It seemed like a good decision at the time to send him down to the mines.

There were other jobs that he had to get done, but he couldn't concentrate on any of them. The High Chancellor was all he could think about. There was something nagging at him, but he couldn't work out what it was. He wanted the man dead, that was something he was sure of. The problem was how he was going to go about it. There were few people in the Grand Cathedral he could trust and he couldn't openly announce that the High Chancellor was in the secret mine. If he wanted him dead, it was a job that he was going to have to accomplish himself.

Suddenly there was a knock on the door that made him jump. He had been so deep in contemplation that he lost perspective of reality. He took a moment to compose himself before he called for whoever it was to enter.

"Sorry to disturb you, my lord." It was Tybalt again. "I became concerned when you didn't join us for the midday meal."

Za'aroz had no idea what the time was. He looked out the window and noticed the sun was well and truly on its downward arc. The day had completely got away from him and he was no closer to his answer.

"I have been in deep contemplation." Was all he said.

"I am sorry to disturb you again, but I thought you would like to know that the army is ready to march. It seems as though the Alliance has run out of ammunition. The bombardment stopped about an hour ago. I am not sure who this general is who is leading them, but it seems as though he doesn't really know what he's doing. I think this is going to be easier than we first thought." Tybalt paused for a moment. "Do you want Cassius to entreat with them first? You never know, when they see the might of your army they may just surrender."

"We don't want to give them a chance to surrender. We want to completely destroy them. The more deaths the better. When this is over the Alliance will be completely destroyed. Tell Cassius we are not to take any prisoners."

Tybalt didn't like what he was hearing, but he was not brave enough to question the Dark Knight's motives. He would do as he was told out of fear more than anything else. He was beginning to think he had chosen the wrong side. It had seemed fun at first. He had lived a mundane life, always doing the right thing. When he had the opportunity to bring a little danger to his life he had jumped on it. It seemed like it would be a good life, he had been promised riches beyond his dreams and women to wait on his every whim. It was a life that he would never have achieved as a High Priest to the God King Emerald. Up until that point his life had been about tending the trees and plants in the inner circle. That was all his life was going to achieve, in-between lectures and prayers. Now he was not so sure that he was going to receive what was promised to him. He needed to look for a way out, somehow. For the moment he would just have to do as he was commanded.

"I will come out and see how everything is progressing shortly," Za'aroz said as an afterthought just as Tybalt was leaving the room.

He would have to show some sign of leadership. He knew that the weak men would need reassurance from their leader. There would be time to seek out the High Chancellor once the sun had set. There would be no action on the battlefield until the morning. Once the sun had set the soldiers would have to return to their barracks and tents respectively. That gave him plenty of time to seek out his prey. The next problem he had was that he had no idea where the High Chancellor was. The mine was a maze of tunnels and shafts and Augustus could be anywhere.

As he walked out of his offices he felt pleased with himself. Despite the small problem of the real High Chancellor everything was going better than planned. It would not be long before he would stand victorious on the field of battle. He only wished that he could take part in the slaughter, but that would soon give away his true identity and that was something he couldn't risk. He would just have to watch the bloodshed from the battlements. At least that would be something.

Chapter 11: Leaving Jarrat

Alaric knew it was time get moving. The army was well and truly on its way out of the city. He carried his bags through the castle until he reached Alena and Eldred's apartment. He thought that some servant would have tried to carry them for him, but that was not the case. Once he reached the apartment that was a different story. There was a group of young pages waiting for his arrival. Two of them snatched up his bags as soon as he put them down and hurried to the stables. The horses would be loaded and ready to leave once they reached the courtyard.

"So are we all ready to go?" he asked.

"Yes!" Eldred replied quickly.

The old wizard seemed to be in good spirits as was Alena. The malaise still hung over Richmond's head as he still believed that the death of his friend and advisor was somehow his fault. It made no sense, but that didn't change his mood. Alaric hoped he would get over it. It would be a long journey if he remained in such a state. Alaric almost wished it wasn't Richmond who was to be his last companion.

"Then I guess that we should get moving. There isn't a great deal of day left," Alaric stated the obvious.

"It will be good to be out in the open again," Alena said as they made their way through the castle. "I have been cooped up inside for too long. Elves aren't made to be inside for long periods of time." There was a note of anticipation in her voice. She had only left the castle briefly to see here father, but that was nothing compared to the amount of time she had been trapped inside. There was a spring to her step that made Alaric happy. He almost felt excited about the trip, if it wasn't for the thoughts that weighed down on him.

There was still no clear destination for their journey. Eldred still claimed that they had to travel to the Isle of Wizards, whilst Alaric felt that he needed to go to the Scorpion Mountain. Both felt as though they were right, but neither of them could be completely sure. In the end Alaric knew it would be his decision. Once in his life he would have followed Eldred's advice without question, but things had changed so much since then. Alaric had grown in ability since they had first left Arsiliac. He knew how to follow his own feelings and make his own decisions, although he had to admit it was nice having Eldred back. At least he would have someone he could ask questions to.

The horses were waiting for them in the courtyard. Alaric was happy to see Adelanta. The pure white elven stallion also seemed happy to see him. He knew they were about to start another long journey and that thought excited him. Like Alena he didn't like being kept inside. He needed to be out in open, able to run free like the wind.

Tormenta, Eldred's white elven stallion, seemed even more excited to see Eldred. The horse had not seen its friend and master since Eldred had been taken in Nostalia. He was keen to have the wizard on his back again.

Alena had been given a white elven mare from her father before Orric left with the army. Lluvia looked pleased when she saw Alena approach. Alena had known Lluvia from when she was a foal and had spent many a day riding on her back.

Richmond was left a young grey mare given to him by Duke Xarles. Although it was nothing like the breeding of the elven horses it looked as though she was a sturdy animal. Although she had no name, Richmond patted her neck and called her a good girl when he mounted.

The four of them rode out of the castle grounds in silence followed by four pack animals loaded with their supplies. They were all glad to be leaving Jarrat. The city had done nothing for any of them, some worse than others. No one looked back at the castle or the city as they made their way along the Remidian-Entero highway to the north-west of the city.

Once they were inside the forest the mood of the group lifted slightly. Even Richmond didn't seem to be as sombre. Alena was happy to be around a large group of trees again. She took in deep breaths as they rode. The smell of pine filled her nostrils and with each breath she felt as though her strength was returning. She had still been suffering the affects of her imprisonment whilst she was inside the castle. Now that she was out in the open she knew that it wouldn't be long until she fully recovered.

It was a warm afternoon as they rode through the woods. As they expected there was no traffic on the highway. They didn't expect to see anyone at least until they reached the next town. It wouldn't be long before the roads to Jarrat were completely open again, but for the moment the duke was playing things safe. There was still enough food and other supplies for the city to last another few months. The trade routes would be open again long before they ran out.

If it wasn't for the nagging feeling in the back of his mind Alaric would have found the ride enjoyable. A cool breeze blew through the forest creating a pleasant atmosphere. He couldn't help feeling the unrest of not knowing their true destination. There was a strict time frame for his meeting with Adder. If he missed it then his home town would be destroyed. He wanted nothing more than to skip through reality, but he didn't know where it would take them. He couldn't risk losing the feeling that kept him going.

As the afternoon wore on Alaric's feeling of unrest continued. He wanted nothing more than to kick Adelanta into a run. The white stallion could sense his rider's anxiety and jumped as he walked. Alaric had to give him a gentle tug on the reins to keep him from breaking into a trot. As much as he wanted to speed up there was little chance the pack animals would keep up the pace.

When the sun started to set they found a small clearing on the side of the highway to camp for the night. Alaric wanted to keep riding, but he had to agree it was the perfect place to stop. He begrudgingly pulled Adelanta to a halt. He looked up at Alaric with a questioning look. All Alaric could do was shrug his shoulders and dismount.

"It's nice to be out in the open again," Alena was the first to speak as they sat around a small campfire.

They had been sitting in silence for almost half an hour with everyone just staring at the flames. It had been uncomfortable and she felt it was time for some conversation. There was a certain amount of confusion with her words as the forest almost completely enclosed them, but they understood what she meant.

"I have to admit that I am glad to see the back of Jarrat. I will be more than happy if I never have to visit the city again." Richmond's words were not what Alena wanted to hear.

Alaric didn't have the heart to tell them they would be returning once he found the Opal stone. Since he didn't know how long that would take he thought it best not to bring it up. A lot could happen in the mean time so there was no point in decreasing his mood any further.

"I think we can all relate to that." Eldred had to agree. "It was not an enjoyable time in the castle's dungeon."

"We should be on the road at first light." Alaric thought it would be wise to change the subject. "We have a lot of ground to cover and little time."

At that moment Alena wished she had not spoken. It didn't seem as though there was going to be anything to lighten the mood. Too much had happened recently for it just to be forgotten. She wasn't going to let that worry her. She was happy to be back in the forest and that was all she cared about. The others could stew in their own malaise.

They spent the rest of the night in silence. It was easier than making conversation. There was plenty for them all to think about. Alena was the only one having happy thoughts.

Alaric was the first to rise in the morning. He prepared a light breakfast for everyone before he packed the animals. He wanted to make sure that when they had eaten they were ready to move again. As much as the others didn't have Alaric's zeal they too wanted to be on the road. Alaric's words were still thick in their minds. Time, as always, was against them.

"What concerns me," Eldred started after they had been riding for an hour, "is that we don't know what Nyrra is doing."

"What do you mean?" Alaric asked.

"I'm sure at some point over the last few months he was in Jarrat. My time in the dungeons is a little sketchy now, but I am quite sure that he visited me. Now I have no idea where he is and what he's doing. That's a very disturbing thought."

"I would imagine he is searching for the Ruby stone." Richmond added.

Alaric looked at Eldred who in turn raised his eyebrows. He had to admit the thought had crossed his mind, but that was the easy answer. Eldred was sure there was more to his movements. He still had three Dark Knights and a rather large army somewhere in the Seven Kingdoms. Nyrra would not have left them all to their own devices, Eldred couldn't doubt that logic. He only wished he could get some idea of what the Evil One was planning. There was nothing in prophecy to help him and that was very frustrating.

"I'm afraid that the easy answer is not necessarily the right one." Eldred had taken his time, trying to find an answer that wouldn't upset Richmond. In the end he just decided to say what was on his mind. "I have a bad feeling that he is planning something terrible. I would feel a lot more comfortable if I knew what that was."

"I'm sure if he had the Stone we would know by now, I guess that is a promising sign." Alena quickly added.

"Is there anyway you can use the Jade stone to find the Ruby stone?" Eldred asked, taking up the change of subject.

"I don't think so. I have only used the stone briefly, but there doesn't seem to be anyway for me to control it. It will show me the direction of the other stones, but not which one specifically. It helped me find the Sapphire stone and the Emerald stone, but when it was said and done I am sure the prophecy would have sent me in the same direction."

At the mention of the Jade stone Alaric had a sudden compulsion to see which direction it thought they should be travelling. He had only just recovered from his recent ordeal with the Topaz stone and he was not sure he wanted to go through that again. There was little point in the end. For the moment Alaric couldn't go chasing around looking for the three remaining stones. The thought of the Sapphire stone brought the memory of Marina back. He blushed slightly at the thought and hoped that no one noticed. He quickly pushed the idea to the back of his mind. There were more important things to think about.

"I don't think that it will lead me to the Ruby stone unless it really wants me to find it." Alaric continued, trying to hide his embarrassment.

The conversation finished abruptly with Alaric's words. They had gone too far off topic and Eldred didn't see the point in returning. There was little that anyone could do except surmise.

Eldred had to make sure the other wizards helped their cause. He knew it was the only way they would survive. They needed the added firepower of the five other wizards, knowing that Minerva was already on their side. At least he would have one ally on the island and that was better than nothing.

Alaric couldn't help feeling the urge to hurry things along. He knew he couldn't push the animals, but there had to be another way. The temptation to jump was almost irresistible, but again he couldn't risk losing his direction. There was a long way to travel and jumping such a distance would be too draining. There had to be another way, but hadn't figured it out yet.

As the morning wore on Alaric felt a strange sensation at the base of his neck. At first he scratched it and it went away, but it soon returned and when it did it intensified. The next time he tried to scratch it away it wouldn't leave. He tried to ignore it, but that also didn't work. When he realised what he had been doing he looked around at the others to see if they had noticed, but they were too involved in their own thoughts.

A thought came to Alaric as they rode. He didn't know where it had come from, but it seemed to make sense. Slowly he started to draw in the energy of the forest around him. In fact he had started drawing in the power before he knew what he was doing. The feeling of the fresh, clean life force of the forest filled Alaric's body with joy. The experience was euphoric. Alaric had almost forgotten how glorious it felt.

The next part of his plan was not going to be so easy and he was not sure how he was going to achieve his goal. The spell that he needed to create was one that he had never used before and one that he had never seen made. He had never tried such a thing before. When he had needed to cast a spell it had always come naturally to him. He knew what he wanted to achieve, but he had no idea how he was going to do it.

It was fifteen minutes before he finally released the energy he was holding in frustration. There was nothing he could do to create the spell that he wanted. When he did the itchy sensation also left him. He wondered, in the end, why it was even there and why it had disappeared. It seemed pointless and that worried him.

They reached the edge of the forest as the sun started to set. Eldred pulled in his horse when he reached the tree line. He instantly knew that something wasn't right, but he had no idea what it was. There was no way, at their gentle pace, that they should have travelled so far. He called the others to a halt and for them to remain inside the forest. There was something about being out in the open that made him uncomfortable.

Until he could work out what had happened they were going no further. There was a good chance there was dark magic at play. He had learnt his lesson when he led them into Dhlark's trap outside the Cloumid Mountains and was not going to make the same mistake twice.

"I think we should make camp inside the forest tonight," Eldred explained.

"What's the matter?" Alena recognised the tone in his voice.

"There is still plenty of light left. Now that we are out of the forest there should be no trouble travelling at night," Alaric interrupted.

"No, we shall stop here for the night," Eldred commanded.

Alaric was about to say something else, but then stopped. He didn't like the tone in Eldred's voice. He was no longer the leader of their group. That title was firmly Alaric's, or at least that was the way Alaric felt. In the end he figured there was no point in arguing. Eldred obviously knew something that he didn't. If there was trouble ahead he didn't want to rush into it.

"Is there something wrong?" Alena asked.

"I'm not sure. We have travelled too quickly for one day." Eldred had debated whether he should voice his concerns. In the end he figured the others might be able to help, or at least Alaric.

"What are you talking about?" Alaric asked.

"It should have taken us at least another two days to reach the edge of the forest. Someone or something is speeding up our journey."

"That's a good thing!" Alaric spoke before anyone had a chance to think too hard. "We are racing against the clock. Anything that gives us an advantage has to be good."

Alaric's logic was sound, but Eldred was not convinced. He ignored Alaric's hasty words and continued with his theory that there was Dark Knight involved, or worse, Nyrra himself.

"I don't have the ability to slow down time, as that is what I assume has happened since we remained moving at a normal pace. It would have taken a powerful magician to create such a spell. I have a bad feeling that it was a Dark Knight," Eldred explained.

"Why would a Dark Knight be aiding us?" Richmond asked. "Wouldn't they be trying to hinder our movements not assist us?"

That was the problem that Eldred was struggling with. It didn't make much sense. It was also the reason why he didn't want to leave the relative safety of the forest. If it was indeed a Dark Knight playing with the fabrics of reality then there would be a good reason for it and it would not be to their advantage. Eldred was afraid they wouldn't be able to move until he was able to figure it out.

"There has to be a trap waiting for us. The most frustrating thing is that I couldn't feel the spell being created. Something so powerful should have sent waves through the air. You didn't feel anything, did you Alaric?"

Alaric simply shook his head and remained quiet. There was something about Eldred's words that was disturbing him. The spell that was created was the spell Alaric was trying to achieve. He knew there was a way to slow down time, the only problem was that he couldn't work out the weaves to create such a spell. If he had then he couldn't imagine who would have been able to feel it. He had not even thought about trying to mask it. It was as if someone was messing with his mind. There was a good chance there was a Dark Knight at play, but even when the thought entered his mind Alaric didn't really believe that was right.

"Are the Dark Knights really that powerful?" Richmond sounded surprised. "I would have thought that you were stronger." He had to admit that he didn't really know Eldred at all. He had heard rumours of the great seven wizards and their island, but he had never met one for real. He had heard tales of great deeds the wizards were able to complete. He hoped they were not just myths and bedtime stories.

"It's hard to say anymore. At one time I would have agreed with you, but now I am not so sure. Their powers have grown over the years where it seems as though mine are starting to wane..." Eldred paused. He wasn't going to mention his next theory, but he thought it was better that they all be prepared for the worst. "There is a chance that this is the work of Nyrra."

Eldred's words brought shocked gasps from both Alena and Richmond. The thought that the Evil One was close by had not entered any of their minds. They knew he was free in the Seven Kingdoms, but it was always better not to think about it. If Nyrra was the one controlling the spell then the final battle couldn't be far away. Without the army for support it was not a good sign.

"I think I would know if it was Nyrra." Alaric wanted to put that thought right out of their minds. He could clearly see their fear and concern on their faces.

"I don't know if you would. He is very powerful. I wouldn't go as far to say his power was limitless, but if he already has the Ruby stone then I would say he was as close as anyone has ever been."

The more Alaric thought on the problem the more convinced he became that he knew what had happened. He had wanted to keep his theory to himself until he knew for sure, but he didn't think that was the right course of action. No one would sleep if they were afraid the Evil One was after them. That would be enough to make the most stalwart of men break down and cry.

"I think it was me who created the spell," Alaric blurted out.

No one knew what to say. They all looked at Alaric in shock. The words didn't really seem to make sense. Eldred thought he was just trying to ease their minds. He was also concerned that Alaric was in such a rush to reach their destination that he would risk their lives. That was something he couldn't allow. No matter what the risks Alaric's safety was paramount.

"I appreciate what you are trying to do Alaric, but this is a serious matter. If we are walking into a trap then we need to be prepared. Underplaying the situation is not going to help anyone."

Alaric knew he wasn't going to receive a positive response. He was ready for such an attack, but he really had no idea how he was going to respond. Deep down he wished he had some idea how he was able to create the spell. At least that way he would sound like he knew what he was talking about.

"I can't explain it, but I am confident that it was me who created the spell." He looked at the group.

"That's impossible." Eldred blurted the words out when Alaric had finished. "There is no way possible that you could have created such a powerful spell without realising and then be able to mask it so I couldn't feel anything riding next to you. There has got to be another explanation."

"What's more likely? That there is someone out there who is helping us save time only to rush us into a trap or that I created the spell by pure chance?" Even as Alaric asked the question he knew how ridiculous it sounded. Neither option was really appealing.

The argument went back and forth. Each time Alaric was more and more confident that it was in fact he who had created the spell, but Eldred was still not so sure. He couldn't believe that Alaric had surpassed his abilities in a matter of months. There had to be something else at play. He could understand if Alaric was using one of the stones, but to create such a spell on his own was another story. It was not something that Eldred could readily believe.

"Just the pure fact that none of us knew we were travelling faster than time is a fair indication that it wasn't you. Maybe it was the Dark Knight who put the thoughts in your mind. It would be a lot easier for him to set the trap if you think it was you who created the spell." Eldred refused to add Nyrra to his list anymore.

It was a compelling argument, but that didn't change Alaric's mind. He knew he had created the spell, he just didn't know how. It was the most frustrating thing that had happening to him in a long time. He wished that he could make Eldred understand.

"I don't know what it is I have to do to convince you that it was me. I am sorry if I have offended your ego, but unfortunately you are going to have to accept the fact there are things that I can do that you cannot." Alaric didn't want to sound arrogant, but there was no other way.

That certainly did nothing to improve Eldred's mood. He had not sat in that dungeon for so long just to be insulted when he was released. It was time the upstart in front of him was taught a lesson. Suddenly Alaric felt something wrap around his body. At first the feeling caught him by surprise, but by the look on Eldred's face he soon realised what it was. It was not something he wanted to participate in, but it seemed as though Eldred wouldn't give him the chance.

The spell was a simple one. Alaric could see the weaves as clear as day. Alaric didn't have to draw in any energy to break it. When he was free again Alaric relaxed. He had proven his point and that was end of it. Unfortunately Eldred didn't feel the same way. The old wizard had used the simple tricks many times when his student became too bold. In his many years he had never had a student defeat him and he was not about to start now.

Alaric was a little surprised at Eldred's attempt to ensnare him. The last thing he was expecting was another attack. Eldred tried again and cast another much more powerful spell. Again the weave wrapped around Alaric and held him tight. The look of surprise was clearly written across his face. The other two didn't seem to know what was happening. Eldred was masking his magic so Alena couldn't feel anything. They sat around the campfire, oblivious to what was going on around them.

There was no way that Alaric was going to let Eldred keep the spell going. Again he could see the weaves and knew exactly what to do. The weaves unravelled like a poorly made scarf. Alaric didn't even break a sweat breaking the spell, whilst Eldred was starting to feel the strain.

Alaric was about to speak, but no words came out. The silence spell was even simpler than the first one. Eldred didn't want him to speak, which clearly made Alaric annoyed. There was absolutely no reason why Eldred should be attacking him. Alaric didn't have any time to break the silence spell before Eldred's next attack. A small bolt of lightning shot from Eldred's open palm. The sudden flash of light made Alena and Richmond, who were sitting, minding their own business, look up. Alaric simply raised his own hands and the lightning fizzled out of existence.

"What are you doing?" Alena asked in horror.

Neither of them answered. It was Alaric's turn to go on the attack. It was clear that was going to be the only way to get Eldred to stop. He still couldn't work out what the old wizard was trying to achieve. It was as if he wanted to die. Alaric was going to make him hurt, but he was not going to go too far until he had to. Suddenly Eldred was lifted from the ground. The move took everyone by surprise. Eldred had not been expecting an attack to come so swiftly and without warning. There was no time for him to counter it. Alaric threw him across the forest until he struck a nearby tree. The blow knocked the wind out of him, but didn't do any serious damage. Alaric didn't give him a chance to recuperate. He cast another spell that dragged Eldred to his feet. Alaric walked over to him.

"What is the idea of this?" Alaric spoke through clenched teeth, although it was not from the strain.

"Please Alaric, put me down!" Eldred was struggling to breathe.

Alaric had not even realised that he was squeezing on Eldred's chest. He quickly released all the spells he had created and Eldred slumped to the ground, panting for breath. He was starting to believe that Alaric could have created the spell to slow down time. The man was much more powerful than he could believe. He knew that Alaric would eventually surpass his own abilities, but he just didn't think it would be so soon.

"Would someone please tell me what is happening?" Alena stood between Alaric and Eldred.

"I think Eldred should do the explaining. I'm not sure if I know what this is all about," Alaric replied.

Eldred nodded his head in agreement before taking a moment to catch his breath. He knew they would understand when he had told them what he was doing and the reason behind it.

"I had to see how powerful Alaric was. If he had created the spell that sped up our journey then he should have no problem breaking my spells, which I am sure you can tell he did with ease." Eldred did his best to explain.

"If that is all you were doing then why didn't you tell me before you started?" Alaric didn't sound convinced.

"It wouldn't have been the same if you were expecting it. That would have made things too easy for you. I am sorry for the ruse, but it was imperative that you didn't know what I was doing." Eldred hoped that would be enough.

"I think that sounds fair enough." Alena looked back at Alaric.

Alaric thought for a moment. He had to admit that it made sense. If Eldred had announced he was going to attack then he would have been able to prepare a quick protection spell. The thing that he didn't like was that Eldred didn't trust him. There was no reason for him to lie. His life would be in just as much danger, if not more, than the others. There would be no advantage to him if they all got captured by a Dark Knight or worse, Nyrra himself. Alaric returned to the fire in silence.

"I am sorry," Eldred spoke after a few minutes had passed without conversation. "I didn't mean to doubt you. What you have to understand is that I have never heard of anyone with such ability and to work that out subconsciously is hard for me to grasp," Eldred spoke candidly.

Alaric could accept that answer. There was little point acting like a spoilt child. Eldred was doing what he thought was best and at least he knew that Alaric's abilities had surpassed his own. Now there was a chance that Eldred would listen to what he had to say. That in itself would make the ordeal worthwhile.

"I understand," was all Alaric said.

They had already stayed up too late. If they were going to get an early start they would need sleep soon. Alaric had no intention of staying up later than he should. The others didn't look as though they were making any move to sleep. Alaric hoped his example would entice the others.

Chapter 12: Fresh Information

Again Alaric woke before the sun rose. Now that Eldred had agreed with the fact that Alaric had created the spell there was nothing stopping them from exiting the forest. Alaric wished he knew how he had created it. It would definitely come in handy the further they travelled. Any time he could save time would increase his chances of reaching the mountain peak.

Although it couldn't be his first priority he still needed to make sure he didn't leave Arsiliac fall under the yoke of Adder. There was no telling what the Serpentant would do.

"We need to be on the road again," Alaric said as soon as the sun crested the horizon.

There were no arguments from the others. Now that it was safe to leave the forest they were all keen to be on the road again. They all wanted to forget what had happened the night before. It was a scary thought at how fast Alaric had progressed. The revelation had not been lost of any of them, even Richmond. Something had changed in Alaric since Nostiria. Eldred wasn't completely sure if it was a good sign or a bad sign.

As the morning wore on the slow pace became frustrating again. Alaric had spent the ride trying to find the answer to his problem. If he had created the spell the day before then he could do it again, but he still had no idea how he had done it.

It was just after they had stopped for the midday meal that Alaric felt the itch at the back of his neck. At first he scratched it without taking any notice, but when the feeling returned there was a sense of hope in Alaric's heart. He slowly started to draw in the energy around him. Again he had no idea what he was going to do with it, but he had a feeling it was the right thing to do. The feeling of euphoria returned and he didn't want to let it go.

The next part was trying to recreate a spell that he had no idea how to. He tried for almost half an hour as they rode before he finally let the energy flow from his body. He was disappointed at losing the glorious feeling, but he knew the dangers of holding onto the energy for too long.

When all the energy had left his body he looked around to see if anything had changed. To his disappointment everyone and everything looked the same. He thought that nothing had happened. At least the itch had disappeared and the feeling that they were running out of time had left him.

It wasn't until they reached a small town along the highway did Alaric realise that the spell had worked. It was mid-afternoon when they started to ride through the town of Martelle. At first he thought everything was normal, but then he realised that no one in the town seemed to notice their arrival. Not only that, but they were moving at a slower pace. He then realised they must be travelling faster than they should be. The people around them moved at a snail's pace. He wondered why he hadn't noticed anything when they were in the forest or out in the open.

The sudden realisation at what was happening made Richmond feel nauseated. He felt like losing the contents of his stomach and it took all his concentration not to. It was quite discerning to watch people in slow-motion. He had much preferred not knowing what was happening around him. There was something very unseemly about the situation. He couldn't wait until they reached the other side of the town.

By nightfall they reached the border city of Albend. Although the city stood on both sides of the border it was ruled by Duke Balin of Remidia. Albend had been ruled by many over the years. The last ruler was from Entero until the current duke invaded almost twenty years ago. He had survived numerous attacks and was the longest running ruler in five hundred years. It was almost getting to the point that the city was no longer a disputed territory.

Once they passed through the gates the reality around them returned to normal. There was still almost an hour before the sun would completely set. Alaric thought it was odd that the spell had worn off without any warning. He thought they would have been at least a few leagues into Remidia. It was a little frustrating, but at least they would be able to sleep in a bed that night.

"We should find an inn." Alaric resigned himself to the fact that they weren't going any further.

"I think we should try and get access to the castle. The duke should have information on what it is like in Remidia. Do you know the duke at all?" Eldred asked Richmond.

"No, I have never had call to come this way," Richmond replied. "But I am sure the duke will welcome a visiting noble."

It seemed as though Richmond was starting to return to his old self. His depression had lessened the further they had travelled from Jarrat. Alaric was pleased he was getting better. He couldn't imagine what it was like to lose his best friend, but unfortunately there was no time to grieve.

They made their way through the streets towards the duke's castle in the centre of the city. It was a small castle, smaller than any Alaric had ever seen. It had been constructed out of stone brought down from the Cloumid Mountains. Despite its size it was a still an impressive structure. It was surrounded by a small wooden wall, more for decoration than defence. There were half a dozen turrets flying the royal flag of Remidia.

That was to let everyone know which kingdom was in command of the city.

The citizens shied away from the group as they rode towards the city. Alaric had a bad feeling they were afraid and that was not a good sign. There was no reason why they should feel that way unless things were bad. Alaric knew they were going to receive some unpleasant news once they reached the castle.

There were two guards standing at the gate. As expected they blocked their path as they approached. Alaric wished for once that someone would just let him in. He'd had enough of trying to convince guards that they were no threat and in fact they were there to help.

"Who goes there?" one of the guards boomed.

"I am Lord Richmond. I am travelling from Jarrat to Remidel and wish to speak with Duke Balin. We have some interesting information that I am sure he will be interested to hear," Richmond explained.

"Do you have the appropriate paperwork?" the guard asked, not impressed at Richmond's title.

That was something that Richmond no longer had. Since his imprisonment all the documents that proved his nobility had been destroyed. The only proof he had was his signet ring, which anyone could have stolen. He showed it to the guard anyway in that hope that he believed him.

"I think that should be enough proof."

Alaric was the only one who knew that Eldred had created a spell. The wizard didn't think it was important enough or strong enough to warrant masking it.

"That looks fine, I am sure the duke will be keen to speak with you." Even as the words came out of the guard's mouth he knew that they weren't right, but for some reason he couldn't help himself.

"Sometimes it's just easier," Eldred said to Alaric as they passed through the gates.

They left the horses in the castle's courtyard. Adelanta didn't seem happy to be left in a stable again. He had only just been let out into the open spaces and the last thing he wanted to do was to be stabled again. Alaric spoke a few calming words to him before they climbed the stairs to the main doors. The other two elven horses didn't seem too concerned and the mare actually seemed happy.

When they were inside they were met by two young serving maids. They looked at the four of them standing in front of them and they started to giggle when they saw Alaric. He simply brushed it aside, but Alena didn't look happy about it. She was about to speak, but Richmond spoke first.

"We wish to speak with Duke Balin. I am Lord Richmond from Bellarome, Darshival," Richmond spoke with a haughtiness in his voice that was typical of nobility. It almost made Alaric laugh.

The two serving maids blushed, turned and hurried away, but started giggling again as they went. Richmond led the group further into the castle, but only by a number of steps before he stopped again. It would have been rude if they had just decided to wander around. Richmond didn't want to start by getting the duke offside.

The castle foyer was small and adorned only by a large painting of King Faxon on the far wall. There were a number of small chairs and tables, but the group decided it would be best to remain standing.

It wasn't long before a smartly dressed man came walking down the hallway. He looked overly confident and there was an air about him that Alaric didn't like. He couldn't put his finger on it, but he made a note to be wary about him.

"I understand that you are Lord Richmond?" The man bowed. "And who are these other three with you? As I am sure you can imagine, these are worrying times and we need to careful with who is allowed to see the duke. It would be the perfect time for some Enteroite to usurp control and you say that you have just come from Jarrat?"

Richmond could understand their caution, but it was still annoying. The only saving grace was they were in no hurry. The sun had not quite set and they would not be on the move until the morning. It would be nice to spend an evening in luxury again. Their stay at Jarrat had been less than pleasant.

"This is the Wizard Eldred, the High-Elf Alena and the Chosen One of the Prophecy and the Saviour of the Seven Kingdoms, Alaric." Richmond used the best titles he could think of.

The castle master looked at them all with a strange expression on his face. He had heard of Eldred before, but the other two were a mystery to him. He had heard of the Chosen One, but he thought the prophecy was only an old wives tale. In the end he decided to take them on face value. He had never seen an elf before, but Alena didn't look like any human he had ever seen. Their story seemed to make sense.

"The duke is in his private chambers. He is interested to meet with you Lord Richmond." The castle master wasn't completely sure, but it was up to the duke and he had already agreed to see them.

The castle master led them through the castle toward the duke's chambers. There were many servants and minor functionaries standing around, trying to act busy. In fact they just wanted to get a look at the new arrivals. Word had travelled fast around the castle, it had been a long time since there had been visitors.

Duke Balin was making a show of shuffling papers when they arrived. He thought it was better if he looked as though he didn't really care. In fact he was very excited at the thought of speaking with another noble. When they entered the room he quickly pushed his paperwork aside.

"Good evening, please, take a seat." Balin offered before the castle master had a chance to introduce them. "That will be all Latimer."

They sat down and waited for the duke to speak again.

Duke Balin was of middle age with a well trimmed brown beard and brown hair. He wore a simple red tunic and leggings. He looked strong and there was little doubt that he had led the siege on Albend to bring it back under Remidian rule.

"There are rooms being prepared for your stay and a meal should be ready soon. I am sure you are tired and hungry from your journey. How long will you be staying?" Balin sounded somewhat excited.

"Unfortunately we will only be staying for one night," Richmond replied. "We have urgent business which leads us towards Remidel." He lied, not thinking it was worth telling the truth. There was no telling who would find out if he did.

"Then I'm afraid you're in for a tough journey." Balin's tone turned grave. "I have been hearing some disturbing things from the heart of the kingdom."

"What do you mean?" Richmond asked.

"Now you have to understand that these are only rumours. We don't get a great deal of factual information being so isolated, but you can make of it what you will." Balin shuffled the papers in front of him until he found the one he was looking for. "It seems as though the Evil One's army is taking over Remidia and the king is doing nothing to stop him."

"How is that possible?" Alaric couldn't believe what he was hearing.

"Now again these are only rumours..." Again Balin had to refer to his paperwork. "It seems as though there is a Dark Knight in the capital and he is controlling King Faxon."

That was not at all what they wanted to hear, although they weren't surprised. All the other kingdoms had been under the control of a Dark Knight at one time or another. As much as Alaric had hoped it would not be the case he knew that it was coming.

"This is indeed disturbing news." Richmond continued. "Do you know if the source of this information is reliable?"

"If I wasn't sure I wouldn't mention it, even though I can't guarantee it, I wouldn't doubt it."

There was a moment of silence as the information sunk in. They all knew that their journey wouldn't be smooth, but things sounded as though they were going to get a lot worse. The one thing that had happened in the other kingdoms was that the enemy had only stayed in the capital city. It sounded as though Nyrra was trying to take control of all of Remidia and that would include Arsiliac.

"Do you know which cities, towns and villages have fallen to the Evil One?" There was only one village Alaric was interested in, but he kept his question broad.

"There have been no confirmed sackings, but I would imagine it won't be long before the reports come in," Balin explained.

"I've noticed you don't seem too worried here," Richmond said. "The gates were open and if there had been more of us it wouldn't have been too hard to defeat your guards."

"My soldiers are out scouting the surroundings. They have been gone for almost a week now. They should be returning any day. We are not going to be taken by surprise." Balin sounded proud.

"That sounds like a very good idea." Richmond praised him.

Before he had a chance to continue there came a knock on the door. A number of serving maids entered with platters of food. It was a welcome interruption. There was little more that needed to be discussed in the presence of the duke.

"What is happening in Jarrat?" the duke asked when they started eating.

That was a question they all hoped wouldn't be asked. No one wanted to re-live that experience. Richmond knew the most first hand, but it was clear that he didn't want to discuss it. Neither Alena nor Eldred looked like they wanted to speak, so it was up to Alaric to explain. He had wanted more responsibility and it was time for him step up. The hardest part would be omitting details without leaving holes in his story.

Balin sat in awe as Alaric did his best to explain what had happened. He couldn't bring himself to ask any questions. He could hardly believe the story was true. There was no doubt that if the rumours were true that Remidia was looking at the same fate. It was something he couldn't allow, but also something he couldn't change. His army wasn't big enough to make any serious dent on the enemy.

"So where is the Alliance now?" the duke finally asked. "Shouldn't they be on their way to Remidel?"

"They are on their way to Castalia," Alaric replied.

Balin actually spat on his own floor. He couldn't believe what he was hearing. He had never thought much of the Castalials. For some reason the traders always seemed to rip him off or at least that was the way he saw it. When he tried to get a council with the High Chancellor to discuss trade discounts, Augustus had simply ignored his emissary. Balin wanted nothing more than to move his army into Castalia, but that was never going to work. He would incite a war that his king would never sanction, thus leaving him to fight on his own. The second, and main reason, was that his army wouldn't even make a dent to Castalia. There was nothing he could do besides accepting the High Chancellor's ruling, which was to say nothing at all.

"Why would they move to help a kingdom that has no respect for the other kingdoms? The High Chancellor sits in the Grand Cathedral and doesn't care what happens to everyone else. The Alliance should be moving into Remidia."

Alaric was somewhat surprised at the duke's response. Surely the man could see what would happen if the enemy gained full control over the Castalial army. If he left Za'aroz in command then it would only be a matter of time. He took a deep breath before he explained the situation to Balin. He didn't really know why he did, there was nothing the duke could do, but he felt as though he should. In the end Balin was still unhappy, but he came to accept the fact.

"Once we are done with Castalia I can assure you that the army will move on to Remidel. If there is a Dark Knight in control then he will not remain there for long," Alaric promised.

Duke Balin looked satisfied with the answer. They had all finished their meal and it seemed as though the conversation was over. Alaric took the momentary silence as an excuse to leave the room. He thanked the duke for his hospitality and much to Balin's chagrin the others followed closely after him.

"I don't think you should have promised Duke Balin that the army would march on Remidel." Eldred scolded Alaric.

Alaric didn't like the tone in Eldred's voice, but he pushed it aside. He could understand where he was coming from. It did seem like the logical place for them go next. If there was indeed a Dark Knight in Remidel then Alaric had located them all. It would make sense for the army to go to Remidel and then Lel Dinion rather than the other way around. He didn't think it would hurt give Balin a little hope.

"I am sure it will be okay. I am sure the army will go to Remidel after it is finished with Castalia. If not there really isn't anything he can do. At least this way he will sleep easy," Alaric explained.

The castle master met them outside the duke's chambers. Alaric had to wonder how long he had been waiting there. Latimer didn't seem too happy, it seemed as though he didn't like the new guests. If they were staying longer than one night Alaric would have been concerned, but he didn't think the man could get up to too much trouble in one.

They were all given a room each for the night. Alaric had to admit he was happy to be back indoors. It seemed like he had spent more nights outside than he did in. Being inside a castle with a soft bed and expensive linen was even better. He could see the moon rising in the sky and knew his time was running out. He stared out the window for a long moment before he turned to go to bed. As he did there was a gentle knock on the door. He thought about ignoring it, but his curiosity got the better of him.

He found Alena standing on the other side with a smile on her face. She had changed from her riding clothes into a close fitting, silk nightdress. Alaric had to take a step back in surprise. He had not been expecting such a visit.

"What can I do for you?" Alaric asked when he regained the power to speak.

"Are you going to invite me it or am I going to have to stand out here all night?" There was a cheeky grin on her face.

"Ah... of course, please come in." Alaric retreated further back into the room. "What is it I can do for you?"

"I thought I might come in for some conversation. We haven't really had any time to talk since my recovery." There was something sweet in her voice making Alaric's heart start to race.

It might have been the place but it wasn't the time for such a tryst. Alaric needed to sleep. He wanted to be on the road again at first light. That being the case he didn't have the heart to turn her away. Instead he offered her a place to sit.

Since they had left Jarrat Alaric had pushed his feelings aside for Alena. He knew he still loved her no matter what had happened with Marina. He felt somewhat guilty, but that wasn't the reason for his aloofness. With the trials ahead of him he didn't have time for romance. He needed to keep his mind on the job at hand, but that had all suddenly changed when she turned up on his doorstep.

The two stayed up late into the night talking. Alaric had forgotten how easy it was to speak with her. He wished they had been able to meet in different circumstances. She pushed him for information about what had happened since she had been taken prisoner. Alaric explained, but had to omit a few details, especially those about Marina.

They both curled up in Alaric's bed when they finally finished talking. Alena was too exhausted to walk back to her room, or at least that was the excuse she used. Alaric was happy to have her lying next to him. He had almost forgotten what it was like to have someone to share his bed. He couldn't think of anything better. For the first time in a long time Alaric had a restful night sleep.

In the morning Alaric slept past the rising sun. At first he woke slowly, seeing the form of Alena lying next to him. He closed his eyes and smiled. For a brief moment he had forgotten the situation he was in. He could have been back in his house in Arsiliac, the only problem with that fantasy was that Alena wouldn't be there. It was that thought that brought him back to reality. He quickly threw back the covers and jumped out of bed.

"What is it?" Alena asked when she was suddenly woken.

"The sun is up and we have already lost precious hours," Alaric explained as he hurriedly dressed.

"Relax. Thanks to your ability to slow down reality we are making great time," Alena cooed. "Who knows when we are going to have accommodation like this again? Why don't you come back to bed?" She patted Alaric's side of the bed to accentuate her point.

The offer was tempting, but Alaric knew he couldn't accept. He had wanted to be on the road before the duke rose for the day. It wasn't that he didn't want to thank Balin for his help, but he didn't want to get caught in another discussion. He knew the duke would want to speak with him again. A knock on the door made Alaric's heart sink. He hoped it wasn't who he was expecting. When he opened the door he knew he was right. A pageboy stood waiting for him.

"Duke Balin has asked if you would join him for breakfast?" the page spoke nervously.

That was the last thing Alaric wanted to do. As much as he wanted to leave he couldn't be rude. The duke had taken them in and had been hospitable. Alaric owed him a little courtesy if nothing else.

"We will be along shortly." Alaric assured him.

"I thought you wanted to get on the road?" Alena asked, after the page had left.

At first Alaric ignored the question. He knew she was right, but it had not stopped him agreeing. There was no real reason for them to remain in the castle. He was sure the duke would understand if they just left, but he still felt as though he should at least stay for breakfast. Alaric knew well enough not to fight the prophecy if it really wanted him to do something.

"Sorry, what were you saying?" Alaric suddenly realised that Alena was staring at him with a concerned expression on her face.

"I thought we were leaving."

"I guess we have to eat either way. I think it would be better to eat the duke's food and save our supplies."

It was obvious that Alaric didn't want to speak any further on the subject and busied himself dressing. Alena was about to speak, but realised the futility of it.

It was not long before they were in the duke's private dinning hall. Eldred and Richmond were waiting for them, they had already started eating.

"So what do you have planned for today?" Balin asked.

Alaric looked at Eldred who in turn shrugged his shoulders. For some reason the duke had waited for Alaric before he pressed for answers. Although it seemed like an innocent enough question Alaric was a little suspicious.

"We shall be leaving once we finish breakfast," Alaric spoke slowly, closely watching Balin's reaction.

"I don't know if that will be possible." There was a hint of a smile in the corner of his mouth. It was only there for a moment, but Alaric definitely saw it. "A messenger came with news this morning. His message was from the Earl of Rizzor saying that the enemy was heading this way. The report is unconfirmed, but we have to take every precaution. All my soldiers and citizens are being moved inside the walls. Once the gates are shut they won't be opened until we know the threat is over."

Alaric had stopped eating and listed intently to every word. It was not at all what he had been expecting. He couldn't believe he had been drawn to such a meeting. He didn't have time to be trapped by an overly paranoid nobleman.

"Then we should be leaving now." Although he was still hungry he couldn't remain inside. Alaric stood as he spoke.

Before Alaric could move from the table there came a knock on the door. A man entered without waiting for permission. He wore a light breastplate with a grey cape flowing behind him.

"What is it sergeant?" Balin didn't mind the interruption.

"Everyone is inside the walls and the gates have been barricaded." The soldier spoke louder than he needed to.

"Very good. See that we have archers on the walls and someone in the watchtower at all times. We don't want to be caught by surprise."

"Yes sir!"

Alaric watched the sergeant leave the room and thought about following. In the end he resigned himself to return to his seat. There was little he could do. He knew it was a mistake coming for breakfast.

Chapter 13: Intrigue

"Are you sure that the Earl of Rizzor is a reliable source?" Eldred asked.

Since the sergeant had left the room the tension had increased tenfold. Alaric had returned to his seat and stabbed at the half eaten slab of ham still on his plate. The action made everyone around the table nervous. Duke Balin watched him carefully, even as Eldred spoke.

"I doubt there would be any reason for him to fabricate such a story." Balin replied.

"It's not unheard of for two Remidian nobles to attack each other. This could be a plot for the earl to take control of Albend," Eldred continued.

"If that was the case then why would he want all our resources inside the city? If he wanted to betray us then he would attack whilst we were unprepared. Anyway, Rizzor is a weathly province. There is no reason for the earl to betray me," Balin explained.

"It still doesn't make any sense," Richmond added. "The Evil One has been concentrating his attacks on the capital cities. There is no reason for him to attack an outlying one. There has to be another reason."

"There is a very good reason for the Evil One to want to take Albend. If he knows that you have reclaimed Jarrat then he would want to stop the main trade route between the two kingdoms. It would make perfect sense for him to move on Albend." On one hand his words made sense on the other it didn't.

"How would the earl know they were coming?" Richmond asked.

"He didn't say in his missive, but I would assume that one of the scouts saw his men on the move."

Alaric slammed his knife into the table. While he had been listening to the others speak he was also trying to work out what was happening. He knew there had to be an explanation. He would not have felt the subtle tug of the prophecy for no reason. The others suddenly looked at him, distracting them from what they had been saying.

"Nyrra must know that I'm here." Alaric's voice was cold. "That can be the only reason."

No one knew what to say. They were expecting Alaric to continue with his explanation. When he didn't speak there was a moment of uncomfortable silence. It took Balin to finally break it.

"Why would the Evil One know you are here and why would he care?" Balin didn't really understand the situation.

"That is a very good question," Alaric was thinking as he spoke. "If indeed there is a component of Nyrra's army coming here there can be no other explanation. It cannot be a coincidence."

"I am sure…" Balin was about to defend his status, but Eldred interrupted him.

"Why would he try and stop you now?" Eldred was just as baffled as everyone else.

"If I knew that then I would know what to do next." Alaric slumped in his chair. "I can only assume that he has some idea of what I'm planning. At least that means I'm on the right track."

There was something underlying in his words, but Eldred was the only one who picked up on it. He wanted to ask what Alaric meant, but he also didn't want the others to know, especially Balin. The duke didn't need to know anything more.

"What are we going to do?" Eldred finally asked.

"There is nothing you can do. You will have to remain here until the threat has passed," Balin spoke quickly before Alaric had a chance to answer.

Everyone then turned to Alaric. They wanted to see his reaction as well as hear his response. He didn't look as though he really cared what the duke had said. He looked as though he was deep in thought. When he regained his senses he realised that everyone was staring at him.

"I think Balin is right." They were all surprised to hear the words come out of his mouth. "We need to know what Nyrra is planning before we go running into danger. Was there anything else in the earl's missive that might give us a clue to what is happening?"

"There was nothing that I was able to gather." Balin sounded excited. "I will send for the letter is you wish to read it?"

Alaric thought for a moment. There might be something in the letter that was worth reading, but he doubted it. The best thing he could do was go to the battlements and try to search for the opposing army magically. If there was an army of evil marching towards them then he was sure he would be able to find it.

"I think I will go out to the battlements and see what I can see." Alaric suddenly stood as he spoke.

"That sounds like a good idea." Balin agreed.

"I think that it would be better if we went alone." Eldred knew exactly what the duke was thinking. Eldred wanted some time alone to discuss matters with Alaric.

Balin didn't look happy, but he had made a small victory. He had wanted to keep the group in the city. If nothing else their presence would reassure the citizens. It would also give him time to formulate a plan.

Alaric was glad to be away from the duke. There was something about the man that he didn't completely trust. He had moved his citizens inside the walls a little too quickly for Alaric's liking. That was a side issue and he quickly put it out of his mind. He had wanted to walk the battlements by himself, but it looked as though he was going to have company. He would have settled for Eldred, but he wished the others had not decided to follow.

No one said anything until they were out in the open air.

"Do you really think that Nyrra knows we're here?" Alena almost didn't want to ask the question.

"I'm not sure." Alaric was trying to concentrate on his surroundings. "But that is what I am going to find out."

"How do you propose to do that?"

"I have a few tricks up my sleeve." A smiled crossed his face.

"Do you care to elaborate?" Eldred asked.

Alaric simply ignored the question. He wasn't exactly sure what he was going to do. He figured that he would be able to sense the evil, but he had no idea how. All he simply assumed was that it would come to him when the time was right. It might not have been the best of ideas, but it was one that had worked for him in the past.

The air was fresh when they reached the battlements. Dark clouds had moved in over the sun creating a gloomy atmosphere. Alaric didn't think it was a good sign. The weather had been perfect the last few days and all of a sudden it seemed as though a storm was brewing. On the positive side at least they would not be on the road if the heavens decided to open.

"Now what do we do?" Alena asked when Alaric brought them to a halt. "There is nothing out there."

The land outside the city was almost flat. From their vantage point they could see for half a dozen leagues in all directions. There would be plenty of warning if Nyrra had an army on the march. Alaric took a deep breath.

"Do you know what you're doing?" Eldred asked when nothing seemed to have happened.

"In a word... no." Alaric sounded upset with the distraction. "But if you let me continue I am sure I will work it out eventually."

Eldred was about to speak, but after Alaric's last comment he thought better of it. It seemed as though Alaric had no real idea what he was doing. What he really wanted was for him to ask for his help, or at least admit that he couldn't do it by himself. That would be better than just telling him what he needed to do.

If Alaric had not been so distracted by his trial he would have noticed the little tickle at the back of his neck. It was frustrating that he couldn't find what he was looking for. He knew what he wanted to do, but that wasn't the problem. He thought the answer would have come to him, but it didn't. Finally he let out a sigh as he gave up.

"Do you need something?" Eldred seemed rather smug, although he couldn't find a sign of anyone either.

"I thought that I would be able to sense if Nyrra was sending someone here, but it doesn't seem to be the case."

Eldred stifled a laugh. "*Sensing* is one of the spells that you learn at an early stage as an apprentice. In fact some learn it as a novice." Alaric wasn't overly happy with what Eldred was insinuating. "Now I can explain to you how to do it if you like."

"Just create the spell and I will be able to copy you." Alaric kept his voice level.

Eldred took a step back in surprise at Alaric's words and he looked at him with horror on his face. Alaric, in turn, also took a step back, unsure exactly what had come over the wizard. There was nothing untoward in what he had said and yet Eldred was looking at him as if he was the Evil One himself.

"What's wrong?" Alaric finally asked.

Eldred shook his head. He was deep in thought and had not realised what he was doing. His expression quickly changed to one of surprise before returning to normal. Alaric's words had hit him like a club and he had to compose himself before he continued.

"Nothing, I just thought I felt something." He lied.

"Well as much as I am enjoying standing here I think it would be good if we got started. If there is no army coming this way then we need to be on the move."

Eldred prepared himself to cast the spell again. Even though he found no sign of an army he thought it was worth the exercise. He was a little dubious that Alaric could copy a spell just by watching it being cast. If he could, then Eldred couldn't imagine what it meant.

Alaric watched him closely as he started to create the spell. In the end he couldn't believe how easy it was. The usual tingling sensation returned to the back of his neck and this time he noticed it. Instantly he knew what he had been doing wrong. He had been trying to search too far too soon. He needed to start the spell small and then expanded it slowly.

"Do you think it would be a good idea to mask the spell? There is no telling who is around," Alaric said before he made his own.

"What are you talking about?" The tingling sensation disappeared when Eldred suddenly extinguished the spell. "I never create a spell without masking it. It's second nature to me now. But the searching spell isn't powerful enough to be noticeable."

Alaric thought it was odd. The tingling sensation must have come from Eldred. There was one way for Alaric to find out. If there was someone else with power to use magic nearby he would soon know about it. He started the spell without even thinking. Instantly he knew that Eldred was right, there was little power needed to mask such a simple spell.

The further Alaric pushed out with his spell the greater the power he needed to use. With each extra push he had to increase the energy needed to keep masking the spell. The feeling of stretching his senses across the land was exhilarating and the further he went the better he felt. As he basked in his own glory a sudden shock filled his body. As he did the searching spell was suddenly broken. Alaric fell backwards and hit the ground. The move was so unexpected that no one was able to prevent him from falling.

"Are you alright?" Alena asked as she rushed to his side.

Alaric rubbed his head. Something bad had happened, but he didn't know what it was. He suddenly felt very exhausted. The spell shouldn't have used that much energy. There had to be another explanation. He looked around to see where he was.

"What happened?" he asked.

"That is a very good question." Eldred sounded concerned. "I don't really know how to explain this, but a darkness seemed to be closing in around you. I thought it would be best if I severed the spell. I'm sorry for the abruptness, but it was all I could do."

With Alena's aid Alaric returned to his feet. He felt as though he had been struck across the back of his head. He wasn't sure what Eldred was talking about, but there was a sense of evil about him. He had found something in the distance, but Eldred had stopped before he could work out what it was. The only way to figure it out was to start again.

"There is something out there." Alaric spoke slowly at first. "I only just found it when Eldred severed the spell."

Again Eldred was amazed. "I searched out as far as the spell could go and couldn't find anything. Are you sure that you found something?"

Alaric had to think for a minute as he was still suffering the effects from Eldred severing his spell. He had to admit when he thought about it he also knew the spell was not strong enough to reach as far as it did. He must have done something to it to give him the extra reach he needed. The answer was in the back of the haze in his mind. Slowly his head started to clear and he remembered what he had done.

"I overlayed one spell on top of the other and by doing so I was able to extend the range," Alaric explained. "There was definitely something on the edge of my vision."

Eldred was stunned. He had been a wizard for more years than he could remember and he had never thought something like that would be possible. He had to admit that Alaric had grown more powerful than he could believe since they had been captured in Nostiria. He wasn't sure if it was a good sign or a bad sign. For the moment he would have assume it was good.

"I think we need to have a talk when this is done." Eldred mused.

"That's fine, but for the moment I need to know what is out there." Alaric returned his attention to the distance. Now that he knew which general area to search, his spell wouldn't require as much power.

Alaric pushed out his senses in the general direction where he had found the feeling of evil. Besides that feeling there was nothing else he could remember about what he had found. Being able to narrow down the search he could concentrate more on what was happening.

It didn't take long for Alaric to find what he was looking for. He couldn't tell exactly how far away they were, but there could be no doubt that the soldiers were marching towards Albend. What disturbed him the most was the fact that there were not just soldiers in the small army. He recognised the disfigured creatures as Orglin. That was not his major concern. He needed to find the person in command. If it was a Dark Knight, or worse Nyrra himself, then they could be in great trouble.

As he searched through the ranks he couldn't find anyone who looked to be in command. There were a few slave masters to keep the Orglin under control, but that was basically it. Comfortable that there was no threat of magic approaching, Alaric slowly returned his consciousness to his body.

"What did you see?" Eldred was the first to realise that Alaric had returned.

"There is an army on the way here." Alaric panted in-between words. The spell had taken more out of him than he had expected. He looked around for somewhere to sit, but there was nothing suitable.

"That isn't good news," Richmond added. "What are we going to do?"

"The more pertinent question is when is it going to arrive?" Eldred spoke before Alaric had chance to speak.

"By the way they were moving I would assume that they are going to be here by nightfall. It looks as though they are pushing hard, but I can't say for sure exactly where they are." Alaric started to feel dizzy.

"Then we should get out of here!" Richmond exclaimed. "Whilst we still have a chance."

"I don't think so." Alaric slumped to the ground.

"Are you alright?" Alena asked.

"I will be fine in a moment. The spells took a lot out of me."

"Then we should leave when you are back on your feet?"

"No! We need to stay and help defend the city," Alaric explained.

"But if the army is only coming to delay us wouldn't it make sense for us to leave?" Richmond wouldn't be dissuaded.

"I can only assume the army is coming this way to delay us, but that may not be the case. We can't leave the city to be sacked by Nyrra. There are enough soldiers and Orglin to overrun these walls. We have to stay and help in their defence. We can't leave the enemy behind us to sack cities at will."

"I suppose we should tell Duke Balin, he will need to be appraised of the situation." Richmond was resigned to the fact that they were staying. He had to agree that Alaric made sense and he was ashamed that his first reaction was to run.

"If you don't mind I think I could use a lie down. Would you tell him what is coming?" Alaric asked no one in particular.

"Of course we will," Eldred looked at Richmond. "I think that you should help Alaric," he turned and spoke to Alena.

The four of them left the battlements. Richmond and Eldred didn't wait for the other two. Alena placed her arm around Alaric and tried to steady him. He thought with a little rest he would have recovered, but he was worse than he had expected. There had to be a good reason why Eldred had severed his spell and he needed to know what it was.

"Easy now," Alena cooed as she helped Alaric onto his bed. "Now, is there anything you want me to get you?"

"No, thank you. I think that you should prepare yourself. I think we will need your skill with the bow once the enemy arrives." Alaric did his best to sound jovial, but it didn't work.

Alena kissed him on the forehead before she left the room. Alaric fell asleep as soon as his head hit the pillow. Alena took one last look at him before she shut the door. She was sure he was going to be okay.

The others were in with the duke's war council. Balin had not wasted anytime when he had received confirmation of the approaching army. The information that Eldred and Richmond brought to the table didn't seem to register. He had never seen an orglin before, let alone fought one. The severity of the situation was lost on him.

"I don't think you truly appreciate the situation," Eldred tried again. "I doubt the army is coming here to take control of the city. If that was the case then there would just be soldiers in the army. The Evil One only uses Orglin when he wants complete annihilation. This is not going to be like any battle you have ever fought."

"What you don't appreciate is that I have defended these walls on more than one occasion. I am sure that I am capable of doing so again." Balin didn't like what Eldred was insinuating.

"You're not listening." Richmond was becoming frustrated. "Orglin are like nothing you have ever seen or fought before. They bring a totally new terror with them. They will throw themselves against your walls until they break or enough have died that they can simply walk over." Although Richmond had not witnessed that first hand Eldred had told him the information would be better coming from a fellow nobleman. Richmond had no doubts.

"If that is the case then why do we even bother?" Balin still wasn't appeased.

"Because we can win!" Everyone looked around at Alena. "This is no time to be stubborn or a defeatist. The time for planning is short and there is no time to waste with petty squabbles," Alena commanded.

"Then what is it you propose?" Balin finally asked.

"The army is approaching from the north. That is where we must set the archers. Once they are in range we need to attack. There will be no negotiations and there will be no treaties. You have to believe me when I tell you that this will be a battle to the death. The winners will be the last ones standing," Eldred explained.

"You are talking all doom and gloom. By the sounds of what you are saying we have already lost."

"That is not our intention. You just need to be aware of the danger approaching us. Once you understand it then you can plan for it." Richmond added.

"So what is your plan?" Balin didn't sound impressed.

"We need to keep the army to the north. We can't let them surround us." Eldred started. "We need to concentrate our attack in one central location…"

"Attack? I thought we were going to defend?" Balin interrupted.

"And that is what the enemy is going to think. We need to take them by surprise." Eldred continued. "We can use the advantage of the walls to rain down arrows upon them. That is how we will keep them from spreading. If they try and flank us we will shoot them down."

The problem with the plan was that they really didn't know exactly how many were coming to attack them. Alaric's description had been vague. Eldred had surmised that there was a battalion of soldiers and a hoard of Orglin. If there were anymore then he doubted his plan would work.

They spent the rest of the morning in discussion. Balin was not completely confident with Eldred's plan. There were too many variables for it to be the solution. In the end Eldred also had to admit that his plan was flawed. On the other hand there were no better ideas. In the end they had a brief outline of what they were going to do and that was better than nothing.

When the meeting was over Alena went to check on Alaric. She was concerned that he had not joined them and she wanted to make sure he was alright. Eldred and Richmond went to check on the soldiers to make sure they were prepared for what was coming.

Alaric was still in bed when Alena arrived. His breathing still sounded laboured. As much as she didn't want to disturb him she knew she had to wake him. If they were going to survive the impending battle they would need his skills. If he was not well rested she didn't know how much help he would be, but she couldn't risk leaving him any longer.

"Are they here?" Alaric woke with a start when Alena roused him.

"Not yet," Alena replied quickly.

Alaric clearly relaxed when he realised where he was. His heart was racing and it would take a little time to return to normal. He looked around to see if there was anyone else in the room. He relaxed a little more when he realised there was only Alena.

"How are you feeling?" she asked.

"Still tired, but much better, thank you," Alaric replied. "I think I could use another few hours sleep, but I take it that by you waking me that isn't going to happen?"

"We need to prepare for the impending battle. Eldred has suggested that the duke takes the attack to the army," Alena explained.

"I don't think that's a good idea," Alaric was surprised to hear Alena's words as he tried to rise from the bed, but he quickly returned to where he was lying. His head was dizzy with the sudden movement. He was sure that it would pass soon or at least he hoped so.

"Are you sure you're feeling alright?" Alena moved to his side and placed a hand on his forehead. He didn't have a fever, which was a promising sign.

"I'll be fine. I just need to take it a little easy for the minute." He paused and thought for a moment. "What time is it?" he asked slowly.

"Just after midday."

"Something is wrong!" he sounded distracted.

"What are you talking about?" Alena was worried.

"The army is closer than what it should be."

"How do you know that?"

"I don't know, but I know it's true. If they keep moving at the same speed then they will be here in a little over an hour."

Chapter 14: Siege

Alaric stood on the wall to the north of the city with Alena, Eldred, Richmond and Balin. Unfortunately he had been right about the army moving in faster than it should. The army had arrived an hour after he left his room. His extra information had been invaluable towards their preparations. They would have been completely unprepared without it. Balin tried to push for more information, but that was all Alaric could give. He didn't want to mention that he didn't agree with Eldred's plan. There would be enough time for that when it happened.

The army came into view long before they were within the range of the archers. Alena had borrowed a bow and a quiver of arrows from the armoury. She wished that she still had her elven bow, but that had been destroyed when she had been captured. She had forgotten to get a replacement from her father. There could be no doubt he would have brought spares with him. Next time they met she would remember, but for the moment it was a moot point. The bow she had would decrease her range considerably, but she was sure she would retain her accuracy.

Alaric watched the army closely. It didn't seem to be moving at any special pace. He wondered at how they could have arrived so quickly. There was only one answer that came to him; Nyrra or one of his Dark Knights had moved them magically. There could be no other explanation and there was still one Dark Knight he had not located. That was something that Alaric had not allowed for and would sway the advantage to the enemy.

"This is not going to be good," Alaric finally spoke.

Everyone heard him, but they all chose to ignore it. They had been somewhat confident until the army appeared on the horizon. Thoughts of their own mortality had been passing through their minds. The last thing they wanted was for someone to voice their concerns, that would only make them a reality.

There was no time for thought, not that they could think anyway. All they could do was watch the approaching army. Alaric was only one who didn't seem completely horrified. Even Eldred couldn't contain his feelings, which didn't help everyone's nerves.

"Well I guess this is going to be harder than we originally thought." Alaric felt the need to speak. "I guess we should get ready."

There was little left to be done. The archers were in place and waiting for the order to fire. The soldiers were still mobilizing behind the gate and there was little they could do to help.

"What do you propose we do?" Richmond asked when he realised the point.

"I think we are going to need some additional assistance." Alaric spoke directly to Eldred even though his gaze didn't move from the army.

"What did you have in mind?" Eldred was glad for the distraction.

"The army is larger than what I thought. I think some magical power might be in order to sway the balance." Alaric sneered.

"Unfortunately I haven't fully recovered from my ordeal in Jarrat, but I will do my best," Eldred tried his best to sound positive.

Alaric didn't like what he was hearing. As much as he was up and about he too was still suffering the effect of his earlier ordeal. He had hoped that Eldred would be able to be useful, but it seemed as though that would not be the case. He still had a trick up his sleeve, but he would wait and see what happened first.

"Hopefully it will be enough." Alaric added as an after thought.

Slowly Alaric reached out with his senses to see if there was a Dark Knight in the group. At the short range the spell didn't take much energy. Alaric was sure he could complete it without taking on anymore strain. It didn't take long for him to realise that there was no one of any real power with them. That was both a good sign and a bad one.

The army started moving at a painfully slow pace. With each passing moment more and more soldiers and orglin came into view over the horizon. There were many more in the army than initially suspected. Those who were able to see them were told to keep their shock to themselves. The last thing Balin wanted was for his infantry and cavalry to know what they were up against. He could only hope that Alaric knew what he was doing, otherwise there would be a lot of dead people at the end of the day.

Alaric remained calm as he watched the army approach. His resolve brought strength to the others around him. Those who were not so close didn't have such a benefit.

"There is no way we can stand up against that army." The Captain of the Archers rushed to where they were standing. He addressed the duke after a quick salute. "We have to abandon the city."

"You will stand strong captain." Balin spoke overly harsh, overcompensating for his own terror. "We will not relinquish the city. This is our home and we will defend it with our lives."

The speech did little to settle his nerves, but it did put his captain back in his place. The captain left barking orders at the archers. Balin was happy that he was showing strength to the others.

"I hope you know what you're doing Alaric." Balin didn't sound too confident.

Alaric ignored the comment. He was too busy concentrating on the sight before him. What he had planned was going to take a great deal of luck and he couldn't afford to miss his opportunity.

"Do you think you could cause some havoc?" Alaric asked Eldred without moving his eyes.

"I will do my best, but I fear that it will not be enough." Eldred's voice remained as calm as Alaric's.

Alaric didn't respond. He had to plan for the worst and that was not something he wanted to do. For the moment he hoped that Eldred could cause enough damage so that Alaric didn't have to step in. Deep down he knew that wouldn't be the case and the last semblance of hope left him.

Eldred started drawing in the energy surrounding him, being careful not to take any from the soldiers. Alaric could sense what the old wizard was doing and a glimmer of hope returned. With the power he was consuming, the spell should be able to do enough damage to give them a good head start.

Slowly the tickle returned to back of Alaric's neck. As it did a grey cloud started to build above the opposing army. Only those standing on the wall seemed the notice. The enemy marched forward regardless when suddenly a bolt of lightning struck down. It landed in the centre of the army followed by a large explosion.

When the dust settled Alaric was disappointed to see the amount of damage it had done. No more than fifty soldiers and a half as many orglin had been killed. Alaric had been expecting so much more. He turned to Eldred to see if that was just the beginning but the wizard was panting and leaning against the wall.

"Do you think you could do that again?" Alaric didn't sound confident.

"I am sorry..." he panted. "That is the most powerful spell that I know. I don't think I could create another one."

Deep down Alaric knew that it was going to come down to him. No one else had noticed that he was wearing the Topaz sceptre at his side. He slowly fingered the velvet covering, not looking forward to what he must do.

The army advanced without much notice of the spell which had killed a number of its members. As he watched the he knew he didn't have long before he had to make his decision.

"What are you planning on doing?" Alena was concerned with the look on his face. At that moment she saw the sceptre at his side. "I don't think that is a good idea. I am sure that we can still defeat them." Even as the words came out she realised how futile they were. There was little chance they would survive without his assistance.

"I don't see that we have any other choice," he said.

Alaric knew there was no more time for thought. The army was almost within range of the archers. Although he couldn't be completely sure, he figured that when the arrows started to fly the army would charge the walls. Once that happened it would be too late. He couldn't risk blowing a hole in the city wall. With each passing second his window to attack became smaller and smaller.

Slowly he lifted the velvet cover from the Topaz stone. Instantly the world rushed in around him, which almost made him fall over. The feeling was instantly followed with a great sense of wellbeing. The world around him seemed to no longer exist. All that remained was a feeling of bliss.

"Now is the time to kill them all." The voice cooed inside his head.

"You are almost right, but we are not going to kill them all." Alaric had to respond. He kept the words inside his mind, although he almost spoke them by mistake.

"Don't trust them. They will betray you in the end! Now is the time you can finish them off." The voice was more persistent.

Alaric didn't have time for such a conversation. He had a bad feeling that it might already be too late. He wasn't sure how long it had been, but it seemed like a lifetime. Returning to reality was not going to be as easy.

"It is time for you to go. I have work to do." Alaric tried to concentrate, but his mind had already started to go fuzzy.

"You can't get rid of me that easily. You need my help if you are going to succeed. If I help you then what are you going to do for me?" There was venom in the voice.

"There is no time for this conversation. If I don't do something very soon then it is all for nothing," Alaric explained, panic creeping into his voice.

"There is plenty of time, there is always time." The voice sounded as though it was laughing, but Alaric couldn't be completely sure. "It is time for you to make me an offer."

Alaric didn't like the sound of what he was hearing. He had overpowered the voice in his head before and he could do it again. He needed to use the Topaz stone's power.

"There will be no bargaining. You will do what I say and that is all you need to know." Alaric thought he heard another round of laughter. "You can laugh all you want, but it isn't going to help you."

Alaric concentrated again and he felt as though there was another shift in reality. Time was starting to return to normal, he was starting to regain control. It was much easier than he remembered. As he regained his senses he noticed that the army was no closer. It suddenly struck Alaric what had happened. Somehow the Topaz stone had managed to stop, or at least slow down considerably, time. The thought didn't have long to stay in his mind. It was time for him to do something about the approaching army.

Once he had released the Topaz stone Alaric instantly felt better. The aches and pains had completely left his body. All he had to do was create a spell that would cause some destruction. As he started to draw in the energy around him he knew the Topaz stone had started to glow, even though his gaze had not left the army.

Slowly the ground started to shake and a dull rumble could be heard. Only those who knew Alaric knew what was happening and even then they were not completely sure. No one had ever seen him in action, or at least not since he had started to realise his true potential. In their minds there was a chance a Dark Knight was in the opposing army. If there was then there was nothing Eldred could do to counter the spell. His own spell had taken too much out of him.

Alaric's eyes started to roll up into his head as he continued to draw in power. Like Eldred he was going to put all his eggs in one basket. He figured one large spell would be better than a lot of smaller ones. Since there was no one of power in the army there really was no one he should target. Just before he released the spell he raised his hand out in front of him. When his arm dropped the spell had been cast.

Suddenly the ground opened up the front of the army. A great explosion followed sending dirt, stones and soldiers flying into the air. Once everything had settled again the earth around the explosion suddenly ignited into a great ball of flame. Anyone or anything that was in range of the fire was instantly destroyed. There wasn't even enough time for them to scream out in pain.

Regardless of the madness around them the army and the horde continued to move forward. Their movements looked as though they were possessed. Even those whose advance brought them into the flames didn't stop moving. It was as if to retreat would have brought them an even worse fate. The sight did nothing to strengthen the resolve of those on the wall. Some of the archers were physically sick at the sight before them.

Alaric didn't move. He was stuck where he was until the spell had been completely finished. Even with the aid of the Topaz stone the strain was obvious. Eldred couldn't believe what he was seeing. He had no idea that Alaric had become so powerful. Things were happening very quickly and he wasn't sure if he completely liked it. He wished he had been around more to assist Alaric in his growth. There was no telling what could happen without the right assistance.

As the flames died down Alaric slowly started to return to normal. All the energy that had left his body during the spell was slowly returning through the Topaz stone. Alaric felt like he could do it all again, but he knew that he shouldn't. The feeling of wellbeing from the stone would only remain whilst he held the sceptre. Once the battle was over he would have to return the velvet hood.

"Fire!" Alaric's voice was hoarse, but he managed to get the words out.

At first nothing happened. The archers were still shocked by what they had seen. The smell of burnt flesh and worse filled the air. They had not realised that the army had moved within range of their bows. Alaric's words did nothing to rouse them.

"You heard the order!" Alena was the first to recover. "Fire for your lives and the lives of those you love."

To accentuate her words Alena fired the first shot. Her arrow sailed through the air. When it came to land it struck a soldier in the chest, killing him instantly. The leather armour they wore was no match for her arrowhead. The death incited the army to increase the speed of their advance. It also forced the archers into action. Suddenly the air was filled with the snapping of bows and a hail of arrows.

Alaric watched as the army sped its approach. The arrows rained down on top of them but both the soldiers and orglin simply ran over the dead. Alaric had no doubt that someone had cast a spell over them. He had never seen such apathy towards comrades and could not believe that any normal man could feel such a way. He knew they were followers of the Evil One, but even that was no excuse.

"Let's go to war!" Alaric smiled as he spoke. He then turned to Richmond. "Are you ready for this?"

"I was born ready," He returned Alaric's smile as he drew his sword. "Let's finish this."

There was still time for the two to make their way to the northern gate. The archers were still firing at the enemy and would do for another minute or two. Once the gates opened they would stop their attack and it would be time for the soldiers to do their job. With a little luck the numbers would now be more even.

Alaric found Adelanta waiting for him at the gate. The white stallion seemed happier to see him than he had in a long time. He could sense the impending battle and looked as though he was ready for action. He jumped around nervously, waiting for his master's arrival. Once he was on Adelanta's back Alaric was ready for war. All that was left was to rally the troops.

"Remember that there are going to be evil creatures beyond these walls." Alaric had debated about telling the soldiers about the orglin. In the end he figured it was better they were prepared, even if it was at the last minute. "There will be creatures that you thought never existed. They will shock you to your bones, but you must remain strong. They will die like anyone else and they will try and kill you like the other soldiers. That is all that you need to know." Alaric hoped his speech was helping. "This is a battle to the death. They will give you no respite and we must return the favour. At the end of the day we will be victorious."

Alaric hoped the battle would be over before the sun set. He estimated there could be no more than an hour of daylight left. The orglin would seem even more frightening at dusk. The time line didn't really seem to fit, but that was last thing on Alaric's mind. There was nothing left for him to do, but ordered the gate to be opened. His heart raced as the time etched ever closer.

"Raise the gates!" Alaric boomed at the top of his voice.

Slowly the gates started to creak open. Adelanta edged his way forward in anticipation. Alaric was glad that Adelanta was just as keen as he was. It was time for Alaric to show his strength once more.

"This is a mistake. We could kill them all. It wouldn't be that hard. Then we can walk away and leave this all behind. We don't need to do this." Alaric thought it was the most inappropriate time for the voice to return.

"There is no time to change now." As soon as his words entered his mind he knew they were wrong. Suddenly the world closed in around him again.

"We have nothing, but time." The voice sounded proud of itself.

"What do you want from me? I am not going to kill my friends and I am not going to use you any further. Now it is time for me to use my physical strength to prevail. Both are important to me." Alaric didn't even know why he was trying to explain.

"I want you to set me free!"

Alaric didn't know what that comment meant and he really didn't care. Although time was not technically passing Alaric still felt as though it was. He wanted to join the field of battle. Adrenaline had filled his veins and with every passing moment he could feel it leaving him.

"It is time for me to go now. I have a battle to win." Alaric kept his statement short.

Suddenly he blinked back into reality. Again the change was so sudden that it disorientated him and he nearly fell from Adelanta's back. Once he had recovered he noticed the gate was nearly completely open. It was time for him to leap into battle.

"Charge!" he screamed as the top of his voice.

Adelanta recognised the command and jumped into action. He broke into a sprint before any of the other horses. The duke's cavalry took the lead with Alaric and Richmond, the infantry would follow behind. Alaric had planned the attack and now it was just a matter of it working. The cavalry was to charge the opposing army and try and make it through to the other side, taking out as many soldiers as they could on the way through. Once there the infantry would attack from the front whilst the cavalry struck from the rear.

It was clear that the opposing soldiers had not been expecting an attack. There was no reason why anyone would leave the safety of their walls and that was one fact that Alaric had been relying on. They continued forward, even though everything in their bones was telling them to stand strong. The orglin didn't seem to care one way or another. They just revelled in the opportunity to cause death.

Alaric slashed out as Adelanta charged his way through the ranks. The soldiers all fought, and died, with blank expressions on their faces. They didn't seem to realise they were being attacked until it was too late. The orglin, though, were a different story altogether. Once the cavalry had left the city they were on the hunt. The smaller of the orglin leapt onto horse and rider alike. The larger ones were able to stand and deliver their attacks. Even with a sword piercing their bodies they didn't slow their advance. Blood, both theirs and others, streamed from their mouths and open wounds. If it wasn't for the stress of the battle the soldiers would have run, scared, for their lives. Once they were in the thick of things there was nothing for them to do except fight.

The plan to reach to the other side didn't quite work out as planned. The cavalry finished up stuck in the middle of the opposing army. Alaric was the last to give up attempting to reach the other side. Luckily he had planned for such an occurrence. If it seemed they weren't going to break through the army then they had to form a circle and attack outward. It would still give the infantry a chance to join the battle.

Alaric took a brief moment to look back towards the city. The infantry all joined the battle and the gates were closed again. That was a relief. At least if they failed in their mission the archers would have a chance to save the city. It was a small victory, but a victory nonetheless. It was only a moment before he realised that there was an orglin racing towards him.

Adelanta was just as affective in battle as Alaric. If he had not been prepared then there was a good chance Alaric would have been killed. The white stallion jumped to the side as the orglin leapt towards them. For his trouble Adelanta received a nasty gash across his flank. Alaric was able to recover from his short reverie and slashed the creature across the back of the neck. The blow wasn't enough to sever the head completely, but it was enough to kill.

Nothing Alaric could have said would have prepared the rest of the army for the orglin. Some carried crude looking weapons, but most relied on their natural features. Large talon like claws and protruding tusks could rip through flesh just as easily as a sword. Their tough hide acted as armour, protecting them from glancing blows.

Their grotesque appearance was backed by their ferocity in battle. The orglin charged at their foe with little regard for their own safety. When they got hold of their prey it took them no time to rip them to shreds. The blood lust only increased their strength and aggression. A missing limb did nothing to slow their attack and the Albend soldiers had to change their tact to survive the onslaught. Half the battle was surviving the pure horror that the orglin brought with their brutal attack. More than one soldier had turned and ran in fear when he saw his comrades being ripped apart and eaten by the evil creatures.

The battle was going well. Balin's soldiers were sustaining injuries, but not as many as the enemy. To help their cause the orglin were easily distracted once there was an opportunity to feed. It didn't take long for Alaric to work out what was happening. The orglin that were feeding were easy to pick off as they had no further interest in the battle.

Alaric sent word to the other soldiers that given the chance they should strike out at the feeing orglin. It would have been better if he had explained the plan before they started fighting, but it was the best he could do. At least he was able to see their advantage. He only hoped that it wasn't too late.

With more death on both sides of the battlefield more and more orglin stopped to feed. Sometimes two or three orglin would fight over the one body. The victor only survived long enough to be skewered by one of the city's soldiers.

When the sun had almost set the sound of a horn could be heard from the castle. That was the signal to retreat. It was a sign that the battle was going well. The plan was to decimate the enemy before retreating, allowing for the archers to shoot the remaining men and orglin.

When all the men were safely inside the castle the arrows started to fly again. As expected the opposing army started to approach the city. To everyone's surprise the remaining orglin started to attack their own soldiers. With the bloodlust on them there was nothing that could stop their feeding. With the men intent on approaching the walls they were not expecting an attack from behind.

Again the orglin were more intent on feeding and tearing the bodies to shreds then they were on attacking the city. They couldn't comprehend the fact that their very lives were in danger. It gave the archers easy targets. Even though it took a number of arrows to take down each orglin it wasn't long until the battle was over. The surviving

Albend soldiers let out a cry of relief when word reached them that they had won. There had been many casualties, but the relief of victory was overwhelming. For the moment they would celebrate what they had achieved.

"Thank you Alaric, I don't know what we would have done if you weren't here." The duke's clothes were drenched in blood. He had already wiped what he could from his face.

Alaric debated whether the army would of attacked if he wasn't there, but he kept that thought to himself. He had to admit that he was glad things had worked out so well. It was sad there was such a loss of life, but there would have been a lot more if he wasn't successful. All in all he would have to count it as a win.

"Your men fought bravely. I would be very proud of them if I was you." Alaric finally responded. He wanted nothing more than to wash the blood and grime of war off his body.

"We shall be celebrating tonight. There will be time to morn the dead in the morning." Balin remained positive.

Alaric was glad when the duke left. He was in no mood for conversation. His battle was not yet over. He still had to struggle with the Topaz stone and when that was all said and done he would need to cover it, draining him of all his extra energy.

"That's right. You know that you owe me now. I kept you going during that war. If it wasn't for me you and all of your friends would be dead."

Alaric was grateful that the reality around him didn't change. He stared out at the chaos before him. Even in the darkness he could still see all the death. He knew the stone was enhancing his eyesight. There seemed to be such a waste of life all over the field. Only the dead orglin didn't concern him. As far as he was concerned the evil creatures didn't deserve to exist.

"I'm afraid to say I have nothing for you." Alaric smiled as he spoke. "It is time for you to go back to sleep."

"Noooo…" the voice screamed in his head until he had returned the velvet cover.

Alaric had wanted to wait until he was inside before he covered the stone, but he didn't have the time to waste. A wave of exhaustion suddenly struck him. He legs wobbled and he regained his balance by holding onto the wall. He refused to let the fatigue get the better of him.

"Are you alright?" Alena quickly moved to his side when she realised he was unsteady.

"I will be fine. I think it's time for me to retire, but I need to wash first." Every word was a strain. "Where is Eldred?" he asked as Alena helped him down the stairs.

"When it was clear that we would be victorious he went to lie down. It seems as though he is in a similar condition as you." She smiled.

Alaric felt somewhat better. At least he wasn't the only one too tired to join in the celebrations. The citizens had already started preparing for the festivities. No one seemed to notice the two as they made their way back to the castle. Alaric was thankful for that. If anyone recognised them then he didn't think he would be able to rest anytime soon.

Once they were back inside the castle Alena had one of the servants run Alaric a bath. It was a little hopeful, but she hoped the bath would be ready by the time they made it back to his room. Luckily his guest room had a bathroom attached. It was one of the only few designed in the castle.

When they finally reached his room the bath was not quite ready. The young serving woman seemed embarrassed at their arrival. It was obvious she wanted to be gone before they returned.

"I'm sorry, it won't take long for the bath to heat." She blushed.

"That's fine." Alena reassured her as she helped Alaric into a chair.

Alena slowly started to undress him. His clothes were stained with blood. She didn't think that any cleaning would get rid of the stains. In the end she decided that it would be better if they were taken away and burned.

The serving woman took Alaric's clothes after she had finished with the bath. Alena slowly helped Alaric into the water. If he had not been so exhausted he might have been embarrassed at her seeing him naked. He had grown a lot since the first time they had met when they were both naked in Elhjem. He still had some shame, but for the moment he didn't care. All he wanted was to remove the filth that had dried on his body.

Alaric had to admit that it was pleasant having Alena bathe him. He was sure if he wasn't so exhausted he would be aroused by the situation. It was a shame that he was so tired, but that was not going to change. Instead Alaric closed his eyes and let the water wash over his body. There was a scent of rose in the water, which made the experience all the more enjoyable. Alaric thought that he could happily drift off to sleep and the only thing that stopped him was the threat of drowning.

It was more of an effort lifting Alaric out of the water than it had been putting him in. His muscles had started to stiffen once he was able to relax, even the heat of the water couldn't prevent that from happening. He did his best to help, but there was little he could do. It seemed as though the last of his energy had washed away with the bath water.

Alena cradled Alaric's head and stroked his damp hair as he went to sleep. There was no doubt that Alena was hopelessly in love with

Alaric. She thought Alaric felt the same, but she couldn't be completely sure. There had been plenty of time pass since she had been imprisoned. He had not mentioned much of what had happened in that time. She had heard that he had been travelling with a woman from Darshival but it was not something she was going to openly ask. If he was going to tell her then he would have to do so in his own time.

Chapter 15: The Journey Continues

Alaric felt surprisingly spry when he woke in the morning. The sun was well on its way up into the sky, but that didn't disturb him at all. He was just glad that he no longer felt like death. In fact he couldn't remember feeling any better, except of course when he was using the Topaz stone. He jumped out of bed ready for the day's trials. It was then that he realised two things. The first was that he wasn't wearing any clothes and the second that Alena had spent the night in his bed again. At first he was shocked, but as the information sunk in he relaxed. He had to admit that she looked beautiful and he felt bad about having to wake her. He had a compulsion to kiss her and there was nothing he could do to help himself, as he did she slowly woke.

"Good morning Alaric," she smiled as she spoke. Alaric thought she was radiant. "It looks like it is going to be a glorious day."

Only a sliver of light shone through the heavy curtains, but it was enough to brighten Alena's mood, not that it needed any. She looked up at Alaric with love in her eyes. Alaric wished he could stay there forever, but he knew that would not be the case. With the city safe he was feeling better, but they would have to be on the road again. He stole himself another moment before he turned to get dressed.

The same clothes as the day before suddenly appeared on his body. The black leather jerkin, long jacket and pants looked as though they had been recently cleaned. What Alena didn't realise was that Alaric had made the clothes with magic.

Alena stayed in bed a moment longer. She also knew they would have to be on the move, but she stole herself a few moments of happiness. She didn't know when they would have the chance again. There was a long road ahead of them.

This time Alaric was not going to be talked into staying for breakfast, even though he was ravenous. He wanted to get a few leagues under his belt before they ate. He only hoped that Eldred was back on his feet. He couldn't stand another delay.

Once they were both dressed they called for a page to collect their belongings. They would have the animals packed before they reached the courtyard. The page also was instructed to gather Richmond and Eldred's belongings as well. Alaric didn't want to leave anything to chance.

They found the two in the duke's private chambers. Alaric was relieved to see that Eldred was out of bed. Although the old wizard didn't look fully fit at least he was up. They all stood when they entered the room.

"A pleasure to see you this morning," Balin's greeting was directed at Alaric, although he left it open for interpretation. "Would you join us for breakfast?"

"I'm afraid we need to be on the road again." Alaric's voice was firm.

"Are you sure that I…"

"Thank you, I am sure." Alaric cut him off. "We need to get moving." He directed his conversation at Richmond and Eldred.

"The citizens will be disappointed. We are preparing a feast in your honour tonight," Balin spoke as the other two stood.

"I'm sorry, but we really need to keep moving. We have a long way to go and little time to get there," Alaric explained.

The duke was about to speak, but Eldred spoke first. "Thank you for your hospitality and I hope that we will meet again someday."

Balin had to resign himself to the fact they were leaving. He had an ulterior motive for wanting them to stay. If word got out of the battle, then other nobles would know that the city's defences were weak. Albend would not be able to withstand another attack for a long time. The duke was concerned that some minor noble might have a run at him. With Alaric he knew they would not stand a chance.

Alaric turned and left before the duke had another chance to speak. He knew that Balin would try and convince him to stay another day and he didn't think he could deny him for much longer. Deep down he did want to stay, so the best thing for him to do was to take away the temptation. He would be happier once they were travelling again.

Leaving the city was not going to be as easy as Alaric had hoped. The page had managed to spread the rumour that the heroes were leaving and it didn't take long for a crowd to appear. During the festivities the citizens were made aware of their role in the battle. No one wanted to miss seeing them before they left. A large crowd had appeared outside the castle. A great cheer erupted when they surfaced.

"What is this all about?" Alaric asked as he mounted Adelanta.

"It seems as though the citizens wish to thank you for saving them." Alena smiled as she mounted Lluvia.

Alaric shook his head and urged Adelanta forward. The crowd was slow to make room as Alaric approached. He hoped they would move. The last thing he wanted to do was run over someone, but at the same time he couldn't wait. When it was obvious that he wasn't going to stop they moved a little quicker to allow them to ride through.

As they started to move the crowd simply looked in awe at the man who had saved their lives. Some couldn't believe such an ordinary looking man could have done such extraordinary things. Others just didn't know what to say. It wasn't until one man couldn't contain his joy any longer that the crowd started cheering loudly. The sound was almost deafening and the surprise of the sudden outcry nearly knocked Alaric from his saddle. He appreciated their gratitude, but he wished they would show it in a quieter fashion.

The noise of the crowd brought more people to see what the hubbub was about. Soon enough the crowd stretched all the way to the Northern gate. As they approached the stench of burning flesh could be smelt from the pyres which had been built since dawn. They had only been recently lit when the wind was in the south. It had since moved to the north and was blowing back towards the city. No more would be lit, but it would be sacrilegious to extinguish those that had. The smell did nothing to waver the citizens' adulation.

Once they were out of the city Alaric led them off to the west. He didn't want to get any closer to the multitude of death to the north. All the bodies close to the city had been dragged away. It would take a few days before all the bodies were burned. He hoped they were ready for what was ahead of them. The smell of burning flesh was bad enough, but those of the orglin was much, much worse. He was glad that he wouldn't be around for it.

"Where are we headed now?" Alena asked once they had circled around the battlefield. It seemed as though Alaric was leading them back towards the highway, but Alena wanted to be sure.

"We keep heading north-west. I am still unsure of our final destination," Alaric replied.

That was not entirely true. Since they had left the city Alaric had felt the tug of the prophecy again. There was still no exact location, but he was fairly sure that it was no longer directing him towards Mount Scorpio. There was little doubt that they were now headed towards the Isle of Wizards, but he wanted to be completely sure before he told everyone. He hoped there was a chance that things might change.

Their journey was going to bring them close to Arsiliac. He had been trying avoid that thought, but now that they were getting close he couldn't help himself. Although he had never really felt connected with Arsiliac when he was living there, he now missed it. The thought of returning home was both fearful and exhilarating.

"Do you think it is such a good idea to stay on the highway?" Eldred asked.

Alaric had to admit that Eldred was right. It wasn't safe. There was no doubt that Nyrra knew they had been in Albend and there was a very good chance that he knew they were travelling north-west. If they remained on the highway then it would only be a matter of time before they ran into more trouble.

"You're right. We need to cross country to stay away from the Evil One." Alaric turned Adelanta from the highway.

He wasn't sure how that was going to work. If Nyrra could see where they were travelling it wouldn't matter where they were. The move did seem to make the others relax a little and Alaric guessed that was a good sign. He had to admit that he did feel better himself once they were off the highway.

The countryside they rode in was filled with rolling hills. There were few trees for shelter and a fresh breeze blew in as the morning wore on. By lunchtime dark clouds had rolled in from the west. They looked as though they contained a bounty of rain. Alaric had hoped they would hold until they reached shelter, but they were not so lucky.

Just after eating a light meal, the heavens opened and the rain came down. It was light at first and Alaric thought it wouldn't be too bad, but soon enough it started to get heavier. Along with the rain the wind increased its intensity. The weather made the day's travel utterly miserable. Alaric kept looking for shelter, but there was nothing. He had hoped to find a small cave in the side of one of the hills, but he couldn't see any.

"We are going to need to find some shelter for the night," Richmond called over the weather as the light started to fade.

"That might be easier said than done," Eldred returned.

Alaric kept scanning the countryside for any signs of shelter. There couldn't have been more than an hour before the sun would completely set. It was a pure guess with the sun behind the dark storm clouds. There was little chance of them resting if they were stuck out in the weather. Alaric wanted to find somewhere for them to stay the night before he lost the light altogether.

"I think I see something!" Alena exclaimed.

Richmond couldn't believe that she had seen anything. He couldn't see more than a few paces in front of himself. Her voice was excited and that was enough to lift all their spirits. It wasn't long before the sight of a small cave came into view. The three men were all amazed at her vision. Alaric could have sworn there was nothing there when he had been looking, but it was there nonetheless.

The cave was large enough for the horses to be brought in out of the weather. The smell of wet horse quickly filled the cave, but it was something they would have to deal with. They couldn't leave the horses outside in such conditions.

Eldred created a small ball of light so they could see their surroundings. The cave was only just large enough for all of them. There was a small pile dried grass on the floor, but that was it. There was nothing that would be suitable for creating a fire. On the plus side it didn't look like the cave was home to any unsavoury creatures.

"It looks as though we are not going to have a fire tonight." Richmond had already started shivering.

"If we can gather some wood I should be able to create a fire," Alaric spoke before Eldred had a chance.

"Any wood will be soaked through and through. There is no way a fire will work." Richmond wasn't happy.

"You let me worry about that."

"If you and Alena gather the wood there will be no problem creating a fire." It was clear that Eldred wanted some time alone with Alaric.

"Oh well, I suppose we aren't getting any dryer standing here." Richmond tried to sound positive, but it didn't work.

Alena took one last look at Alaric before she left with Richmond. She wanted to make sure that he was alright. There was little expression on his face to give away his emotions. She had also picked up on Eldred's subtext and was concerned at what he wanted. They had had a successful day in the saddle and there should be no reason for intrigue.

"What is it you want?" Alaric asked before Eldred had a chance to speak.

Eldred paused for a moment to survey the situation. It was obvious that Alaric was in a confrontational mood. He had to tread carefully if he was going to get the answers he needed.

"I need to speak to you about your abilities." He started slowly.

Alaric then noticed that Eldred was completely dry. There wasn't even a pool of water at his feet. He realised that there was still so much for him to learn. He wished he knew how to create such a spell. He started shivering to accentuate the fact and he instantly wished that he hadn't.

"It is a simple enough spell to keep yourself warm," Eldred explained.

There had to be an explanation why Alaric didn't feel the tell-tale tickle in the back of his neck when Eldred had created the spell. It must have been a very weak one or it could have been the fact that he was very cold.

"Would you please create the spell again? I will copy it." Alaric's teeth chattered as he spoke.

"Unfortunately it is not a spell that should be used once you are dry. There is a high chance you will cook yourself from the inside out if you do." Alaric wasn't sure if that was the truth. It didn't seem right to him, but he didn't want to question it. "There is only one way for you to learn and that is for me to teach you."

That was not the only way, but again Alaric didn't want to point that out. If Eldred simply walked outside the cave then he would be wet again in a matter of moments. He wanted to see what Eldred had to say first and if it didn't work he could always fall back on copying him.

"You don't need to draw in any energy for this spell. What you carry inside you naturally will be enough. To create the spell all you really need to do is feel the heat deep inside you," Eldred explained.

It did sound simple enough, but Alaric wasn't sure if he understood correctly. It didn't sound like any spell he had created in the past. Nevertheless Alaric attempted the spell as Eldred had instructed. He searched for the heat, which apparently was already inside him. At first nothing happened and Alaric thought Eldred must have explained something incorrectly. Just when he was about to give up he suddenly felt warm again. It was so instantaneous that Alaric almost lost the spell in surprise. He held on just before it disappeared and it wasn't long before he was completely dry. When all the water had left his clothes he started to heat up even more. With a gasp he extinguished the spell before he caught on fire. He now knew what Eldred had been warning him about.

"It is good to see that you can follow instructions." Alaric wasn't sure if it was a compliment or not. "Now I need to get some information from you." Eldred paused, not knowing how to broach the subject. "I am a little concerned at how you know so much magic now. When we left you were just learning and knew very little. Now it seems that you have surpassed me, or at least in some respects."

"I don't know what you want me to say."

"I need to know what happened, how you learnt the spells that you know."

Alaric knew that the conversation would happen eventually, but it still didn't make it any easier. He really had no idea how he knew what he knew. It was really a matter of necessity. Whenever he needed a spell he was always able to create it. Also he was able to recreate any spell that he saw being cast or even the remnants of a spell if it hadn't been created that long ago.

"I can't really help you with that because I don't know. It just happened when I was in Kiarome. All of a sudden I was able to create spells and I have grown from there. It seems that I know what I need to know when I need to know it." Alaric explained as best he could.

Eldred thought for a moment. It didn't really make sense, but there seemed to be no other logical explanation. There was a more important question that he needed answering.

"How is it that you can recreate spells that you see?"

That was something he had hoped Eldred would be able to explain to him. He should have pre-empted the question and asked it himself. It seemed as though he was going to have to come up with an answer, he had no idea what it might be. He hoped that by talking it out an answer would come to him.

"Well, you know when you create a spell there are... I suppose for lack of a better word you would call them weaves? Alaric started as best you could.

Eldred returned with a confused expression on his face. It seemed that he didn't know what Alaric was talking about and that made him suddenly self-conscious. He stopped what he was saying and waited for Eldred to respond. When nothing came he thought he better ask the question.

"Why do you look so confused?"

Eldred suddenly composed himself, not realising that he had let his confusion show. "I don't understand what you are saying about seeing the spell."

"You know, the weaves." Alaric returned.

"I don't see anything when someone creates spells."

Now it was Alaric's turn to be confused. He didn't know what Eldred was saying. He had to admit in the beginning he couldn't see the weaves, but he just figured that it was something that came to sorcerers and wizards when they grew in power.

"Then this is indeed somewhat disturbing." Alaric was finally coming to understand what was happening. "Anyway, when someone creates a spell I see what I can only explain as a colourful weave. All I need to do to recreate the spell is to recreate that weave."

"I don't know whether this is a good or bad." Eldred mused.

"Well I can't see how it can be a bad thing." Alaric almost sounded offended.

"No, I'm sure that it isn't a bad thing. Even so I really need to discuss this with the council." Eldred sounded as though he was talking to himself. "Please continue..."

Before Eldred could finish his sentence Alena and Richmond returned to the cave. They were both dripping with water. The rain had not eased since they had left. They both held two piles of wood in their arms. There looked as though there would be enough to keep the fire going for most of the night. At the very least there would be enough to cook their dinner and take the chill out of the air. Neither of them seemed to notice the tension or the fact that the other two were completely dry.

"Put some the wood in the middle of the cave," Alaric instructed.

Alena did as she was asked, whilst Richmond put his wood off to one side. Alaric shot Eldred a quick look before he returned his attention to the wood. He had planned to just light the wood on fire and then rely on the flame to dry out the wood, but he figured he could use the same spell to dry the wood out first.

The spell worked just as planned. With the wood dry it was a simple spell to light it. The mood instantly changed once there was a fire burning brightly. It would still take a while for Alena and Richmond to dry out, but at least they were much more comfortable. Once they had warmed up and eaten they all went to sleep.

In the morning they had hoped the rain would have subsided, or at least eased, but it was not to be. If anything Alaric thought the storm had increased in intensity. They stood at the mouth of the cave and watched solemnly.

"Do you think this could be a spell?" Alena asked.

"No, I think I would know if there was magic at play." Eldred didn't sound completely sure of himself and he looked to Alaric for reassurance.

"No, this isn't the work of Nyrra or any of his underlings. This is natural weather and just our bad luck." The revelation did nothing to raise their spirits.

"So, what do we do? Are we going to wait for this to pass over?" Richmond asked.

"I'm afraid not. We can't lose any more time than we already have."

Once the decision had been made there was no reason to delay. The horses, even Adelanta, didn't seem keen to leave the cave. Alaric had to coax the white stallion out and as soon as they were out in the weather he wished he had not made the decision. From the cave the rain looked threatening, but it was nothing compared with the added bite of the wind.

The day continued much as it started. The rain poured down and the wind blew through. Early in the afternoon the thunder and lightning began. Great bolts of lightning shot down around them, the occasional tree being its landing point. None of them liked being out in the open on horseback, but again there was no place for shelter. Eventually they came across a small farming community and even though there was plenty of daylight left they look the opportunity to shelter from the storm.

"Do you know this place?" Richmond called over the storm to anyone who could hear.

"I have never seen any village on any map before, not that I really know where we are," Eldred called back. "I guess there is only one way to find out."

Like all villages, no matter how small, there was a tavern. That looked like the best place to start. It was doubtful there would be an inn, but it was worth a try. Eldred was sure that if he passed around some gold he would find somewhere comfortable for them to spend the night.

There was no stable at the tavern for the horses, just a hitching post out the front. The animals didn't seem too happy at being left out in the rain. Even Adelanta, who was normally stalwart in all conditions, started to buck and try to pull away from the post. Alaric whispered some calming words to him, which seemed to take effect.

The tavern was all but empty when they entered except for the barman and two other men sitting in the far corner. It looked as though they had been drinking for a long time. They didn't bother looking up when the group entered.

"Don't get many strangers here." There was something about the way the man spoke that didn't sound right to Alaric. "In fact I would say you were the first in many a year."

"How do you get supplies?" Alaric asked without thinking.

"Our horses are out in the weather, is there someplace we can stable them for the night?" Eldred asked before the barman could reply.

"We are also looking for rooms if you have any?" Richmond added.

Only Alena remained silent. There was something about the way the men acted that didn't seem right to her. She was about to speak when the barman beat her to it.

"Name's Bryce, Bryce the Barman." He smiled and offered his hand in a friendly manner.

There was something very peculiar about the situation, but Alaric was not going to be rude. He shook Bryce's hand and as he did it felt like a bolt of lightning shot down his arm. He stumbled backwards catching himself on a nearby table before he fell.

"Are you alright sir?" Bryce sounded surprised.

Alaric shook his arm. It felt numb and hard to move. He started to feel hazy, as if someone had drugged him. He was certain there was something wrong. He opened his mouth, but no words came out.

"I think you should sit down. You look like you are about to fall over." The barmen sounded jovial.

The other three didn't seem to be taking any notice of Alaric. They looked at the barman as if they were waiting for an answer. Alaric did as he was instructed. His head was swimming and he wasn't sure how long he could remain standing. Sitting down didn't make him feel any better.

"What's happening?" Alaric's mouth was dry and the words hurt the back of his throat.

"Don't try to talk. You will only make matters worse."

The room started to spin. In the moments he could focus he saw the other three lying on the tavern floor. Now he definitely knew something wasn't right, but he had a sneaky suspicion that it was too late.

"That's right. Just let it wash over you." Bryce started laughing.

Alaric tried to stand, but his legs couldn't take the weight. For a moment he forgot where he was, but then the memory came rushing back. He fumbled at the velvet covering the Topaz stone. Before he realised what was happening he saw Bryce standing over him.

"I don't think you will be needing that anymore." Bryce's voice had lost all familiarity.

The barman took the sceptre from Alaric's belt. Alaric tried to stop him, but he had no strength left. It was all he could do to keep his head up. He looked up at the man and thought he saw something flicker. He tried to focus, but to no avail.

"That's right. Time to drift away…" that was the last thing Alaric heard.

Chapter 16: Friend or Foe

When Alaric woke his head was aching. He felt as though he had been hit over the head with a cudgel. At first he couldn't remember what had happened or where he was, but then it came rushing back. The shock hit him suddenly and he sat bolt upright. He half expected to be bound, but that was not the case.

"Relax, Chosen One." The voice hissed. "I am not here to hurt you."

"What do you want?" Alaric was about to look up, but his aching head stopped him.

"Drink this, it will help you."

A pouch was dropped at his feet. Alaric realised how dry his mouth was, but just before he let the water pour down his throat he paused. There was no telling what was in the pouch and what it would do to him. He knew there were some evil potions in the Seven Kingdoms and he didn't want to fall into another trap.

"Don't worry. If I wanted you dead then poison would be low on the list."

Alaric knew that he recognised the hiss in the voice, but his head was still fuzzy. The words did make sense though. He didn't know how long he had been unconscious, but he was sure there would have been ample opportunity to kill him. With that thought in his mind Alaric look a long draught from the pouch. Once he had quenched his thirst he felt much better. As he looked up he saw a figure dressed in black.

"Do I know you?" he was still confused.

"In a manner of speaking. We have met a few times before."

It was the hiss in the voice that was bugging Alaric. He knew it was significant. On the plus side he wasn't bound. If the man's intentions were to imprison them then it would make sense for him to be bound. He wished that his head was clear, he needed to be able to think.

"It seems you are still suffering from my spell." For a moment Alaric's heart jumped. He thought a Dark Knight was standing before him. He tried to jump to his feet, but his body was still too weak. "I'm Viper." The serpentant recognised the concern on Alaric's face. As much as he enjoyed tormenting Alaric that was not the point of their meeting and if anything if would only prove to hinder his goals.

Alaric was somewhat confused again until the memories of Viper came rushing back to him. He was not sure if he was supposed to be afraid or not. The creature had made no move to harm him, but he was sure his motives were not pure. Slowly he came to his feet before he spoke.

"Where are the others?" Alaric asked.

"They will take a little longer to recover."

Alaric looked around to survey his surroundings. They were still in the tavern, which was a surprise. The two drunken men were no longer there, although Alaric doubted they ever were. The others were still lying on the floor and his first instinct was to see if they were alright, but he remained where he was. He needed to know Viper's intentions before he turned his back. There was something very unseemly about the situation.

"What are you doing here?" Alaric forced the question.

Although Alaric couldn't see inside Viper's robe he could tell what he was thinking. His senses had almost completely returned and he needed stay sharp. He felt for the stones, but none of them were there. Panic suddenly filled his heart.

"Don't worry, the stones are safe. I have no intention of stealing them from you. I know what they can do and they are more trouble than they're worth. I just needed to make sure that you weren't tempted to use them." He pointed to the bar where Alaric could see the stones, still with their velvet covers. He wanted to make a dash for them, but figured it wasn't the right move. For the moment he would have to trust the serpentant. "I will return them to you when we finish speaking."

Alaric wasn't sure if he believed Viper, but he accepted what he said. There was no point in doing anything until he found out what Viper wanted. At that moment he realised that Viper was holding a great amount of energy. It was obvious that he didn't trust Alaric. There was no chance for him to counter. He knew as soon as he started drawing in energy then Viper would attack. He thought he might be able to mask the fact, but at such a close range he didn't think it would work. He had to admit that he was at the serpentant's mercy and he would have to be very careful.

"Well I guess you should start talking then. There is obviously a very good reason why you are here." Alaric steeled his voice.

"Now we get down to business. I hate to admit it, but I need your help." The words lingered in the air.

Alaric couldn't believe what he was hearing. The creature was pure evil and he wanted Alaric's help. Things were not making sense. It had to be some kind of a trick.

"I and my kind are not what you think. Nyrra has twisted us to his will, but that is not who we are. I need your help to free us from his tyranny."

He had to admit that Viper did sound genuine, not that he really knew what a serpentant actually sounded like when they were being sincere. There was no way he could trust Viper, but he still couldn't discount it. He needed more information before he made his decision.

"And what if I don't believe that your motives are true?" Alaric tried to sound as suspicious as possible.

"Do you have something in mind for me to gain your trust?"

There was nothing that came to mind, but he was sure it would come to him. If Viper was telling the truth then he could indeed be a valuable ally. That was something that Alaric had to bear in mind. The serpentant s were very powerful and if he could get them all into the Alliance then it would be a great advantage.

"I think you should explain your motives." It seemed like the best place to start.

"That's fair enough." They were both starting to relax, although Viper still held onto the power inside him. "A long time ago, more years than I can remember, Nyrra imprisoned me and my kind. Over the years some of my brothers have grown accustomed to their captivity. Eventually they grew to believe that Nyrra was their true deity. They forgot he had betrayed the Goddess to her demise. I have never forgotten that betrayal and I have been waiting for such an opportunity to come along. I will free my kind from his yolk if it's the last thing I do."

"It could very well be the last thing that you do." The voice came from Eldred. Neither of them had noticed that the others had started to come to. The wizard had only just managed to get to his feet, whilst Alena and Richmond remained on the floor. "Nyrra doesn't take too kindly to traitors and I don't take to kindly to torturers."

Alaric could sense that Eldred was about to do something dangerous. He wasn't sure if he knew the amount of power that Viper held. If he tried to attack then he would certainly be killed.

"Relax Eldred, we're just talking." Alaric tried to calm him.

"Do you know what he put Alena and me through when we were his prisoners? I didn't think so. This creature deserves nothing more than death."

"I was just doing what I had to. It was the only way to keep up the ruse that I am still a faithful servant of the *Great Lord*." Viper defended his actions.

"That is no excuse. I should strike you down where you stand."

"Trust me when I tell you I could have done a lot worse. I couldn't leave you unscathed, but I did the best I could."

"Enough!" Alaric boomed. "I know he has wronged you and Alena and no one wants revenge for that more than myself, but now is not the time."

Eldred shrunk back from Alaric's harsh words. Each time that he thought things were returning to normal, Eldred realised how much Alaric had changed. The strength of his character was amazing, but it did nothing to reassure him.

"Thank you Alaric." Viper was grateful.

"Don't thank me yet." Alaric's rage was coming to boiling point. "I know you are holding a great deal of energy, but don't think for a moment that I can't kill you." It was a bluff, although Alaric thought that he might be able to do it, but the anger in his voice was convincing.

Viper almost let the energy leave his body out of pure shock, but he knew if he did that then Eldred would kill him. He held the magical power for protection, not to be aggressive, but he knew there was no point in trying to explain that.

"As I was saying, it is a case of the enemy of my enemy is my friend." Viper was hoping that his words were getting through. "We have a common goal and it is better if we work together. Trust me when I say I don't like it as much as you, but it is the only way we are both going to achieve our goals."

"There was never any love between Serpentine and the race of men. It was no coincidence that Nyrra was able to betray your Goddess. She walked straight into his trap." Eldred spat the words.

"What are you talking about?" Viper didn't like what he was hearing.

"She conspired with Nyrra to destroy the world of man. Elves, dwarves and any other living creatures were to be destroyed." Eldred spoke as if he was teaching a lesson.

"That is a lie. She would never join forces with Nyrra."

The conversation was again straying from its course. Alaric wanted it to return, but he also needed to know what they were talking about. In the end he decided to let the argument play itself out, at least until he gained what he needed to know.

"It is fact, whether you wish to believe it or not. Just because you are enemies with Nyrra it doesn't make you our ally. Your kind tried to destroy us in the past and there is no reason why you wouldn't again. You will always be hated by us as we will always be hated by you." Eldred was sure of himself.

Viper didn't seem so sure of himself. He knew there was some truth to Eldred's words, but it went against everything he knew. When it was said and done all that he knew, at least his most recent memories, had come from either Nyrra or one of his Dark Knights. He couldn't be completely sure if he could trust Eldred, but there seemed no good reason for him to lie. Viper really didn't know what to believe.

"Regardless of the past and what you believe to be true it doesn't change the here and now. Nyrra is my enemy, for the moment at least. Once he is dead then we can sort out old differences. For now you need my help as much as I need yours."

"He's right," Alaric said. "Nyrra is the enemy now, he is the biggest threat and the one we must destroy. You no longer need to convince me of your motives, you now have to convince me of your worth."

Viper wasn't expecting such a response and he had to think quickly. Originally he had his speech planned, but things had not gone to plan. He wasn't so sure he should use his original excuse. It seemed as though Alaric was going to be harder to convince than he thought. He also knew that he couldn't wait too much longer or Alaric would become even more suspicious.

"I am not the only serpentant roaming the Seven Kingdoms. The other six are here somewhere and if I am not mistaken they are all being controlled by Nyrra. If we run across any I should be able to convince them to join our plight." Viper wasn't too confident with his own words. It wouldn't be that easy to convince the others to turn against Nyrra. He had been their father for so long. "Remember that I have been living with the enemy for a long time. I can give you an insight into their mindset. I can tell you what they have been doing."

Alaric had to admit that could be handy, but he wasn't sure it would be enough to trust the creature. When it was said and done it could still be a trick to lull them into a false sense of security. On the other hand, if he was telling the truth, he would be an extremely useful and powerful ally.

"Don't listen to him Alaric." Alena's voice was broken and it sounded as though she was about to burst into tears. "He is a traitor. He tortured me so many times."

That had to be something Alaric couldn't take into account. He knew that Viper had done some terrible things, but he wasn't on trial for that. As the serpentant had said 'Nyrra was the enemy now'. Once it was all over then they would get their vengeance.

"Okay, for the moment I will say that I trust your motives." The others were about to protest, but Alaric silenced them with a wave of his hand. "For starters you will release the energy that you have been holding throughout this conversation. You will not draw in any power or create any spell without my expressed acceptance. You will do what I or anyone else tells you to do. If you don't like these rules then you can turn around and walk away."

"There is one more problem." Eldred spoke slowly. "He cannot come with us to our destination."

"And where might that be?" Viper asked without thinking.

"That is none of your business. See Alaric, he is just here to spy for the enemy. I knew we couldn't trust him."

"Relax Eldred. I don't believe he's a spy, but I also agree with you. He doesn't need to know our destination, but he will be travelling with us."

Viper looked at Alaric and then at the others. Alaric and Eldred looked as though they were both ready to strike. Richmond also looked wary, but not aggressive. There was a chance he would be killed once he lowered his defences. On the other hand he wouldn't be able to achieve his goal if he didn't take the risk. In the end he knew that he had no choice and let all the energy he was holding seep out of his body.

"Very good. Now you might be able to give us some information." Alaric also relaxed.

Viper stepped away from the bar as Richmond stepped forward. It didn't look as though it was an aggressive move, but he wasn't sure. The last thing he wanted was to end up dead. Richmond, on the other hand, had no thoughts of killing the serpentant. His main priority was to see if there was anything to drink. He found nothing. That was not a promising sign.

"Why is there nothing to drink back here?" Richmond asked.

"That is a very good point," Eldred said. "Where are we and where is everyone?"

"I can answer those questions quickly and easily. This is the small village of Woodville, although you could hardly call it a village. Nyrra has already brought his men through here and either captured or killed everyone. There is a small store room through that door behind the bar. There are still some supplies left," Viper explained.

It seemed as though things were getting worse in Remidia. As far as Alaric knew it had only been the major cities in the other kingdoms that had been attacked and some only by espionage. He didn't want to think about his home town, but he couldn't help himself. Meeting Adder on top of Mount Scorpio might be a moot point anyway.

Richmond quickly moved to see what was in the storeroom. There was surprisingly more than he thought there would be. He found two large barrels of wine and more food than they could take with them. At the very least they would be able to restock their supplies. For the moment he was only concerned about the wine. There would be time to eat once he had settled his nerves.

They were all glad to see Richmond return with the barrel. A sudden crack of thunder reminded them that the horses were still out in the rain. They had no idea how long they had been unconscious or what time of day it was, but regardless they needed to find shelter for the animals for the night.

"There is a stable, or at least what will pass as a stable at the back of the tavern. I am sure it will be suitable for the night. Otherwise there are other stables attached to farming houses," Viper explained.

Richmond took a long draught from his goblet before slamming it down on the table. He scolded himself for forgetting about the horses and also the fact that he couldn't relax. No one wanted to leave Viper alone, not that he was expected to do anything untoward. Alena and Richmond volunteered to stable the horses for the night so Eldred and Alaric could keep an eye on him.

"I guess if they are going to take care of the horses we should see what we can make for dinner." Eldred wanted to keep himself busy. "You can stay right where you are." He spoke to Viper when the serpentant stood to help.

"You need to trust me if we are going to get along." Viper returned.

"Get one thing straight." Eldred turned around to face him. "We are never going to get along. Keep your wits about you because given half a chance I will kill you." Even though Viper was the serpentant it was Eldred's voice that contained the venom.

Viper chose to ignore the comment. Instead he turned to face Alaric. This was the Chosen One, the one who was supposed to kill Nyrra. This was the moment he had been waiting for. Now he was able to devise a plan that would free the others, but that would have to wait. For the moment he would have to bide his time and gather enough information for him to use.

"So what is the plan from here?" Viper tried to sound as casual as possible and talk without his usual hiss.

Alaric ignored the question. He wasn't about to give Viper any more information than he already had. Their plan would remain a secret. For the moment he would be happy just knowing where, exactly, they were. He had never heard of Woodville before. It seemed to be a completely isolated village with no road leading out. If there was no trade route then it wouldn't be on any of the maps he had seen.

"Where exactly in Remidia is Woodville?" Alaric asked.

"I would say it is about ten days south of Remidel and three days to the east. Of course being so isolated and not on any of the maps it is hard to be precise," Viper explained.

"That can't be right." Eldred had returned from the storeroom and caught the end of the conversation. "We couldn't have..." Eldred stopped himself before he gave too much away.

"What do you mean?" Viper knew something was happening and he wanted to know what it was.

"It seems as though we were blown off course in the wind and rain." Alaric covered quickly for Eldred's blunder. "But that's alright, we are still on our course."

Viper thought for a moment and came up with one conclusion. They were travelling towards Remidel, that could be the only answer. If that was indeed the case then he had information they would need to know. It would be the perfect opportunity to gain their trust.

"You are heading to Remidel?" it was more of a statement than a question. "That is the only way you could have ended up here."

Alaric looked at Eldred and did his best not to smile. Viper had given them the perfect opportunity to throw him off their trail. If they let him believe they were going to Remidel then they could continue in peace. When he realised their course wasn't taking them to Remidel it would be too late for him to betray them.

"Yes, we are moving towards Remidel." It wasn't a complete lie, just a well worded response.

Viper smiled under his hood. It was auspicious for him to remain covered, that way no one could see his expressions. It was not the only reason for the hood, but it was definitely handy.

"Do you think someone could start a fire?" Richmond called as he came in from the weather. He was dripping wet, as was Alena.

Alaric hadn't noticed the cold. It was a promising sign that he was learning how to regulate his body temperature without having to think about it. That was good for him, but it would do nothing for the two who had been out in the rain. Before Alaric could rise Viper sprung to his feet. He wanted to show that he could be useful. There was a pile of firewood in the storeroom that would be perfect to heat the room. Once the fireplace was full Viper was about to light the wood when Alaric called out.

"I will let you off with a warning this time, but if you do it again I will strike you down." Alaric's voice was firm.

It took Viper a moment to realise what Alaric was talking about and then he realised what he was doing. He was about to use magic to start the fire and that was a no-no. He had relied on magic for so long that he didn't know how to start a fire without it. He looked at the wood and wondered how he was going to get it lit.

"Move out of the way." Richmond almost pushed him out of the way as he grabbed the tinderbox from the mantle.

It wasn't long before Richmond had a blazing fire burning and Eldred had their dinner cooking. All that was left was for them to relax with their wine, as much as they could with the serpentant watching them.

"Are there beds in this place?" Eldred spoke after a long silence.

"There's the owner's quarters, but I think that it might be a little small for all of us," Viper replied, happy that the silence had been broken.

The more conversation he had the more he felt like they were accepting him and that was what he was trying to achieve. He wouldn't be able to push his own agenda if he wasn't trusted. There was something disconcerting about the situation. It was as if he had traded one evil master for another. He much preferred it when he could rely on his own judgment. Now he had to answer to others and that in itself wasn't pleasing.

"I think that it would be better for us to stay here tonight. The rest of the village is a bit of a mess." He explained before anyone could question him further.

"The village looked fine when we rode in." Richmond was suspicious. "I'm sure that there will be somewhere more suitable for us to rest." To accentuate his point Richmond yawned openly.

"That was a little trickery on my part. I figured that you would be more coercive if you were relaxed. If you rode into a village in ruin you would be on your guard." He was somewhat pleased with his excuse.

Alaric wasn't sure if he believed what Viper was saying. There was only one way to find out if he was telling the truth. Slowly he made his way to the door. As he approached he could hear the screeching of the wind outside. If he opened the door the gale would fill the room and extinguish any heat created by the fire, but he couldn't just trust the word of a serpentant.

As he opened the door he was hit in the face by the cold wind. The rain pelted down and the small veranda gave little protection. He shut the door behind him so the room didn't lose all of its heat. It also didn't help his eyes with the firelight coming from behind.

With the storm clouds covering the moon it was pitch black outside and it took Alaric a long moment before his eyes became adjusted to the dark. Again he used the advantage of magic to enhance his eyesight. As he peered into the night he could see that the buildings were not as he remembered them. Windows were broken, doors hung off their hinges and some had even been burnt to the ground. There was no doubt that Viper was telling the truth. It again struck home how close Alaric was coming to the final battle. With that thought in his mind he returned inside the tavern.

"It seems as though he's telling the truth. The village is in utter ruin." Alaric explained.

"Why would Nyrra want to destroy such an isolated town?" at first Alena looked at Alaric and then to Viper.

"What?" he asked defensively.

"There is no reason for Nyrra to worry about such an insignificant village," Alena repeated.

"I do not know the mind of Nyrra. From what I have learned he will destroy anything that he comes near. I can only imagine that this was such a place."

"That is a lie." Alaric knew there was something wrong with his words. "That is not the reason for the destruction or the reason why you are here. Now I think you should start telling the truth."

Viper had been hoping not to explain his actions, but it seemed as though he was going to have to. He had to be careful how he worded things.

"I was instructed to come here and lay a trap for you." He started slowly. "Once the villagers had all been killed I sent the soldiers to search for the next village and I waited here."

"So Nyrra knew we were coming here?" Alaric sounded surprised.

"Not exactly. He knew that you would be coming this way. Once we arrived here I had a feeling that you would be arriving soon. That is why I wanted to get rid of the soldiers." Viper hoped they believed him.

"So you ordered the deaths of innocent men and women and children?" Richmond couldn't believe what he was hearing.

"It was either them or you. Which would you have preferred me to do?"

"We could have defeated the soldiers. You should have waited here with them." Eldred wasn't happy. Even though his words made little sense it didn't register with him. There was nothing the serpentant could say that would appease him.

Viper knew he wasn't going to gain anything from telling the truth, but he didn't have any other option. It was going to be an annoying twist of events. It looked as though it was going to take a lot to gain their trust, but he was going to make sure he got it.

"Then I am sorry to say that I made the wrong decision, but you can be assured that I was attempting to do the right thing." It was all Viper could say.

"What if the soldiers return here?" Richmond asked.

"I don't think they will be coming back. They are too busy searching the surrounding countryside for you. They will keep going until they are told to stop."

"Then we should stop them," Alena said.

"You know that I would like to, but we don't have time to be fighting every battle. We have to hope that eventually they will come to a village that will fight back." Alaric almost felt sick at the thought.

"Alaric is right. I have no idea where the soldiers would be now. It could take us many days to find them," Viper added.

"Well I think it should be time for us to get some rest. I think we have gained everything we need to know," Alaric suggested. "We have another big day tomorrow."

There was no denying Alaric's comment. It was getting late and they would have to be moving early to make up time. As much as they didn't want to sleep with the serpentant in the room no one had the energy to complain about it. At least their bedrolls and clothes had dried by the fire and their surroundings were a little more comfortable than the night before.

Alaric was the last to sleep. He needed to stay awake a little longer to make sure that Viper was not going to betray him. He couldn't be sure the serpentant was asleep, but eventually he was satisfied. If he was dead in the morning there was nothing he could do about it.

Chapter 17: Shoretown

Alaric was surprisingly relieved when he woke the next day. When he went to sleep he was sure that Viper wasn't going to try anything, but in the back of his mind he was uneasy. He was a step closer to trusting the serpentant, but there was still a long way for him to go.

Alaric had another problem to work out. It wouldn't take Viper long to realise that he was speeding up their journey. He wasn't sure if that was something he wanted him to know. There was no way Viper could join them and not know what he was doing.

The storm had past late in the day, but they were still drenched when they stopped for the night. They had found a small grove of trees that would give them some shelter. Viper quickly realised what Alaric had done. He waited until he was alone with him before he mentioned it. They had all gone to collect firewood for the night and Alaric and Viper were the first to return.

"How is it that we have travelled so far today?"

Alaric had known the question was coming, but he still hadn't worked out the answer. He didn't want to tell the truth, but lying would be extremely difficult.

"I don't know what you are talking about." Alaric feigned innocence.

Viper thought for a moment. It was obvious that Alaric knew what he was talking about and he knew that he would need to tread lightly if he was going to get answers.

"It seems as though we have travelled a great distance today, more than what we should have. I know this grove and I know that it is more than a day's ride from Woodville." Viper kept his voice level. He didn't want to give away the fact that he knew Alaric was lying.

Eldred returned with an armful of firewood which he dumped in the middle of their campsite. He could sense the tension between the two and was instantly concerned. First he lit the fire then he looked around to see where Alena and Richmond were. They were still out collecting firewood, but he didn't think it would be long before they returned.

"What did I miss?" he asked casually.

"Nothing." Alaric was glad for the distraction.

"I was just mentioning to Alaric that I believe we have travelled further than we should have today." Viper was not going to let it rest as Alaric had hoped.

"Of course we have." Eldred replied. "It is quite a simple spell to speed up our movement. I create it every morning before we leave."

Viper didn't like what he was hearing. He knew it wasn't a simple spell. If it was then he would know it himself. He also didn't believe that

Eldred had created it. It seemed as though it was going to be more difficult to get the answers he required.

"I don't suppose you would show it to me?" even if Eldred did know the spell Viper doubted he would share it with him.

Eldred just gave him a dark glare and shook his head. He still hadn't accepted the fact that Alaric had let Viper join their party. He had read nothing in the prophecy about it and now there was no chance to refer to the great tome. If the serpentant knew of its existence then there was no doubt in Eldred's mind that he would steal it. The prophecy was far too valuable to take that risk. At least they would be free once they left for the island. If Alaric wanted to keep the serpentant alive then he would not be able to travel with them. The Council of Wizards wouldn't let him live if he stepped foot on the island. It would be a death sentence. In fact Alena and Richmond shouldn't be going either. The island was supposed to be for wizards only, but if that was truly the case then Alaric wouldn't be able to travel there either. However there was no other option and he was sure the other wizards would understand.

"No, I guess not. You know if you told me I might be able to take some of the strain." It was worth a shot.

"No thank you. As I said it's not much of a spell." Eldred hoped he was right. Alaric didn't seem to be suffering any effects from it. He was sure if it was causing him any trouble he would have mentioned it.

"We appreciate the offer, but you still have a long way to go if you want to gain our trust." Alaric added ending the conversation.

Before Viper had a chance to push any further the others returned from their foraging. As well as the wood Alena also carried two small rabbits. No one had even noticed that she had taken the bow and arrows she had received from Albend.

"I thought it might be good to have some fresh meat." She smiled warmly until she saw Viper.

Alaric doubted that Eldred and Alena would ever trust him. He could only imagine the pain and suffering he had put them through. He wished he could be done with the evil creature, but he knew that he couldn't. There was still a part for him to play and it was time Alaric got some answers.

"What is your brother, Adder, up to?" Alaric asked suddenly as they were eating their evening meal.

"I'm sorry, what did you say?" Viper looked up from what he was doing.

"Adder, what is he doing?"

"Why do you ask?" Viper wasn't sure if it was a trap or not.

"I will be the one asking the questions." Alaric wasn't going to give away any unnecessary information.

Viper was really getting frustrated. It was very hard for him to give the right answer. "I don't know what he's doing." It seemed the easiest response, at least until he knew more. It wasn't a complete lie, he really had no idea what Adder was doing.

"Then it doesn't seem as though you are any use to us." Alaric stood as he spoke. In Alaric's mind Viper must know what the other serpentants were doing. He picked up his sword and then moved back towards Viper. "Tell me something I don't know."

"Don't be so hasty." Viper put his hand up in a sign of surrender. Alaric kept the sword point close to his face. "I know something very important. I know that you are walking into a trap."

"What are you talking about?" Eldred snapped and then he remembered that as far as Viper knew they were travelling to Remidel.

"There is a Dark Knight in Remidel, Dargoz. He has taken control of the city and by the looks of things most of the kingdom," Viper spoke quickly.

"What's his plan?" Alaric didn't sound convinced.

"I don't know. I only know what Ra'naroz told me." Viper was starting to panic.

"And where is Ra'naroz?" Alaric kept the question going.

"I head a rumour that he's dead, but I don't know if it's true." Viper shrank back.

"How did he die?" Alaric wasn't going to ease up.

"I heard that Nyrra killed him for failing to capture you and letting you gain the Topaz stone." Alaric touched the sceptre subconsciously. "Knowing the Great Lord I wouldn't be surprised at all if it was true."

Alaric had to admit that he had felt a shift not long after Ra'naroz had escaped. There had been so much happening at the time that Alaric had thought nothing of it. It was all starting to make sense. That thought brought a smile to his face. The Dark Knight would have thought he was so clever getting away from Alaric. He could only imagine the look on Ra'naroz's face when he was being slaughtered by Nyrra. He was glad that another Dark Knight had been killed. It was just a shame that he couldn't do it himself.

"I see, well that is some good news, but let's get back to Dargoz. I think you should tell us everything you know about him." Alaric was interested to find out about Dargoz. He was the one Dark Knight that he had not met and anything he could find out would be an advantage. He wasn't sure when he would be able to confront him, but that didn't matter.

"I know that he is masquerading as a dwarf. I can't remember his name exactly but…"

"Gilgi!" Eldred interrupted and spat the name.

"Yes, that is it, you know him?" It seemed like a good chance to gather some information of his own.

"Yes, he is the son of Golgi and the leader of the Dwarven Guild in Castalia. He comes from a long line of usurpers and betrayers. I should have guessed that he was a Dark Knight. I guess if I had been able to spend more time with the army I would have been able to tell." Eldred berated himself.

"Don't blame yourself Eldred," Alena's words were soothing. "There was nothing you could have done."

Viper watched the exchange carefully. He wasn't sure, but he thought it might be something useful. He turned away before anyone noticed him staring.

"What is he up to?" Alaric asked, realising that they had gone off topic.

"I don't know for sure, but it seems as though his job is to keep the Remidian and Dwarven army inside the walls of Remidel. Whilst he does that, Nyrra is free to cause mayhem throughout the kingdom." Viper surmised.

"This is indeed troubling," Alaric mused. "Is there any other information you would care to share with us?"

"I have not been to Remidel myself, so I can't give you any more information, but I can tell you that I wouldn't advise a journey in that direction."

Alaric thought about telling him that they weren't headed for Remidel, but he figured Viper would learn soon enough. At the rate they were travelling it would be sooner rather than later. He had to make a decision fast of what he was going to do with Viper when they made the journey to the island.

For the moment it was better he believed what he believed.

"I think I might get some sleep now. We have another long day ahead of us." Alaric stopped the conversation.

"Yes, I suppose we do." Viper spoke under his breath.

Alaric was able to relax a little more that night. There was no point in stressing about the serpentant's intentions. If he wanted them dead then it would only be a matter of time. For the moment he would just relax and hope they had made the right decision.

It took them another two days to reach the oceanside town of Shoretown. It wasn't until they were able to see the sea that Viper realised they were not going to Remidel. He was amazed at the fact they could travel so quickly and yet he didn't know how. The spell had to be powerful indeed and if that was the case then he should be able to feel who had created it. At the very least he should see the affects of the casting. No one could create such a spell and not show it. Viper didn't like what that meant.

The only way to gain passage to the island was by boat. Of course Alaric could transport them through the fabric of reality, but Eldred strongly advised against it. Besides the fact that it was against everything he believed in, there was a good chance that they would be killed upon arrival. The other wizards wouldn't like someone entering unannounced. Alaric had to agree. He didn't want to get the other wizards offside. He was going to ask a great deal of them and he couldn't risk them saying no.

It was late in the afternoon when they reached the town and it was too late to gain passage to the island. No one would sail the waters during the night. It was said that the waters were cursed, but Alaric figured it was a spell to stop people arriving after dark. Be that as it may they would have to find lodgings.

Eldred entered the inn they found by himself. He didn't want Viper to hear the conversation.

"What brings ye to our lil' old town." The owner of the inn spoke with a thick accent.

"We need transport to the Isle of Wizards," Eldred spoke openly.

It struck home how long it had been since he had been to the island. He used to know everyone in the town, but that was a long time ago. It would have made life easier for them if he explained who he was, but he didn't want the rumours to start. Instead he would have to try and talk or at least pay his way through.

"Fraid ye might be out of luck there friend." The innkeeper made a show of wiping down his desk, obviously not willing to offer up any information.

"Well for starters we will be needing rooms for the night." Eldred would come back to his questions. He wanted to get the others settled in first. More to the point he wanted to make sure that Viper remained in his room.

"Hmmm... that could also be a problem." He didn't sound interested.

Eldred was starting to become annoyed. It was obvious that the innkeeper wanted gold, but it was a matter of how much. He would have to play the game for a little longer and luckily he had time on his side, for once.

"I couldn't imagine there would be too many people here this time of year, with the costal storms and all," Eldred replied casually.

"That isn't the problem."

Eldred was starting to lose his patience. Instead of getting angry he simply dropped a gold coin on the desk. He knew that would get the answers he required.

"The wizards have informed us that they don't want anyone staying in our inns. Now normally I wouldn't listen to such orders, but they are paying in gold and more than I could make accepting guests." He tossed the coin in the air and smiled.

"Well I am sure that you can make an exception on this occasion." Eldred feared that he was going to have to reveal his identity. At first he dropped another two coins on the desk to see what would happen.

"Ye can keep doin' that all night, but it won't help. We can't go against the wizards. Until they lift the embargo no one comes or goes." The innkeeper looked sad at the fact. He really wanted to take the gold.

Eldred sighed loudly. He had really hoped he could have remained anonymous. There was nothing he could do about it. The only way he was going to get what he wanted was to reveal his identity. At least he had that up his sleeve.

"How long have you been here?" the innkeeper seemed taken aback at the sudden question.

"What?"

"How long have you been in Shoretown?"

"All of my life. Why do you ask?"

Eldred looked around to see if anyone was listening "I was just wondering why you would be running an inn in Shoretown and not know when you are speaking to a wizard."

At first the innkeeper thought he was lying. It was easy enough to claim to someone that you were a wizard, it wasn't the first time someone had tried it. But he had to admit that there was something different about the man standing before him. If he was wrong and he let the group stay and this man wasn't who he said he was then he would be in great trouble.

"And wha' is ye name?" he asked cautiously.

"My name is Eldred and if you mention that fact to anyone else then you are going to wish you were never born."

Even though he had never met the wizard the name Eldred was synonymous around the village. He doubted anyone would use it if it wasn't him. He quickly made the decision that the man was telling the truth.

"I am sorry, me lord." He quickly changed his tune. "If I had known I would…"

"I know. That is in the past. Now I would like some rooms for my friends and myself." He dropped another coin on the desk.

"Of course, me lord, but I can't take ye money. As I said, the wizards pay our way." He turned away from Eldred as he called out to the page.

"What do ye want?" the page was a lot older than Eldred had expected. He was a lage man with a balding head. He didn't look like he had washed in over a week.

"We 'ave visitors." He sounded pleased with himself.

"Don't be daft Vance, we haven't had guests in o' a year. Now stop messin' around an' tells me what ye want?" At that moment he saw Eldred standing in front of the desk. A confused expression crossed his face.

"No, take the bags to our finest rooms." Vance smiled. "And then see to the others. I am sure that they 'ave horses that need stabling. It is 'bout time ye did somethin' useful."

Eldred smiled, it was clear that the innkeeper was enjoying himself. It would have been a long time since the page had needed to work. He didn't really look too happy about it. Eldred had already spent too much time trying to convince the innkeeper he needed to stay. He needed to find passage to the island and he needed to make sure they were on the move at first light.

"Where might I find passage to the island?" Eldred asked.

"The ports 'ave been closed for almost a week now. Normally there are regular shipments of supplies comin' in, but we be instructed to only allow those comin' from land."

That seemed very strange to Eldred. It was almost as if the rest of the council knew he was coming and didn't want to give him access. There would have to be a boat to take him across the straight, after all he did sit on the council. No one could refuse him passage, but it would seem as though he would have to reveal his identity again.

"I take it the captains would be in the taverns?"

"Ye would be correct. The Sailor's Arms would be the best place to look. That's where most of the captains drink. But I wouldn't hold ye breath. Although the captains are still in town most of the sailors have left. There isn't much to do in a town like this if you're used to being on the open seas. The only reason some of the captains have remained is because of the wizards. They said they can't leave."

There was something very strange happening in the town. He had never heard of the council making such outrageous rules. He could understand their concern, but there was no reason to take it out of the townsfolk. He knew they had spent too much time on their island.

"Thank you. I will see what I can do." Eldred nodded his head before leaving the inn.

He found the others waiting outside. It seemed as though the page had yet to take their possessions. Eldred figured it would be just as easy to leave them inside the inn. The light was starting to fade and he wanted to be inside the Sailors Arm's before the captains were too inebriated.

They left the horses out the front of the inn. Alaric was certain that the elven horses would protect Richmond's mare if someone came along and tried to steal them. Alaric had to admit that he had not seen anyone on the streets since they had arrived. That thought started to weigh on his mind as they made their way to the Sailor's Arms. Eldred had not explained anything since he had left the inn. All he had said was that they needed to find a captain.

"So you are going to the island?" Viper asked as they walked.

"That is not your concern. Wherever we are going you are not coming with us." Eldred didn't like Viper's tone.

"What are you talking about?" Viper sounded shocked. "We agreed that I would be coming with you."

"We agreed to nothing," Alaric spoke harshly. "You will wait here for our return."

As far as Alaric was concerned that was the end of the conversation. He quickened his pace so Viper didn't have a chance to question him further. Eldred had also moved on ahead. He didn't want to waste any time, or risk giving away too much information. Viper already knew too much and that could be very dangerous. He had wanted to leave him alone on the mainland, but that wouldn't be safe either. They would now have to leave Alena and Richmond behind to keep an eye on him. That in itself could be very dangerous. He had no idea what the best move was.

The tavern was full of people when they arrived. They all had the look of seafarers about them. Eldred doubted very much that they were all captains. He didn't think Vance knew what he was talking about when he said all the sailors had left. He was sure there would be enough seamen to take them across to the island. Eldred let out a quick sigh of relief before he controlled himself, it was not over yet.

"I'm looking for a captain!" Eldred boomed over the din.

Alaric was suddenly on guard as he saw everyone in the room turn to look at them. They didn't look too happy about being interrupted. Alaric had no idea what Eldred was thinking. He thought it would have been much better if he had kept things quiet. The last thing they wanted was to gain more attention.

"Why do you want a captain?" only one man spoke. He sat the bar staring into the bottom of his tankard. He didn't look up as he spoke.

"That is our business for the moment." Eldred wasn't going to give anything away.

"Then I don't like your chances." Another man spoke.

"We haven't been able to sail in a long time." Another said.

"Then you should be all keen to take to the water again," Eldred said with a smile.

"We can't. We've been grounded. The wizards have told us to remain in port until further notice. We have not had any further notice, so we must remain in port."

"I have a lot of gold and am willing to pay for the service." Eldred wasn't going to give up so easily. He could have just revealed his true identity, but he had a feeling that wasn't the right thing to do.

That brought a lot of murmurs throughout the room, but no one was willing to put their hand up. It didn't matter how much gold Eldred had, they were sure it was not enough. They couldn't go against the wizards.

"Damn it." The man sitting at the bar slammed his tankard down. "Isn't there a captain here with a set to take on the wizards."

"You keep quiet Blaine, this has nothing to do with you. You gave up that right a long time ago."

"And what about you Fremont? Isn't it time that you stepped out from underneath the shadows. You're a captain, it should be your choice whether you sail or not." Blaine turned around for the first time.

He had a short trimmed, dark moustache and goatee beard. His hair was strangely combed and neatly cut. He looked somewhat out of place. The rest of the bar was filled with rough, unkempt looking men. There was something about Blaine's appearance that both intrigued and worried Alaric. He could only hope that Eldred knew what he was doing.

"Bah, go back to your ale. I've had enough of this nonsense. Be warned if you are going to deal with Blaine," barked Fremont.

The rest of the bar had gone back to their drinks and started to ignore the visitors. Fremont made a point of speaking with his small group, trying to make the others feel uncomfortable. When it was obvious that it wasn't working he returned to his normal conversation.

"What was that all about?" Eldred asked.

"Not much good without an ale." Blaine tipped his tankard over to accentuate his point.

Eldred's shoulders dropped. He hoped that it wasn't just a ploy to get free drinks. Either way Blaine looked as though he was going to be their best chance, so Eldred ordered the man an ale.

"What should we do?" Viper asked as he looked around the bar. It didn't look as though anyone really wanted them to be there.

"Just shut up and wait," Alaric snapped.

"Tell me what you need?" Blaine asked after he took a long draught.

"We are looking for passage to the island." Eldred didn't waste time getting to the point.

"Hmm…" he took another drink as he thought on the question. "That is indeed interesting."

"I think it is time for your friends to leave." The barman spoke in a gruff voice.

At that point Alaric noticed there was an air of hatred in the room. He didn't think it would be long before someone started trouble. He thought it would be a good idea for them to leave, but they couldn't without a captain.

"This is a bar for seafarers only." He repeated.

Blaine looked at the barman and then around the bar. They were not receiving any friendly looks from the patrons. It would only be a matter of time before trouble ensued. Blaine had a sneaking suspicion that it would be the other sailors who would suffer.

"I think we should move on," Blaine suggested. "There are better places to discuss such matters."

Eldred nodded. It seemed as though Blaine was the captain who was going to help them. Eldred had to admit that there was something very familiar about him and that was a promising sign.

"Where do you think you're going Blaine?" the barman was clearly not happy. "You know that you aren't supposed to speak with strangers."

"Bah!" he spat on the floor. "I'm sick of all these rules. I am going to have a drink with my new friends. Now if you don't mind I would like to purchase a bottle of rum."

As much as the barman didn't want to help Blaine he couldn't pass up the purchase of a bottle of rum. He quickly snatched a bottle from behind the bar and plonked it down.

"That will be two gold crowns." He sneered as he spoke.

The price was almost five times the normal price. Instead of looking angry Blaine simply looked at Eldred who in turn dropped two gold coins on the bar. He figured it would be easier than trying to haggle with the barman. They had already stayed too long.

There were a few sailors standing between them and the door when they turned to leave. Alaric thought there was going to be trouble and drew in a small amount of energy. As much as the sailors didn't like the strangers they also didn't want to start any trouble. They were always wary of people who wanted to travel to the island so the sailors simply stepped aside as they walked out of the tavern.

"Getting mighty stuffy in there," Blaine spoke before using his teeth to pull the cork out of the bottle.

Once the cork was free Blaine took a swig. He thought about offering the others a drink, but returned the cork instead. He wasn't going to waste the rum, he wasn't sure when he could afford another bottle. If the men weren't on the level then he would have to make it last.

"Where are you taking us?" Alaric asked after a while.

"I have a small shed by the docks." Blaine didn't look at Alaric as he spoke. There was something in his voice that didn't fill Alaric with confidence.

They travelled the rest of the journey in silence. There were a few people on the streets, but no one seemed to take any notice. No one wanted to risk their plans being overheard. There was no point in taking any silly risks. All would be revealed once they reached the shed.

It was apparent when they entered the shed that it wasn't only a shed, but also Blaine's place of residence. A bedroll and linen was spread out in a corner. Alaric looked around, but he couldn't see what Blaine had used for his waste. That thought was especially disturbing. There was a small makeshift table made out of a plank of wood and two small crates, with crate chairs around it.

"This is not what I expected," Eldred said as he looked around the shed. "You say that you're a captain?"

"Well that is not exactly true, or at least anymore." Blaine took another swig from his bottle.

Viper took a step forward. "I knew we shouldn't have trusted this man. Let me finish him off!"

"Stand down Viper!" Alaric barked. "Let's hear what he has to say for himself."

Chapter 18: Captain Blaine

"Please, have a seat." Blaine took another swig from the bottle of rum. It was clear he was nervous about what he was about to say.

Viper was the last to be seated. He still wanted to attack Blaine, but it was obvious that Alaric wasn't going to let him. He shot Blaine an evil look before seating himself. Being dressed in a robe with hood drawn over his face made it a futile gesture. The last thing they wanted was questions about their reptile looking companion.

"Now I think you should explain to us why we bought you an overly expensive bottle of rum." Eldred's voice was sombre.

Blaine took another draught before slamming the bottle down on the makeshift table. Alaric wondered if the man was sober enough to plead his case. It might be easier if he just let Viper have his way with him. He cringed at the thought and pushed it to the back of his mind. No matter what the man had done nothing could warrant such a punishment.

"I was a captain, not that long ago." Blaine reached for the bottle, but Alaric snatched it away. It was clear that he wouldn't get it back until he had finished his tale. "It was not long after word came in that we could no longer sail from this port that I decided to take my ship out. I had just made a few repairs to my vessel and I wanted to make sure she was still seaworthy. It seemed as though this was considered a breach of the council's edict and my licence was revoked. My ship was sold out from underneath me. My crew took up with other captains. Even though there was no work, the wizards were paying all expenses. Extra crew meant extra gold, at least in the short term. Once they are allowed to sail again then I am sure my men will be out of work."

The story wasn't making Alaric feel any more confident. He had a very bad feeling that things weren't going to work out. What he couldn't understand was why the man brought them to his place of residence if he couldn't come through with the goods. There had to be more to the story.

"So, that doesn't really explain anything," Eldred said. "I think you should get to the point if you want your rum back."

Blaine looked at the bottle that Alaric still held. He had to admit that he did want the rum back, although he knew he would feel better in the morning if he didn't. If all went to plan that would be when he was sailing his ship again, although he wasn't sure if he should reveal that. When it was said and done he didn't believe that he had a choice if he wanted it to work.

"Some of my crew remained with my ships new owner. These are my most trusted of men and they have remained loyal to me."

Things were starting to make sense. Although he had not given away the ending Alaric realised what he had planned. He wasn't sure if he liked it or not, but with the way things were he didn't think they had any other option.

"So you want us to steal your ship back for you?" Alaric didn't wait.

"Well I don't really see it as stealing. The way I figure it, the ship was stolen from me in the first place. I am just getting my property back." He smiled an evil smile.

"You were paid, I don't see the discrepancy." Alena didn't sound pleased.

"I was paid about half the value of the ship. Since no one can set sail, no one needs extra vessels. In truth I was lucky to get what I got, but as you can see that hasn't lasted me long. Now it is time for me to get my own back." Blaine eyed the bottle of rum.

"I don't like the sound of this." Eldred stood. "We will find other means of transport."

"That is all well and good, but you won't find anyone else to take you. All the other Captains are too afraid, especially after what happened to me," Blaine spoke quickly.

Eldred had already turned to leave, whilst the others remained seated. When he heard Blaine's words he stopped. He knew he was right. There was no coincidence that they were sitting in a shabby old shed. It was not an ideal situation, but it seemed as though it was the one they were in.

"Okay, let's say for argument's sake that I might be interested in your deal. What do you have in mind?" Eldred returned to the make-shift table.

"Now that's more like it," Blaine knew they were starting to believe him. "I have a number of men on the ship who are still loyal to me. Once I have given them the word they will slip something in the other crews' drinks."

"We don't want to kill anyone!" Alaric interrupted.

"Relax, I am not planning anything that will see me in the hangman's noose." Alaric was dubious on that comment. "There is a nasty little herb that I have procured for such an occasion. It will put them to sleep and give them a nasty headache when they wake, but that is all."

That really didn't put Alaric's mind at ease. He had been drugged himself and knew that it wasn't a pleasant experience, but it didn't seem as though there was any other option.

"If you don't like that idea I could dispose of the crew," Viper offered.

Alaric wanted to strike the serpentant, but refrained. Blaine gave the creature a strange look at the sound of his voice. It was as if he was seeing Viper for the first time, although he couldn't see any features under his robe. He tried to peer into the hood, but that didn't do any good. Alaric glared at Viper who understood the unspoken threat.

"So if you are just going to steal a ship then you won't need the gold. I think our help in returning your ship would be sufficient payment." Eldred didn't miss a beat.

Blaine looked at their faces as he thought for a moment. There was nothing on their expressions that gave away their true feelings. He didn't think that Eldred was serious, but he couldn't be completely sure. If he was going to successfully get the gold then he would have to come up with a good excuse.

"Of course that would be the case, if it was just up to me…" He kept a close eye on Eldred's face, nothing had changed. "My crew are going to want payment. They have families to feed and as you can imagine their pay has not been that great."

"I thought you said that the wizards were paying all costs?" Eldred didn't sound impressed.

"Just because the wizards pay the Captains it doesn't mean that the coin filters down to the crew. Of course they have to be paid, but the rates for remaining in port are a lot less than on the open seas."

Eldred had to admit that made sense. He had been hoping to save the remainder of their gold, but when it was said and done he would be able to restock once they reached Čarolija Island.

"Very well. We will pay the fee."

"Good. Then we need to be on our way to the docks." Blaine stood from the table.

"Docks?" Alena asked. "Surely your crew wouldn't be there at this time of night, especially since they can't sail."

The situation had always been suspicious and Blaine had done nothing to ease their minds. They were all used the swings of the prophecy, but that still didn't make it better. Alaric had a bad feeling they could very well be walking into a trap.

"Don't you worry about that. Everything is taken care of." There was an evil glint in Blaine's eye.

"We need to go back to our inn and get our things. We will meet you at the docks when we are done."

They all left the shed together. Blaine moved on towards the dock, whilst the others left for the inn. Alaric was glad that they had a moment to think about what they were about to do. He was still not sure they were doing the right thing. There was no pull from the prophecy and that was never a good sign, although there was a little too much happening for it to just be a coincidence.

"Now what are we going to do?" Alena asked when they had everything packed. "We have paid for the rooms and I don't think we should rush into anything that could see us dead."

"I have a good feeling that Blaine is on the level. He will see us safely to the island, I am sure of it." Eldred tried his best to reassure her.

"You could always explain that you are on the Council of Wizards." Viper suggested what they had all been avoiding. "I am sure that the captain's will be falling over themselves to help. It would be a much simpler solution."

As much as no one wanted to agree with the serpentant they had to admit his words made sense. It would be a lot easier than taking a risk on a captain who had his commission taken away from him. The only problem was that Eldred didn't want everyone to know who he was. It was bad enough that the innkeeper knew. When Viper pushed for more information he refused to give any. All he said was that there was a good reason for remaining anonymous.

"Then we should keep moving." Viper tried to act inauspicious.

"You are remaining here." Eldred was happy with the change of subject. "There is no way you are coming to the island."

"And you can be sure that if you cause any trouble while we are gone you will pay for it when we return," Alaric warned.

Viper wasn't happy with the situation, but there was nothing he could do about it. He had always wanted to visit the wizard's island, but it seemed as though the opportunity would pass him by.

They stopped when they reached the front desk. Vance was still sitting there, although it was obvious there would be no more customers that night. He smiled when he saw Eldred approach.

"What can I do for ye, me lord?" Vance asked.

"I am leaving for the island. I will be leaving two of my friends behind." Alaric had made the decision that Alena would be coming with them. As much as Eldred didn't think it was a good idea he couldn't say no. "I would appreciate it if you looked after them," Eldred replied.

Richmond did not like being left behind with Viper, but he knew he couldn't go with them. What he didn't understand was why Alena was going. From what he had gathered no one who wasn't a wizard or worked for the council was allowed on the island. All he could do was trust that Alaric was doing the right thing. He didn't think he would lead her into danger.

"Of course. They are more than welcome to stay." Vance shivered after he spoke. There was something very unnerving about one of the wizard's friends. He wished that he would go with them, but he couldn't say anything. To go against the wishes of one of the seven would be disastrous. "And no I don't need any more gold." Vance spoke quickly as Eldred produced his money pouch. He had already pushed his luck and didn't want to cause any problems for himself. He didn't know what the other six wizards would do if they heard he had been taking gold from Eldred.

"I thank you for your assistance and I will make sure that you are properly compensated." Eldred smiled.

Viper walked out of the inn with the others. He was still trying to sneak his way across to the island. It annoyed Alaric, but he didn't want to say anything in front of the innkeeper. Once they were outside Alaric took a moment to see if anyone was in the street before he started on Viper.

"Get back inside the inn!" Alaric snapped. "This is your last warning. If you are disobedient again then you will suffer the punishment." To accentuate his point Alaric drew in a small amount of energy, enough to create a dangerous spell.

Viper raised his hands in defence. He knew he had pushed too far, but it was worth a try. He needed to know how far he could go before Alaric would retaliate. Unfortunately it wasn't as far as he had hoped. He returned to the inn without saying a word. There was no point speaking any further, it would only prove to get him into more trouble.

"I will keep an eye on him," Richmond assured them before they left, although Alaric wasn't sure what Richmond could really do if Viper wanted to caused problems.

Alaric was much happier once the serpentant was gone. It had been hard for him to relax with the creature nearby. Although Viper had done nothing to break his trust there was little chance Alaric could forgive his past crimes. What he had done to Eldred and Alena was unforgivable.

With the energy inside him Alaric's senses were suddenly heightened. For the first time he noticed the smell of the salt water as they walked towards the docks. Ever since he had learned how to block out the temperature around him he had dulled his other senses.

As they neared the docks Alaric was not so grateful that his sense of smell had returned to him. The first smell that filled his nose was that of rotting fish guts. Although the fishing ships were not allowed to leave the docks there were still those who would fish from the pier. The catch wasn't as good, but the demand was still there and that meant the prices were on the way up. Even a small catch was a good day's work.

The smell was almost enough to make Alaric wretch and he soon wished his senses would return to normal. The stench of fish guts was only one of the putrid smells on the docks. Although Alaric couldn't place them he knew they were not pleasant. He could only hope that once they had set sail then the stench would disappear. He didn't think he could stand much more of it.

The docks were dimly lit by a few lanterns. Since no one could sail there didn't seem to be any point in lighting the area properly. It made it a dangerous place by nightfall. Some of the more unsavoury types would inhabit the area after dark.

"What 'ave we here?" A small gang were leaning against a group of crates outside a boatshed.

"We have business in the dock, none of which is yours." Eldred spoke casually.

They continued past, but it was obvious the gang was not happy with the response. Alaric hoped that there wouldn't be trouble, but he doubted it. The gang had the air of those who always got their way. He wasn't in the mood for a fight, but it seemed as though he wouldn't have a choice.

"I would appreciate it if you didn't follow us." Eldred turned around to face the men who were behind them. "Our business is no concern of yours, but if you keep following then that may change."

"We will be on our way for a slight fee. You see times are tough and we need to make gold anyway we can." Even in the dull light they could see an evil grin on the man's face.

"Unfortunately our gold has already been spent. We have nothing to offer you," Eldred explained.

"Well, it looks as though the pouch on your waist is telling me a different story. I am sure that I can lighten your load a little."

Alaric drew his sword as a pre-emptive measure. He didn't think the gang would put up much of a fight. Although they each carried a cutlass on their belts he didn't think that they knew how to use them. Alaric guessed that they had been stolen from some poor, unlikely victim.

"There is no need for that. As ye can see there be seven of us and only three of ye. I am sure that ye dun want to end up dead on such a fine evenin'." The leader spoke with confidence.

"I think you should reassess your plans. There is no need for bloodshed," Alaric said. "If you leave now then we can forget this ever happened."

"I don't think so." The leader drew his cutlass, followed shortly by his six companions. They were ready to fight, but no one made a move forward.

"Harlon, what in the Gods names are you doing?" the voice came from behind them. Alaric recognised it as Blaine.

The situation suddenly became very confusing. Both sides seemed to recognise the captain, but no one knew what he was doing there. According to the directions he had given Eldred the ship was still another dozen births away.

"This is none of ya business captain. We just doin' what we can to stay afloat, as it were," Harlon replied quickly.

"I told you I was goin' to get me boat back, now it is time for ya to return."

Harlon stopped to think. His old captain had told him that he would return, but Harlon had not believed it. He and his seven friends had not been able to gain employment with any of the shipping companies or private captains. They had resigned themselves to a life of drunken thuggery.

"Ye dun 'ave a ship. What are ye goin' get us to sail?" Harlon was not completely convinced.

Harlon had been first mate when Blaine had been captain. He had refused to take on new work on the grounds of the captain's dismissal. He didn't want to take employment with someone who was scared of the wizards.

"Milt is readying the ship as we speak. We will set sail before dawn."

"Hah!" Harlon scoffed. "Ye know what happened the last time we set sail without permission. I ain't goin' through that again. We'll stay here and earn our gold the old fashioned way."

"These three want passage to the island. I figure it's a good opportunity to plead my case to the council."

"Then what do you want us for?"

"I need ye to complete me crew. I promised ye places on me ship and now I am 'ere to do good on it."

Harlon looked at the others. There was nothing on their faces to show their opinion. Harlon had been the senior of the seven when they were on Blaine's ship and he had assumed the role as their leader on the docks. The other six would do whatever Harlon decided, although he didn't really want the responsibility.

"Very well, looks like we set sail again boys!"

The other men cheered as they put away their swords. They were glad that they didn't have to fight and also that they had gainful employment again, even if it wasn't strictly legal it was better than what they were doing. They were born to be on the open sea and they hated being stuck on dry land for so long. It the end there was no real choice to be made.

"Let us be off. I am sure there'll be a guard around 'ere sooner or later." Blaine was happy with the response.

Alaric finally relaxed and sheathed his sword. He was also glad that he didn't have to fight. He knew that times were tough for these men and they really didn't deserve to die. He would have some stern words with the rest of the council once they reached the island. It was very remiss of them to enforce such a law.

There was a new spring in the captain's step as they made their way towards his ship. Alaric noticed that he still held the bottle of rum in his hand, but he had not drunk any more since they had left his rundown shed. Alaric thought at least that was a promising sign. He didn't think it was a wise idea to sail with a drunken captain.

It wasn't long before they reached the birth of Blaine's ship, the *Windy Princess*. It was a four mast vessel and looked to be in good condition. Men could just be seen moving around on the deck when they arrived. All the lanterns had been extinguished to hide their movements. If anyone saw what they were doing then they would alert the night guard and their little escapade would be over.

"There she is, the *Windy Princess*, the finest boat on the water," Blaine said with a great amount of pride in his voice. "She is finally home again."

It was hard to gauge the true impression of the boat in the darkness although its silhouette looked impressive. Alaric wondered how something so large could sit up in the water. It didn't make any sense to him.

The three were given the guest cabin to share. Although it was not as nice as the captain's cabin it was a lot nicer than the sailors' quarters. Half a dozen hammocks hung around the walls. Alaric knew that they were for sleeping, but he wasn't quite sure how they worked. The ship swayed slightly as the tide started to shift and Alaric felt his stomach start to twinge.

"You don't look too well?" Eldred asked, a wry grin on his face.

"I don't know. The smell of the docks wasn't doing me any favours, but that has disappeared. I hope I am not coming down with something." It had been a long time since he had been sick and he didn't want to start now.

"I doubt that's it. Once you start using magic your immune system is all but impenetrable. The only way you can get sick is if someone injects the disease directly into your body." The smile had not left his face.

"What do you think it is then?" Alaric felt his stomach churn again as the boat suddenly lurched to the right.

"Seasickness." Eldred laughed, although he was the only one to see the joke.

"I thought you said…"

"It is not a disease," Eldred explained. "It is due to the motion of the boat when it is on the water. It is strange that it is having such an affect already. Normally it doesn't take hold until we set sail."

It didn't make a great deal of sense to Alaric, but he did know that if things continued it wouldn't be long before he saw his evening meal again. That thought in itself was almost enough to make him vomit. It took a lot of willpower to keep the contents of his stomach where it should be.

"I don't think this is going to be a pleasant experience for you." Eldred added.

When he finished speaking Eldred left the cabin. Alena said that she would remain to make sure Alaric was alright. Eldred wasn't sure if she was feeling the same. Elves were a land creature and very rarely took to the water, not even the rivers and streams that inhabited their lands. He wouldn't be surprised if Alena was also starting to feel seasick.

The main deck was full of action when Eldred arrived. The captain was standing by the wheel watching the action happening below him. In the dark it was hard to see, but it didn't stop him. Eldred made his way through the bustle until he reached him.

"How long until we sail?" Eldred kept his voice low.

"An hour at most. We are still set to beat the sun." Blaine didn't take his eyes from the scene in front of him.

"You are going to attempt the exit through the Mouth in the dark?"

The Mouth was a small outlet leading out of the bay around Shoretown. Normally a straightforward task during the day, but at night it was a completely different story. There wasn't much clearance on either side and a ship could easily run aground on the jagged rocks on the port side and on the sharp coral on the starboard. Only the most skilled of captains would attempt the Mouth at night and very few would succeed.

"There is little choice. If we wait until daylight then we have little chance of making it to the Mouth, let alone making it through. Since my last little voyage the Council ordered privateers to guard the bay and make sure that no one leaves. Of course this only happens during daylight hours. As you see we have no choice but to risk the Mouth at night." Blaine almost sounded excited as he explained things to Eldred.

Eldred wasn't happy with his excuse. He was sure there would be enough time if they were to leave on daybreak. On the other hand he didn't want to take the risk.

"Can you make it through the Mouth without light?" Eldred asked.

"There is a small beacon on the bow. That will give me enough light to see where I am going."

"Then won't the privateers see you?" Eldred asked.

"Yes, but by the time they realise what it is it will be too late. Once we are through the Mouth I doubt that they will follow."

Eldred didn't like the plan at all. Blaine was leaving far too much to chance. It was almost a better idea for Eldred to explain who he was, but that was still not preferable. There was a reason why the Council had disallowed ships to sail from Shoretown. It was as if they were deliberately trying to stop him from returning. Until he was sure of their motives he couldn't let too many people know who he was.

It was two hours before dawn when the *Windy Princess* was ready to set sail. Alena and Alaric had managed to get some sleep in the meantime, once they had figured out how to use the hammocks. Eldred had remained awake. As much as he would have liked to get some sleep he didn't want to risk being taken by surprise.

As the boat moved into action so too did Alaric. The jolt from the boat gave him such a shock that he fell from his hammock. He hit the floor hard before he knew what was happening. He looked up to see Alena standing before him.

"Are you alright?" She asked, a little amused.

"I'll be fine." He replied as he picked himself up. "What's happening?"

"I think we have set sail."

"Well at least it's not as bad as Eldred had said."

The rest had settled Alaric's stomach and he no longer felt like vomiting. He put his illness down to a lack of sleep. It seemed the most obvious reason.

"Let's go and watch from the deck," Alena suggested.

The night was still thick in the air as they reached the main deck. It was lit only enough for the sailors not to bump into each other as they moved around and they could see a light shining at the front of the boat.

They found Eldred leaning over the bow staring at the murky water below him. He was lost in thought when the others arrived. He didn't notice until they were standing right next to him.

"Good morning. I didn't think I would see you until the sun rose." Eldred greeted them.

"A little hard to sleep with all this movement," Alaric explained.

"I suppose it does take some time to get used to sleeping on a moving vessel." Eldred smiled.

Alaric brushed away the comment. The cobwebs of sleep were completely gone as he peered out in front of the ship, trying to see where they were going. The light from the beacon was only enough to light the water directly in front of them. Standing so close to the light made it impossible to see any further.

"How long will it take for us to reach the island?" Alaric asked.

"Normally it's a two or three day voyage, but I was hoping with your aid that we could make it by nightfall." Eldred kept his gaze on the water.

Alaric thought for a moment. He had never been on a ship before and had no idea how to speed their journey. He could try and shift it through the fabric of time, but the risk of them ending up on the bottom of the sea was too great. He had no idea how he had increased their travelling on land, let alone how to do it on water. He was curious to see what Eldred had in mind.

"We can increase the strength of the wind. That should significantly increase our speed and it shouldn't be too noticeable that we are tampering with things," Eldred explained.

That seemed to make sense to Alaric, although he was not completely sure it was the right thing to do. Too much wind and they could easily rip the sails from their masts. He felt as though there had to be a better option.

"I will see what I can do." Alaric drew in a small amount of energy.

"Not yet Alaric," Eldred did his best not to raise his voice. "We need to make sure we are through the Mouth before we go any faster, otherwise we will end up on the sea-bed."

The *Windy Princess* suddenly heaved to the left as the right side of the ship scraped across the bottom of the bay. The three were almost knocked off the bow as they tried to steady themselves. Curses could be heard from around the deck, but it wasn't long before Blaine had them back on track.

That was last time Blaine grounded the ship as they made their way through the Mouth. Luckily the little accident didn't make any holes in the hull. The only thing that it achieved was to make Alaric's stomach start to churn again.

The sun slowly started to rise as they passed through the Mouth. The opening was a lot smaller than Alaric had expected. There could be no more than a few hundred paces on either side of the ship and only half of that was navigable in a ship the size of the *Windy Princess*. Alaric was impressed at Blaine fortitude.

Chapter 19: On the open sea

The crossing didn't quite go to Eldred's plan. He had hoped he would have been able to use Alaric's skills to speed up the voyage, but it was not to be. Once the *Windy Princess* had left through the Mouth the wind picked up on its own accord. The water soon became choppy, causing the ship to sway and list. The added movement did nothing to calm Alaric's stomach, which had already started to churn again. There was no way he could create spells feeling the way he did. It didn't take long before Alaric was heaving over the side. He needed to be tethered to one of the masts to stop him from being hurled overboard.

Alaric wasn't the only one who was struggling with the rough conditions. Shortly after he started leaning over the side Alena had joined him. Eldred had to laugh at their plight, although on his first journey to the island he had felt the same way. He thought about increasing the wind by himself, but with the sea in such a condition he didn't think that it was wise.

They had not travelled far before dark storm clouds moved across the sun. Blaine screamed at the sky as he tried to keep control of his ship. He had remained at the helm after they had passed through the Mouth, although it was normally not his job. He was wishing he had passed the job over to the helmsman, but there was nothing he could do.

"This doesn't seem natural to me. The sea shouldn't be this rough this time of year and those storm clouds came in awfully fast," Blaine called out over the raging wind.

"I think I might know what is happening." Eldred returned.

He could feel the hand of magic involved in the weather as the rain started to fall. There had always been a certain amount of protection surrounding the island, but this was a little excessive. The spell was hindering anyone coming to or leaving the port. That was something that Eldred couldn't abide. He was going to need speak to his brothers and sisters. He felt as though they had overstepped their edict.

"So do I." Blaine replied, although he really had no idea.

Eldred moved to where Alaric and Alena where leaning against the side of the ship. It took great skill to walk across the deck with the ship heaving the way it was. It was clear that Alaric was going to be of no use to him and he doubted he would be able to counter the spell of the other wizards by himself. For the moment he would have to suffer through the weather like everyone else.

"What's happening?" Alaric's voice was weak from all the vomiting. Eldred strained to hear him over the storm.

"It seems as though the other wizards have set a trap for us."

"Why would they do that?"

The rain poured down and lightning crackled around them. The wind whipped around them making the situation even more unpleasant. Alaric wanted to just curl up and die. There was nothing he could do to get comfortable and Alena was in the same condition.

"I have no idea," Eldred yelled even louder as the storm intensified.

Alaric threw his head over the side of the ship in just enough time to not get any vomit on the deck. He had thought that he had emptied his stomach, but it seemed as though that was not the case.

"I see you are not well." Hanlon had been told to check on the guests, whilst Blaine still battled with the storm.

"Thank you for stating the obvious, is there something we can do for you?" Eldred spoke on the invalids' behalf.

"Blaine asked me see if you were alright, it seems as though he cares for some strange reason. I, myself, am more than happy to let you sit here and suffer." Hanlon didn't like Eldred's attitude.

"What can you do to help?' Alaric gasped for breath as he spoke.

"There is some medicine in the captain's cabin for seasickness. I just thought that you might appreciate some, but it seems as though you are fine." Hanlon turned to walk away.

"Wait!" Alena and Alaric cried out in unison.

"Come on then." Hanlon chuckled to himself as he made his way towards the cabin.

It took Alena and Alaric a lot longer to reach the cabin than Hanlon. They had to untie themselves from the mast and struggle across the deck. They were not used to travelling on a moving surface and they needed to be careful. A wrong step and they could end up flying overboard.

Once they arrived at the cabin Hanlon held two small glass vials. "Drink these and you should be fine in half an hour or so." His skill keeping his balance with the rocking ship impressed Alena and Alaric who had to sit down before they fell down. Luckily the chairs were nailed to the floor.

Neither of them waited for another offer before snatching the vials and downing the liquid. It took all of their willpower to keep the medicine in their stomach.

"Don't worry, it won't be long before you feel better... If you can keep it down." Hanlon laughed as he left the cabin.

Neither Alaric nor Alena wanted to move until the medicine started to take effect. The captain's cabin looked more comfortable than their own. A large double bed was nailed to the floor at the far end of the room. There was a desk as well as a table and the chairs they sat on. The bed was what held their attention. It looked so comfortable and the way they felt it looked even better.

"Do you think the captain will mind?" Alena asked the question they were both thinking.

"To hell with him," Alaric made the decision.

Even with the ship constantly heaving lying in the bed made them start to feel better. They were confident they would survive until the medicine worked. The only thing that worried them was the risk of vomiting in the captain's bed.

True to the first mate's word it took half an hour for the medicine to work. They remained in the captain's bed until they felt better. They were both thankful that Blaine remained at the helm whilst they used his cabin. As soon as they could, they returned to the deck.

"Are you feeling any better?" Eldred called over the storm.

If anything the weather had worsened since they had been in the cabin. Alaric couldn't believe it was the Council who had caused such terrible conditions. Now that he was feeling better he could sense the magic involved and he had to admit that it was the only reasonable excuse.

"Much, thank you. Now what do you say we do something about this terrible weather?" there was a cheerful tone to his voice, even though he had to yell.

Eldred tried to smile, but the wind whipped at his face making it impossible. He was glad that Alaric was back and there was a chance they could stop the storm. The spell would be powerful, but being so far from its origin meant it should be possible to break.

Alaric didn't wait for Eldred to start drawing in the energy around them. The feeling was different than anything he had felt before. He put it down to the sea water; it seemed a logical enough theory. It didn't take him long to find the end of the weave that he had been looking for. He had to admit that the spell was more complicated than he first thought.

"What are you doing?" Eldred asked.

"You will see in a moment," was all Alaric could say.

He tugged at one of the threads, but nothing happened. The spell was something he had not come up against before. He plucked at another thread and still nothing. It took him a moment, but then he realised why the spell wouldn't unravel. It had been created by five wizards, working together on a common goal. The threads were all intertwined, supporting each other when Alaric tried to unravel them.

"This is a complicated spell." Alaric yelled once he had given up on his original idea.

"That's why I need your help." Eldred called back.

"It would be a lot simpler if this storm wasn't raging around us."

"Yes, but that's kind of the point though," Eldred laughed.

"Do you have any idea how to break the spell?" Alaric asked.

"No, but we need to find the source of the spell. It should be easier to stop from there." At least Eldred hoped so.

Alaric scolded himself for not coming up with the idea himself. He had gone for the easy option when he should have thought about it. The start of the spell would be a lot easier to unravel than at the end. The problem was that he didn't know how to find the start. The weaves were so entrenched in each other that it would be impossible to follow one back to the beginning.

"How do we find the source?" Alaric called back.

"Try and concentrate. Try to let your mind wander," Eldred explained.

That was easier said than done with the ship moving so violently. It took most of Alaric's concentration to remain upright. He knew there would be a simple spell that would help him and before long his feet were anchored to the deck. The ship's rocking didn't seem to have any effect on him anymore and he wished that he had released the spell before the ship started moving. It would have stopped him from feeling so sick.

When he was sure he wasn't going to end up over the side, he was able to concentrate on the job at hand. He knew that Eldred had already started searching for the start of the spell and knowing the direction of the island would be a great advantage to him.

"I've found it! I will guide you..." Eldred called out.

Alaric didn't wait for Eldred to locate him. The start of the spell was a little more organised than that of the tail. All the threads were neat and ordered. Alaric didn't think it would be too hard to dispel it. He knew not to rush into action. There were likely to be traps along the line. The wizards would be prepared for his attack.

With no particular reason Alaric started plucking on the threads. The first snapped away with little effort, that was not what Alaric was expecting. He knew that it was more than likely a trap.

"You need to be careful. I have already sensed that there is trap somewhere within the spell. I am sure that there will be more."

Eldred was trying to be of some use, but he had to admit, if only to himself, that he had no idea how to stop the spell. The spell was created by five of his brethren and it would take more than one to dispel it, unless that one was Alaric. Eldred had no idea how he could do what he could do, but he guessed that was why he was the Chosen One.

Alaric continued to pick at the threads, carefully checking for traps. There were a few shock spells and fire spells, but they were easy enough to avoid. He was afraid that eventually there would be something more dangerous. The traps had only slowed an already laborious process.

After an hour had passed it was clear that Alaric was starting to struggle. Even with the rain beating down on top of him and the spray from the seawater it was obvious that he was sweating profusely. His skin was white and it didn't look as though he would remain conscious for long.

The storm had died down a little since he had started snapping the threads, but not enough to make the voyage any safer. It would lessen the weaker the spell became, but it would not dissipate until the spell was gone.

"You need rest Alaric!" Eldred called over the storm. "You can't finish by yourself."

Alaric ignored Eldred's words. Although his body didn't look well he didn't feel it. Whilst he was wrapped in the protection of the energy around him he would be fine. He knew that he could finish what he was doing. He was strong enough and Eldred's words only strengthened his resolve.

The distraction from Eldred didn't come at the best of times. Suddenly Alaric tugged on one of the threads and was suddenly sent flying across the deck until he stuck one of the masts. The blow knocked the wind out of his lungs, but it also saved him from being sent overboard. The movement of the ship now affected him again. The energy he had been holding instantly left this body and with it all he strength he had left.

"Are you alright?" Alena was the first to his side. No one else noticed as the crew were still struggling to control the ship.

"In a word… No." his voice was weak and only just audible.

"We need to get him off the deck?" Eldred said.

That was not as easy at is sounded. The steps to the lower deck were at the other end of the ship. It was hard enough walking by themselves without the added stress of carrying Alaric.

"This is stupid." Alaric called as he was dropped for the second time as the two tried to keep their balance.

"We don't have much choice. The crew are busy with the ship and we need to get you off the deck," Eldred explained.

"Go and get the Topaz stone!" Alaric yelled as best he could.

Eldred stared down at Alaric. It was not something he was expecting to hear. He wasn't sure if it would be a good idea. Alaric had battled with the Topaz stone before, and won, but Eldred was still not sure it was the right decision. The storm was more of an annoyance than a danger. He was confident that Blaine was a skilled enough captain to get them to the island.

"I think it would be better if you rested," Alena suggested.

"Just get me the stone." Alaric wasn't up for conversation.

Alena stayed with him to make sure he didn't roll off the ship. It was unlikely, but Alena didn't want to take the risk. One violent dip and Alaric could easily go flying over the side. It was also a good excuse to get close to him. The wind and rain whipped around them, but Alena didn't seem to notice. All she could see was Alaric.

It wasn't long before Eldred returned with the sceptre. He made sure that the velvet cover stayed over the Topaz stone whilst he was touching it. Contact with the stone was the last thing he wanted. He didn't want Alaric to have contact with the stone either, but there was little he could do.

Alaric forced himself to sit up when Eldred handed him the sceptre, Alena did her best to help. He stared at the velvet covering for a moment and despite the pouring rain it was completely dry. It was not something he wanted to do, but he knew that it was the only way he would be able to stop the storm. Slowly he undid the pull strings and removed the velvet cover.

A bright yellow light radiated from the stone when it was free of its bonds. It bathed Alaric and the deck around him in a warm glow. Instantly Alaric felt better and he returned to his feet. He knew that it wouldn't be long before the voice returned inside his head.

"I was wondering when I was going to see you again." The voice sounded somewhat annoyed. "I must admit that you have gone further than I thought without my help. Where are we going now?"

The question seemed odd. It was as if the stone wanted to have a general conversation with him. The question caught him so off guard that he answered it without thinking.

"Noooo!" the voice screamed in his mind. "You cannot take me there. You must turn around."

The sound in his mind caused him to drop to his knees in pain. Alena and Eldred watched in horror, not sure if there was anything they could do to help. Alena placed her hand on his shoulder and instantly a bolt of electricity shot threw her body. She was knocked backwards and crashed into the side of the ship.

"What's wrong?" Alaric spoke with his mind voice.

"The wizards' cannot be trusted. They have their own agenda. We shouldn't go there." The voice was convincing.

"I don't think they are going to do anything. I need them to complete my goal. I have a job for them to do," Alaric responded.

There was a moment of silence in Alaric's head. He felt as though the stone was thinking about his words. It wasn't quite so confident as it had been in the past.

"Hmmm… Well don't say that I didn't warn you." There was no confidence in the voice.

"Before you go."

"Yes."

"I need you to make sure that I don't lose the extra energy you have given me." Alaric thought it better to ask than to order the stone to help.

There was another moment of thought before the stone answered.

"Very well. I will help you this time, but don't be expecting it all the time." The stone started to shine even brighter before the light almost completely blinked out. "Now I want to go back to sleep."

Something very strange had happened. It was the first time that a stone had been happy to return to its velvet prison. Alaric returned the velvet cover and tucked the sceptre into his belt. It was time to get back to the job at hand.

"Are you alright?" Eldred asked.

"I haven't felt better in a long time."

There was something that Eldred didn't like about Alaric's new disposition. He didn't even notice that Alena was still lying against the side of the ship. He was focused on the distance, somewhere out in the storm.

It was time for him to finish unravelling the spell. He felt much more confident and quickly started to draw in the energy again. He felt even better with the power filling his body, it was like he had been born anew. He felt as though he could take on anything.

There was a disturbing expression on Alaric's face which made Eldred retreat to where Alena was slumped. She was conscious, but only just. He sat down and let her head rest against his shoulder. As much as he wanted to take her below deck, he didn't want to leave Alaric by himself. He wasn't sure what he could do, but he had to stay.

Alaric quickly found where he had left off. He saw things a lot clearer than he had before. He plucked at the weaves and they unravelled at his touch. The further he came to unravelling the spell the more traps he came across. With his new heightened senses he found them easily and quickly extinguished them.

It seemed to Alaric like it was only a few minutes, but in fact it took him two hours to completely finish what he was doing. When he was done his body was drenched in sweat, but the storm had subsided. This time he remained on his feet as if they were nailed to the deck. Although he was drained of energy he would not let himself collapse. He had succeeded and he was going to bask in his glory.

He looked around and was surprised to see it was late in the day. With the storm blocking the sun it was hard to gauge the exact time, but Alaric was sure that more time has passed than it should have. He looked around, but neither Eldred nor Alena were near him. In the end Eldred had decided that it was better if he made sure Alena was comfortable. It wasn't good for her to be out in the storm in her condition, she needed rest. He figured that Alaric knew what he was doing, or at least he hoped he did.

The crew were looking around in confusion. They couldn't figure out why the storm had stopped so suddenly. In the many years they had been at sea they had never seen anything like it. Alaric suddenly became very self-conscious when he realised that everyone was watching him. The exhaustion then suddenly got the better of him and he became weak at the knees.

Without speaking Alaric decided that it was time to rest. He was disturbed at the stone's warning of the wizards' intentions and he didn't want to be taken by surprise. He had a feeling he was going to need all the strength he could muster once they reached the island.

He found Eldred in their cabin. He looked around for Alena, but she was not there. He collapsed onto one of the hammocks before he spoke.

"Where's Alena?"

"She's resting in the captain's cabin. She was hurt quite badly," Eldred explained.

Alaric tried to remember, but he couldn't think of an occasion when she had been hurt. He assumed she must have been knocked off her feet by the ship when he was concentrating on the spell and decided not to push any further. It seemed a logical conclusion.

"And what about you Alaric, are you alright?"

"A little tired, but nothing a good night sleep isn't going to fix. I will be ready once we reach the island." There was something ominous in his words.

"Very well, you get some sleep. I will see what I can do to speed this journey along." Eldred ignored his concerns.

Eldred didn't wait around to see Alaric fall asleep. Now that the storm had been broken there was a lot of work for him to do. It was obvious that Alaric wasn't going to be any help until he had rested, which wasn't ideal. Like Alaric, Eldred too wanted to have all his wits once they reached Čarolija Island. It had been a long time since he had seen his brothers and sisters and the last time he left it had not been on such great terms. Although it was many years ago he was sure they had not forgotten.

His first port of call was to speak to the captain. It was the first time that Blaine had moved from the helm since they had started their journey and he looked as though he was beaten. Eldred didn't really want to give him the news that his bed was already taken and he was going to have to sleep with his crew.

"Do ye know anytin' 'bout tis storm?" Blaine didn't sound happy.

"It was a spell created to keep travellers away from the island. It has been taken care of." That was the only explanation that Eldred was going to give. "Are we still on course?"

"It is hard for me to tell. Won't know 'til nightfall and I can see the stars to truly gauge our location. In that storm we could 'ave been blown anywhere," Blaine explained.

"Very good." Eldred slapped him on the shoulder. "You look as though you need some rest. I suggest you get some sleep."

"That's a very fine idea." Blaine started to move off.

"Oh, but Alena is using your quarters. You will have to bunk with the crew," Eldred spoke quickly before walking away. He didn't want to speak any further on the matter.

Blaine turned around as the words sunk in, but Eldred had already left and he couldn't be bothered chasing after him. He was exhausted and all he could be bothered doing was sleeping and he really didn't care where it was.

Eldred was happy with the captain's response. There was still at least another two hours before nightfall. With any luck Eldred could have them closer to the island than anyone would have expected. Since no one knew where they were they would blame the storm for their extra distance and no one would ask any questions. On the other hand it would take Eldred a little time to find out where they were. There was no point speeding their journey if they were heading in the wrong direction.

To Eldred's surprise they were closer than he had thought. It seemed as though the storm had actually blown them closer to the island than if the weather had been clear. It didn't make any sense to him. There was no point in the wizards' creating a spell if it helped them find the island. He felt that Alaric had a hand in things, but he couldn't be sure. He knew that it was something that he was never going to get to the bottom of and he had more important matters to deal with. He needed to get them a lot closer before nightfall and he had little time to accomplish that.

Since they were waiting for the stars to direct them the captain had ordered the sails be lowered and their journey slowed as much as possible. This both helped and hindered Eldred's plans. The ship bobbed and swayed in the water which was much more pleasant than the violent thrashing of the storm. It was now much easier for him to concentrate on the job at hand. The other problem was that the crew would notice if the ship started moving at a faster pace, so not only would he have to increase their speed, but he would also have to change the crews' perception. That was not going to be an easy task.

Eldred took in a deep breath before he started drawing on the power around him. The first part of the spell was much harder than the second. He had to sense out everyone on board and change their perception one by one. On a rare occasion if there were two people in close proximity he could do them both at once.

When he was sure no one was going to notice his tampering Eldred pushed all his energy into moving the ship. Slowly at first the ship started to pick up speed. Eldred looked around to see if there was anyone who looked like they saw what he was doing. When he was comfortable they didn't, he continued with his spell until he was happy with the speed they were travelling. With a little luck he thought that they would be hitting the beach around lunchtime the next day.

Chapter 20: Isle of Wizards

It wasn't until early afternoon that they reached the southern beach. It had taken longer than Eldred had hoped, but it was still a much shorter journey than if he hadn't tampered with things.

Blaine had made the decision to take things easier. He eased the sails and kept them going at a restrained pace, much to Eldred's chagrin.

He was uncomfortable at the distance they had travelled, even though Eldred had tried to assure him that it was due to the storm. The explanation did nothing to ease his mind. He felt that the wizard's were drawing him nearer, although he couldn't fathom why.

No one was happier to be on dry land than Alaric. The potion for the sea-sickness had worn off by mid-morning and he was violently ill again. Alena had managed to gain her sea legs remarkably quickly. As Alaric ran his fingers through the sand on the beach, he thought it was the most natural feeling in his life. Although it was a new sensation it felt somewhat familiar, but he figured it was just the assurance of being on land again.

"Well I guess this is where we say our goodbyes." Blaine stood near the longboat on the beach.

"And how do you think we are going to get back to the mainland?" Eldred wasn't happy.

"But… I don't think them wizards are goin' to like me bein' here," Blaine blathered.

"Thanks okay, you go." Alaric sounded much better. "I think I will be able to work out something a little more pleasurable."

Eldred didn't like what he was hearing, but on the other hand Blaine was relieved. The captain wanted nothing more than to be on his way, although he didn't really know where he could go. If he went back to Shoretown then he would surely end up on the gallows. It had been a long time since he had been on the open seas and it seemed as though that would be his life for a long time. He was sure that he would be able to find some cargo needing to be transported somewhere.

Blaine didn't wait for Eldred to respond. He returned to the longboat and helped the other crew push it back out to sea. He was sure that given half a chance Eldred would have made them stay. He had pushed his luck enough and now it was time for him to get moving again.

"Are you sure that is a good idea?" Eldred asked.

"Too late now!" Alaric smiled. "I am sure between all of us we will be able to work our way back to the mainland."

Alaric's words did nothing to instil any confidence in the other two. He had no doubt that he would be able to get them all back and there was no way he was going to travel by boat. The experience had been enough for him to last a life time.

"I really think that it's time we get moving. I am sure that your friends are dying to meet us." There was an evil glint in his eyes.

Eldred simply shook his head and made his way up the beach. The residence of the wizards was in the middle of the island, about a two hour walk. There was no doubt that the wizards knew of their arrival. Eldred had not bothered trying to mask their presence. He knew the spell to make it possible, but figured it was not the right time to use it.

Alaric took a deep breath as he walked up the beach. There was something very familiar about the salty air. It smelt fresher than the air in Shoretown, almost as if it was cleaner. Alaric couldn't explain it, but he felt as though he was finally coming home.

The scent was familiar but that was all. There was nothing else about the Island that Alaric recognised. The sand on the beach was new to him. He had seen plenty of sand in the Southern Wasteland, but this was completely different. It was pure white and looked soft as snow. He wanted to kick his boots off, but decided against it. There was no time for frolicking.

The trees surrounding the beach looked strange to him. As they walked towards the small village Eldred explained that they were palm trees. A variety of strange looking fruit hung in the canopies. He didn't ask what they all were, he figured he would find out in due course.

As they continued towards the heart of the island more and more grass appeared underfoot. There was still the faint sign of sand, but not as much as on the beach. Alaric felt a slow peace pass over him as they neared their destination. He wasn't sure if it was the serenity of the Island or a subtle spell he had not been able to detect. He hoped that it was the former.

Alena was the first to notice the animals grazing around the land. Alaric recognised goats, cows and sheep, but there were also some animals that didn't look familiar. He asked Eldred what they were, but no response came. They were getting close to their destination and he didn't want to be taken off guard. He was still unsure of the reception he was going to receive.

"They know we are here!" Alaric said.

"What?"

"They know we are here. I can feel them scrying for us." He explained.

Eldred suddenly stopped. "What do you mean? I can't feel anything."

"Hard to say exactly, but I just know that someone was searching for us. I think they already knew we were coming, but they didn't know who we are, now they do."

Eldred didn't know whether he should feel relaxed or tense. He had been trying to figure out if they were looking for him, but he had not found any sign of a spell. It seemed as though Alaric had just *felt* the spell. It was getting scary how powerful Alaric was becoming. He knew that the other wizards' would not be happy. Eldred would have to be careful exactly how much information he gave them and he would have to warn the others to do the same.

"You need to be careful, both of you, with what you tell the others. Let's just say that they don't share the same views as I do with regards to the prophecy and the part you are to play. Some believe that you will become too powerful for your own good."

"And you are starting to believe them?" Alaric sounded defensive. He didn't like what Eldred was insinuating.

Eldred ignored the question and kept walking. He couldn't answer because he didn't know how to. He wanted to believe in him, he had spent most of his life believing in Alaric, but all of a sudden he was having doubts. Things were happening that he was not prepared for and that was something that always made him wary. He didn't want to give any response to Alaric's accusation until he was sure of what to say.

Alaric wasn't happy, but he continued nevertheless. He had noticed that Eldred wasn't as forthright with him as he would have liked, not that he had ever been that open. It almost seemed like Eldred was afraid to share any information with him. Alaric was beginning to think that he should take the prophecy back. There could be vital information that he was missing.

Suddenly Alaric's heart skipped a beat when he looked up and saw the back of a timber building in front of him. The building was raised three feet off the ground by long footings. Alaric couldn't imagine the sea level rising so much that they would be necessary, but he couldn't question the design.

"Here we are," there was a hint of pride in his voice. "This is my home."

When they reached the front of Eldred's house they could see there were seven buildings surrounding one central one. Each of the dwellings was made from materials from each of the wizards' home kingdoms.

Eldred's house was built from the timber from the Great Eastern Forest on the border of Hondin Lel and Avalon. The roof was made from thickly woven grass from the plains of Avalon. It was a simple design, but somewhat magnificent.

The building in the middle of the Wizard's village was much larger than the others. That was the meeting house and where Eldred was sure all the other Wizards would be gathered. It was the only building that had been constructed from materials on the island. The timber was cut from the many palm trees. Although it was called the meeting house it had many other purposes.

There were other buildings on the island, but they were separate from the main village. They housed the wizards' functionaries, those who prepared the food and cleaned the houses. There were also houses for novices and apprentices, but they had been vacant for many years. It would be one of those buildings that Alena and Alaric would be staying in, although in one sense Alaric had surpassed any apprentice who had ever studied at the Island, but on the other he was still as ignorant as a novice.

"What sort of reception do you think we are going to get?" Alena asked as they approached the meeting house.

"Hard to say. It has been a long time since I was here."

Eldred paused at the bottom of the stairs. A moment of loss and remorse passed over him. It had been too long since he had been home, but there was no time for self pity.

"Well, we were wondering how long it would take for you to join us," Drake spoke when they entered the meeting room.

Eldred looked around the room before he spoke. As soon as he walked in he knew that something wasn't right. There was a tension in the air that was obvious to everyone. It didn't take long before his eyes fell on Minerva and Brielle and he was quick to realise the situation.

"It seems as though I have come at just the right time," there was no humour in his voice.

"I would say that is an understatement. Can you please tell these fools, that time is running out and I need to return to Castalia," Minerva spoke abruptly.

"Please Minerva, calm yourself," Gwydion spoke softly. "There is still time left for us."

"You have spoken far too much over these past few days," Brielle snapped.

"I have plenty more to say," there was more to Minerva's words than what was spoken.

Alaric was trying to understand the scene before him. He was glad to see that Minerva had made it safely from Castalia, but things were not as they should be. He needed to be careful with the information that he had if he was going to get the wizards to do what he wanted.

"So I see that nothing had changed since I left," Eldred's voice was thick with disgust.

"Please, Eldred, have a seat and introduce us to your friends." Gwydion was the voice of reason.

Eldred did as he was told. He figured that it would be easier if he moved on. There was no point in fuelling the flames of their argument. There would be enough time for that later. For the moment he needed to get everyone on board.

"This is Alena, Orric's daughter of Elhjem and this is Alaric, The Chosen One."

There was a mixed response from around the room. There were still those who doubted the legitimacy of the prophecy and the players within it. Eldred knew they weren't going to receive a warm welcome.

"Why is it you have brought this *Elf* to our island? You know the rules," Brielle's voice dripped with venom.

"So, what is it that should make us believe that this is the Chosen One, my brother?" Ulman barked, ignoring Brielle's comment.

Brielle opened her mouth to re-ask her question, but Eldred spoke before she had a chance. She didn't like being ignored and her disapproval was clearly written across her face. She would wait, but she would not be brushed aside so easily.

"He has done things that would amaze all of you. His strength is far beyond what any of you can comprehend. You cannot still doubt the validity of the prophecy," Eldred explained.

"There is still much that we don't understand." Gwydion said. "We cannot rush to a decision that will affect the entire Seven Kingdoms."

"And what do you know of the Seven Kingdoms?" It was rhetorical question "You have already taken too long to make your decision. Minerva will tell you. She has, at least, been outside of the Island in the last hundred years, albeit only for a short time." Eldred's words would bring offence, but there was no time to stand on ceremony.

"That's right. I have been trying to tell you that we can no longer sit in our isolation. It is time we return to the mainland and lend our strength to their cause," Minerva added.

Her words earned her a strike across her face from Brielle. None of the newcomers could believe what they were seeing. They knew something was wrong when they entered the room, but they had no idea how bad things were. To make matters worse Minerva did nothing to defend herself.

"What is this all about?" Eldred demanded.

"That is enough Brielle!" Drake scolded.

"What have we told you about striking Minerva?" Althea added.

"I am sorry, but she has been warned." There was no sincerity to Brielle's apology.

"Would someone please tell me what is happening here?" Eldred was at a loss. He couldn't work out where things had gone so wrong.

Alaric was watching everyone closely. There was definitely something underlying in the conversation and not just between Minerva and Brielle. There was a subtle spell in the air. He had not noticed it when he had entered the room because the entire island was shrouded in magic. When he took his time he was able to feel something that he had missed before. He didn't know exactly what the spell was, but he was sure that it had something to do with Minerva.

"We have instructed Minerva, as we will instruct you, to remain on the Island until we have made a decision on our next course of action," Gwydion explained.

"That is an outrage!" Eldred slammed his fist on the table and stood.

Suddenly there was a shift in the air. Before anyone had a chance to react Eldred was forced back into his seat. Alaric realised that with the magic aura surrounding them it was very hard to pick up on new spells. There was no way he would have been taken by surprise if it wasn't there. He half lifted himself out of the chair to see if he too was trapped, but found that for the moment he was still free to move.

"What is the meaning of this?" Eldred glared around the table.

"I am sorry brother, but we feel as though it is necessary. We can't have any rash decisions being made. The only way to be sure we are making the right decision is through contemplation." The words seemed odd coming out of Ulman's mouth.

"I demand that you let me go!" Eldred boomed.

"You can scream all you like, I did, but it will do you no good." Minerva forced a smile.

Alaric thought about searching for the spell, but decided against it. There was something happening and he needed more information before he reacted. He didn't want to get the other wizards offside, at least not yet. There was still a little time before they had to leave.

"Please, you must relax Eldred." Althea tired to soothe him.

"Now you can tell me what you are doing bringing an *Elf* here. You know our rules," Brielle finally had her chance to get an answer.

"She is here because I brought her. She is my guest and you will treat her as such for as long as we are here," Alaric said, raising his voice as he went.

"Who do you think you are to speak unbidden?" Brielle sneered.

"I am Alaric and I am here because I am the Chosen One. Whether you want to believe it or not it doesn't change the fact." Alaric remained calm. "I will be treated as an equal as will Alena. We are not here to beg for your approval, you can be sure of that." Alaric wanted to make sure that he didn't give too much away.

"You will be treated like any other visitors to this island and that is to say…" Brielle wasn't allowed to finish her rant.

"We will do what we can to make your stay comfortable." Drake finished her sentence.

Alaric didn't really know what that meant. He was sure it wasn't the answer he was looking for, but at least it was civil. Eldred was trying to calm himself, but it wasn't working. He knew that he wasn't going to be welcomed back with open arms, but he couldn't believe they would do such a thing. It was against the Council rules to detain a member of the Council or prevent them from practising magic.

"I think that you have had a long journey and you should rest for a while. It is not a pleasant voyage across the sea." Gwydion suggested, although it wasn't really a suggestion.

"And where might I be residing now?" Eldred spoke through clenched teeth.

"Your house has been kept for you. It is clean and ready for your return," Ulman explained. "Things have changed around here, but you are still part of the Council."

Eldred wasn't impressed with the response, yet there was no response that would have appeased him. He was surprised with Alaric's attitude and knew that he could break the spell. He couldn't work out why he hadn't, but he had to accept that he knew what he was doing.

"Yes, I guess you're right. Things will look much better after we have eaten, bathed and had a chance to rest." It was obvious that he didn't believe his own words.

Eldred stood again, this time he was not hindered. Alena also rose, but Alaric remained seated.

"Is there something else Alaric?" Althea asked.

"No, I was just thinking. Everything is fine. We will get some rest and then return a little later in the day. Would someone kindly show me to where we will be staying?" he looked at Minerva as he spoke.

"That is fine. I will show you where to go," Brielle said quickly before Minerva had the chance.

It didn't seem like it to anyone else, but Alaric had won a small battle. He had managed to get the Council to speak to him and also managed to get one of them alone. He would have preferred to speak with Minerva, but anyone would be suitable. He wasn't sure how much information he could gather from Brielle, but it was better than nothing.

"So what is happening here?" Alaric asked as they left the common room.

"What do you mean?" Brielle spoke surprisingly softly. She was taken aback by the question.

"It seems as though everything is falling apart. You have been holding Minerva prisoner and it seems that you want to do the same with Eldred. I am sure that this is not the way you normally treat people on the Island."

Brielle didn't know what to say. It was clearly written on her face that she wasn't happy with Alaric's accusations. She opened her mouth to speak, but then thought better of it. She was still unsure about him. She had never really believed that he was the Chosen One, or that there even was a Chosen One. When Nyrra returned, the seven of them would put an end to his mayhem.

"It is none of your business what we do here. Our judgment is final. You are not even a wizard. You're lucky we don't put you in the gaol." Brielle sneered.

"I would really like to see you…"

"We are grateful for your hospitality," Alena interrupted.

Alaric wasn't happy with Alena, but he had to admit there was little point in upsetting Brielle so soon. There would be plenty of time for him to open their eyes, but he would have to do it very carefully. One wrong move and he risked losing their support and that was something that he couldn't afford.

Brielle looked at Alaric, waiting for an apology, but none was forthcoming. She frowned as they reached their destination. There were a number of small huts not far from the wizards' houses. There were no guest houses, just those for the worker's and the trainees. Fortunately there were no apprentices on the island, leaving a number of huts free.

"You will be staying here. Your food will be brought to you. If you want anything washed leave it at the front door. For the moment you will need to stay inside. Don't go wandering around the island." Brielle spoke as if she was speaking to a novice.

Alaric didn't like the tone of her voice, but he let it slide. He knew that he needed some rest. He was still feeling a buzz from the Topaz's energy, but he knew that wasn't the same as a good night sleep. He knew that he had some time up his sleeve and it was the first time in a long time.

"This is a little small," Alena said when they were inside.

The hut they were in was reserved for the head novice. The other novices were required to share a hut of similar size with three or four others. The only advantage with being the head novice was having a room to themselves. Beside a small bed was a small table and one chair. It was not suitable for two people to reside. Alaric was giving some serious thought to returning to common room.

"I guess we will just have to make the best of it." Alena continued when Alaric didn't respond.

"What? Oh… Yes… I will have a word to the wizards if you like."

"No, this is fine." There was a strange expression on Alena's face as she spoke.

Alaric wasn't sure exactly what it meant until she suddenly launched herself at him. Alaric took a step back to brace himself as she wrapped her arms around him. Without waiting for permission she pressed her lips against his. At first Alaric didn't know what to do, but it didn't take long for him to remember.

The kiss seemed to last for an eternity before Alena finally pulled her head back, keeping her arms firmly wrapped around him. She looked at Alaric with a large smile on her face as he blushed slightly. It had not been what he was expecting, but the kiss brought back some good memories.

"Why did you do that?" Alaric stammered.

"I have been waiting to do that for a long time." It was Alena's turn to blush. She slowly let him go and took a step back. Alaric suddenly wished that he had not said anything. "I am sorry… I didn't mean…"

Alaric didn't wait for her to finish her statement. Although his mind had been too preoccupied to think of such things it was now all he could think about. He moved to her side and scooped her up in his powerful arms. Alena squeaked in surprise before wrapping her arms around his neck. The smile returned to her face. Alaric thought she looked more beautiful than she ever had been.

The bed, although it looked small, was surprisingly accommodating. Soon all of Alaric's worries washed away and it was like he was in another world. All the troubles that had been plaguing him were suddenly washed away and for a moment he was truly happy.

Although it had not taken long he had managed to cover both himself and Alena in sweat. He lay back and looked around the room for a place to bathe. He wasn't surprised to see that there was no water or tub. Suddenly there came a knock on the door. They looked at each other, not sure how to react. It wasn't what they had done anything wrong, but they suddenly felt very self-conscious.

The knock came again and Alaric got out of bed, wrapped a small towel around his waist and opened the door. Standing on the other side was a nervous looking woman. Alaric guessed that she would be no older than fifteen, but he couldn't be sure. Her features were like nothing like he had ever seen before. Her face was round and her skin had a slight yellow tinge underneath a sun-bronzed tan. It looked a touch leathery, but soft at the same time. She had long blonde hair that fell around her breasts and she wore a soft, lace dress with no design on it. In her arms she carried a large platter of food.

"I was instructed to bring you some food." She did her best to curtsy, but it was awkward under the weight of the platter.

She moved into the room without being instructed and carefully placed it on the table. Once she was done she turned and quickly moved to leave. Before she was out the door Alaric spoke.

"I would appreciate it if you could bring us some water to bathe. It has been a long journey and we need to clean ourselves." Alaric blushed slightly at the half-lie

"Of course, and if you need something else you know what to… Oh. Sorry I forgot that you are not a wizard." She left before Alaric could respond.

Alaric wasn't sure what to make of the comment. When she was gone Alaric returned to the bed where Alena was still lying. This time he realised how small the bed truly was. It would not be easy for them to both sleep at the same time, but for the moment he didn't mind the forced closeness.

"So what do you think is going on around here?" Alena asked as she lay in his arms.

"I don't know, but what I do know is that things aren't right. There is something seriously wrong with the wizards. It is almost like they can't see what is right in front of them. Still there is nothing we can do about it for the moment."

Alaric gently moved her head from his shoulder and moved to the table. He was suddenly very hungry and the smell of fresh fruit and spiced meat was irresistible. Alena rested her head on her palm as she watched him eat. She couldn't believe how far she had gone. She had to admit that she didn't think that she was ever going to make it out of the dungeon in Jarrat.

"You should eat something, this food is good." Alaric didn't recognise any of the fruit on the platter, but it all tasted wonderful.

"I will shortly," she cooed.

It was going to be a fun afternoon and for the moment they could both forget where they were and why they were there.

   ***

"What do you think of Alaric?" Gwydion asked the remaining wizards when Alaric, Alena, Brielle and Eldred had left the room.

"I can sense no real strength in him," Althea replied. "If he was as strong as Eldred claimed I would have been able to feel something, and I couldn't. Whoever he is he has mediocre strength at best."

"I agree, I couldn't sense anything from him," Ulman added. "He is physically strong, but that is about all I can say for him."

"I don't think you should all be so rash to judge." Drake spoke calmly.

"You know something, don't you?" Althea accused.

Drake shook his head. "I just know that I have been around long enough to know not to believe everything at face value."

"You know as well as we all do that if we can't sense the power then it's not there." Ulman returned.

Gwydion watched and listened to the conversation carefully. He smiled when he realised what Drake was thinking. If it was true then things were much worse than he thought, but on the other hand it also gave them a fair advantage.

"There is another reason." Drake wasn't going to just give the answer away.

The others thought, but couldn't come up with an answer. They had already made their decision that Alaric wasn't the Chosen One, if in fact the Chosen One actually existed. There was no other explanation they could come up with and therefore didn't believe that another answer existed.

"Just tell us what you're thinking!" Althea spoke harshly.

Drake sighed. "For one moment I wish we could see outside of our own beliefs." It was as much a dig at himself as it was at the others. "For a moment we have to think about the consequences. There is a chance that we can't feel Alaric's power because he is blocking us…"

There was a long silence as the news sunk in. Althea and Ulman couldn't believe what they were hearing, although they knew it was very good reasoning. They had not come to the conclusion on their own because the idea was extremely scary. They had been studying the effects of magic for a long time and for someone so young to be more powerful with little to no training was unthinkable.

"I have seen him do things that I can't explain," Minerva finally spoke, although he wasn't sure the others really cared what she had to say.

There was not going to be an answer until they were able to speak with Alaric again and that wouldn't happen until the next day. In the meantime they would all return to their own houses to reflect on what had happened.

Chapter 21: Revelations

Alaric wasn't going to wait to be invited to leave the hut the next morning. At first he was happy to be sleeping so close to Alena, but as the night wore on it became frustrating. There wasn't enough room in the bed for them both to spread out comfortably. One of them had to squeeze in to allow the other to be relaxed and for most of the night it was Alena who got the most room. Their living conditions were unacceptable. It wasn't so much the room they had been given, he had slept in worse, it was the lack of respect it showed. It was obvious to him that the wizards had no respect, not that he was really expecting anything less. It was time for them to understand that he was no novice or whatever else it was they thought of him.

"Do you want me to come with you?" Alena asked from the bed.

"No, you relax. I think it will be better if I do this on my own," Alaric smiled as he replied.

He wished he could have stayed with Alena. All his worries had washed away the day before when there was just the two of them. The light of day brought everything back. He had a lot to do if he was going to convince the other wizards that it was their time to help.

"What should I do? I don't want to stay in this small hut all day," she was somewhat sulky.

"Go for a wander around the island. I am sure there is plenty to see." He wasn't sure if that was true.

"But what about the Wizards?"

"Let me worry about them. You just enjoy yourself. Once we leave here I don't think that we will have another opportunity to relax." With that Alaric left the hut.

The sun was shining brightly outside and the morning was already growing hot. Alaric had stopped using the spell to control his body temperature. He didn't want to give the wizards any clues to his abilities, although it was one of the weakest spells he knew. He walked with his shirt open and his sleeves rolled up, for some reason he felt as though it was appropriate. There was a subtle cool breeze that felt good against his skin.

The scent of salt water filled his nose as he walked towards the main building. There was something very refreshing about it. It was the first time Alaric could ever remember actually being relaxed. The only problem was that he knew it was all about to change. Once he reached the Council it would be all over again, but he would enjoy the walk while he had the chance.

Alaric knew his reception would not be a welcome one when he reached the Council, but it was the best way to announce himself. He was relying on the fact that they would try and restrain him. That would be the first time they realised he wasn't who they thought he was.

The five wizards were sitting around the table when Alaric arrived. He wasn't surprised to see that both Eldred and Minerva were missing. The others didn't look happy to see him. Alaric thought it would be better if he spoke first, he didn't want to give them a chance to get on the front foot. If he was going to achieve his goal then everything would have to go to plan.

"Good morning all, I trust you all slept well last night." It was a pleasant greeting, but designed to infuriate the wizards. He knew they would not like his casual attitude.

"I believe that you were told to stay in your room until we called for you," Brielle snapped.

It was at that moment that Alaric noticed the extra magic in the air. He knew that his suspicions were coming true, but he was prepared. Soon enough he felt someone reaching out for him. The spell wanted to wrap him so tight that he couldn't move, but Alaric protected himself. The spell itself was a weak one, showing how little the Council thought of him. If they had tried harder than they would have been able to trap him. Alaric quickly realised that it was Ulman who had created the spell. He wanted to retaliate, but that would hinder what he was trying to achieve.

"Please, that is no way to treat a guest." Alaric helped himself to a chair when he finished.

"Just what do you think you are doing?" Gwydion was aghast.

"We have a standing tradition that you have just broken. No one outside of the Council is allowed to sit around this table." Althea said as she looked at the few chairs around the outside of the room.

Alaric could have chosen to sit in any of those chairs, but to prove his point he didn't. They needed to learn that they were no longer in the past. The rules they once lived by were no longer applicable and it was Alaric's job to make them see what they were missing.

"Well, I guess there is nothing I can do about now," there was a smugness in his voice. "It is now time for us to move on."

"This is not time to move on. We will make all the decisions. We will be the ones who decide the fate of the Seven Kingdoms," Althea was babbling.

"I think it is time for us to listen," Drake spoke for the first time since Alaric arrived. "We have been too narrow-minded for too long."

"Do you wish to sit in contemplation with Eldred and Minerva?" Brielle asked.

"When will you stop Brielle?" Drake remained calm. "When we are all in 'contemplation', as you like to call it."

"It is contemplation." Brielle objected.

"You can call it whatever you like Brielle, it isn't going to change the fact that we have imprisoned them."

Alaric smiled as he listed to the conversation. He was slowly starting to have the impact that he wanted. For the moment he was happy to let them come up with their own realisations. It would make things so much easier if they did.

"We have never and would never imprison our own. That is not what this council is about," Brielle retorted.

"Think about it for a moment," Althea sounded defeated. "You have to admit he's right. We have imprisoned our own and this is unforgivable."

"But there is a reason why they are in contemplation." Brielle wouldn't give up. "They have tried to subvert our command. Errr... I mean our decision."

"It is over Brielle." Gwydion had also come to the realisation. "We have done the wrong thing and now we need to make up for it."

Brielle stood from the table and stormed out. She knew that she had spoken poorly, but she would not back down. She left more from embarrassment than anything else.

"Hold, Ulman!" Drake could sense the spell he was preparing. "We can't make an error to correct one."

"How are we supposed to free the others? Brielle was the one who created the spell. You all know that Council rules dictate we cannot break anyone else's spell." Ulman wasn't happy.

"I am sure she will come around eventually," Gwydion said.

"If it helps, I could break the spell for you," Alaric offered.

Everyone had forgotten his presence. They all turned and looked at him when he spoke. They had confused expressions on their faces. They weren't quite sure what he meant. They were all sure that he couldn't break a spell that one of them had created. None of them realised that Alaric had broken the spell to create the storm, they had just presumed it was Eldred who had broken the rules.

"And what pray tell will you do?" Ulman accused. "Do you think that you could break a spell that one of us created? I have seen it all from our apprentices and novices, but this arrogance is something different. Who do you think you are?"

Alaric kept the arrogant smile on his face. He had made a conscious decision to portray that image. He figured it was the best way to keep the wizards thinking. If he simply submitted then he would achieve nothing.

"I am the Chosen One and if you think that comes lightly then you are all grossly mistaken. If you would like for me to demonstrate I would be more than happy to."

No one knew what to say. As much as they didn't believe that he could break the spells Brielle had created they also didn't want to be proven wrong. No one wanted to make the call. They sat uncomfortably waiting for someone else to speak.

"We can sit here all day, but that is going to get us nowhere. Now if you don't mind I would like Eldred and Minerva to join us. We have much to discuss," Alaric snapped

There was an uncomfortable silence as they tried desperately to decide what the best plan of action was. No one wanted to agree to Alaric's suggestion, but in order to refute him they had to come up with something better. No one knew what to say. Eventually it was Gwydion who spoke.

"We will have Minerva and Eldred brought here, but they will remain in their so called chains." It seemed like a fair compromise.

Although it was a small victory it wasn't enough for Alaric. He wasn't going to accept anything less than what he wanted. He had the upper hand and was not going to relinquish it so easily.

"That is not enough," Alaric snapped, surprising everyone. "You will release the two or I will release them for you."

When he finished speaking he felt more than one of them probing. He increased the power of his shield, just to be on the safe side. The last thing he needed was to allow himself to be imprisoned. If that happened there was little chance he would be able to achieve his goal.

"I would suggest you stop doing that." He looked at all of them. "I might just lose my patience and that is something you don't won't."

There was something in the threat that made the others take pause again. Things weren't working out quite as they thought they would. In fact it was nothing like they thought. They figured that Alaric would be Eldred's submissive pet and that they would soon realise he was not the Chosen One.

"Very well, I assume by your lack of response that you are happy for me to remove the spell?" it was more of statement than a question.

Again there was no response. Alaric had hoped they would say something. He really didn't want to break their rules, but it seemed as though he didn't have a choice. He needed to show them he was serious and that would only happen if he followed through with his threats.

It would have been easier if he had waited for Eldred and Minerva to arrive, but he didn't want to. He had to be decisive to prove his strength. He had wanted to take baby steps and not overwhelm the others, but that was getting him nowhere.

The energy around him was clean as he drew it in. There was something very refreshing about it. It was almost like it was the purest form of energy in the world. Alaric wanted to savour the moment, but he knew he had to continue. First he sought out Eldred. He was making his way to the common room. The spell was surprisingly complicated, but it didn't take Alaric long to unravel it. He did so carefully as not to bring pain to Brielle. It wasn't that she didn't deserve it, he just didn't want to let her know what he was doing.

When he had finished with Eldred he moved on to Minerva. He found her still in her house. There was something very different about the spell that surrounded her. It had been there for longer than Eldred's and had lost some of its potency making it much easier to free her.

"So are you going to wait for them to arrive? Is that your idea?" Ulman scoffed.

Alaric had to smile to himself. They had no idea what he had just achieved and that would hold in his favour. They would all be surprised when they realised he had already broken the spells. It was another step in the right direction. Alaric just kept his mouth shut knowing that Eldred would be joining them shortly to prove his point.

"So it seems as though you have come to your senses!" Eldred didn't wait for greetings as he entered the room.

"What are you talking about Eldred?" Gwydion asked.

All Alaric did was smile. He was going to wait for them to come to their own conclusions again.

Eldred looked around the group in confusion. When he realised that Brielle wasn't there, it slowly started to dawn on him what had happened. He wasn't sure why Alaric had not explained the situation, so he wasn't going to reveal the surprise.

"Why is it that you have called me here?" He changed the subject.

"It is time to discuss the future," Althea said.

Before anyone had a chance to speak further Minerva stormed into the room. There was a look of rage on her face and Alaric could tell she was holding a great deal of power. It was something that he had not been expecting and all he could do was hope she wasn't going to do anything rash.

"So it takes a stranger to the island to finally do the right thing!" Minerva knew who had freed her. "What do you all have to say for yourselves?"

"What are you talking about?" Drake asked.

It took a moment for the other wizards to realise she was holding onto so much energy. Once they realised they knew what had to have happened. No one wanted to believe that Alaric had been able achieve such a feat without them noticing. They were slowly starting to understand, but it was just the beginning.

"What I am talking about is my imprisonment. I am just wondering how long you were planning on keeping me prisoner if Alaric had not set me free?"

"You were never a prisoner. We just had to make sure that you didn't leave," Althea tried her best to explain.

A sudden slapping sound could be heard and Althea's head flew back and to the right. Her hand quickly rubbed the left side of her face. Minerva's face softened for a moment and Alaric almost thought he saw the start of a smile before it hardened again.

"Would anyone else care to placate me?"

"No one is placating you." Ulman also received the same treatment after he spoke.

"Something is happening and we are not quite sure what it is. I am sure that you and Eldred might be able to shed some light on it." Drake took the risk.

"You could wake up and see what is happening around you." Minerva spared Drake the same punishment as the others. "Things are happening that we didn't expect and if you don't listen to what we have to say then everything will be completely destroyed before you even realise. It won't take too long for the Evil One to come here once he has conquered the Seven Kingdoms."

It was the first time she had been a given a chance to speak freely since she had returned from Castalia. She didn't know which words she should get out first.

"I am sure that things aren't that bad." Althea couldn't believe what she had heard. She simply looked at Alaric and Eldred. Alaric didn't respond and Eldred simply nodded.

"This is only the tip of the iceberg," Alaric said. "Much has happened and there is still plenty to do."

No one mentioned anything about Alaric speaking out of turn and that forced him to smile. He placed his hand up to his mouth to hide the fact. The last thing he needed was for the wizards to think that he was becoming arrogant. He was slowly starting to get them to come around and he didn't want to do anything to ruin it.

"So what do you expect us to do?" Ulman asked the table. He didn't want to directly ask Alaric the question.

"We need to fight!" Eldred responded. "We can no longer sit on our island and ignore the world around us." He used the word 'we', but it was obvious he was talking about the six other wizards.

"Our place is fading." Gwydion spoke the words that no one wanted to say. They had been avoiding telling Minerva and Eldred, it was something they wanted to discuss between all seven on the council.

"What are you talking about?" Eldred sounded confused.

"This is why we haven't left the island," Ulman's tone had dropped. "There is a problem with the Seven Kingdoms and our place in it."

"This doesn't make any sense. You need to explain yourself better," Eldred snapped.

"I think we should wait for Brielle to join us before we go any further." Gwydion suggested, looking at Alaric as he spoke. "I think it would be best if Alaric wasn't here."

"There is nothing we can say that he will not hear. It will be better if we listen to his input," Eldred returned.

"Then I think we should send for Brielle," Alaric suggested.

As if on cue the door opened and Brielle stormed in dragging a half-naked Alena with her. There was a wild look on her face only overshadowed by the expression on Alena's. Alaric's initial reaction was to jump out of his seat, but he thought better of it, he could sense she was holding a held a great amount of energy.

"Look who I found frolicking on the beach?" Brielle was almost foaming at the mouth.

She shoved Alena into the room. Her body was strangely stiff and it took Alaric a moment to realise what had happened. When he did he started to fill with range and instantly let a flow of energy fill his body without thinking about the consequences.

"Just what do you think you are doing?" Alaric stood as he screamed.

"You were told not to go wandering around the island. We have strict rules and they need to be adhered to." Brielle had not noticed the change in the room. All she could see was her own superiority.

"You do not give me orders," Alaric spoke between clenched teeth. "Release her now!"

Brielle had no idea of the danger before her. She didn't realise that Alaric was holding an immense amount of power. He could have easily brought the building down around them and if he wasn't careful there was a good chance that he would.

"I will not…" Was all that Brielle could get out before she was sent flying across the room, the blow knocking the wind out of her. What happened next was much more painful. Alaric stripped away the spell that held Alena causing a great deal of pain to the creator. If Brielle had been able to breathe then she would have been gasping for breath. In the end her lungs just started working again before she lost consciousness.

When she came to, Brielle couldn't believe what had happened. She looked at the other wizards assuming that one of them had broken her spell. It didn't take too long for her to realise who did it and that did nothing to calm her nerves.

"Who do you think you are to do that to me?" she snapped.

Alaric was in no mood. Once Alena had been released she moved to Alaric's side, who in turn helped her into a chair. He needed to concentrate if he was going to truly teach Brielle a lesson.

"I am one of the Council of Wizards and it looks as though it is time for me to teach you some manners," Brielle barked.

It wasn't the time that Alaric had wanted to prove his dominance, but he had been forced into it. It was clear that Brielle was going to try and test his abilities. The fact that she thought she was so much stronger was going to make things a lot easier for him.

Brielle tried to wrap Alaric in the same spell she had kept Alena. It was a weak spell and Alaric easily deflected it. It would have been the perfect time to retaliate, but that would not prove the point he was trying to make. He could sense that the other wizards had also taken the opportunity to draw in more energy. Alaric didn't think that they would join in the fight, but he had to be prepared for it.

When it was clear that Alaric was not going to be trapped Brielle stepped up the pace. Her next attack was a volley of invisible punches. Alaric simply placed an invisible wall between himself and her attack. It wasn't long before Brielle realised her efforts were futile.

A droplet of sweat appeared on Brielle's brow, which brought a smile to his face. She was not going to stop there. She had forgotten what they were fighting about, but that didn't matter. All she knew was that she had to teach this upstart a lesson and she couldn't stop until she reached that goal.

Her next attack was a little more visual. Without thought she created a small ball of light and threw it towards him. The ball crackled as it flew through the air, but Alaric simply raised his hand as it neared him and the ball blinked out of existence. It was time for Alaric to put an end to the battle.

Before Brielle knew what was happening she felt a strong pressure against her skin. It felt as though her entire body was being squeezed. Once the sensation stabilised Alaric lifted her a foot off the ground. There was nothing she could do to defend herself. She fought to draw in more power, but Alaric had cut her off. She could feel the energy around her, but there was nothing she could do to harness it.

"Now I think it would be time for us to have a little chat." There was no strain to his voice. That in itself surprised Brielle.

The wizard looked around the room for support from her brethren, but it didn't seem as though any of the wizards wanted to help. In the end, for the sake of bringing the stand-off to a close, Drake decided to step in. He sent a small spell Alaric's way, more so to distract him than to do any real harm. It didn't have the desired effect.

Alaric swung his arm around until his palm pointed at Drake. He quickly had the wizard wrapped up in the same spell that still held Brielle. Drake had no idea what had hit him. Not only did his spell have no effect on Alaric he was now a prisoner himself. He didn't know how he could have been so stupid. It was a novice mistake to get caught in the same trap. What he couldn't understand was how Alaric could hold both spells and not be suffering a huge strain. To look at him he was as calm as if he was on a sunny afternoon walk.

"Now I wouldn't advise anyone else to jump in. I can do this all day, but I can't guarantee that my spells will hold their integrity. For those who don't know what that means I could potentially suffocate one of you accidentally." Alaric smiled as he spoke.

At first no one knew what to say. Even Eldred was surprised at what he was doing. He knew that Alaric was growing stronger, but he couldn't believe the rate it was happening. It seemed as though he had completely lost track of Alaric's abilities.

"Enough!" Brielle could only just be heard. "Enough!"

Alaric released Drake first, but he held Brielle for a moment longer before letting her go. There was something about her that didn't sit right with him. She was definitely going to be the hardest to get to see reason, but that wasn't going to dissuade him.

"This isn't the way I wanted things to happen, but you gave me no choice." Alaric smiled. "Now if you would like to take a seat we can continue."

Brielle didn't want to do what Alaric said, but the expression on his face worried her. The pain and embarrassment was still thick in her mind and would be for a long time. She would have to bide her time if she was going to get her revenge.

"What were you saying Gwydion?" Alaric said when they were all seated.

Brielle looked around the table wildly. She knew that something important had happened and it was something that she was not going to be happy with. The fact that Alaric seemed to be leading the meeting made things worse. There had been a serious shift in power.

"I am sure you have also felt it." Gwydion looked at both Eldred and Minerva. "Our power is waning." The words hung in the air.

"I must admit that I have been feeling somewhat faded, but I just figured it was the result of my imprisonment," Eldred mused. "What does this all mean?"

"It means that we aren't going to be as much use as you think in this upcoming battle of yours," Brielle snapped.

"It's not just our battle, it's yours as well," Alena returned with just as much venom in her voice.

"She will not speak at the Council," Brielle returned.

"You will hold your tongue Brielle," Alaric's voice was stone-cold. "I will decide what happens now. You have lost your rights."

"Please Alaric, calm down. Talking this way is not going to get us anywhere." Eldred tried to diffuse the situation.

Alaric had to admit that he was right, but he still couldn't have Brielle speaking in such a manner. Her superiority complex needed to change and change quickly. That was the only way that Alaric could think to solve the problem.

"Please Gwydion, continue," Alaric said calmly.

"It is hard to explain. We have been trying to figure out where this shift has come from."

"I think that it is obvious," everyone was surprised to hear Alena speak again. "It is a ripple effect from Nyrra breaking out of his prison."

"But…" Brielle started.

"You know she is right. We have all thought it. We just didn't want to believe it." Drake cut her off.

Alaric had to smile to himself. He was finally getting somewhere. They were starting to realise that they could no longer sit back and wait for events to unfold. Things were coming along quicker than he thought.

"It is time for us to rejoin the Seven Kingdoms," Ulman voiced his approval.

"But…" Brielle tried again.

"There are no buts Brielle," Minerva sneered. "This is what we have to do."

"Please, Brielle is still part of this conversation. Let her speak." Alaric could see something in her eyes and wanted to know what it was.

Brielle was taken aback by Alaric's support. She had been so against the man that there was no way she would believe that he would help her. She took a moment to compose herself before she continued.

"If we have lost our power, then what are we going to achieve by leaving the Island?"

"That is a very good point." Althea had to agree.

Alaric had his doubts they were truly losing their power. His strength had only been increasing since he arrivedand he couldn't believe that Nyrra was truly affecting things that much. It seemed as though he was going to have to turn the tables and teach the wizards to use magic again.

"We have little choice. I will do what I can before we have to leave, but the fact remains that we will have to. It will not be long before Bern and the Alliance reach Castalia. They will need all the help they can get if they are going to be able to defeat Za'aroz."

The mention of the Dark Knight did nothing to regain the wizards' already dwindling confidence. Alaric could hardly believe the sudden change in them. He had wanted to make them malleable, but he thought that he may have gone too far. Without speaking he looked at Eldred for support.

"Alaric is right. We can't just sit here and feel sorry for ourselves. We need make a stand and fight. Was have defeated Nyrra once before and we can do it again." The short speech was uplifting.

"It still doesn't change the fact that our power is waning. There is a good chance that Za'aroz will kill us all." Drake had also become despondent.

Alaric didn't know what to do. On the plus side the Council seemed more united, or at least they weren't at each others' throats any more. There was still time for them regain their confidence, but once the full moon was high in the sky he would have to leave them, one way or the other.

Chapter 22: Out of their Comfort Zone

Alaric took the chance to relax. It was going to take them all a little while to come to terms with the fact that they were going to have to leave the comfort of the island. Alaric was going to enjoy the ambience of his surroundings. It was the first time he could really appreciate the magical aura of the island. There was a sense of peace that he hadn't truly noticed when they arrived.

Alaric and Alena frolicked in the sea and walked along the white sandy beaches. Alaric thought for the moment he was truly at peace. He knew that it wouldn't last for long, but he was going to savour every moment.

While the two spent their days and nights together the Council did what they could to try and understand the situation. In a matter of hours Alaric had turned their entire world upside down. In the end they had to admit they were expecting it. There was no way they could remain in isolation whilst the rest of Seven Kingdoms were pushed into war. It was time for them to take a stand.

It wouldn't be long before the moon was at its fullest and Alaric had to meet with the wizards again. He had given them enough time and he needed to get things moving. He hoped that they had been able to resolve their differences and had come to a conclusion.

"Welcome Alaric, I am glad that you could join us this morning."

"Thank you Gwydion. I think it is time that we came up with a plan."

There was no response initially, but eventually Eldred spoke. "What is it that you had in mind?"

"In two days time the moon will be at its fullest. That gives me just under thirty days to reach the pinnacle of Mount Scorpio."

That brought laughter from around the room. It was a strange resonating sound that seemed out of place. Alaric didn't see what the joke was and became quite annoyed. He took a deep breath, calming himself, before he asked the obvious question.

"What's so funny?"

"We are sorry Alaric," Drake apologised when he realised that it wasn't a joke. "There is no chance you can reach Mount Scorpio in thirty days. It will take at least seven days for a ship to arrive to take us back to the mainland. Even if we affect the wind it will take another two days to get there. There is no way we can reach the mountain in thirty days."

"Hmmm, it seems as though you have a lot to learn."

"What's that supposed to mean?" Brielle snapped.

"Alaric has worked out a way to speed up travel, or more so I believe he slows down time. He did it on our journey from Jarrat to

Shoretown. If he says he will be on the peak of the mountain in less than thirty days then he will be there."

"So, that means we are going to Mount Scorpio?" Althea asked.

"No," Alaric replied. "I am going to Mount Scorpio. You are going to Castalia. You have to help the Alliance against Za'aroz. The seven of you must stick together now. It is the only way you will regain your power."

"But I will be travelling with you." Eldred wasn't happy. "You will need my help against Adder."

"What has the Serpentant got to do with anything?" Gwydion sounded concerned.

"That is who Alaric is meeting on top of the mountain," Eldred explained. "You need me with you. I have read it in the prophecy."

Alaric thought Eldred was grasping at straws, but if he was right then it changed everything. There was no real reason why he thought all seven of the Council needed to travel together. He figured they would all be able to draw on each others strengths, but that was only a guess.

"I will have to consult the prophecy before I make any decisions," Alaric mused.

"You put too much faith in that book," Brielle almost spat the words. "The prophecy is just a silly children's story."

Alaric wanted to explain how untrue that statement was, but he couldn't be bothered. There were more important matters to discuss. There was little time and he needed to teach them a lot.

"Be that as it may, I will make my decision before we leave," Alaric replied.

"So what are we supposed to do against Za'aroz?" Gwydion asked. "I have heard that he is growing in power."

"You need to have more faith in yourself. I don't know what it is you're concerned about, but I am sure it's not as bad as you think."

"Well I couldn't do anything to stop you," Brielle added. "I would say that means we are losing our power. There is no way a few years ago you would have been able to do that."

Alaric didn't want to have to explain that he had already surpassed her abilities, even when she had been at her peak. He had surpassed all of them and he wasn't even close to reaching his potential. There was something very empowering in that thought. He pushed it aside and returned his attention to what was important.

"There is a lot you need to know. For starters I will need to teach you how to jump through the fabric of time. You will only have a few days to reach Castalia and this is the only way you can do it."

"Why do you believe that we need to go to Castalia? Surely our abilities would be better used elsewhere," Ulman protested.

"We have to rescue Castalia from the clutches of the Dark Knight," Minerva spoke with passion.

"Minerva is right, but that is not the only reason why you must go. As I am sure you know Za'aroz is masquerading as the High Chancellor. At the moment he is in ultimate control of one of the largest single armies in the Seven Kingdoms. If Bern fails in his task then Nyrra will control the Castalial army and everything as we know it will be over." He paused to let the words sink in. "You need to help make sure this doesn't happen."

"How do you suppose we stop Za'aroz without everyone thinking we have killed the High Chancellor?" Gwydion asked.

"Now where is the fun in that? If I had all the answers it would be too easy. There may be something in the prophecy to help, but I wouldn't count on it."

"Bern is going to try and free the real High Chancellor. He is trapped in the diamond mine under the Grand Cathedral and I don't really know how he is planning on finding Augustus. Bern knows how to get into the mine, but I still don't know if that will do him any good. The mine is a warren of tunnels and shafts. To find one person in all of that is going to be next to impossible. Finding his way out is also going to be a problem. I am sure that Za'aroz is prepared for what Bern is trying to do. He will increase the security in the mines for sure." Minerva was starting to talk herself out of returning to Castalia. She recalled the plan Alaric had explained to her as best she could.

Alaric had to admit that he had no idea how Bern was going achieve his goals, but then he really didn't know how he was going to achieve his own. He didn't know how he had gone as far as he had, but the wheels were in motion and that was all that mattered.

"We have to trust that he is going to find the High Chancellor. That is what we have to plan for and that is why you need to go to Castalia. Bern will not be able to defeat the Dark Knight on his own," he stated.

"He is right," Eldred returned. "We need to trust that everything is going to work out for the best. Worrying about it isn't going to solve anything. We need to concentrate on fixing the problems we can."

"So what do we do now?" Drake asked.

"It is time for some training," Alaric replied.

"There is not enough time. To train a wizard takes many years of study," Brielle scoffed.

"The training is not for me." Alaric winked and smiled at Brielle.

"How can you be so arrogant as to presume..." Brielle couldn't believe what she was hearing.

"He is right Brielle," Gwydion interrupted her. "If we are going to succeed then we are going to need all the help we can get."

"Good, now let's get started." Alaric rose from his chair.

***

The training was intense. There was much to learn and little time to learn it. Not only that, but Alaric had to make sure he didn't burn the wizards out. They would need all the energy they had if they were going to reach Castalia in time and defeat the Dark Knight.

"Do you think they are ready?" Alena asked as they lay in bed together.

"I have no idea, but I also have no choice. The moon is full and they have to leave in the morning, as do we."

That thought had been weighing on him all night, except for a brief period of passion. He wished he had another week or two with the Council and then he would be confident they were ready. He thought about using the Topaz stone to cure their fatigue, but it was something he didn't want to risk. It was odd that none of them had asked him about the stones. It was almost as if they were deliberately avoiding the subject.

He wasn't looking forward to the next stage of his journey. He had a very bad feeling about his meeting with Adder. There could be no doubt it was a trap. What he couldn't work out was why Viper was so willing to help him. If the two were working together then his life could be over very soon.

He sat, naked, on a chair while Alena stayed in bed. He had felt the need to get up before he slept. There was a lot weighing on his mind and Alena knew that.

"I think I'm going to miss this place." Alena continued when Alaric didn't elaborate. "There is a sense of peace that I haven't felt in a long time."

"It's the magic aura that surrounds this island. It is no coincidence that the wizards chose this place to reside," Alaric explained.

"What are you talking about?" Alena was surprised to hear him speak his mind and didn't quite understand what he was saying.

"I've been trying to locate it over the past few days, but I've had no luck." Alena had wondered where he had been going on his various strolls around the island. "Whatever it is it has a huge amount of power. That's what creates the calming effect."

With that he ended the conversation. Alena knew there was no point in pushing any further. It was a little idiosyncrasy that she had grown used to no matter how much it annoyed her. There was no way she would get any extra information from him.

"What's our next move?" she asked.

"We travel to the Scorpion Mountain." There was no elaboration.

"Are you sure that is the right move. I am sure that it would be better if we helped those in Castalia."

"I can't risk Adder destroying Arsiliac." Alaric stared out the window at the moon as he spoke.

"I see no reason why he would destroy your home town. The village is too insignificant."

"I promised Bern that I wouldn't let anything happen to his family. I can't go back on my word."

That excuse was flimsy and Alena knew it. There was something else drawing him towards the mountain and she wasn't going to let it rest.

"Please, tell me what you are thinking?" Alena spoke softly.

"There's something waiting for me at the mountain."

"You know it's a trap," she couldn't help herself.

"I know that, but I don't know who is setting it and who it is meant to capture. I don't know what it is, but I do know that I have no choice but to go. I have been feeling it more and more every day. I am being drawn to the mountain and whatever it is that is waiting for me."

There was a darkness in Alaric's voice that frightened Alena. She wished she had not spoken. The feeling of being at peace had completely gone. His lack of feeling had taken all of her happiness and she felt depressed.

"I'm sorry." Alaric returned to the bed and wrapped his arms around her. Alena felt a little better, but his words still had their affect on her. He held her even closer when he realised that she was still tense. "Everything will be alright. I will be ready for whatever it is that is waiting for us."

That made her feel a little better and she physically relaxed in his arms. There was nothing she could do to change the situation. Alaric had made up his mind and they would be travelling towards Mount Scorpio in the morning. All she could do was enjoy the last night on the island. Slowly the peaceful aura drifted over her and she fell asleep.

In the morning Alaric was the first to rise. He left Alena sleeping and went to see what the wizards were doing. He had hoped that Eldred had changed his mind, although at the same time he still hoped he was coming with him. Either way he would be a great asset and a great loss. He would have to leave the decision up to the old wizard.

"Good morning Alaric." It was a surprisingly cheerful greeting from Gwydion.

The wizard stood at the front of the main building with Drake and Althea. Their respective bags were packed and they looked as though they were excited with the days prospects. It wasn't at all what Alaric was expecting.

"I must admit I am surprised to see you here, ready to go."

"And you would be right to be sceptical, but that's the funny thing. We were all sceptical with your plan, of course with the exception of Eldred and Minerva, but this morning we all woke up with a renewed spring in our steps. It seems as though we are all keen to see some action again. It has been a long time since we have fought the forces of evil," Gwydion explained.

The fact that Brielle was absent was not lost on Alaric. She had been the most hostile since he had arrived and it seemed as though that hadn't changed. He had hoped that by teaching her a lesson in civility it might have mellowed her aggression. She had listened to Alaric's instruction and learnt the spells he had taught, but that was as far as it went. He was concerned that her motives for subserviency were not pure.

"Where are the others?"

"Minerva, Ulman and Eldred have gone to find Brielle. It seems as though she has slept in this morning," Drake spoke casually.

Alaric didn't like the sound of that. They would need her assistance if they were going to defeat Za'aroz. He was beginning to think that he had made the wrong decision in leaving Castalia, but there was nothing he could do about it. The tug of the prophecy was undeniable and he knew that he had no choice. If anything he felt as though he had remained on the island too long.

They waited in silence until the others joined them. Brielle didn't look happy when she saw Alaric. The expression on her face only changed for a second, but it wasn't lost on him.

"I guess I was asking too much to sleep in on my last day at home."

"I know that you like your sleep, but unfortunately the time for sleep is over. Once we are done you can sleep as long as you like," Gwydion explained.

"I guess you're right," Brielle smiled.

"Now, you all know what you need to do?" Alaric asked.

"Small jumps to conserve energy," Ulman repeated.

"I'll take the first jump, which is the longest and then rest for most of the journey," Gwydion added.

"We need to make sure that we arrive in Castalia with the ability to fight," Brielle sounded somewhat excited.

"You need to be careful. I have a bad feeling that Za'aroz will be expecting you." It was the first time Alaric had mentioned his fears. The feeling had hit him four days ago and he wanted to wait until the last moment before he mentioned it.

"Don't worry Alaric, we weren't expecting this to be a walk in the park. We have been fighting the Evil One for a long time. We know to expect the worst and then everything else is a nice surprise." Ulman spoke with a gruff voice.

"Easy brother, there is more to this than what we have faced in the past," Eldred warned.

Eldred's words hung heavy on the group. Alaric wished he had not spoken and dampened their spirits. There was plenty of time to realise the severity of their situation, but he couldn't deny Eldred his concern for the others.

"You all need to keep training while you travel. You will need to keep your skills sharp if you are to defeat Za'aroz," Alaric continued.

"We have been doing this for a long time," Gwydion sounded a little perturbed. "You don't have to worry about us."

Alaric wished that was the case. They were not prepared for what they were about to do, but then he wasn't prepared when he started either. Now he was stronger than anyone could believe. He could only hope the six wizards would also grow in the same way.

"And what of you Eldred?" Alaric changed the subject quickly.

"Nothing has changed. I have started this journey with you and I plan on finishing it in the same manner."

Alaric felt better hearing his words. There was something comforting about his confidence. Now it was time to send the wizards on their way and find Alena, then it would be time for them to leave.

"I think that is enough. Now it is time for you to leave. I hope that you all stay safe. This is but the start of your journey." Alaric smiled.

When Alaric finished speaking the wizards suddenly blinked out of existence. He had felt the power growing inside Gwydion ever since he had arrived. It was no surprise when they suddenly left, leaving Alaric and Eldred standing alone.

"Well I guess there is nothing left for us to do?" for some reason Alaric didn't want to leave.

Ever since he had arrived at Ĉarolija Island he had felt at home. The magical aura had washed over him and gave him a contentment he had only ever felt holding one of the *Stones of Power*. It was so powerful that he didn't want to leave.

"The *Well of Water* is on the north side of the island. That is what gives it its magical aura," Eldred explained as he recognised the expression on Alaric's face. "This is the reason why were drawn to this island so many years ago."

It was all starting to make sense. Alaric had felt his power growing ever since he had arrived and he couldn't work out why. The spells he had created should have caused him more fatigue than they had.

As much as he was glad for the explanation he had hoped that it was part of his increased power.

"It's time. I wish that I could stay," Eldred lamented. "It has been so long since I have been here and now it is time to go again. I guess I am just being silly."

Alaric wanted to comfort him, but he couldn't admit that he too wanted to stay. He thought that if he did then he might just not leave and that would be disastrous. He had to accept the fact that it was time to go.

It wasn't long before Alena arrived with a number of servants carrying their bags. Alaric smiled when she reached them.

"Well I guess that is it then. The next stage of our adventure begins."

Before anyone else could speak they suddenly blinked out of existence.

Chapter 23: Deep in the Mines

The small group had been wandering through the mines for over an hour with no luck in finding the High Chancellor. On the plus side they had not run into any more guards. Every time they heard the sound of metal chipping on stone, however, they had to check for guards. Each time they found a miserable looking person working at breaking the diamonds away from the walls. Each time Bern's heart broke a little more and the rage increased inside him.

"This is hopeless," Bern sighed when they stopped for a rest.

"We can't give up." Hadar recognised the tone in his voice. "If we don't find the High Chancellor then this plan won't work."

Bern knew that he was right, but he also knew that they couldn't continue wandering aimlessly around the mines. There were too many branches and levels for them to search them all one by one. It would only be a matter of time before they lost their direction and covered the same ground. There had to be a better way. Ever since they had arrived he had been waiting for the prophecy to aid them, but it had not happened. There was nothing drawing him in any direction.

"I have an idea," Delbert spoke softly. "What happens if we allow ourselves to be captured? Surely we would be taken to one of the leaders and then we could make them tell us where the High Chancellor is."

They thought on the idea for a moment. On face value it seemed good enough, but it wasn't until Hadar spoke that they realised it wasn't.

"If we get captured then they will take our weapons for sure and that would not be a good result. I am sure that the guards are not used to taking prisoners and I am sure they would see us dead before they take us to their leaders." Hadar's words lowered their rising spirits. "But I think it's right. We need to find the captain-of-the-guard. I think that would be the only way we are going to find the High Chancellor."

"How do you propose that we find the captain" Delbert asked. "I doubt any of the guards are just going to take us to him."

"Then I guess we shouldn't give them the option. The next time we run into a slave master we should make sure we keep him alive." Bern had to agree.

Time was running short. It would only be a matter of time before the Dark Knight would send the Castalial army out to fight the Alliance. Bern had to make sure that he located the High Chancellor before that happened. There was no chance the Alliance would survive a frontal attack from the full Castalial army.

"Well at least it seems as though we have a plan now and that has to beat wandering around these mines aimlessly." Hadar smiled.

The sense of direction picked up everyone's spirits again. They had an end in sight, even if it was a risky task. The last time they came up against the slave masters there was little chance to take them prisoner. It seemed as though they would rather die than be captured.

With a new direction no one wanted to sit around and it wasn't long before they were on the move again. Bern led the way with Hadar, listening carefully for the sound of footsteps. The sound would be the first indication they were coming close to their goal, but that was not as easy at it sounded.

Another hour passed and they had not come across a single slave or master. There was something strange about that. They had descended two levels without realising it. They were concentrating so hard on the sounds around them that no one noticed the gentle downward slope.

"This isn't good!" Bern commented when they stopped again. "I have a very sneaky suspicion that we are lost."

"I think you are right!" Hadar sounded dejected.

It didn't take long for the mood of the group to drop again.

"What do we do now?" one of the bandits asked.

"There is nothing we can do except back track," Hadar replied. "It looks as though we have just wasted an hour that we didn't have."

Bern's attention was suddenly distracted. There was something or someone nearby. He couldn't explain what it was, but he knew it was there. He felt as though the prophecy had something to do with it, at least that was a promising thought.

"Let's get moving." They started back the way they came when Hadar realised that Bern hadn't moved.

Bern didn't respond. He was trying to locate the direction of his feeling. He knew that whatever was out there was close by and he had to find it before he left. The feeling would not leave him until he did what it wanted him to.

"Bern!" Hadar grabbed his shoulder, shaking him from his reverie.

"What? Sorry, what were you saying?" Bern looked confused.

"We need to retrace our steps if we are going to find a slave master.'

"Not yet."

"What do you mean?" Hadar was becoming concerned. "We have already lost too much time. We can't afford to waste anymore."

The words made sense, but nothing was going to drag Bern away. He needed to find the answer to the unasked question. There was something important ahead and he couldn't leave until he knew what it was.

"I must go on," was all he said.

"You're not making any sense. Bern we have to get moving."

"What is the hold up?" asked Delbert.

"Bern thinks there is something ahead," Hadar surmised.

"What is it?" Delbert asked.

"I don't know," Bern replied. "But I need to find out."

It seemed as though Bern had returned to normal, or at least as normal as the others had grown used to. He took a torch from a nearby wall. He didn't know why, as all the tunnels they had been down had been sufficiently lit, but he took it anyway.

"Oh well, let's go see what it is." Delbert knew there was no point in arguing.

"I should go alone."

"I don't think that is a good idea," Delbert retorted.

"I will go. You stay here with the others," Hadar added.

The solution didn't seem to appease either side, but no one commented further. Bern had already moved off down the tunnel and had turned a corner out of sight. It was a deliberate move to try and dissuade Hadar from following. Both men knew that it wasn't going to work. Hadar also grabbed a torch from the wall and hastened his step.

They had not been travelling long before the torches on the walls became sparser and sparser until eventually there were none. Hadar didn't think it was a good sign. It was clear that no one came down so far anymore. There was no chance that the High Chancellor would be in these parts. If he was then Hadar doubted he would still be alive. Either way he felt as though it was going to be a wasted trip. Bern continued on with purpose, which was the only thing stopping Hadar from speaking.

Bern had no idea what he was looking for. All he knew was that he couldn't turn around. The tug of the prophecy was too great for him to resist. Even if he wanted to there was nothing he could do. The strong pull had piqued his curiosity. There had to be something important ahead.

After a short walk they came to a crossroads. Bern stopped in the middle and looked at his options. He really had no idea which way he should go. It was strange. Normally when the prophecy tugged at him it had a definite direction, or at least it did when it mattered.

"Which way do we go?" Hadar asked when Bern didn't move.

Bern didn't answer straight away. The wrong choice could lead them anywhere and if they got lost there would be no coming back. Before he made his decision he wanted to make sure it was the right one. He investigated the three tunnels. The first two he found the entrances thick with spider webs and the floor covered in dust. The last one had spider webs brushed aside and there were scuffed footprints in the dust. The prints only led in one direction. Whoever had made them was still there and obviously the person Bern was meant to meet.

"I guess this is the way to go." He poked his torch through the entrance.

"Are you sure?" Hadar questioned.

"No, but it seems as though it would be the logical course."

When the flaming spider webs died down Bern started into the tunnel. As soon has he walked out of the small crossroad cavern he felt much better and that was a good sign. If he was heading in the wrong direction he would hope that the prophecy would let him know. Either way he had made his decision and he could only hope it was the right one.

They had not walked for long before they could hear the sounds of scratching coming from somewhere in front of them. Bern stopped suddenly when he heard the noise and Hadar nearly ran into him. The big man cursed softly under his breath.

"I'm sorry, but there is something ahead," Bern spoke in a whisper.

"What is it?"

"If I knew that I wouldn't have stopped."

Hadar was about to ask another question, but Bern stopped him with a wave of his hand. He wanted to listen to the scratching to determine if it was human or animal. Whatever it was would be alerted to their presence by the torch light, but it was a necessity. Without the light then they would be too vulnerable. With that thought in mind he decided that it couldn't be a human. Whatever it was had to have the ability to see in the dark.

"We need to be careful when we proceed. The light will give away our   position before we can see what we are up against," Bern explained.

Hadar strained to hear the scraping. He couldn't gauge how far away it was. He was surprised that Bern could even hear it before they stopped, he couldn't hear a thing over their own footsteps.

Bern started again, keeping the pace painfully slow. He didn't want to disturb the creature scratching away. There was no doubt that he needed to know what it was. The further they continued the louder the scraping became. Whatever was making the noise didn't know they were coming.

Finally, after they rounded a corner, they saw what they were looking for. Bern gasped in surprise and nearly dropped his torch. There was a man resting on his haunches looking at them. His eyes were almost completely shut as he strained against the sudden light. The rags he wore were dirty and only just hanging from his body. Bern tried to see what he was scratching at, but the man protected the wall. His dark, dirty, patchy hair hung around his shoulders.

"It's mine!" his voice was cracked.

"Who are you?" Bern asked in awe.

He couldn't believe that such a creature existed. It was clearly human, but also not. He was bent over and Bern was sure that he wouldn't be able to stand up straight. By the looks of his skinny body he had been in the mines for a long time. There was dirt all over his body with a ring around his mouth. Bern couldn't imagine what he ate to remain alive in such a place.

"Who am I...? Who am I?" the man repeated the question.

"I think this man has lost his mind," Hadar whispered.

"Lost my mind? Lost my mind?" the second question he asked himself. "How do you lose your mind?"

The question floated off in the silence. Neither man knew how to answer it. Bern wished that the prophecy was still urging him forward, but it had stopped. Whoever the man was it was the one the prophecy wanted him to find. He had no idea what he was going to do with the wretched creature. His first thought was to put him out of his misery, but he didn't think that was the right thing to do.

"We need to get out of here. We have already wasted enough time." Hadar had had enough of the strange man.

"Get out of here! Get out of here? We all want to get out of here." The man picked at something in his fingers with his teeth. It looked as though he was deep in thought, but neither of them could be sure. "That is not allowed. They won't let you out. They never let you out."

"Come on Bern, we can't waste our time any longer."

"Bern... Bern? Where have I heard that name before?" the man perked up at the sound of Bern's name. "Bern... So familiar. Stay in the dark and keep to your mark. Wait for your turn until you meet a man named Bern. A man named Bern... A man named Bern."

The incessant rambling was starting to get on Hadar's nerves, but at the mention of Bern's name he relaxed a little. He wanted to hear what the wretched man had to say and was no longer so keen to keep moving.

"Who told you that?" Bern spoke in a calming voice.

"A man, a man, a man, a man, a man..."

"What man!" Hadar boomed.

The sound of the large man's voice rattled the wretched man even further. He cowered against the wall, but there was no where for him to retreat. His breathing became laboured and Bern thought he was going to lose consciousness. He buried his head in his arms in an attempt to hide.

"It is okay, he's a friend." Bern tried to soothe him.

"A friend?" he looked up at Hadar with a confused expression on his face. "The man said nothing about a friend."

"Who was the man?" Bern asked softly.

"Don't know, don't know. Didn't say his name. All he did was set me free. He told me to wait here for you and that's what I did."

"This is getting us nowhere." Hadar had lost his patience again. "We have to get going."

"Run away big man. This is nothing to do with you," the strange man said.

Bern shot Hadar a stern look. They weren't going anywhere until his curiosity had been sated. There was something very peculiar about the man and for some reason Bern knew that he was important. For what? He had no idea.

"Tell me what happened?" Bern asked.

"Slave I was, many, many, many years. Unfairly treated I was. Imprisoned for a crime I didn't commit. Wanted to die I did. Working away, digging for diamonds, but they wouldn't let me, no they wouldn't. Kept me alive they did, to dig for their dirty, dirty diamonds. One day a man came to me, yes he did. He told me to come deep into the mines and wait for a man named Bern. I didn't want to, not at first. I wanted to die. That's all I wanted, but he wouldn't let me, no he wouldn't. He told me that I had to wait and wait for you I did. A long time I waited, a long, long time..." He slowly drifted off.

"What have you been living on?" Hadar couldn't help himself.

"Bugs and bats and other unfortunate creatures. No one wants to live in this place, no one should live in this place. It is not fit for living, no it isn't..."

Hadar wished that he hadn't asked the question. He felt suddenly sick in the stomach. He had lived in the wild before, but nothing like this man had suffered. He suddenly felt very sorry for him. He couldn't imagine what it had taken to live in such a place.

"Did the man tell you what he wanted you to do?" Bern was also starting to become frustrated, but he held his tone.

"Man, man, who's the man? Who's the man? No. Don't know the man. Never said his name, never said what he wanted."

That was frustrating, but at least they were starting to get answers. He couldn't imagine the life the man had been living over the years. In fact he had no idea how long the man had been living alone in the dark. It wasn't going to be easy to getting any answers from him.

"Do you know your name?" Bern tried, a lot softer than Hadar.

"Name, name, name, name... What's my name? What's my name?"

"Please think hard. What's your name?" Bern asked again.

The man looked away and stared into the darkness. Bern figured it was better than the incessant repetition. With any luck the man might be able to remember something.

"Yes, my name. It is... Ze... Oh now what is it again. I know it's in here someone. You must forgive me. I haven't heard my name spoken in many a year." He sounded a little more coherent. "Zenon? Zenon Verloren."

His last name sounded like someone from Darshival, but the given name was one that Bern didn't recognise. It was a strange name, which seemed fitting for the situation. At last they were starting to get somewhere. Zenon also seemed a lot happier.

"It is nice to meet you Zenon. My name, as you already know, is Bern and this is Hadar." Bern made the formal introductions. "Now do you have any idea why the man wanted you to meet us here?"

"Meet here, meet here? Who have we met here?"

It seemed as though Zenon was regressing. Bern had hoped that he was getting better, but it didn't seem to be the case. He didn't know what to do. There had to be some way to get answers out of him. There was a reason they were there and he needed to stay until he realised what it was.

"You met us, you crazy old coot." Hadar had had enough. "This is ridiculous Bern. We have to get back to the others."

"Bern... Bern... Bern... That's right! I am here to meet Bern. A man told me to meet Bern here. Do you know where he is?"

Bern had to admit that Hadar was right. Zenon had lost any sign of recovering his senses. There also seemed little point in remaining in the tunnel. The least they could do was bring Zenon with them and hope that his memory returned.

"Let's get going," he sounded resigned.

Hadar was relieved to hear the words come out of Bern's mouth. The crazy man had taken up too much of their time. As much as it wasn't the right thing to do Hadar would be happy when they left Zenon behind. It wasn't the nicest of places to live, but he seemed to be doing alright.

At the sound of Bern's words Zenon went back to what he was doing on the wall. Bern was a little taken aback, but Hadar had already started making his way back towards the others. Bern didn't know what to make of the situation. It seemed as though neither of them understood what he was trying to achieve.

"Come on Bern, let's go," Hadar called.

"Are you coming with us?" Bern asked Zenon.

The man didn't seem to notice Bern's question. He suddenly sneezed and then almost jumped out of his skin when he saw Bern watching him. It was as if it was the first time he saw him. The situation was becoming even more annoying. It wasn't until he spoke before Bern relaxed a little.

"Time to go already? Oh well… I guess I can always come back later. More time, more time…"

Zenon left what he was doing and started following Hadar. Bern remained behind in shock. He had a bad feeling that Zenon was going to get worse before he got better. He could only hope that he would be of some use, otherwise he would be very annoyed with the prophecy.

"Why are we going this way?" Zenon asked as they made their way back to the others.

"We are meeting our friends. They are waiting for us a little further along," Hadar explained. He seemed to have accepted Zenon was coming with them.

"Oh… Okay…"

Bern remained a few steps behind, watching the two of them closely. Zenon remained crouched over as he walked half a step behind Hadar. It almost looked like he was Hadar's pet. Zenon looked up every now and then at Hadar. Bern could only imagine what he was looking for.

It didn't seem to take anywhere near as long to reach the rest of the group as he expected and he was glad to see them. Wandering through the mines was starting to get to him. The close walls and the darkness was something that he thought he would never get used to. He much preferred the open air. He had to push that thought aside or he would risk going insane. For the first time he could completely understand how Zenon was feeling.

"What did you find?" Delbert asked, seemingly not noticing a hunched over creature at Hadar's side.

At first Bern thought Delbert was joking, but then he realised that he hadn't seen the man. Bern wasn't sure what to say.

"We found this wretched creature gnawing at the walls not too far away." Hadar sounded exasperated.

"Zenon, my name in Zenon…"

Delbert looked down for the first time with a confused expression on his face. He wondered why he hadn't seen the man when Hadar arrived. There was something very peculiar about the new arrival. He wondered why Bern had brought him back. There didn't seem to be anything extraordinary about him, but he thought he better give Bern the benefit of the doubt.

"Is that what you were looking for?"

"I believe so. All I know is that I don't feel the urge to continue." Bern was still coming to terms with the situation himself. He wasn't sure how to explain it.

"So who is he?" Delbert was still confused.

"Zenon, Zenon Verloren… Listen, listen, listen, listen… If you want to know you have to listen."

Delbert stared at the strange man whose attention had returned to the floor. He didn't really know what to make of him. Hadar and Bern both had confused expressions on their faces.

"Would anyone like to explain what is happening here?" he asked when no one else responded.

"Yes we would, but we have no idea ourselves. All I know is that the nagging feeling of the prophecy has gone. I would have preferred it if it had led us to the High Chancellor, but we found him instead."

"High Chancellor... High Chancellor?" The name set Zenon on another rant. It looked as though he was deep in thought, but no one could be really sure. They thought to be on the safe side they should wait. Even Delbert was curious at what he was going to say next. "He's an evil man," Zenon said when he realised everyone was watching him, or at least that's what the others perceived. "Don't find him, no, no, no... You don't want to find him, he's an evil man."

"What do you mean?" Hadar couldn't help himself.

"Mean... Mean? Yes he is mean. The High Chancellor... The man said 'you're no good, you need to spend time in the mines'. Yes I remember... How could I forget? Never forget, no, no, no never forget..."

"Is he okay?" Delbert whispered in an attempt to speak over Zenon.

"I don't know, but I would suggest that he has been down here for a long time. That would be enough to send anyone crazy. There are glimpses of someone inside, but not often," Hadar explained.

"You know I am standing right here." The comment confused everyone. It almost sounded as though he was sane, which meant his previous ranting could have been an act.

"Are you alright Zenon?" Bern asked.

There was no answer. It was as if he didn't even hear the words. Bern was becoming even more frustrated. It was as if the man was playing a game with him. The problem was that there was no way to say if he was telling the truth or not. He felt that they were walking into a very dangerous situation. Without warning Hadar kicked out at Zenon and struck him on his left arm. The blow was enough to knock him over. Everyone was in shock at the sudden attack. Zenon returned to his feet and retreated away from Hadar, a look of pure horror on his face.

"Don't do that again," Bern's voice was strict.

"I'm sorry, but..."

"Sorry, sorry, sorry... We are all sorry... That's what he said, yes he did. We are all sorry and there is nothing we can do about it. Move on, move on... Sorry, sorry, sorry..."

They were just going round and round. Just when it seemed as though Zenon was coming good he would slip back into his insanity. Bern wondered if the sanity was the act and his current state was real. Either way they had more important matters to work out.

"We need to keep moving if we are going to find the High Chancellor."

They had wasted too much time on Zenon. He had made no sense and there seemed to be no good reason for them to keep him around. At the mention of the High Chancellor he scooted across the floor and grabbed Bern's legs. The large man was tempted to kick him the same way Hadar had, but he restrained himself. It would not be a good example.

"No, no, no... Not the High Chancellor... He is an evil man. You don't want to find him. He put me here, yes he did... Can't be trusted, no he can't... Don't find him, don't find him, can't find him..."

"Please Zenon. We have no choice. Our mission hinges on finding the High Chancellor. We don't have a choice." Bern tried to explain.

"Choice... Choice? You always have a choice. Make the choice to leave the High Chancellor alone. He is a bad man... Yes, he is a bad man... Put me down here he did, but I will get my revenge."

"He is a prisoner here too. Depending on how long ago you were imprisoned it might not have been him who put you here. There is a Dark Knight in control of the Castalia now." Bern didn't know why he continued to explain, but he thought it might help.

"No, no, no... It was the High Chancellor, yes it was, he put me here... He put me here many, many, many years ago... Long time, long time here... He can't be trusted, no he can't..." Zenon's rambling was getting worse.

Bern let out a sigh of frustration. He was seriously considering leaving Zenon in the mines, but he knew that wasn't an option. Regardless of the tug of the prophecy he couldn't leave anyone in such a place. That would be too cruel a punishment and no one deserved such a fate.

"Either way we can't stay here any longer. We need to find the slave masters if we are ever going to get out of here," Hadar sounded resigned. He was starting to feel sorry for the strange man.

"Get out, get out, get out...? Yes, yes, yes... Zenon wants out, yes he does... Zenon can help, yes he can..."

"What are you jabbering about?" Delbert snapped.

"Help, help, help... Zenon knows the way. He can find the slave masters. He knows where they are, he know how to avoid them..."

Things were starting to improve. It was the first time that Zenon had started to make sense, even if he was still talking in riddles. There was a chance the strange man could help them on their way and that could only be a good thing. He didn't need to know that they were still searching for the High Chancellor.

"Are you sure that you trust him?" Delbert was not so convinced that Zenon knew what he was talking about. "He might have been left here to lead us astray. I think it would be better for us to return to where we started and start again. That is the safest option."

"Return, return, return...? How do you return...? Do you know the way back...? Zenon knows, yes he does... He has lived in the caves, he knows the way... You don't know the way... You will get lost. That is one thing for sure." There was something knowing in his words that made them all very uncomfortable.

They all knew he was right. No one was exactly sure of the way they had come. It would only be by pure chance that they came out where they started. Their best chance of finding the High Chancellor alive was to put their trust in Zenon. It was not something he really wanted to do, but the prophecy had led Bern there for a reason and he had to put his trust in that.

"Zenon is right. We don't know the way. I say if he says he knows then we have to trust him. What other option do we have?"

Bern's question fell silent. No one had any other ideas. There as no other choice, but to accept Zenon's help.

"Then I suggest that we keep moving."

Chapter 24: Discovery

Once Bern had given the order Zenon scampered back the way they had come. Bern looked at Hadar and Delbert before shrugging his shoulders and following after him. The peculiar man seemed to be on a mission and nothing was going to slow him down. Bern figured it was the thought of freedom that urged him on and he couldn't blame him.

Zenon seemed to move through the mines with no real direction. After what Bern estimated to be an hour, but was in fact only ten minutes, he brought them to a stop. Bern saw a look of concern on Zenon's face and his heart sunk. Instantly he figured that the man had got them lost and that could only mean trouble. There was no time for such problems.

"Why are we stopping?" Hadar asked when he reached the two.

"Shh, shh, shh... Keep your voice down. There is someone ahead, yes there is..." Zenon warned.

Bern quickly drew his sword and prepared himself. He listened intently to try and gauge the situation, but he couldn't hear anything. After a tense wait he let out a sigh of relief and turned to the strange man. Zenon was crouched in front of him, seemingly waiting for instruction.

"There is no one there Zenon. I can't hear anything," Bern didn't sound happy.

"There is someone there, yes there is... Zenon can hear, yes he can... At least three, maybe four... They are not slaves, no they're not... They are talking, yes they are... Zenon can hear them, but not what they say... Slaves don't talk, no they don't... They just work, work, work..."

Bern had to admit he had a point, even if he couldn't hear the same thing. He figured that spending all his time in the mines had heightened his senses. It was the only explanation for it. Zenon seemed so certain there was someone ahead that Bern couldn't doubt him. If it ended up being voices inside the man's head then it would be the last time he listened to him, but for the moment he would have a little faith.

"Be careful. There are some men ahead and I don't think they are friendly."

Bern ordered then men into single file, with Hadar and Delbert directly behind him. He wanted Zenon to go further back, but he wouldn't leave them. If they came into trouble he wanted the two men at his side and Zenon protected by the others. At least he had the first. He needed to make sure they were able to take a least one of the men prisoner. It was the best chance of finding the slave masters and ultimately the High Chancellor.

Slowly they made their way forward. They didn't want to alert whoever it was ahead of them to their presence. Zenon moved closely behind Bern. He had a nervous twitch about him that didn't make the others feel comfortable. Bern was too busy concentrating on what was ahead to notice what was happening behind. Slowly he started to hear the sound of voices in the distance. The tunnels echoed the sounds, making it impossible to know exactly where they were coming from.

Every sound coming from behind him echoed inside his mind. Each time it happened he stopped the group and instructed them to be quiet. Bern's fear was that the noise would alert whoever was ahead of them. He was relying on surprise as an ally, he didn't need their position to be given away by sloppy soldiering.

The sound increased until they rounded a corner and came out into a small cavern. Four slavers were standing around talking. None of them noticed Bern enter the room. Zenon disappeared back into the tunnel, the sight of the slavers sent a shot of fear through his body. It wasn't until Delbert entered the cavern did the slavers realise they were there.

"Well, this is a bit of surprise." Although none of them really seemed surprised.

That didn't do anything to relieve Bern's nerves. It seemed as though they were expected, which was not a good sign. Bern was hoping for a surprise to put them off guard, but instead the four slavers didn't seem to sense any danger at all. There was no room for any of the others to enter the cavern and Bern suddenly realised they were in a very bad position.

"We are looking for a slave master." There didn't seem any point in playing games.

"There will be a big reward for bringing these in," one of the slavers spoke casually.

"We are not alone. There is a group of men in the tunnel behind us. There is no way you are going to be able to take us all prisoner." Bern tried to reason with them.

"That would be if we were alone, but that is not the case."

Bern's heart dropped. He realised that the slavers were stalling for time. There were four entrances into the cavern. One, the way they came, one blocked by the four slavers and two others. It wasn't long before three more slavers came in from each entrance. There was little room between the two groups and fighting wasn't an option. The advantage was definitely swayed in the slavers favour.

"We don't want to fight. We just want you to take us to the slave masters." Bern repeated.

"And that is exactly where we want to take you. If you would kindly hand over your weapons we will be on our way." The slaver spoke with a smooth voice, unlike the others they had met.

"Unfortunately that is not an option," Hadar took half a step forward, sword in hand. "We can go peacefully or you can lose all of your friends. The choice is yours."

Hadar's words brought laughter throughout the cavern. The numbers were clearly favoured to the slavers inside the cavern, but outside there was an unknown number. No one knew how many the other side had. A battle wasn't going to be good and the close quarters wouldn't make fighting easy.

"I doubt you will be around long enough to go any other way. Now the Masters are interested to speak with you, but at the same time they would be just as happy if we drag your corpses back with us. The choice is entirely yours."

"Don't listen, don't listen… This one is not what he seems, no he isn't… There is something to him, yes there is…" Zenon had appeared from behind the others.

Bern had to admit that he had the same opinion as Zenon. The man was large and dirty, like the other slavers, but there was something more in his eyes. There was a knowledge there that the others didn't have.

"And who is this strange little man?"

"No one, no one, no one…"

"He is no one you need be concerned about. Now I feel as though we are at an impasse. As I am sure you can appreciate we cannot surrender and I am sure that you can't just let us go," Bern explained.

"So what is it that you're suggesting?"

Bern was hoping the slaver was going to come up with a suggestion as he had no ideas. There was a chance that they could kill all the slavers and save one to show them the way, but there was an even better chance that at least one of them would be killed in the fight.

"Hadar and I will come with you," Hadar couldn't believe what he was hearing. "You can leave the others to find their own way out." He was grasping at straws.

The slaver thought about the offer. He knew there were more men in the tunnel behind them. He could hear them shuffling around, although he had no idea how many there were. It seemed as though it was good offer and he would look good in the eyes of the slave masters for bringing in prisoners. It wouldn't matter how many they brought back.

"Hand over your weapons and we have a deal."

"Not on your…" Hadar barked.

"That is fair," Bern interrupted as he relinquished his sword.

"What are you doing?" Hadar spoke between clenched teeth.

"Trust me!"

Hadar begrudgingly gave up his weapon. He would have much preferred to fight his way out. He was quite confident that he could kill them all, but he had to defer to Bern. It seemed like a strange plan, and hoped Bern knew what he was doing.

"Let's move!" the slaver commanded.

"Give me a moment." Bern turned to Delbert.

"What are you doing?" Delbert whispered.

"Once we are gone you are going to get attacked. I have faith that you will be able to kill them all. Once you have done that follow us to the Slave Masters."

"What if we are too far behind?" Delbert didn't sound confident.

Bern looked at Zenon, but didn't say anything. The strange man was cowering in the corner. He didn't seem to have any understanding of the situation. It was a risk, but one he had to take.

Three of the slavers, at great risk to their own lives, manoeuvred their way between Bern and Delbert. Even with their weapons drawn they were no match for the three men. Their only saving grace was that Bern and Hadar were coming peacefully. There was no reason for them to attack now that they were disarmed. A gentle poke in the back was all that was needed to get Bern and Hadar moving. The slaver who had been doing all the talking led the way out.

With the extra room in the cavern a number of bandits and slavers entered. There was little room to battle, but room nevertheless.

"What do we do now?" Delbert asked no one in particular.

"Kill them, yes, yes, yes... kill them all..." Zenon retreated as far away as he could without leaving the cavern.

"The masters will 'ave their prize," one of the slavers drawled. "Don't see no reason to keep 'em alive." He started laughing when he finished and was that echoed by the other slavers in the cavern.

The cavern was evenly matched. Not including Zenon there were five on both sides. There was no room for anyone else to join the battle, at least not until someone had died and even then the corpse would make it difficult.

"Let's show them what it means to be a King's Forest Bandit," Delbert called out, louder than necessary.

His words were followed by a rousing cry from the other bandits, even those at the back of the tunnel. There was no doubt they were prepared for what was ahead of them. They needed to dispose of the slavers as quickly as possible and then chase after the others.

Even though both sides were prepared for battle neither wanted to start the fray. There was little room to move and they only just realised that the battle wasn't going to be as easy as they originally thought. The slavers were used to the tight conditions, but they had never had an opponent who fought back. The most they had done was whip the slaves who weren't working fast enough.

The bandits had their own issues. Although fighting in the forest wasn't completely open, there was more room to move. It was a tactical nightmare that really didn't play to anyone's advantage.

The standoff remained for the next few minutes as both sides tried to work out the best way to attack. There seemed to be no good way to start. In the end it was Zenon who forced their hand. The wretched man had scratched a piece of rock from the wall and he hurled it the closest slaver striking him on the head.

"Attack, kill them, kill them all…"

It was Zenon's words more than his actions that spurred the bandits to fight. The rock throwing had taken everyone by surprise, no more so than the slaver who was struck. With the words still echoing throughout the cavern Delbert saw his opportunity to strike. He slashed the reeling man across the side of his face, slicing off two fingers as his did so. Although it wasn't a killing blow it rendered the slaver useless in battle.

The other slavers were quick to react. Delbert took a step backwards and nearly tripped over one of his men. He recovered just in time to block a wild swing. The fight wasn't going to be an easy one to resolve.

***

The lead slaver walked with purpose, but with no great speed. He did his best to try and ignore those walking behind him, but he couldn't help himself. There was a question that he wanted to ask, but he couldn't bring himself to speak. He wanted to know how they managed to sneak into the mines without being seen. It didn't make any sense. No one should be able to get past the main guards.

Bern hoped that he had made the right decision. He knew they were heading in the right direction, but it was a matter of what was going to happen when they arrived. Without their weapons there would be little chance for bargaining. He would have to rely on his power of persuasion.

The further they travelled the more torches lit the walls. It was a fair sign they were still on track. Neither Bern nor Hadar had any idea how the slaver knew where he was leading them. There didn't seem to be any recognisable markings on the walls. When they stopped for a small break Bern couldn't resist asking the question.

"How do you know where we are going?" he asked casually.

A broad smile appeared on the leader face. "You don't last long down here if you can't find your way around. Many a slaver has been lost in the tunnels, never to be seen again."

Bern simply nodded his head. It made perfect sense, although it still didn't explain how he was able to find his way. He figured that he had pushed his luck far enough and he let the conversation die. There was little point is continuing just to satisfy his curiosity.

After a short rest they were on the move again. The next tunnel the slaver took them in sloped gently upward. As they moved the sound of metal hitting stone could be heard echoing through the tunnel ahead. Bern thought it was a good sign they were nearing their destination.

Now that they were getting close Bern gave some serious thought to disarming and killing their captives. He didn't think that it would be too hard. Besides the slaver who had done all the talking he doubted that any of the others would know how to use the weapons in their hands. It would be easy for them to succeed, but there was always the chance that one of them could get killed. It wasn't the risk that deterred him, but the fact that he didn't know how many other slavers were waiting for them. It was obvious that the slavers were looking for them and they would soon be reaching a heavily guarded area. It was better for them to see how things played out before making any rash decisions.

They rounded a corner and came out into the main mine. Bern had to stop himself from looking up to see where they had come in. He kept his head bowed and tried not to draw any attention to themselves.

Hadar looked around the mines and all the wretched souls working there. He wondered if one of the men was the High Chancellor. He had no idea what the man looked like and no idea how they were ever going to find him. He could only hope that the slave masters had an idea.

The wall remained roughly cut as they neared the slave masters' quarters. Bern had expected the wall to become smoother which was not the case. It seemed as though no one really cared for the aesthetics of the place. Bern really didn't know why he had thought it would be different.

The lead slaver stopped them outside a crudely cut, timber door. His demeanour had clearly changed since they arrived, there was a touch of fear in his eyes. Bern wasn't sure if it was a good sign or a bad sign as he waited intently for the slaver to speak.

"You need to be very careful what you say to the slave masters. They are not known for their patience. If I was you I wouldn't speak until you are told to."

Bern didn't reply.

The slaver opened the door and led the way inside. Bern and Hadar followed whilst the other slavers stood outside looking at each other. They weren't sure what they were supposed to do. The situation had never come up before, but as a rule they weren't allowed inside the slave masters' quarters. After a nervous moment they disappeared back into the mines.

"Ah, Armando, I see you have returned." The slave master who sat at a small table only looked up briefly. He spoke with distain in his voice. "I suppose you have failed me again."

Armando dropped his prisoners' weapons on the floor as a sign he had succeeded.

"These are the men you have been looking for, Slave Master Genero. I have done as you have asked." Armando took a step back as he spoke. He was taking a risk speaking so abruptly to one of the slave masters, especially one like Genero.

His words brought Genero's full attention. He stopped what he was doing and looked up at the group. It was more than he was expecting, but he knew it wasn't all of them. He didn't know the exact amount, but he knew there should be more than two. He considered them carefully before he called out to his fellow slave masters.

"Curt, Emil, get in here!"

"What do you want?" Curt called out as he burst into the room. He cut himself short when he saw the two men standing behind Armando. "What have we here?" A sneer appeared on the slave master's face.

"These are the two you have been looking for," there was a touch of pride in Armando's voice.

"Two?" Curt asked. "I thought there were more than two?" He looked at the other two slave masters.

"Yes there were more than two we were looking for," Genero agreed.

"The rest have been taken care of. They will not bother us anymore."

Bern had to smile at that last statement. He had faith that Delbert and his group of bandits would make short work of the slavers. He had no doubt they were on their way to rescue them, not that they really needed rescuing just yet.

"Did we ask you to take care of the other invaders?" Curt sneered.

"Ah, um… well… no sirs, but I thought…"

"You thought? That was your first mistake. No one asked you to think. Get back out there and find the traitors who have invaded our mines." Genero dismissed Armando with a wave of his hand.

The slaver stiffened his jaw as he turned. There was no reason to keep the others alive. It was clear that the two he had brought were the leaders. Whatever information the slave master's needed they would gain from them. He wanted to teach the three arrogant pigs a lesson, but he knew it wasn't the time. Instead he steeled himself and left the room.

"So this is not such a good day for you two," Genero laughed once the door was closed.

Neither of them replied.

"It seems as though you have stumbled on something that you shouldn't have," Curt added. "Now it's time for you to answer some questions."

Again Bern and Hadar remained quiet. Hadar wanted to speak, but he had promised himself that he would let Bern do all the talking. He didn't think that his temper would do them any favours. He wanted nothing more than to pick up his weapon and kill the three Slave masters.

"You are wise not to speak out of turn. Most slaves would be on the floor grovelling by now," Emil sounded suspicious, making it sound less of a compliment.

"That just adds to the mystery," Curt added.

"Okay, enough of this chit chat, it is time to get down to business," Genero stood as he spoke. He walked to where the weapons lay on the ground. He picked up Bern's axe and studied it carefully. "Can't say I have even seen a weapon like this before. You two are quite the enigmas. Now the question we would all like to know is how you managed to find your way into the mines without anyone seeing you."

Bern remained silent and Hadar followed his lead.

Genero fingered the blade menacingly. He wanted to intimidate the two men, but was failing miserably. No one had ever stood up to him before and he didn't like it. Even though he held a weapon, he really didn't feel as though he had any advantage.

"Lost your tongue? Well I am not surprised. Curt, let's see if you can make them remember how to speak," Genero continued.

Curt didn't look happy with being singled out. He had been quite content staying at the back of the room. He took a nervous step forward before stopping again.

"Emil, I think this is more your line of work. You like to get answers out of the slaves." There was an evil grin on Curt's face which wiped the smile from Emil's.

"Why do I have to do it? This is your show Genero. You should do the dirty work."

Hadar smiled to himself. He had to admit he wasn't sure why Bern had remained silent, but now he did. By not speaking and not breaking down he was having more of an effect then if they were to make threats. The three slave masters had no idea what they were up against and that scared them. Bern would have to speak soon, but in the meantime Hadar was enjoying himself.

"Very well. It seems as though my friends don't have the stomach for such work. I on the other hand am quite happy to deal out torture.

Let's see how long you remain quiet when I start cutting you." Genero didn't make any move forward. He was hoping the threat would be enough to get them talking.

Bern thought for a moment. It didn't take him long to figure that his silence had served its purpose. It would only be a matter of time before one of the slave masters would have to follow through on their threats and that wouldn't prove anything.

"We are looking for the High Chancellor. We believe that he is being held captive here in the mines," Bern spoke before Genero moved.

It wasn't what anyone was expecting, but it was good enough for Genero to stop. It was a start and that's all that mattered to the slave master. Now it was time for him to get the answers they were after.

"That is the why, but for the moment I am more interested in the how. Tell me how you managed to sneak past the guards, through a locked door and into the mines undetected with so many men."

"That is not important. What is important is the location of the High Chancellor. You of all people should care for his safe return." Bern had a bad feeling the conversation was going to go around in circles.

"I think you have misread the situation. You are our prisoners and therefore you will answer our questions," Emil said from the other side of the room. He made sure that he was safely behind Genero.

Bern raised his hand as he sensed that Hadar was about to say something. The duke had tried his best to remain silent, but it was becoming more difficult. He was glad that Bern had stopped him. He wasn't sure what he was going to say, but he knew he would enflame the situation.

"I repeat. I thought that you would want to find the High Chancellor. He is your ruler is he not?" Bern ignored the question.

"Our ruler is whoever sits in the Grand Cathedral and I believe that the High Chancellor is still there."

The other slave masters knew that was not true. They had been the ones who had helped Za'aroz hide the real High Chancellor in the first place. He had offered them high positions of power once the war was over and being such simple minded people they believed him.

Bern looked at Hadar. They both knew there was deception at play. He knew it wasn't going to be easy to get answers and he was prepared for such a response.

"We know that he is here and we know that you know where he is. Now if you want to keep your lives I would suggest that you tell us," Bern spoke coldly, his words sent a shiver down Hadar's spine.

The words didn't have their desired effect on the slave masters and Genero started laughing. His two companions weren't so sure it was a joke, but they too started laughing when Genero looked at them. They didn't want to seem weak. It was obvious that he was the strongest of the three and that was not lost on Bern. He knew that there was no point in trying to crack him. If he was going to be successful then he would have to get to the others. They both looked nervous as he eyed them carefully.

"You speak a lot for a prisoner. I am sure you won't be so talkative once you have been whipped a few hundred times. Then we will see what you have to say for yourself."

Genero took a step forward as he spoke, expecting the two men to retreat. Instead both Bern and Hadar stood their ground. They weren't going to let the slave master get the better of them. It was going to be a battle of wills and they had no choice, but to win. Bern's next move was going to be vital to both theirs and the High Chancellor's survival.

Chapter 25: Discovery

Delbert had learnt early in the battle that they needed to hold the advantage of numbers in the cavern if they were going to succeed. The slavers had much greater numbers in the tunnels, but there was only room for ten men to fight at any one time.

Although the slavers were an unruly bunch they were still able to take a life. It was more from luck than any real skill. The bandits were used to fighting in the forests of Darshival and not in the confined space of a cavern. This was evident when the battle started. One of the bandits tried to push forward into the fray and tripped over one of his companions. The slaver in question couldn't believe his luck and almost took too long to drive his sword into the bandit's back.

Seeing the dead bandit gave the slavers a false sense of their own abilities and they pushed forward allowing one of the other slavers to enter the cavern. The numbers favoured the slavers and if they weren't in such tight conditions they might have been able to overpower Delbert and his bandits, but that was not the case. Delbert retreated as far he could before starting his attack. There was little room for the fifth and sixth slavers to join the battle, but the bandits had to be wary of them nevertheless.

Once the initial shock was over the bandits grew accustomed to the conditions a lot quicker than the slavers. It wasn't long before the advantage swung back towards the bandits and Delbert was able to make light work of the slaver he was fighting. Once he was dead Delbert pushed forward with his attack. The last thing he wanted to do was to allow the cavern to fill again.

Having a strong leader also held in the favour of the bandits. Delbert ordered the fighters at the front line to back out of the cavern too allow fresh bandits to join the battle. He rotated his men every five to ten minutes. This tactic allowed them to remain fresh, like the slavers coming to refresh their fallen comrades.

The next problem that threatened to destroy the flow of the battle was the piling up of the dead bodies. It was no real advantage to either side of the fight. The clutter helped the slavers who really had no idea how to fight. It didn't allow any flow to the bandits' attacks. On the other hand it didn't take long before they had to climb over the bodies to enter the cavern.

It was Delbert who commanded his bandits to start dragging the bodies out. Anything that impeded the battle wasn't good in his eyes. He wanted to make sure that the rest of his men stayed alive. Losing one man was too much in his book and he wasn't going to lose any more.

Delbert remained in the battle until his muscles ached. There were more slavers than he had thought. Another bandit was happy to join the battle, even more so when he saw who he was replacing. It was time for Delbert to watch from the sidelines.

After the first few slavers dropped to the ground the remaining group started to panic. They had joined the party expecting to be victorious. They had not thought for a moment they would have been defeated. As a slaver they had very rarely had anyone put up a fight and those who did never lasted long. They were more suited to using whips than the crude swords they held. Even though they were losing the slavers still pressed forward. They had been given an order and they knew what would happen if they didn't succeed. The thought of death was much more appealing.

The rotation of the bandits fighting gave away any advantage the slavers had. They pushed their attack forward as to allow only four slavers into the cavern at any one time. Having only four attackers on their own side allowed room for those not fighting to remove the dead bodies. Delbert had to smile from the entrance to the cavern. Things were working out better than he thought they would. He had to admit he didn't have a lot of faith in Bern's plan, but at least it hadn't cost them all their lives.

The battle was fought fiercely on both sides, but in the end there was no real competition. Besides the man who died at the start of the battle there were only a few minor injuries.

"What do we do now captain?" one of the bandits asked.

"Once everyone has been patched up we will follow the others. They have gotten a good head start so we will need to hurry."

"How are we going to be able to find them?" another bandit, who was taking the opportunity to rest, asked.

That was one question he had hoped no one was going to ask. He really had no idea how he was going to find his way in the mines.

"Ah…"

"Ask Zenon… Zenon knows, yes he does…"

Everyone had forgotten about the strange man who had retreated when the fighting had started. He appeared again when everything was over. If anything he looked excited. Delbert wasn't sure if he would in fact know the way, but there didn't seem to be any other choice. It would only be pure luck if he they were able to find the way themselves. Trusting the crazy man was the only option.

"Okay Zenon, show us the way!"

Little did Delbert know the effect his words would have on the man. Zenon jumped to his feet and scooted out the same tunnel Bern and Hadar had been escorted into.

"We're not ready to go yet," he called after Zenon, but he had already disappeared.

Delbert looked around the cavern. There were confused expressions on everyone's faces. No one knew what to think. Delbert could only hope that Zenon had the sense to realise that no one was following him and return. There was a nervous wait in silence until he suddenly reappeared.

"Come on... Come on... No time to waste, no there's not... Have to find Bern, yes we do..."

Again Zenon didn't wait for a response before he turned and left the cavern. This time Delbert wasn't going to let him get away. He moved out of the cave followed by the rest of his group. He knew that Zenon was right. There was no time to waste if they were going to rescue Hadar and Bern, as well as the High Chancellor.

Zenon skipped on ahead and then waited for the others to catch up. Although there were more torches on the wall there were still patches of tunnel that were completely black. Delbert wondered how he was able to see without the aid of torchlight. He knew if it was him he would be surely be banging into the walls. Zenon didn't really seem to notice the difference.

After they had been travelling for what seemed like hours Delbert grabbed hold of Zenon just as he was about to take off again. He wanted to make sure the crazy man did in fact know where they were going.

"Yes, yes... Zenon knows were he's going... He takes different route to the slavers, yes he does... He takes a route that no one knows about... No one will find us... No one will know we are coming..." there was something that resembled a smile on his face.

Once he had finished his explanation Zenon wriggled free from Delbert's grip and continued on his way. Delbert wanted to speak to the others, but he didn't want to lose the strange man. He felt as though they were coming close to their destination and this time Zenon didn't wait for the others the catch up to him. He just figured that they were on the move.

Delbert moved as quickly as he could through the various tunnels in a vain effort to catch the strange man. Once they had left the cavern there were no torches on the walls to light the way and the torches they carried only gave off so much light. Delbert was concerned that they were going to lose Zenon in the darkness. Each time they came to a crossroad Delbert was able to see a mark on the wall that Zenon had left indicating the direction they needed to take. If Delbert was impressed before with Zenon's ability to move in the dark he was now completely speechless. He could only hope that he did indeed know where they were going.

They didn't see Zenon again until they reached a large cavern. The cavern was large enough for everyone to fit inside and Delbert was surprised to see that the cavern was completely lit. He didn't think it was a good sign and had a bad feeling that Zenon had brought them into a trap. The strange man stood with a broad smile on his face.

"Here we are, here we are…" He seemed very proud of himself.

"Where are we? If you have brought us into a trap then I will not rest until…"

"No trap, no, no, no… This is the way, yes it is…" Zenon hopped up and down as he spoke.

Delbert let out sigh of anguish. He was really becoming frustrated with Zenon's antics. He had a bad feeling that time was running out for Bern and Hadar. The more time they wasted the more chance they would end up dead. He wanted nothing more than to reach out and throttle some sense into the strange man, but he figured in the end that would be counterproductive.

***

Genero remained standing in front of Bern for a few minutes. He was unsure of himself and he was getting no support from his colleagues. It seemed as though they were waiting for him to make the decision. All he could do was stand and watch Bern. He had never had anyone stand up to him before, unless it was someone of greater standing than him. When that happened he always backed down, but this was something completely different and he didn't know what to do.

In the end Genero decided that he held the weapon and therefore he held the power. If Bern wasn't going to co-operate then he would taste the bite of his blade. He took two steps forward and that was all Bern needed to strike. He saw by the expression on Genero's face that he was planning to attack and knew that he had to counter.

Two more steps and Genero was within striking distance. Bern had remained still and stalwart up until that point, but when the slave master raised his arm to strike Bern reached out and as and grabbed his wrist. He quickly gave it a sharp twist and he pried the sword loose from Genero's hand. A look of pure horror crossed his face, but Bern was not finished. With his free hand Bern struck out at his neck. The blow caused Genero to drop to his knees, gasping for breath.

The other two slave masters watched on in horror. They couldn't believe what they were seeing. Hadar remained behind Bern, but by his stance they could tell that he was ready to rush in at any moment.

Bern wasn't finished. He'd had enough of the slave master. He knew if he was going to find the High Chancellor it would be the other two who would give him the answers he needed. Keeping a grip on Genero's wrist he spun the man around with one quick movement. When he had him in position he released his wrist and gripped his chin and the crown of his head. Bracing himself Bern then gave a sharp twist. The subtle twang indicated that he had successfully snapped Genero's neck. He then let the body sink to the ground.

The other two slave masters were trembling with fear. They had not expected such a thing to occur and had no idea what to do next. If they had any senses left they would have been inclined to flee, but they both stood frozen to the ground. All they could do was hope that Bern wasn't going to kill them.

Bern smiled an evil smile as he walked to where their weapons lay on the ground. He returned Hadar's to him first before collecting his own. He moved slowly, deliberately, baiting his prey. He could see the fear in their faces and he wanted to play on it. They would be more appeasing if they feared for their lives.

"Now I didn't want to do that." Bern acted as though it was their fault Genero was dead. "If you co-operate then no one else needs to die here today."

"Yes sir, we will help. We always wanted to help. It was Genero who said not to," Emil started grovelling.

Bern had to smile to himself. It was all too easy. They were going to get the answers they were after.

"Where is the High Chancellor?"

"He is in the back room. We brought him here 'cause we knew you were coming. We can go get him for you if you like." Curt stumbled to get the words out. He too wanted to look as though he was trying to help.

"I think we shall go together. Don't want you two sneaking out the back, now do we?"

"Oh course not, me lord, we would never do such a thing." The lie was evident on Emil's face.

"Of course we will show you where the High Chancellor is." Curt was visibly shaking.

Neither of them made any sign of moving and Bern had to refrain from laughing. He wouldn't be surprised if one of them messed their pants. He thought about it for a moment, but then decided that it would be too cruel. Instead he indicated for one of them to move.

Emil was the first to regain his senses. Again it was the fear of dying that forced him into action. What Bern didn't know was that Hadar was fingering the blade of his short sword. In the end that is what urged the slave master to move.

Bern followed after Emil, whilst Hadar kept a close watch on Curt. "I think you and I will stay here."

Hadar took a step forward when he finished speaking, which was mirrored by Curt taking a step back causing him to bump into the wall. He turned around in hope of finding an exit, but there was nothing there. It was Hadar's time to have a little fun, since Bern had had it all so far.

There were six beds in the room, each with their own small table. It was obvious that the High Chancellor wasn't there. Bern felt that Emil was moving a little too keenly towards the back of the room. Although Emil and Curt were good friends he wouldn't think twice about sacrificing his fellow slave master to save his own life.

"Stop there!" Bern boomed as Emil's hand touched the door handle.

"W...w...what?" Emil stammered.

"What is on the other side of the door? I don't want any surprises. As you know I don't like surprises. It makes me do rash things."

"The High Chancellor is behind this door," there was something in Emil's tone that Bern didn't like. Although he was scared he was still thinking about his escape.

"What else is waiting for us behind the door?"

"What do you mean?" Emil tried to play innocent, but the stammer in his voice betrayed him.

"Do you really want me to repeat the question?" Bern snapped.

"There are five guards watching over the High Chancellor," Emil sounded dejected.

"And what would have happened once you opened the door?"

Emil lowered his head. He really didn't want to answer the question, but he knew what would happen if he didn't. "I would have entered the room. Once you followed you would have been killed."

Bern doubted they would have managed that, but at least they would have tried. There was no need for more dead bodies, although he would take great pleasure in killing the scum that ran the mines.

"Well you better go and tell your friends to put their weapons down and back up away from the door."

Emil opened the door and then stood back. "This is slave master Emil, I am coming in unhindered."

Emil took a deep breath before he entered the room. Bern made sure that he remained a safe distance from the door. There was no way he was going to trust the slave master. He didn't think the man would betray him, but he wasn't going to take the risk. There was too much at stake for him to be complacent.

"What's this all about?" Bern could hear a gruff voice come form inside the room. "No one is supposed to enter without Genero's expressed permission."

"Who do you think you are talking to?" Emil's voice went suddenly hard. "Genero is not the boss around here. You will do what you are told and you will like it."

"Erm..." it was another voice in the room that stammered.

"We were given orders and we follow them," another voice pleaded.

"Be that as it may but I am here to tell you what to do and you will listen."

"I'm sorry Emil, but if you recall you yourself told us not to change the rules for anything. We are to remain here and guard the prisoner at all cost. It doesn't make any sense what you are saying..." Bern knew that it was only a matter of time before the guards realised that Emil was under duress. It seemed as though he would have to teach them a lesson, it's just a shame they wouldn't be alive at the end to remember it.

Suddenly a man's head popped around the corner and looked at Bern. The missing look of surprise told Bern that he had been expecting to see someone he didn't recognise. When he was sure Bern was alone he disappeared back into the room.

"Who is that? He doesn't look like any slave master I have seen before." The guard kept his voice low, but Bern could clrealy hear him.

"Of course he is not a slave master. He is from the Grand Cathedral and if you ask any further questions you will taste my whip on your back."

Bern was surprised at the quick wittedness of the slave master. The man might have just avoided a fight.

"Are you sure that it is a good idea to let him in here. We are not supposed to let anyone see the prisoner."

"Again you are thinking and no one told you to think. Now drop your weapons and stand to attention." It had been the disarming of the guards that had concerned Emil the most. He tried his best to sneak it into the conversation and hoped they would just listen to him.

That was not the case. "Drop our weapons?"

"Enough Jay, do you want to get us flogged?" a softer voice spoke.

"This isn't right." Jay pushed his way past Emil and out into the room. He had his sword drawn, but lowered in a non-threatening manner. "Who are you and what business do you have here?"

The other four guards also wanted to see what was happening. It was more out of morbid curiosity than any real desire to support their fellow guard. They saw that Jay had drawn his sword they all followed suit. They felt better being armed as there was something very threatening about they way Bern stood.

"What do you all think that you are doing?" Emil appeared in the doorway, his face bright red. "Get back inside."

"This situation isn't right Emil. You have lost your nerve and you are not fit to command." Jay didn't take his eyes from Bern. "Now I would advise you to tell me who you are and what you are doing here?"

Bern brandished his sword as the guard said his spiel. It seemed as though Emil had completely lost control. That didn't seem to faze Bern, he was already expecting a fight.

"I am here for the prisoner. You have all been relieved of your duty," Bern tried to sound as officious as possible.

"What is your name and rank?" Jay wasn't going to be dissuaded so easily.

"That is none of your business. All that you have to know is that I out-rank you and that's all that matters. Now I believe your were given an order to drop your weapons. I suggest that you listen." Bern didn't miss a beat.

"Where is Genero? He will get to the bottom of this." Jay insisted.

"Genero wanted to stop me and he is now lying dead on the floor. Now unless you want to share his fate I would suggest that you drop your weapons," Bern threatened.

Jay looked back at Emil who in turn nodded his head. It seemed as though the guard couldn't believe what he was hearing. Bern had a strange feeling that Jay was closer to the slave master than anyone thought. He didn't think his threat was really going to have the effect that he wanted.

"Then you will join him soon." Jay looked to his left and right. "I think it's time to teach this fop a lesson."

When he finished speaking Jay charged forward. He had expected the other four guards to follow, but that was not the case. Bern was able to simply side-step the attack. Once Jay was off-balance Bern brought the blade of his sword down on the top of his head. The blade sunk in, killing the man instantly. When the body dropped to the ground Bern had to stand on Jay's chest to pull the blade out of his head. If the other guards had joined his charge it would have been the perfect time to attack, but they still remained standing at the other end of the room.

"Does anyone else what to question my authority?" a drop of blood dripped from the end of his sword to accentuate his gruesome point.

The guards all looked at each other before dropping their weapons. Their first thought was to run for safety, but that meant passing

Bern. He still held his sword menacingly and no one wanted to take the risk of upsetting him. Instead they all dropped to their knees and placed their hands on their heads in a sign of submission.

"Now, let's get down to business. I think I would like to inspect the prisoner now Emil." Bern casually strolled towards the room. He was confident that no one would try anything else now that he had asserted his authority.

Bern walked confidently into the cell room knowing that there would be no more surprises. Even so he still held his sword in front of him. The first thing that hit him when he entered to small cell room was the smell. There was a mixture of stale sweat and human waste. His initial reaction was to retch, but he held on.

After he was able to recover from the sickening smell Bern was able to look around the room. The room was split in two, divided by iron bars. On his side of the room there were five stools and five wooden cups. On the other side of the bars was a man wearing tattered rags huddled in the corner. He didn't notice that Bern had entered. Large blood stained welts showed where the man had been whipped repeatedly.

"Are you the High Chancellor?" Bern asked softly.

The man in the corner slowly looked up. He shielded his eyes from the torch light. When he saw Bern he shook his head and buried his head back in his arms.

"It's alright. I have come here to help you. I am not here to hurt you."

The huddled figure didn't move. Bern tried to keep his voice as soft as possible, but that wasn't as easy as it sounded. Over the months as leader of the army his voice has taken on a harsh tone that was hard to remove. He hoped it was enough to calm the High Chancellor. He couldn't imagine what it would have taken to reduce such a strong leader into a dribbling mess.

"I'm not falling for that one again." Finally he spoke, his voice was strangely defiant.

Bern looked at the lock on the door. It had rusted over the many years. Taking a high swing of his sword he brought the blade down on the lock, shearing it in half. The lock clinked to the ground and the door opened ajar. Hearing the sound forced the High Chancellor to look up.

"What do you want?" the confidence had left his voice.

"I told you. I'm here to rescue you Augustus."

Slowly the High Chancellor came to his feet. He looked unsteady and still unsure of the man standing before him. He didn't look as though he was ready to leave his cell.

"I am General Bern of the Alliance army. We need your help and in return I will save your life." It wasn't really the appropriate time to discuss such matters, but Bern continued anyway. "We need your army if we are to defeat the Evil One."

"Get me out of here and you can have whatever you wish." The High Chancellor took a tentative step forward.

Before he could leave the cell there came an all mighty crash from the front door to the slave masters' quarters. The sudden noise caused Bern to spin around. Although he couldn't see what was happening, he had a bad feeling that things were about to get ugly.

Chapter 26: The High Chancellor

Delbert looked at Zenon. He wanted to strike the strange man in frustration. He had brought them to a dead end, which didn't make any sense. There was a no reason at all why the cavern should be lit. There wasn't enough time for Zenon to light all the torches before he arrived, or at least he assumed there wasn't. It all seemed very suspicious.

"You have brought us to a dead end Zenon. What are we supposed to do now?" there was anger in his voice.

"No dead end, no, no, no... This is the way, yes it is... No one knows... No one but me..." Zenon was hoping from one foot to the other in excitement.

It only made Delbert want to strike him even more. He couldn't see how the man could believe that they weren't lost. There was no other exit to the cavern other than the one they entered in. He turned to his men and was about to address them when Zenon spoke again.

"Come help, it's easier if you help..."

Delbert turned around and saw Zenon readying himself to push a large boulder. The rock had blended in with the stone wall and Delbert had not seen it. He wasn't sure what was behind it, but it could be the only reason for Zenon's excitement. Without another thought he moved to help the strange man.

The boulder moved out of the way easier than he thought it would. He didn't know if it was the weight of the rock or the strength of Zenon. Either way he didn't have time to find out. The freshly moved boulder revealed a small tunnel cut into the wall. Zenon looked even more pleased with himself than he did before.

"This is the hole... This will take us to the slave masters, yes it will... Now is the time..." Delbert could have sworn there was more to his last comment, but he couldn't be sure. It was hard enough to keep up with Zenon at the best of times.

"Well then lead the way," Delbert offered. He wasn't going to let Zenon follow behind him. Whatever was waiting for them on the other side of the tunnel, Zenon would see it first.

"Yes, yes, of course... Don't be afraid, nothing to be afraid of... Zenon will lead the way..."

He didn't wait for further conversation before disappearing into the tunnel. That wasn't at all what Delbert was expecting, but it did relieve some of his tension. He still had a bad feeling they were being led into a trap. The problem was that he had no choice. There was no turning back, that would certainly be a death sentence.

"Be prepared for whatever we might run into when we get to the other side of that tunnel. I don't trust Zenon and we need to be careful. I don't want to lose anyone else. Those who are injured come through last," Delbert commanded.

"But sir, we can still fight."

Delbert wasn't sure who had said it. He looked around the cavern, but no one wanted to make it known. He thought about speaking again, but he didn't see the point. He knew that his men would do as he ordered and he didn't need to berate anyone for being foolishly brave. Taking a deep breath Delbert plunged into the darkness.

The tunnel wasn't large enough to carry a torch. The only light that came in was from the cavern until someone else entered the tunnel. Delbert could hear his breathing getting heavier and heavier as he continued. The closeness of the tunnel and the darkness was very disturbing. On more than one occasion he bumped his head on an obstruction protruding from the roof. Each time he cursed loudly, partly for the pain and partly to warn those behind him. He had no idea how Zenon was able to travel apparently unhindered. He couldn't hear how far ahead the strange man was, but he was sure he would hear if Zenon had bumped his head.

The further they continued in the tunnel the more bends and corners there were. These were worse than any obstacles. There was no way to tell when the tunnel would take a sharp turn until he hit the wall in front of him. All he could hope was that all the bumps and bruises were worth while. The first time he came to a sudden stop it caused a chain reaction behind him, everyone just continued on until they ran into him. He learnt quickly to call out when there was a change of direction.

After what seemed like an age Delbert could see a small sliver of light ahead of him. When he turned one more bend he could see an opening. Once he reached the exit he paused. He hoped the men behind him would be able to see well enough to stop as he didn't want to risk calling out. If there was anyone waiting for them he didn't want to alert them of their presence, although if it was a trap he was sure that Zenon would have sprung it.

First he listened. It didn't sound like there was anyone on the other side. If he poked his head out then someone might see him. His heart was racing as he strained to hear something. Suddenly Zenon's face appeared looking back into the tunnel.

"Come on, come on, no time to waste… Let's go, let's go…"

If there had of been room Delbert would have jumped with fright. He had not heard the man move at all. The sudden surprise was very disturbing. He was grateful that it was Zenon and not a slaver greeting him.

Delbert quickly pushed himself out of the tunnel and sprung to his feet. Looking around he realised there was no one there. They had come out into another cavern, similar to the one before. The relief was obvious on his face. The cavern was lit in a similar fashion, only this time he didn't worry about wondering how it came to be lit. He waited for everyone to arrive before he spoke.

"Now where do we go?" he asked.

"Outside is the main mine. We follow around the wall for a short while and then we reach the slave masters' quarters. There you will find your friends." Delbert took a step backwards. For the first time Zenon had spoken in a coherent manner. There was a new sharpness about his appearance that had not been there before.

"Who are you?" he breathed the words.

"All in good time," Zenon whispered. "Time to go, yes, yes, yes..."

"Let's move out men. Stay on your toes, there are enemies everywhere," Delbert barked as he regained his composure.

It was at that point that Delbert realised that again there was no other exit. He was about to speak, but then thought better of it. He knew that there must be an exit somewhere hidden and he would just have to wait for Zenon to show it to them.

"Come on, come on..."

Delbert spun around to see Zenon's head seemingly sticking out of the wall. He had no idea where his body had gone. He wondered if he was starting to see things. The closeness of the mines was starting to affect his mind, but then he realised it was an optical illusion. The passage out of the tunnel was blending into the outer wall. It would be nearly impossible to find the exit if you didn't know it was there.

The corridor leading out of the cavern wasn't as long as Delbert had expected and all of a sudden they came out into the mines. He looked back at his men walking out and he could see the corridor, but when they were done he couldn't. The same illusion affected the other side of the corridor. Delbert was amazed. It would have taken a long time to design such a passage, if it was indeed man-made.

"Let's keep moving, there is no telling who is around." Zenon took on his more controlled persona.

Delbert shook his head, but didn't comment. It wasn't worth the effort of asking the question. In the end he figured it would be much easier to continue and wait for the answers. He was sure he would find out soon enough who the strange man really was. It was time to rescue Bern and Hadar and nothing else mattered.

Zenon continued to lead the way until they reached a large wooden door. He stopped out the front and looked around nervously. When he was sure there was no else there he spoke again.

"This is it!" Zenon hoped from foot to foot.

"Step back," Delbert commanded as he stepped up to the door. It looked solid enough, but he knew that it wouldn't take too much to knock it down. "Jaeger, come here!"

A large man stepped out from the group. He was larger than any of the other men in Delbert's command and his muscles bulged under his shirt. He looked keen to help, knowing what was about to be asked of him.

"This door looks pretty sturdy. Let's see what you can do about it."

Jaeger dropped his shoulder and braced himself for the impact. As much as he knew he could break the door down he also knew that it was going to hurt. Taking a deep breath he charged and put all his weight against it. The once solid door shattered as if it was made of twigs and the rest of the bandits followed inside with a roar.

***

Bern rushed past Emil, leaving the High Chancellor cowering in his cell. His only thought was getting to Hadar's aid. By the sound of the roaring voices he assumed there was a fair contingent of slavers coming to attack. He could only hope that there weren't too many.

When he arrived in the front room his heart almost skipped a beat when he saw Delbert and the other bandits standing before him. Then he saw Zenon standing next to Hadar, hoping from foot to foot. He thought the man looked as though he was about to crawl out of his skin. There was no telling if it was from nervousness or excitement.

"Would you stop that, please," Bern snapped, but then softened his voice.

"It's good to see you general," Delbert saluted as he spoke.

"And you too captain." Bern returned the salute.

"Did you find the High Chancellor?"

For a moment Bern had forgotten about the scared man in the prison cell and then he remembered Emil and his heart skipped a beat. The slave master was alone with the High Chancellor and it would be the perfect opportunity to run a sword through the prisoner's gut.

"Yes, yes, the High Chancellor, is he here?" Zenon asked excitedly.

Bern ignored Zenon and turned around. When he walked into the second room he was surprised at what he saw. Emil was prostrating on the ground whilst the High Chancellor was standing in the doorway. It seemed as though the slave master was praying for mercy.

"It is good to see you High Chancellor." Bern lowered his head slightly, but that was the extent of his respect. He wasn't sure what the correct protocol was, but he figured there wasn't really time for anything else. The Alliance would face the full brunt of the Castalial army and the man standing before him was the only one who could stop them.

"Get me out of here!" Bern wasn't sure if it was a plea or command.

"You aren't going anywhere!" the voice came from behind Bern. He recognised it as Zenon, but it sounded a lot more controlled. It sent a shiver down his spine.

"This isn't the time for your games Zenon. We appreciate your help, but now it is time for us to leave," Bern stressed.

"Oh no Bern. We are not leaving just yet, not until you have all the facts. Isn't that right Augustus?" there was venom in his voice.

"Who are you?" the High Chancellor peered at Zenon. He thought he recognised the voice, but couldn't figure out who it was.

"I'm the man who you betrayed many, many years ago." Zenon moved in front of Bern cautiously.

"What are you talking about? What is the meaning of this general? Are you here to rescue me or question me?" It seemed as though his strength and confidence was returning to him.

"Step back Zenon. This isn't the time or the place for your nonsense," Bern snapped.

"This is exactly the time and the place." Zenon made no attempt to move. "Tell them Augustus. Tell them what you did to me all those years ago."

"I don't know what you are talking about. If I have wronged you I am sorry, but I command a kingdom and I can't remember every person I have dealings with. Now, please general, I would like to get moving."

"Of course, but it is it not that easy. The Dark Knight has assumed your mantle. We need to get you cleaned up before we return to the Grand Cathedral." Bern explained.

"We are not going anywhere before he admits the truth."

Zenon had found a short sword on the floor and had picked it up. He held it tentatively. It did look that at one stage in his life he had known how to use it. He directed the point at the High Chancellor. Bern felt like striking the strange man, but refrained. Something was telling him that he should listen to what he had to say.

"What is the hold up?" Hadar boomed. "It will only be a matter of time before we are inundated with slavers."

Bern had wished that he had slain the guards instead of letting them run free. He knew Hadar was right. They would surely gather all the other slavers and return to attack.

"Okay, spit it out Zenon. We don't have all day to play games. Get to the point or we will keep moving."

"He knows what he has done and he needs to admit it. If he doesn't admit it then he will just deny it." It seemed as though Zenon wasn't going to return to his broken speech pattern.

"I honestly don't know what you are talking about." The High Chancellor took a step forward, but went no further as Zenon waved the sword at him. "What do you want from me?"

"Think hard, think very hard."

The High Chancellor let his shoulders drop in frustration as he tried to remember where he knew Zenon from. He knew that he recognised the man, but he couldn't for the life of him work out where. Suddenly his heart skipped a beat.

"No. That's impossible. It can't be you. You should be dead by now," there was pure horror in the High Chancellor's voice.

"What are you talking about?" Hadar boomed from behind the other two men.

"Just wait. It's finally coming to him." There was a wry smile on Zenon's face.

"But it can't be you. It isn't possible." The High Chancellor was aghast.

"Spit it out man, we don't have all day," again it was Hadar who boomed the command.

"He is Julius, but he shouldn't be alive. He should have died many years ago." He knew that he shouldn't be saying anything, but he couldn't help himself. It was as if something or someone was compelling him.

"Do you want to help things along Zenon? We really need to get moving," Bern was starting to become nervous. It wasn't just the fact they were in a vulnerable position, but the Alliance would soon be at war, if they weren't already. The sooner they left the sooner he could stop the battle.

"I think you should explain Augustus. This is your story to tell." Zenon, or Julius, continue to menacingly waver his sword at the High Chancellor.

"Can we just get out of here Julius? I will tell them everything once we are out of the mines."

"He makes a good point Zenon, we need to get moving. Surely this can wait until we have everything sorted out." Bern had to agree.

"We go nowhere until he admits the truth. Only then can we get everything sorted out, as you call it," he took a step closer as he spoke.

"Okay, okay, I will tell you." The High Chancellor put his hand up in front of his face in a defensive gesture, not that it would have done anything to protect him against a sword. "It is quite a long story, so I think you should prepare yourselves." Upon hearing that Augustus hoped Bern would to order them to leave, but he didn't.

"Very well. It was over twenty years ago. I was a young man. From an early age I was being primed to be High Chancellor when the time was right. There was much dissention in the Grand Cathedral and the High Chancellor at the time had many enemies. The High Chancellor was my uncle and since he didn't have any children of his own I was the most likely to succeed him. There would be little opposition as long as he didn't name another successor."

"Can you get to the point?" Bern barked.

"I told you that it was a long story." He defended.

"You can cut to the chase Augustus. You know what it is they need to hear."

"Fine. My supporters conspired to kidnap Julius and place him in the mines. Once he was gone I would take the mantle of High Chancellor. I was young and excited and could only dream of power. I didn't know what I was doing," he was speaking directly at Julius. "You have to believe me when I say that I didn't know you would survive this long. I was told that the average life span of someone in the mines is five years."

"And that is supposed to make it right? You gave me a death sentence for your own gain," Julius snapped.

"I'm sorry uncle." The High Chancellor dropped to one knee.

With a gasp Bern finally realised what was happening. He returned his attention to the man who he had been calling Zenon. He could see that man had disappeared and it was now Julius standing before him, although something still didn't seem right.

"But it can't be possible uncle, you should be over sixty by now and you don't look a day older than when you were imprisoned." Augustus had to think back, but he was sure he spoke the truth.

"It seems as though I wasn't meant to die down here. Now it is time for me to take back what was mine."

Bern realised it was the man's age that bothered him. He couldn't be the old High Chancellor. He remembered the stories he heard when he was a child. The High Chancellor was in his forties when he was deposed. If anything the man before him looked younger. That being the case Bern had seen enough to know that he really didn't know anything and that anything was possible. It seemed as though the two men knew each other and that was enough for him.

"So what does this mean?" Hadar asked, clearly confused.

"It means that once this is over there will be a new High Chancellor in charge," Julius spoke before Augustus could.

"This isn't going to help our situation," Bern said. "We need to restore Augustus to power. It's the only way that we can remove the Dark Knight," Bern contested.

"That is not going to happen." Julius lowered his sword and turned to face Bern. "General you must return me to power. I have waited for this day. It is all that has kept me alive over the years. Now it is my time again."

"He has a point Bern. This could work better for us. If we return with two High Chancellor's then we should be able convince the Council of High Priests that there is a Dark Knight masquerading as one," Hadar added.

Bern had to admit that Hadar made a good point. He hadn't really thought how he was going to remove the Dark Knight. Za'aroz was more powerful than the small contingent of soldiers he had with him. He had to rely on the soldiers within the Grand Cathedral and they had to believe they had the true High Chancellor.

"I guess we don't have much choice. I suppose two High Chancellor's are better than one," he resigned.

"I'm sorry general, but I don't think anyone is going to believe that these men are or were even once were High Chancellors," Delbert added.

"You're right captain, we need to get them cleaned up before go much further," Bern turned to Emil. "Is there somewhere we can clean these two and give them fresh clothes?"

Emil looked somewhat confused. It had been many years since he had been able to wash in something other than a bucket of water. He didn't think that was what Bern had in mind. It didn't take Bern long to realise the error in his question. They would have to enter the Grand Cathedral if they were going to find the suitable facilities.

"Well it looks like we are heading into the Grand Cathedral. Linus!" Bern called.

For most of the journey in the mines Linus had stayed at the back of the group. They needed to keep Linus alive if they were going to prove who the true High Chancellor was. The group had protected him and kept him out of harms way. When they entered the Grand Cathedral it would be Linus who would lead the way.

"Yes." Linus emerged from the small group of bandits. "What can I do for you?"

"Do you think that you will be able to talk our way into the Grand Cathedral?" Bern asked.

"I would doubt that guards would know who I am. I can try, but that is the best I can offer." Linus didn't sound confident. "I doubt they would know a High Priest of Jade from a common scullery maid. And if they did I'm sure it is only because the Dark Knight has warmed them to imprison me on sight."

It was a good point. Even if the guards had heard his name, there was no chance that they would know what he looked like. He was going to have to rely on another plan if things were going to work out. Things had already started going off the rail and he didn't need any more surprises.

"Okay Emil, it seems as though we need your assistance," Bern smiled an evil smile.

"No, I can't do that. The High Chancellor will kill me if I help you," Emil didn't think before he spoke.

"I will kill you if you don't help us," Bern spoke before either of the real High Chancellor's had the chance. "Now let's get moving."

Bern wasn't going to wait around for an argument. He could feel time was running out and he was starting to become edgy. All of a sudden he really wanted to be out of the mines. Levelling his sword, Bern wanted Emil to know that he meant business. The slave master had remained on the floor, intent on not moving. Taking one look at Bern's face it told him that if he didn't there would be consequences.

"Fine I will help you, but you have to help me in return. You have to protect me," Emil whined.

"You will receive no such..." Augustus started.

"Do what we ask and we will make sure that Za'aroz doesn't touch you."

Bern turned around and winked at Augustus with the same evil grin on his face. The look stopped the High Chancellor from saying anything more.

"Fine, I accept your word. I will do what I can to get you out of the mines." Emil came to his feet. He looked at the others nervously still unsure of the situation. If he turned his back on the others he was sure he would receive a knife in his back and if it was up to Augustus he would.

"What about this one?" Hadar asked, pointing at Curt who was huddled up in the corner of the front room.

Curt had hoped they would forget he was there. He was trying his best the fade into the background, but was unsuccessful. He started shaking, the fear evident on his face. There was a pensive look on Bern's face as he thought about the second slave master. He didn't want to take Curt with them, he knew that for sure, but the question was what to do with him.

"Hadar, what we do with traitors?" finally Bern spoke.

"With pleasure general!"

Hadar grabbed his sword and took two large steps forwards. Curt put his arms up to protect himself, but it was a futile exercise. Hadar drew his blade through his chest and into his heart. The slave master died instantly followed by a sharp squeal from Emil. Hadar had to place his boot on Curt's shoulder to pull his blade out. Once it was free blood started to squirt from the wound. "Now, let's get moving." Bern smiled.

Emil led the way out of the slave masters' quarters followed by Bern, Hadar, and Delbert, the two High Chancellors and Linus and then the rest of the group. The slave master was fearful for his life. Not that long ago he had been the one to make the decisions, or at least he'd had a choice in them, and now his life was in the hands of another. If he was going to get out alive then he needed to be very careful.

The three leaders kept a close eye on Emil. No one trusted him, although they were sure he wouldn't try anything. He knew that he would be the first to die if there were any problems and that was something he wanted to avoid.

"What's this?" one of the guards spoke to his companions.

There were a total of six guards standing in front of the large, double doors. The captain was conspicuously missing. Bern didn't think that it was good sign. He couldn't imagine why there wasn't a captain on duty. Even without that fact he could tell that something was amiss.

"You are a slave master, aren't you?" one of the other guards spoke. "What business do you have here," by the tone in the guard's voice he didn't think much of the profession.

"You have no business here. You know slave masters aren't allowed to approach the Holy Gates." The original guard sneered.

"I am here to escort these men from the mines. You will be pleased to hear that they have completed their inspection and everything is fine," Emil spoke nervously.

The guards looked at one another, trying to work out what Emil was talking about. They had only just started their shift and it looked as though the men before them had been in the mine for longer than that. The problem was that no one had told them there were soldiers inspecting the mines, not to mention the fact that the men before them looked like mercenaries, not soldiers. The situation didn't seem right at all.

"We have not been told anything of this. Who are they and what are they doing here?" the first guard asked.

"Who we are and what we are doing here is none of your business." Bern stepped forward. "All you need to know is that you have to let us through. We have important matters to report on."

"I don't think so and do not address me again. Slave Master, tell what is happening and do it quick else you'll taste my blade."

"These men, they need to get into the Grand Cathedral. That's all you need to know." Emil was starting to fall apart. He wasn't smart enough to be able to outwit anyone.

"Where is your captain? He will have the information you need." Bern took a risk.

"There are no Captains on duty today. It seems as though they are all needed elsewhere. For all intents and purposes I am the captain today." The first spoke smugly.

"And what, pray tell, is your name?" Bern wasn't going to back down.

"My name is Nuncio. Now I suggest that you explain yourself quickly or else we are going to have trouble." He almost snarled.

Before Bern could say anything more Linus stepped forward. Nuncio didn't seem to take any notice of the priest as his gaze was fixed on Bern. It was obvious that he was the man in charge.

"Nuncio? Son of Silas?" the name Silas brought Nuncio's attention to Linus.

"How did you...? Who are you?"

"I am the High Priest Linus. I knew your father when he was alive. He was a good man. I used to bounce you on my knee when you were a child."

Nuncio thought for a moment before he peered at Linus. He knew the name and there was something so very familiar about the man standing before him.

"What is a High Priest doing in the mines?" Nuncio asked.

"That is not your concern is it?" there was a smugness to Linus' voice that didn't seem right. "Now are you going to let us pass or will I have to speak to your mother?"

The last threat seemed to have the most weight. Nuncio was suddenly very uncomfortable. He could feel everyone's eyes on him and he felt his face turn red with embarrassment and that was even worse. All he wanted was to get the group as far away from him as possible.

"Well I guess that a High Priest may enter the Grand Cathedral." He forced the words out.

"Thank you Nuncio. I will be sure to tell your mother what a fine young man you have grown into, next time I am speaking with her."

Linus stepped forward and was quickly followed by the others. They didn't take more than a few steps before Nuncio stopped them.

"And where do you think you're going? You know slave masters aren't allowed out of the mines. Turn around and back you go," Nuncio commanded.

Emil thought for a moment. In the end he decided that he had a better chance of survival in the mines and not with Bern. He turned to leave, but Linus spoke quickly before he had the chance.

"I have requested the slave master come with me. He has some information that is vital to the survival of Castalia." It wasn't a complete lie.

Nuncio didn't sound overly happy, but the more they remained the more uncomfortable he became. When it was said and done he didn't think that the slave master could get up to much trouble.

"Very well, get out of my sight. I don't want to see any of you down here again," he didn't want to be rude, but it seemed to be the only way to save face.

Bern wasn't going to push the point. They had managed to gain entrance into the Grand Cathedral and that was all that really mattered. As much as it all seemed like a great effort, and it was, it was nothing compared to what they were about to do. Taking on a Dark Knight without a number of wizards by your side was suicide.

"Thank you, thank you," Emil grovelled at Bern's side as they walked.

"I wouldn't be too grateful. I am yet to decide whether or not to kill you." Bern wasn't in the mood.

"But, but, but you said you weren't going to kill me."

"No, I said I wouldn't let Za'aroz kill you. I said nothing about myself." Bern chuckled to himself. "Now let's find somewhere to get cleaned up."

Chapter 27: Battle

"Well this is awkward," Sorrell commented from his vantage point.

The sun was high in the sky and the armies had still not met. The longer they waited the more nervous everyone became, but also the hope of reaching a truce grew stronger. As much as no one believed it was true there was still a chance. The longer they waited the greater chance there was of Bern achieving his goal; not only that, but the heat of the day would soon make fighting difficult for both sides.

"I almost feel like offering their command over for tea and biscuits," Jarwe joked.

As soon as the words came out of his mouth he wished he hadn't spoken. From their vantage point at the front of the line the Commanders could see a number of flags being waved over the Castalial army. It was common practise to use flags bearers to relay orders across a large army and they didn't come much larger than the one from Castalia. It had its advantages and disadvantages. It was a great system for getting information throughout the army in a hurry, but it was easy for the enemy to know exactly what was coming. The flags being waved were blue and had a picture of a foot in the middle.

"Looks like they are sending a small contingent of infantry in against us," Sorrell stated the obvious.

"Get the catapults to fire some more debris onto the field. That should make it a little harder for them to reach us," Jarwe ordered.

Throughout the morning the Alliance had been lobbing debris onto the battlefield. It was both out of boredom and technical advantage. More obstacles on the battlefield meant the opposing soldiers had to advance in smaller numbers. It also lessened the amount of ammunition they had to fire.

"Archers, ready your bows," Jarwe shouted at the top of his voice.

The command was passed throughout the Alliance which meant Jarwe had avoided using his flag bearers. There seemed to be enough time for the command to reach all the archers and he didn't want the enemy to know what he was doing. As much as he didn't want to order the deaths of the Castalial soldiers he didn't have a choice. It was either that or the Alliance soldiers would die and that was less than acceptable.

"Well I guess we didn't come out here for nothing," Hulkan sounded less than impressed. "Let's try and keep the bloodshed to a minimum."

Pernian stifled a laugh. He had never heard a dwarf back away from violence before. He made sure that no one saw him as he figured it wouldn't end well if they knew he was mocking.

The first row of infantry started to march onto the battlefield. It didn't look like they were in any hurry to reach them. Jarwe almost didn't want to signal for the archers to start firing, but he knew once he lowered his arm the shooting would begin. He waited for almost a full minute once the soldiers were in range before he dropped his arm. Shortly after, the twang of bowstrings resonated through the air. There was a moment of breathlessness as the arrows arched before they came to hit their targets. Then the sounds of screams filled the battlefield.

"Another volley," Jarwe boomed at the top of his lungs.

The soldiers who escaped the barrage of arrows were unsure if they should continue or retreat. There was still a lot of ground to cover between them and the Alliance. Although the attack didn't make sense there was no sound of retreat. If they turned around they would be treated as traitors so there was nothing they could do except push forward.

The Alliance's archers reloaded and then waited for the official order to fire. Once they were all ready Jarwe's orders were relayed and the arrows were released again. The infantry stopped their advance and watched in both shock and horror as the arrows flew towards them. To everyone's amazement the arrows reached their pinnacle and then blinked out of existence.

"What in the Gods' names has happened?" Wojtek gasped.

"Where did the arrows go?" Sorrell followed his advisor.

"The Dark Knight!" there was fear in Pernian's voice.

"This is not a good sign," Jarwe added.

The infantry stopped their advance. They were just as confused as everyone else. They assumed the trick must have been from their side, but they couldn't work out who could have done such a thing. The High Chancellor had always limited the amount of magic users in the city.

As everyone stood in amazement the air started to crackle.

"This can't be good," Jarwe looked around.

No one knew what was happening, nor could they do anything about it. Dark clouds started to fill the skies and although no one knew what was coming they knew it wasn't going to be good.

Without warning a lightning bolt shot from the sky and landed deep within the Alliance. The bolt fried thirty soldiers on the spot and sent another fifty flying through the air. The sudden attack was more of a shock than the disappearing arrows. There were cries and screams throughout the Alliance, but the soldiers held their position.

"What do we do now?" Sorrell asked, a slight amount of fear in his voice.

Jarwe didn't know what to say. He had been enjoying being in command of the Alliance again, but now he really wished that Bern would return. He had no idea what he was supposed to do. How could he defend against lightning? There was no telling where it would strike next. At least the Castalial army had stopped their advance. Until they knew what was going to happen next they weren't prepared to advance any further.

Suddenly the air started to crackle again. This time they all knew what was coming. Everyone looked around nervously, wondering if there might be a place to hide, but that idea was futile. There was nothing that would stop the lightning bolt from striking them and there was no telling who it would destroy.

Jarwe didn't know what was worse. When the lightning sturck or waiting to see when it was coming. The air was thick with electricity and he knew it would only be a matter matter of time. The worst part was that there was nothing he could do about it. They lacked the magical strength to repel a Dark Knight's attack.

Without any other warning a bolt of lightning shot down again. This time the bolt landed in the earth in front of the army. Dirt and rocks shot harmlessly into the air. When the dust settled there was a large crater about twenty feet in front of the command group. Jarwe thought that could only aid their defence and broke out in a fit of laughter. The others thought he was going crazy until they realised what he was laughing at.

"We should send him a thank you letter," Sorrell joked.

"Maybe we should go one step better and send another volley in. If he is busy stopping arrows then he won't be able to throw lightning at us," Pernian suggested.

As Pernian finished speaking the air started to crackle again.

"That is not a bad idea, and it seems as though we should do it quickly before he strikes again," Jarwe agreed.

Jarwe quickly raised and lowered his arm. He knew that the message would be relayed to the archers without him having to speak. All he could do was sit on his horse and wait to see what happened.

The air continued to crackle as the call to ready the archers resonated throughout the Alliance. The Castalial army remained motionless. No one from the other side knew what to make of the situation. Something was happening and it was too bizarre for them to comprehend. They weren't entirely sure, but it seemed as though whatever was happening it was to their favour.

Before another lightning bolt struck down another volley of arrows was sent into the air. Jarwe hoped that would stop the attack and put the Dark Knight on the defensive again. It would only be a matter of time before they ran out of arrows, but at least they were buying Bern more time. With every passing minute there was a chance he would reach his destination and stop the onslaught.

Everyone watched the arrows as they started to arc in the air. The electricity remained and Jarwe didn't think that was a good sign. There was a sudden silence as the first of the arrows reached their pinnacle. It was at this point that the other arrows had disappeared and it was what both sides were hoping for. It was not to be and the arrows remained on their deadly trajectory. It seemed as though Za'aroz was not worried about them and by the time the Castalial infantry realised it was too late. Some of the soldiers had enough time to lift their shields to protect themselves, the rest just had to hope there wasn't an arrow heading in their direction.

As the arrows started to hit their marks another lightning bolt shot down from the sky. It forked out just before it struck the army, increasing the amount of damage. It seemed as though the battle was going to be fought at a distance. Although this was what Jarwe had been hoping for he hadn't factored in the magical strength of Za'aroz.

"Should we retreat?" Jarwe asked his fellow commanders.

"Where to? Do you have any idea what sort of range he has on those things?" Pernian asked.

"No, but I know we can't stay here any longer. All we are doing is giving him target practice. We gain nothing by staying here," Jarwe retorted.

"Remember that we are trying to act as a distraction for Bern." Hulkan remained calm as he watched the madness unfold around him.

Neither army knew what was happening. They were taking hits on both sides of the battlefield without really gaining anything. Panic was starting to set in, but both sides remained strong. They wouldn't move another step until they were commanded.

"Be that as it may we can't sacrifice the entire army just to give Bern a distraction. It is time that we move the army away from the city. We have done all that we can for him." Jarwe turned around, although he still didn't have the heart to voice the command that would surely seal Bern's fate.

With each lightning bolt the sky started to darken. The clouds were so dark that it was hard to see the faces of the soldier's standing behind them. Jarwe wondered if they were still holding strong or whether their hearts were starting to fear the unknown threat that shadowed them. As that thought filled his mind the air started to crackle again.

"Should we fire more arrows general?" Wojtek asked nervously.

"No, there is no point in causing more death. They aren't coming any closer and at the moment aren't a threat. Now let's start the retreat." Jarwe finally let the words past his mouth.

Before anyone could pass on the order another lightning bolt shot from the heavens. This time it didn't get a chance to reach its target. Before it was able to strike deep into the heart of the army it fizzled out of existence. If the disappearing arrows had come as a shock no one was prepared for the latest surprise. Again neither side knew what to think about it.

"What is that?" Sorrell pointed to the north as a faint light appeared on the horizon.

"I don't know, but whoever or whatever it is I hope it is here to help. I don't think I could handle another enemy right now," Jarwe tried to sound jovial, but it didn't work.

The light soon blinked out and the battleground became dark again. The sky had grown even darker since the last attack. Still no one had carried out the order to retreat and Jarwe was not about to repeat himself. They all wanted to see what would happen next, even if it did mean their lives.

The light suddenly appeared right in front of them and Jarwe needed all his strength to stop from falling from his horse. All the animals at the front of the line shied away from it. Hulkan, who was the only one on foot, was the first to see the six figures in the centre of the light. Instantly he drew his war axe, although it was more of a reaction than anything else. He didn't really think that his weapon would do anything against those he faced.

"Who are you?" he boomed as the others still tried to regain control of their horses.

There was laughter from inside the light as it slowly started to fade. Hulkan wasn't sure what was so funny, but he thought better of asking the question. Whoever it was would reveal themselves when they were good and ready. The last thing he wanted to do was to upset them.

"I'm sorry," a women's voice spoke. "I forgot that you can't see in the light." She giggled slightly again.

The light slowly reduced in size until it was a small luminescent ball. It then rose until it was floating six feet above their heads. The ball shone out so those in the command group could see and be seen by the new visitors standing before them.

"There, I think that is better," Althea spoke again.

"You would Althea. Some of us would have gotten it right in the first place," Minerva sniffed as she spoke.

"Enough you two!" Ulman boomed. "I am sorry, it has been a long journey and we are all tired and grumpy."

"Speak for yourself Ulman, I am as fresh as a daisy," Althea retorted.

"Only because you haven't done anything for a few days," Minerva couldn't help herself.

"Okay, I think we have heard enough bickering for one day. We still have work to do or have you two ladies forgotten that?" Gwydion spoke abruptly.

"I think we would all like to know who you are?" Jarwe had regained control of his horse and was trying to gauge the situation before him.

"We are the Council of Wizards, has it really be that long that no one recognises us any more?" Gwydion's question was rhetorical.

Jarwe let out a sigh of relief. As he did he felt the air start to crackle again. He knew that the wizards had saved them from Za'aroz's last attack, but he wasn't sure if they could to do it again. There was no doubt that the Dark Knight knew at least one of the wizards was there. He would be forced to increase his attack to counter the opposition.

"We are about to be attacked again," Wojtek spoke with his head lowered. No one knew if it was a sign of being tired or a sign of deference.

"Don't worry about that. The army is protected for the moment," Ulman sounded pleased with himself.

"We need to talk. There is no telling how long the shield will hold and once it breaks the army will be vulnerable again." Minerva explained. "Where is Bern? Have they made it into the Grand Cathedral?"

"We don't know. He left yesterday and we haven't heard anything since," Jarwe explained.

"Then we must assume that he is still alive," Minerva didn't sound confident.

"What should we do now?" Althea asked.

"I was hoping you might be able to answer that question?" Jarwe replied.

"With all due respect general I wasn't speaking to you," there was no humour in her words.

"Now, now Althea. You know Alaric wanted us to report to the Alliance," Gwydion soothed.

"He told us to report to General Bern, he said nothing about the Alliance. It is bad enough that we have to take orders from him I can't from this lot."

Sorrell looked at his advisor and smiled. He had never really liked those who practised magic. There was something very unseemly about the craft. He much preferred the feel of steel. It was tangible. You could actually see the person coming to kill you, unlike the wiles of magicians. It seemed as though the very masters of the craft were under their control. That did seem like a very cruel twist of fate. He was going to look forward to commanding them, but for the moment he would have to play nice. He could see their value, at least while they were under attack from a Dark Knight.

"You are splitting hairs Althea. We are here to help, not to command. The sooner you remember that the better." Gwydion was not going to stand for any of her nonsense. "Now what is it that we can do to help?"

"As it stands I'm not sure what else you can do out here. The Castalial infantry hasn't made a move since the lightning started crashing down. We want to try and avoid as many deaths as possible, there have already been too many. As long as you can hold back the lightning then that is about all we can ask." Jarwe was still trying to come to terms with everything.

"We can do that, but not for much longer. We have to get to the source of the attacks if we are going to stop them," Gwydion explained.

"Then you will have to attack the Dark Knight. As far as we know it is he who is causing the lightning." Jarwe replied.

"Then we need to make our way into the Grand Cathedral," Minerva suggested hopefully.

"I am not sure if that is the greatest of ideas. We are weak from our travelling. We should rest," Brielle whined.

"There is no time for rest. Alaric told us that we needed to fight Za'aroz once we arrived. If we are not strong enough then we are not worthy," Gwydion retorted.

"Then we need to go to the Grand Cathedral and defeat the Dark Knight," Minerva said again.

"Can you get inside the Grand Cathedral? If you didn't notice there is a large army between us and it seems as though it has taken Bern a long time to reach his destination," Sorrell asked.

"We have a few tricks up our sleeves. We shall be able to enter the Grand Cathedral undetected," Minerva smiled.

"Well I guess there is nothing more to do now, except to say thankyou for the assistance." Jarwe was still unsure of them.

"Save your thanks for when this is over. For now all you have to do is stay alive. Now let's keep moving. Minerva, do you know somewhere we can safely land?" Gwydion asked.

"Of course, I know just the place." She winked at Gwydion before closing both eyes.

They stood still for almost a minute before they suddenly disappeared. Again the horses whinnied and shied away. There was something very disturbing about how they just vanished. At the very least they could have shimmered out of view, it would have made it a lot easier for everyone.

"Well that was something I wasn't expecting," Dorn was the first one to speak. "What do we do now?"

Again Jarwe had trouble regaining control of his horse. The animal didn't like the suddenness of the wizards appearing and then disappearing. Once he regained control he realised that the sky was lighter than it had been. Although it was still dark they could now see the outline of the city walls behind the battlefield. The Castalial army still hadn't moved and it didn't look like they were in any hurry.

"I think it's time we made our retreat." It was more of a suggestion rather than a command. "They can't fight us if we are no longer here. I think we have done everything that we can without open confrontation."

"I think that's a good idea," Lord Pernian agreed. "Too many have died and there will only be more death if we remain where we are."

"Send out the command to start the retreat. Slowly at first. We don't want to scare the Castalial army into action. Send the back and side flanks first, then one battalion at a time. Make sure they are ready to turn around if we get attacked."

"That is not in the rules of combat. They cannot attack a retreating army." Wojtek couldn't believe what he heard.

"I doubt that Za'aroz has ever heard of the 'rules of combat' let alone willing to command by them. If he orders the army to move they will move, they believe that he is the most holy of holies. They believe that he is the High Chancellor himself and they will do whatever he commands," Jarwe replied. "We have to be prepared for an attack at all times and hope and pray that it doesn't come.

Once everyone understood Jarwe's point-of-view the commands were sent throughout the army. It would take a few hours to successfully pull the Alliance back from the field. He had to come up with another way to prevent their attack. He didn't think that the army would remain motionless for that long.

***

Bern felt a lot better after they'd a chance to bathe and change clothes. At first they had just gone into the guards' quarters to clean the High Chancellors, but in the end they had all decided to wash and change. A fresh load of uniforms had been brought down from the laundry. He decided that travelling through the Grand Cathedral dressed as guards would be a lot easier than wearing their current clothes. No one argued. Everyone wanted to wash away the sweat and grime from the desert and the mines.

Hadar and Bern sat in a room by themselves. They had invited Delbert to join them, but the captain had insisted on staying with his men. He wanted to make sure they attended to their wounds. The last thing he wanted was for them to turn septic because his men were too proud to show pain.

"What are we going to do with those two?" Hadar asked as the two High Chancellors took their baths.

"I have no idea. This was not something I had been expecting," Bern replied.

A few other guards came and went whilst they were there, but none of them seemed to take any notice. It wasn't strange for new guards to arrive without any warning. There were changes in the shifts which also meant some guards never met others. All they had to do was look the part and for the moment they all looked, strong, angry and over-worked.

"Well you better make a decision soon. Once they have shaved we need to be on the move again. You have to decide which one you are going to put on the throne."

"Why does it have to be my decision?" Bern didn't sound happy. "Who am I to decide who the next High Chancellor should be?"

"You are General Bern!" Hadar put unnecessary pomp to his voice before breaking out in laughter.

"I hate to think what this thing has come to when a poor farmer is deciding on who rules a kingdom." Bern shook his head, but had to laugh at the same time. "Anyway, there is still time. With a little luck Za'aroz might make that decision for me."

"I guess you're right. There are more important matters at hand. How are you planning on taking down Za'aroz? The last time I checked you had no magical abilities, or at least none that you can call on consciously."

That was something that Bern had been trying to ignore. He knew that the entity was still inside him and he knew that it had powers of its own, but he had no idea if it would be enough to defeat a Dark Knight. There was no telling if the entity would even show up to help. Either way Bern was not looking forward to the confrontation. He didn't think it was going to end well.

"How are you to coping?" the question came from the door. They both turned around to see Linus.

Neither man knew how to answer the question. They had not been overly religious men in their lives and were not sure how to speak to a High Priest, at least not in a spiritual sense.

"Don't be afraid, I am not here to judge you. I am here to assist you."

"We are just discussing how we are going to overthrow Za'aroz," Bern finally said.

"Hmm, there is no easy answer to that one. I know that he has many followers. I am sure there are some who actually know who he is. It will be hard to convince them that Augustus is the true High Chancellor," Linus mused

"What if we put Julius back on the throne? That would eliminate the problem of the double High Chancellors," Hadar added.

"I think you would have a harder time convincing people that Julius is still alive than Augustus being the true High Chancellor," Linus returned. "Our job is to get Augustus back in power. What happens after that is none of our business."

Bern only wished that was true. He would love nothing more than to just walk away, but that's not what they were there for. They were there to make things better, no matter what that meant, but he had to admit that Linus made sense. He would have a better chance convincing everyone that the current High Chancellor was a Dark Knight than trying to convince them that a long dead High Chancellor was still alive. He had to pick the fight he was more likely to win.

"Very well, we will push for Augustus, at least until we have Za'aroz sorted," Bern sounded decisive.

They relaxed for the remainder of the time they had in the guards' quarters. It wasn't long before all the soldiers were dressed as guards. Julius and Augustus were the last to surface. They had a little more work to do to make themselves look presentable. Beside the uniform Bern thought he could see the strength and dignity required to be the High Chancellor in both men.

"Okay, let's get moving," Bern stood.

"Before we go," Augustus spoke nervously.

"There is no time for this, we have to get moving," Julius interrupted.

"What is it Augustus?" Bern didn't sound overly interested.

"It's just that I haven't eaten in two days. Could I eat something before we leave?"

Bern was surprised to hear the once High Chancellor actually asking for something. He wasn't sure if it was a good thing or a bad thing. Either way he had to admit that he himself was starting to get hungry. He figured there was no point in fighting the Dark Knight on an empty stomach and there was a very good chance it was going to be their last meal.

They found what they were looking for in the mess hall, which was in fact just another small room. It was designed for those who were forced to work a double shift. There were some supplies of bread, cheese and dried meat. It wasn't enough for all of them, but with what supplies they still had left there was enough for a good feed.

No one spoke as they ate. Everyone had a lot weighing on their minds. They were about to face a Dark Knight and that was enough to make the hardest of generals run screaming like a little girl. When they had agreed on the mission no one had thought about the end result, now that they were faced with it they weren't sure if they wished to continue. Unfortunately no one had a choice.

Once they had all eaten they moved out. Normally it would look a little strange with so many guards wandering around downstairs at the one time, but with the current situation no one would think twice. With their new disguises they would be able to move freely throughout the Grand Cathedral.

"How do we find the Dark Knight?" Bern asked Linus as they started to climb the stairs.

"I assume that the chapel will be the best place to start. If he is not there I am sure that someone will be able to point us in the right direction."

"Very well, let's make for the chapel!"

***

Za'aroz stood on top of the outer wall of the inner city. It was the best place to watch the battle without over extending his powers of sight. The least strain he could put on himself the better. He had a feeling that he was going to be tested soon enough.

It had not taken him long to take part in the battle. The hunger of death started to overpower him when the first of the arrows started to hit their mark. He didn't care which side of the battlefield the deaths occurred, then he realised that he was in command of one side. After blocking a hail of arrows, a relatively simple trick, he had to think on how he was going to cause a lot of death and destruction.

For many years Za'aroz had loved lightning as a form of destructive magic. There was something very exhilarating about the feel of electricity in the air. It would take a little more energy to produce and it was harder to control, but the decision had already been made.

The first of the bolts struck the army and caused a moderate amount of damage, but he knew he could do better. He built up a great source of energy as he prepared his second attack. He concentrated too much on the power and the direction was off, the bolt landed harmlessly in the battlefield. Za'aroz cursed himself for being too anxious.

Another flight of arrows filled the air, but Za'aroz ignored them. He was too focused on his next attack to care about the Castalial soldiers.

Any death was good death and he was going to add to it, not detract from it. The arrows hit their mark and the soldiers screamed out in pain. The sound of agony filled the Dark Knight with elation. He couldn't wait to bring down more pain to the puny men.

His next attack struck the heart of the Alliance. The lightning forked causing more death than the original bolt. Za'aroz couldn't help himself. Without thinking he burst out laughing. Those standing around looked at him with a mixture of surprise and horror on their faces.

"What is it, Master?" High Priest Tybalt could have ripped his own tongue out of his mouth. He looked around to see if anyone noticed the faux pas. With all that was happening around them it was hard to gauge a reaction.

"Be quiet Tybalt," Za'aroz scolded him. "I am trying to concentrate."

Za'aroz had already started preparing his next attack. The air sparked around him as he drew in more and more energy. Those who didn't know better thought it was a divine presence surrounding their great leader. The sky grew ever darker, which made the sparks even more luminescent, but that didn't deter Za'aroz. His body was full of bloodlust and nothing was going to stop the carnage.

As the lightning bolt struck down from the sky it suddenly disappeared. Za'aroz took an unsteady step backwards in horror. He couldn't believe what was happening. He had not noticed anyone in the area with enough strength the stop his spell. He had been so focused on his own attacks that he had not realised what was happening around him. He was now vulnerable, especially since he was out in the open.

"I need to go back inside," Za'aroz's voice was weak.

"Of course my lord." Tybalt bowed in servitude.

Za'aroz had not been looking for an answer. He was talking to himself as much as those around him. He had a sudden urge to flee. Without thinking of the consequences he suddenly disappeared.

Chapter 28: The Real High Chancellor

The chapel was empty when the group arrived. Although it was strange, no one was going to question their luck. They were able to secure all the entrances and exits to the room, creating a greater area of defence. If nothing else it would give them a chance to discuss their next move.

"This doesn't make any sense. In all my years as a priest I have never known the chapel to be completely empty. Even when the High Chancellor isn't present there is always someone either praying or cleaning," Linus explained.

"This isn't a good sign. I'm sure that it is around midday and yet it is very dark outside," Bern mused.

Suddenly there was a bright flash of lightning.

"That was close," Hadar said as he moved to the window.

"That wasn't natural., Bern explained.

"What do you mean?" Linus asked.

"Can't you feel the electricity in the air? That lightning bolt was made by magic."

"That can't be good. There is only one person I know who could do such a thing." Linus didn't need to voice his thoughts.

Bern followed Hadar to the window. It was impossible to see what was happening outside of the city in the darkness. He looked towards the sky and knew that the clouds weren't natural. His heart skipped a beat when he thought about the ramifications of what Za'aroz was doing. The army was defenceless against such an attack.

"We have to help them," he blurted out.

"You must remain here!" a voice spoke inside Bern's mind.

"What?" He was so taken by surprise that he spoke loudly.

"No one said anything Bern." Hadar watched him carefully. "Where do you want us to go?"

"Nowhere."

Bern turned around and walked back into the chapel. It seemed the entity inside of him wanted him to remain where he was. He couldn't see why, but then he had no idea where else he should go. Now he needed to familiarise himself with his surroundings. If he was going to battle a Dark Knight then he would need every advantage he could get.

The many pews had been pushed to the side, to allow for the weekly cleaning. The dust on the floor showed that the task had yet to be done. At the far end was a small dais with a lectern and two candelabras on either side. A large throne was on another platform slightly higher than the dais. There was a large open space behind the throne with a door leading out to the High Chancellor's private chapel.

There was a large space in the middle of the chapel suitable for a battle, but Bern didn't know if that was such a great thing. He had no idea what it would take to defeat the Dark Knight, but he was sure that it wouldn't involve manual weapons.

"Are you there?" Bern spoke with his mind-voice, although he wasn't really sure what he was doing. He needed to contact the entity, but that was something he had never achieved in the past. "I need your help." All he was met with was silence.

"What do we do now?" Delbert asked when he had his men in place.

"Now we wait." It wasn't the words anyone to expected to hear.

"What are we waiting for?" Hadar asked.

That was the question that Bern hoped he wouldn't have to answer. He had no idea what they were waiting for and he knew that it was not a great plan. All he did know was that they had to stay and that was what they would do.

"I'm not exactly sure, but I think that we will find out soon enough."

Hadar new better than anyone in the room what that meant. Linus was about to ask a question, but Hadar shook his head. It was neither the time nor the place for such a conversation.

As the minutes passed the tension grew. There was no sign of the Dark Knight and there was no guarantee that he was going to show. Bern paced around the room, making sure he stayed close to the windows, each time looking out over the city. Each time he looked he hoped he would get some sign of what was happening outside of the city walls, but each time he got nothing.

"We can't wait here much longer. There are men dying out there." Linus was guessing, but he was pretty sure it was true. "We need to reassess and keep moving."

Bern was at one of his many stops by a window. He didn't turn around when he heard Linus' words. There was nothing he could do to reassure the priest that they were doing the right thing. He no longer knew that he was doing the right thing. All he knew was that they needed to wait and there was no explaining that to Linus, so he remained silent.

"We have to keep calm, Linus." Hadar walked over to the priest. He didn't want the soldiers to hear his words. "Bern is doing what he thinks is best. We have to trust him." The explanation was feeble, but it was all Hadar had.

Suddenly the air started to shimmer in front of the dais. Bern was the first to notice and he called for the others to prepare themselves. At first he couldn't see what it was, but he still knew what was coming. Slowly two men started to coalesce. Bern recognised one of them as the imitation High Chancellor, the resemblance was amazing. There was no doubt that it was Za'aroz, but he had no idea who the man next to him was.

"Tybalt, I should have known that you would be grovelling at the feet of a Dark Knight." Linus didn't wait for Bern to speak. He spat on the floor when he finished. Bern was surprised at his reaction.

"You were always a disappointment Linus. You could never see past your own nose. This is the way of the future and you will burn like everyone else," Tybalt sneered as he spoke.

Bern kept his gaze on Za'aroz. The banter between the two priests was irrelevant. There was something off about the Dark Knight and he was going to have to play things very carefully. They weren't set up to fight him.

"Hah! You are a traitor. I could understand if you were a High Priest of Ruby, but Sapphire, there is no reason for you to turn. You are a disappointment and a disgrace." Linus returned.

"That is how simple-minded you really are. You don't believe that there are worshippers of the true Great Lord in your own congregation? It is no wonder we were able to infiltrate so high in the Grand Cathedral."

Bern knew that something was definitely not right. There was no way that Za'aroz would let one of his subordinates speak on his behalf. There had to be a reason and Bern was loathed to make any move until he knew what it was.

Za'aroz simply surveyed the chapel whilst Tybalt and Linus did all the talking. It didn't look like he was going to speak any time soon. He seemed as though he was content to just be watching and listening.

"Your treachery is about to come to an end." Linus suddenly realised that everyone in the chapel was watching him. He suddenly felt very self-conscious and wished that he had kept his mouth shut.

"What do we do now?" Hadar whispered to Bern, taking advantage of the distraction.

"Enough of this rubbish," Bern look a step forward. "Za'aroz, you are to surrender control of Castalia to the Alliance. You have usurped power and shall be punished accordingly." Bern wasn't sure where the words were coming from, but it seemed as though it was the right thing to say.

"I take it you are General Bern..." Tybalt started.

"Be quiet you wretch." Za'aroz spoke for the first time. "You will speak when I ask you to."

There was something different about Za'aroz's tone. It was different to that of the High Chancellor, where it had been the same before. Bern noticed for the first time that the fake High Chancellor's hair was thinning a lot more than the real one. The more he looked the more flaws he noticed in Za'aroz's appearance. He didn't know what it meant, but he felt as though it was very significant.

"I will surrender nothing and you have no authority here. I am the High Chancellor and I rule Castalia." There was a waver in his voice as if he doubted his own words. "Guards!" he boomed.

Although they had not seen any guards on their way to the chapel they didn't believe there were none around. One thing Za'aroz had not noticed was that Bern's soldiers held all the doors. Any entering guards would be caught in their trap. When the guards heard the call of the fake High Chancellor two doors opened.

The guards rushed into the chapel straight into the soldiers. The first few through the doors put up a short fight until they were disarmed and the remaining guards simply surrendered. Bern had to smile when the last of the guards lowered their swords Things had worked out better than he thought.

"It seems as though you have underestimated us Za'aroz. That'll be your first mistake. Are you prepared to make another or one will you surrender?" the smile remained on Bern's face.

If Za'aroz was surprised he didn't show it. If he was concerned about losing all his guards no one could tell. His face remained like stone and his body language gave nothing away. He simply looked around the chapel and surveyed the situation.

"It's seems as though you are lacking something, General Bern." His face remained passive although Bern was sure there should have been a smirk.

"And what might that be?" Bern asked.

"From what I can tell there is no one here with the ability to create magic. I would have thought someone with your reputation would be smarter than that."

Suddenly there was an itch in the back of Bern's mind. At first he tried to scratch it away, but he quickly realised that it wasn't physical. There was something that wasn't right about Za'aroz and he couldn't continue until he knew what it was. He wished that the entity would just let him know.

A drop of sweat appeared on Bern's brow as he tried to figure out the riddle. To his surprise Za'aroz made no move to attack after his revelation and then it finally hit him. The Dark Knight had been battling with the Alliance and was out of energy. He was struggling to keep up the façade of the High Chancellor.

"You are not the High Chancellor," Augustus stepped forward before Bern had a chance to speak. "I am the High Chancellor."

It was not what Bern was expecting and he wished the man had remained quiet. They were all in great danger if the Dark Knight regained his energy. There was little time for conversation.

The sight of Augustus took Za'aroz by surprise, although it did nothing to change his façade. He had thought that the real High Chancellor had been taken care of. It was something he had been relying on to keep up the ruse, but that had all changed.

"Well this is something that I was not expecting." He looked at Tybalt, but was unable to show any expression on his face. "I thought that I made myself clear when I said the High Chancellor wasn't to be found again." He decided to let his words state his feelings.

"But you said we couldn't kill him, you said that he might come in handy." Tybalt starting shaking.

Za'aroz wanted nothing more than to strike the snivelling little worm, but that would prove nothing. He had more pressing matters to deal with. With every second that passed he could feel his energy regaining. It wouldn't be long before he could fry everyone in the room and that was exactly what he was planning to go. In the meantime he would just have to keep playing the game.

"Well I guess there is no point in keeping up this charade." Slowly the image of the High Chancellor changed. Although the spell didn't take a lot of energy to keep going it did take up some and Za'aroz didn't have any to waste. In its place was a figure wearing a black robe with the hood covering his face. "Now let's see what we can do about ending this silly little show."

"You will pay for what you did to me."

Augustus charged forward without thinking about the consequences. Za'aroz simply swatted with his hand and sent him flying across the chapel before he came within striking distance. Augustus crashed into the wall and slumped to the ground.

The High Chancellor's private guard didn't know what to make of the situation. They had watched, who they believed was the true High Chancellor, transform into the hooded figure before them. Now they watched Augustus being attacked by the figure and there was nothing they could do about it. They had been disarmed by Bern's soldiers who were protecting the true High Chancellor. It was more than they could comprehend.

"I expected better from you General Bern. Stories of your exploits have reached my ears, but it seems as though they are all lies. You have come to attack me unprepared and now look at what is happening. It is time for your party to end. It's a shame really. I would have expected more from the Cursed One's greatest friend. Oh well..."

Bern knew that his window of opportunity was starting to close. He drew his axe and moved towards the Dark Knight. Before he was able to reach his target he froze. No matter what he did he couldn't move forward. Slowly he started to slide backwards as if someone was pushing him. Although he was locked in place he was still trying to move forward. It seemed as though his will power was working against Za'aroz's spell.

"It seems you are growing weak Za'aroz," the words came out of Bern's mouth, but they weren't his own. "The last time we met you were much stronger."

The words put Za'aroz off and he released the spell. Bern stumbled forward, but made no further advance. He still had control of his body, but the entity was controlling the words coming out of his mouth.

"What are you talking about? We have never met before today," Za'aroz sounded confused.

Bern smiled, the entity had Za'aroz rattled and that was a promising sign. He had no idea how he was going to defeat the Dark Knight, he only hoped the entity knew what it was doing.

"Well, be that as it may, your power is still waning. Now I think it would be a good idea for you to surrender. We may even be merciful if you do."

"Whatever you are, you aren't strong enough to defeat me." Za'aroz watched Bern carefully. "Regardless of whether I surrender or not there will no longer be an army for you to command. I have set the wheels in motion and the two armies will shortly be destroying themselves." He laughed loudly when he finished.

It was a cheap jibe, but it had its effect. Bern had almost forgotten that the two armies were fighting each other outside of the city. Little did he know that the fight had still yet to start. As far as Bern was concerned with each passing moment more blood was being shed on the field.

"I'll have the High Chancellor send word that the battle is over," Hadar suggested. He tried to keep his voice low, but Za'aroz still heard him.

"Yes, you might be right. Now that the High Chancellor has returned the army might believe his orders to retreat. It's a shame that no one will hear his commands." The Dark Knight laughed.

Augustus had made his way to one of the exits in anticipation of the new plan. When Za'aroz finished speaking he waved his hands in the air. Instantly the sounds of bolts being slammed shut could be heard from the doors. No matter how hard he tried he couldn't get the door open.

"You see. There is nothing you can do. Even if you defeat me the Great Lord has won. Without an army you cannot defeat the Great Lord. He will be victorious."

"It is time to end this. You have been in here for too long. Soldiers, circle in."

The High Chancellor's guards had their weapons returned to them. The soldiers were sure they no longer posed a threat. The guards were always loyal to the High Chancellor, only they believed they were following the real one. Now that they realised their folly they were prepared to fight and die for their mistake.

Slowly the guards and the soldiers started to enclose the Dark Knight. There was little point in protecting the doors if they could no longer be opened. What they didn't know was that there was little point attacking Za'aroz. There was only a very slim chance that their attacks would be effective.

At the very least Za'aroz thought they could rush him if they wanted to try and kill him. The slow attack only gave him more opportunity to prepare his own. His strength was still returning, but even in his weakened state he would be able to defeat the approaching men.

Suddenly one of the guards dropped to the ground. His neck bulged and it didn't take long for those around him to realise it had been broken. This realisation stopped their advance. There was no reason why such a thing should have happened. They knew the Dark Knight was powerful, but it was something they weren't expecting.

The soldiers on the other side of the chapel kept their methodical approach. They moved deliberately trying to gauge Za'aroz's next move. They couldn't be dissuaded by one death.

The next attack was more dramatic. Without warning the head of one of the soldiers exploded. Blood, brain and skull fragments coated the men nearby. The attack was enough to stop everyone from moving. No one could have expected such a thing to happen. Two guards covered with blood vomited on the ground. They had seen blood and death before, but nothing like that.

"What are you doing Bern? You are needlessly wasting lives." Hadar again kept his voice low, although it was harder than he thought.

Bern kept his mouth shut. He knew, no matter how quietly he spoke, Za'aroz would hear what he said. His plan was reliant secrecy. He couldn't let the Dark Knight now what he was about to do. He wasn't sure himself. He could only trust the entity knew what it was doing.

"I have to thank you Bern, this is more entertaining than I thought it would be," Za'aroz sneered as he killed another guard.

"Enough," Bern cried out as the air in the chapel started to ripple.

"Enough? This is not enough," there was a touch of concern in Za'aroz's voice.

It was obvious by his tone that he wasn't the one causing the ripples. Bern figured that was what he was waiting for, although he had no idea what was about to happen. Either way, the Dark Knight was rattled, giving Bern the advantage.

Suddenly a man appeared next to Bern causing him to jump in surprise. He didn't recognise him and had not expected him to be so close. Not long after that another man appeared followed by three women and another man. They were all dressed in robes. The three women carried staffs, while two of the men had swords in scabbards at their sides and one man, the largest of the three, held a brutal looking claymore.

"We are the Council of Wizards, but I think we shall hold formal introductions until we have finished with the Dark Knight," Gwydion, who was standing next to Bern, said. "Now Za'aroz, you will pay for your crimes."

Before Za'aroz could respond his arms were pinned to his side and the air was sucked out of his chest. He wanted to double over, but he was being held upright by an invisible force. Although no one could see through the hood they all imagined there was a look of horror on his face.

There was a moment of silence in the chapel before Za'aroz was able to free himself. Both Althea and Drake dropped to their knees. They had taken the brunt force as Za'aroz broke the spell. The Dark Knight shook his arms as a sign of his freedom. Now it was time for him to counter-attack.

He raised his arms towards Gwydion and Bern. The air crackled as he prepared his spell. Two shots of blue lightning fired from his fingertips towards them. The bolts only managed to get half way across the room before they blinked out of existence. Bern wasn't sure which wizard blocked the attack, he was just grateful that they did.

"Surrender and accept your punishment. You are only going to make it harder on yourself," Gwydion offered.

"Don't make me laugh. I have survived much worse than anything you can dish out."

"Suit yourself."

The air started to crackle again and the floor started to rumble.

"Don't destroy my chapel," Augustus cried out as mortar started to fall from the ceiling.

"This isn't your chapel," Julius yelled from behind the dais.

No one had noticed that the deposed High Chancellor had made his way around to the back of the dais. On the way he had picked up a sword from one of the fallen guards. The sudden noise caused Za'aroz to spin around, letting go of the spell he was trying to create.

Without a second thought Julius plunged his sword into Za'aroz's stomach. The Dark Knight pulled the blade up to the hilt, ignoring the pain, so Julius could see into his hood. What Julius saw sent fear shooting through his heart. Where he expected to see flesh there was just bone. Deep in the eye sockets was a yellow light that pierced the depths of his soul. In a state of panic Julius let go of the hilt and took two steps backwards until he fell onto the throne.

A rage brewed inside the Dark Knight. His full attention was now on Julius. Taking two steps forward he stood over the former High Chancellor. He made his hand into a claw and reached out. He didn't grip Julius, but it didn't take long for everyone to realise what was happening. Julius scratched as his neck as his gasped for breath. Za'aroz gripped tighter and tighter with his spell until Julius' face started to turn red. No matter what he did he couldn't suck any air into his lungs.

Before Julius lost consciousness Za'aroz was struck on the back of his head by an invisible force. The blow brought him back to the dangers in the chapel and the sword that was still protruding from his stomach. Begrudgingly he released the spell and returned his attention to the others, but not before he lifted Julius from the throne and sent him flying across the room.

With his attention back in the chapel he looked around to see who had created the spell that struck him. None of the wizards gave away anything. He was surprised they didn't use the chance to do more damage. That was a concern that they were planning on doing something with more power.

"Well I guess it is time to stop toying with you." He aimed his comment at Bern, although it was meant for everyone. There was a slight strain to his voice and he stifled a cry when he pulled the blade out. He tossed the sword to one side in disgust. There was a viscous green liquid on the blade that everyone assumed was the creature's blood.

"Now!" Gwydion called out.

All at once the wizards released the spell they had been conjuring. The air shimmered around the Dark Knight before he was suddenly struck across the side of his head. That was the first of many blows. The attacks came from all angles and there was nothing he could do to stop them. The distraction from Julius was all that the council needed to create their spell.

The attack continued for five minutes before it finally came to an end. When it was finished Za'aroz dropped to his knees, his head lowered. It looked as though there was no more attack left in him, but that was not to be taken for granted. Althea recreated her spell that wrapped Za'aroz and kept him from moving. She also lifted his head so he faced them.

"Now I think it is over Za'aroz. Are you prepared to surrender?" Gwydion asked again.

Laughter started from deep inside the hood. It was a sickening sound that sent shivers down everyone's spines. Bern couldn't imagine what was coming next. The wizards remained calm which helped his nerves.

"What is your answer?" Ulman boomed.

The laughter slowly died down. "Do you honestly think that I would let you capture me so easily? I have a little trick up my sleeve."

When he finished speaking Za'aroz started to slowly fade. He only managed to become half transparent before he was brought back to reality. There was no laughter from the Dark Knight this time.

"Did you really think that we would let you get away like that? You really are more arrogant than I could have thought." Gwydion mocked. "Now I take it you have made your decision?"

"Do your worst. I will revel in the fact that the Great Lord will roast your flesh for his own enjoyment."

Bern knew that it was time for him to finish the job. As he walked forward he could only hope that the Dark Knight didn't have any other tricks ready.

"Well at least you have the strength to do it yourself." Za'aroz sneered

Bern looked into the hood and saw that same yellow eyes that scared Julius. His heart skipped a beat, but then he steeled himself. He wasn't going to falter as he lifted his blade over Za'aroz's head. Taking a deep breath Bern swung his short sword with all his strength. The blade cleaved through Za'aroz's neck a lot easier than Bern was expecting and it took great control for him to keep his balance.

Za'aroz's skull head rolled across the floor until it landed at Gwydion's feet. His body simply disintegrated leaving a flat robe on the floor. At the same time the spell that was keeping the door locked dissipated. Bern let out a sigh of relief. It was finally over, or at least for the moment.

Chapter 29: A Chance to Relax

"I think it's time that you tell your army that it's time to surrender," Hadar was the first to speak.

"Yes, of course."

Augustus took a dozen of his guards and left the chapel. He thought it would be safer to have backup in case he was questioned. It would seem odd that he had decided to back flip on his previous orders.

Once Bern had disposed of the Dark Knight his legs started to wobble. The ordeal had taken more out of him than he expected. He wanted to sit down, but the situation didn't call for it. Looking around he could see that the wizards were also feeling the strain.

"I think we should retire to the High Chancellor's private quarters. I feel as though there is much that sill needs to be discussed," Bern suggested. "Foremost we need to decide who is going to be the High Chancellor."

"I think that decision might be made for us," Hadar pointed to where Julius was collapsed against the wall.

"Are you okay?" Bern asked after he rushed to Julius' side.

Julius coughed once and a trickle of blood appeared at the side of his mouth. He gasped for breath, but it didn't sound like much made it into his lungs. His face was pale and he didn't look well. He let out a gurgled laugh, but there was little humour in it.

"It seems as though I have made things easier for you," he coughed again, bringing up more blood. "It's a shame really. I lasted so long in the depth of the mines. So long that I thought my mind was going to break and as you saw it almost did. Now it seems as though I won't be able to reclaim my heritage," He coughed again and brought up even more blood. "I really thought that when I found you I would be High Chancellor again. I was going to do things so much differently."

Bern placed a reassuring hand on his shoulder. "Rest now, I am sure one of the wizards will be able to help you." That brought a weak smile to Julius' face.

"Can someone help?" he asked Gwydion, still not knowing his name.

"Althea, see what you can do."

The youngest of the wizards glided across the room. Although she was many centuries old she didn't look a day older than twenty. Her dark brown hair hung in ringlets around her shoulders. Her yellow robe was made from silk and despite the constant travel it was spotless and looked freshly ironed. It swished around her ankles as she almost floated towards the dying man.

Althea knelt beside Julius and placed her hand on his forehead. Instantly he felt a warm sensation pass through his body. After a few seconds Althea pulled away sharply. She almost fell backwards and had to brace herself from toppling over.

"What is it?" Bern asked.

"There… there is nothing I can do," Althea sounded horrified.

"What do you mean Althea?" Gwydion sounded shocked.

"His lungs have been crushed as has his oesophagus. They are too mangled to be repaired. I'm afraid there is nothing I can do." She retreated as she spoke as if Julius was contagious.

Bern returned to Julius' side. "I am sorry."

"That is alright. It is my time to die. I have lived too long as it is and I have completed my purpose. There is one thing I ask of you to make my sacrifice worth while."

"Name it."

"Don't let Augustus return to power. He was a wicked High Chancellor. You need to select a new High Chancellor, someone who will repair the damage of the past."

Before Bern could answer Julius gasped his last breath. His deathly stare remained fixed on the throne that was once his. Bern thought there was something peaceful about him. He couldn't image the courage he would have needed to survive in the mines, but now he was finally able to rest. The problem was that he wasn't sure if he had the authority to replace Augustus or if he even wanted to.

"Come Bern, let us go to some more relaxed surroundings. I know my colleagues won't mention it, but I could really use a seat," Gwydion tried to sound jovial.

Bern had to agree. With Julius' death his fatigue came rushing back. He had to brace himself to be able to stand. He wanted nothing more than to relax, but he knew that wouldn't happen until at least nightfall. Once he was finished with the wizards he would have to visit the army. The others would like to know what was happening.

"Delbert, see that the High Chancellor's body is properly prepared for the funeral. The people should know what he went through for their freedom," Bern ordered. "Linus and Hadar, you come with me."

Once they were all seated in the High Chancellor's quarters Gwydion made the introductions. Bern did his best to memorise the names, although in his current state it wasn't easy.

"Have you seen Alaric?" Bern asked before anyone else had a chance to speak.

"He left the Island when we did. He was heading towards the Scorpion Mountain. I would imagine he would be there by now," Gwydion explained.

Those words sent both a feeling of relief and a feeling a fear racing through Bern's body. His family was safe, at least from the reprisal of the serpentant. The next problem was the reason why Adder wanted Alaric to meet him at the summit. Whatever it was it couldn't be good and Bern could only hope that Alaric was prepared.

"He instructed us to come here to help you and it seemed as though we came at just the right time," said Brielle.

"I thank you for your help, but now it is time to plan our next move." Bern pushed aside the snide comment. He wasn't sure if Brielle was deliberately being rude or that was just the way she was. Either way he didn't have time to waste worrying about it.

"Where are you planning on taking the army?" Minerva asked.

"I don't know." Again Bern would have to wait for the pull of the prophecy to give him direction, although he thought he could hazard a guess. It seemed as though Remidel was the next logical choice. There were rumours that a Dark Knight had taken residence in the palace as were the rumours coming out of Lel Dinion. "I will just have to wait as I always do."

"That doesn't seem like the best of plans," Brielle scoffed again.

"Behave yourself, Brielle," Ulman barked. "You must forgive our sister. She is a little upset about having to leave her home.

"Be quiet Ulman. I don't need anyone to make excuses for me. I find this entire escapade to be completely ridiculous."

Bern let out a sigh. The last thing he needed was to listen to inane bickering. He had much more important things to worry about.

"If there is nothing else to discuss I really should make my way to the army. There is much that needs doing." Bern stood and instantly wished that he hadn't.

"Of course. I think we all need some rest before we have any serious conversations," Drake added.

"Very well then. I am sure that Linus will be able to find you all somewhere to sleep." Bern suggested as the high priest nodded his head. "I'll speak to you when I get back."

"I think I can help you get to the army." Drake stood as Bern did.

Before Bern had a chance to speak the two men faded out of the room. They appeared on the small hill where the command group still watched over the battlefield. Word had just reached the Castalial army that they were to return to the city and the retreat had already started. Although no surrender had been made it was obvious that the fighting was over.

Their sudden appearance didn't seem to startle anyone. Only the horses seemed to get a surprise. The tell-tell shimmering in the air announced their arrival before they appeared. It was something they had tried to stop, but had yet to figure out how to do it, not that they knew if it was even possible.

"It is good to see you again general," Jarwe was the first to greet them.

The other commanders greeted Bern warmly before anyone continued speaking.

"It seems as though you have achieved your goal?" It was more of a statement than a question.

"The Dark Knight is no more and we have control of the city. The High Chancellor will be restored to power." Bern didn't want to think about the decision he had to make and the others didn't need to know.

"So we will be on the move again?" even as he asked the question Jarwe knew the answer.

"There is still much to be done here. We will need to restock our supplies and more to the point we have to mobilise the Castalial army. That will take time. The city is still in turmoil from the Dark Knight's touch. I promise you that we will be on the move again as soon as possible. For the moment the soldiers should rest. Once we move we will have to march hard to our next destination."

"I guess there is little point in asking what that destination might be," Sorrell added.

"You would be right." Bern didn't want to let them know his suspicions. There was no point in putting the idea into their heads. "When it is time to leave I will know where we have to go."

"Very well. I think we should return to the command tent," Jarwe suggested. "Corporal." Jarwe called out.

"Yes general!"

"Tell the army to stop the retreat and return to camp. The battle is over."

"Yes general!"

"Let us return to the command tent."

There were no arguments from the others. Although they had not done any fighting it had still been a draining day. The threat of battle and the strange events had taken its toll. With the threat over they would revel in the chance to relax. That wouldn't last long so they needed to make the most of their opportunity.

"Has Gwydion brought you up to speed with what has been happening out here?" Jarwe asked when they were all seated.

A numbers of servants had laid the table in anticipation of their return. Platters of food filled the centre of their table with jugs of wine in-between. Once they arrived the servants started pouring the wine. As much as Bern really didn't feel like drinking alcohol he figured that it would be rude not too. As soon as the dark liquid touched his lips he was glad he had made the decision.

"No, there has been little time for conversation," Bern replied after taking a long draught.

Jarwe, with the help of the others, explained what had happened since Bern had left. Although there were some disturbing parts to the story there was little that Bern had not expected. He knew that Za'aroz wouldn't stay out of the battle and was grateful in the end for that. It was the Dark Knight's participation that had left him weakened for their confrontation. There was no telling how things would have ended up if Za'aroz had been at full strength. He was surprised there were so few casualties.

Once they had finished their story Bern gave them a brief description of what he had been doing. He omitted the story of entering the mine shaft as he figured it was better if not too many people knew the secret way into the mines. He explained about the old High Chancellor, how he had been deposed and his dying request of Bern's.

"That is indeed a tough decision to make." Sorrell added.

"And I am not sure if that supersedes your authority. We are not here to take command of the kingdom. We need to be very careful," Jarwe warned.

Bern was both grateful and concerned with Jarwe's advice. He was glad that Jarwe used the word 'we' to describe the decision making process. He was hoping for more of a positive response. He knew there would be people against him if he did make a decision, but that was the role he had been forced to play.

"It's not something I am looking forward to, but I feel as though it is something we need to decide on. There are pros and cons and it isn't going to be any easy decision to make." Bern took another long draught of wine. He wished that he could just sit back and drink himself into a stupor.

"I don't think it is our place to choose a new High Chancellor. If anyone should do it then it should be the people of Castalia."

"Has this ever been done before?" Bern asked.

"A new High Chancellor is generally chosen by their predecessor." Jarwe explained.

"Although it is not widely known," Orric spoke for the first time. "When a High Chancellor is deposed it is The Council of High Priests who decides who the supplanter will be."

"Is that what happened with the last High Chancellor?" Bern asked.

"That I don't know. It was widely spoken that Julius died of a disease. I think only a select few know exactly what happened," Orric explained.

"I'll need to think on this one. For the moment I think we should just enjoy the time to relax while we have it." As much as he appreciated their input he knew that it had to be his decision. He had the information he needed. Now he just needed to make up his mind. He felt, however, it had already been made up for him.

***

Bern stood on the balcony of his apartment and stared at the sky. He felt so exhausted that he thought he could fall asleep at any moment, but he still didn't go to bed. Drake had transported him back to the Grand Cathedral when they had finished with the command group. He would have preferred to camp with the rest of the army, but it was more convenient for him to stay in comfort. He wanted to speak with Linus before he made his decision. It was going to be harder than he thought. When he returned Augustus had resumed his role as High Chancellor. He seemed as though he was trying to make amends for his past mistakes, although it would take a long time for that to happen.

There was no moon in the sky and Bern knew what that meant. Somewhere to the north Alaric would be on the top of a mountain. Although the balcony faced the west, Bern felt as though he was looking straight towards Mount Scorpio.

Although Bern had never physically been to the mountain he had memories from many years ago. There was something about the mountain that was missing from his memory. He knew it was something important, but there was nothing he could do about it even if he could remember. Nevertheless the feeling was bothering him. There was some kind of horror waiting for Alaric, he knew that, and he could only hope that his old friend was up to the challenge. It was that thought that was still in his mind when he finally fell asleep.

Chapter 30: Return

Back at the inn the air shimmered. Richmond stood and grabbed his sword, but Viper didn't look at all interested. Before long three figures appeared, it was Alena, Alaric and Eldred. When Richmond realised who it was he physically relaxed.

"Thank the Gods you are back. I was starting to worry." Richmond greeted them.

"That is an understatement," Viper didn't look up as he spoke. He didn't sound overly enthused at their return.

"I know the morning is pressing on, but are we going to get moving?' Richmond sounded hopeful.

"It's good to see you too. No, we won't be leaving until tomorrow. We have had a busy time and need a little rest," Alaric explained.

Richmond thought that he looked fresh enough, but when he looked at Eldred he realised what he was talking about. The old wizard looked even more aged than when he left. Alaric had insisted that Eldred transport them from the island and the spell had drawn a lot of energy. Alaric could have easily created the spell, but he decided that Eldred needed the practice. As much as Eldred didn't appreciate Alaric telling him what to do he had to admit it was important that he learned the new spell. Alaric also wanted to be prepared for an attack from Viper, as much as the serpentant claimed to be on their side, he still didn't trust the creature. The last thing he wanted was to get caught out.

"I guess I will be able to survive for one more day, but I can tell you this town is really starting to get to me," Richmond explained.

"Stop your whining. At least you were allowed to leave this room," Viper snapped.

"Don't worry, snake, you didn't miss anything. This town is less than impressive," Richmond returned.

"Okay you two. I am sure things weren't as bad as you say. I don't know about you, but I'm hungry. Let's see what Vance has for us." Alaric tried to remain calm. He really didn't have the patience for more bickering. He had heard enough from the wizards.

"Am I allowed out now?" Viper asked with surprising deference.

Alaric shook his head and sighed, more out of annoyance than the answer to the question. When he realised what he was doing he thought he better speak. "I am sure that you won't get into any trouble, but make sure that you keep you face covered."

For the first time Alaric noticed that Viper no longer had his hood up. After the first couple of days Viper had stopped wearing his heavy robe. He figured that since he was virtually a prisoner in the room there was little point in trying to hide. Richmond had grown used to the sight of the serpentant. His green, scaled skin no longer affected him. He had even grown used to yellow eyes and forked tongue. He didn't think that anyone else would be so comfortable around the creature. As much as he hated to admit it he actually thought Viper wasn't such bad company.

"Welcome back Lord Eldred," Vance suddenly sprang into action when he saw them enter the common room.

Viper quickly returned his hood before the innkeeper could get a look at him. The sight of a serpentant would certainly get people talking, even if they didn't truly know what he was.

"I'm a lord too, it would be nice to get some respect," Richmond mumbled.

Alaric thought about berating the Darshivallian Lord, but figured he had already suffered enough. Although he wasn't a spoilt nobleman it seemed as though he had his limits. In the end Alaric didn't think it was such a bad thing.

"You have no idea how insufferable this place is. The town has a bad smell of fish, all the time. The townsfolk are grumpy, for which I don't blame them. There is nothing for them to do. A seaside town that isn't allowed to set sail is not a recipe for contentment. Add to the fact that they don't like strangers and you can imagine how unpleasant it has been for me. On more than one occasion I was lucky to leave a tavern with all my teeth in tact. The sailors can get quite mean when they are drunk," Richmond spoke when they were seated.

"I am sure that you will be better for the experience. Were you able to gather any information whilst you were here or have you just been drinking your days away?" Alaric asked.

"Can I get ye anythin' else, me lord?" Vance asked.

"Just some privacy please, my good sir." Eldred was short, but didn't want to sound rude.

"Of course," Vance sounded a little hurt.

"Funny you should ask," there was no humour to Richmond's voice. "Just the other day I heard a rumour that pretty much confirms what Viper told us about Dargoz being in the Remidian palace. It seems as though the Dark Knight has managed to burrow himself into a position of responsibility."

"How can you be sure? If the Dark Knight is in control of Remidia then I doubt he would make it well known. Dargoz is arrogant, but he isn't stupid," Eldred questioned.

"No, but a small merchant train arrived in town a couple of days ago. They were looking for sea passage, obviously not knowing that no ships were sailing. They came from Remidel just before the city was locked down. I think it would be easier if the man I met explained it to you himself. I am sure he is still in town." Richmond turned his head to face the innkeeper. "Vance!"

"Yeah, what ye want." Even though Richmond had been paying his way Vance refused to give him any respect. "Have Holt go find that trader, what was his name? That's right Mercer. He should be at the Drowning Duck."

Alaric didn't think it was a good sign if the merchant was in a tavern and this time of day. The midday sun had only just started its downward arc. At least they would get to speak with him before he became too intoxicated.

Vance looked at Eldred who in turn nodded his head. "Of course, me lord!" he said before he left the room.

A serving woman entered shortly after with their midday meals. They all ate in relative silence and were almost finished when Holt returned with the merchant.

"Hello Lord Richmond. I was surprised when I didn't see you at the Duck." He only noticed the newcomers after he had started speaking. "So these must be the friends you were talking about. By the way the others were speaking I almost thought you had made them up."

"Everything I have told you was the truth. Please, have a seat. Vance! An ale for my friend!" Richmond barked.

"So you really are a lord?" Mercer asked.

"Yes, I am Lord Richmond of Bellarome, Darshival, but that is a side issue. This is Eldred, Alena and Alaric and this is... err..."

"Vlad, my name is Vlad," Viper did his best to take the hiss out of his voice.

Mercer stared at Viper for a moment, transfixed by the darkness within his hood. Just when he thought he could see a face the darkness returned. He shook his head and returned his attention to the others, suddenly feeling very self-conscious about staring.

"Of course, Vlad, I don't know where my mind was. Anyway, I would appreciate it if you told my friends what you told me, about Remidia." Richmond continued.

"If the ales keep coming, I'll keep talking," he smiled as the serving girl placed down his mug. "I'm a wool merchant. I transport wool from the northern lands once a year to the more temperate kingdoms. Even Castalia has use for woollen cloaks, if you would believe it."

Alaric kept a wry smile to himself. He remembered wearing the thick robes in the desert. It wasn't a pleasant memory.

"I was on my way south when I came across another merchant heading north. I recognised the man and stopped to talk with him. It seemed odd that he would be carrying a full load away from the capital.

When I asked him about it he told me that the city had been closed and all the trade routes where being shut. Now let me tell you, this isn't the first time I have been turned away by a competitor under the guise of helpful information. As much as I know the man, trust is a completely different story. Now what I tell you next you must keep to yourself. I only tell you this because you are friends of the good lord here. Now I have spent many years in the capital and over the years you learn a thing or two. Anyway, the point of the story is, when I arrived at Remidel, true to his word the gates were shut and no one was allowed in. I drove my wagons to a stable I know not far from the city. At the inn that night I was told the same story. No one was allowed in or out of the city, it was in complete lockdown. Little did they know there is a secret way into the city. There is a small drain to the north. It isn't pleasant as it carries all the sewerage, but if you have a strong stomach and a change of clothes you can sneak in.

Now what I found out once I was in the city I could hardly believe. I was told that the king has a new advisor, a dwarf no less, and he is the one calling the shots. He is the one who has shut the city and by all accounts has caused havoc for the rest of Remidia."

"What does that mean?" Alaric was concerned.

"Well these are only rumours, but apparently there are some evil creatures roaming freely through central Remidia and the king is doing nothing to stop them. His Royal Army is stationed in the city and not moving. The regional nobles have been left to fend for themselves. From what I've heard they are looking after their own cities and leaving the small towns and villages to fall."

Alaric slammed his hand down on the table and swore. "Damn Faxon and Hawthorne. How could they let their kingdom go to ruin?" He already knew the answer.

"Calm yourself Alaric," Eldred soothed. "There is nothing we can do about it now."

"Do about it? What would you do about it?" Mercer waved his mug at the innkeeper as he spoke.

"Nothing, of course. But Alaric is from Arsiliac, so he is obviously concerned." Richmond cut into try and stop the merchant from thinking too hard on the situation. It didn't work.

"So what's a noble from Darshival, a countryman from Remidia, a woman, a member of the Council of Wizards and a strange hooded man doing in Shoretown?" He didn't recognise that Alena was an elf and had not given her much attention.

Eldred shot Richmond an icy glare. He could only hope that Mercer had the good sense not to repeat what he heard. There was little chance that would happen, but Eldred would do his best to try and prevent it.

"What you hear here you do not repeat. I have no doubt that you understand the hold the Council has on Shoretown. If you betray our confidence I will make sure it is the last thing you do." There was no humour in Eldred's voice.

Mercer suddenly went red in the face and looked at Richmond. His expression showed fear and a bead of sweat just added to his guilt. Richmond felt his heart skip a beat. He knew that he had done the wrong thing.

"Do you want me to take care of it?" Viper's words sent a chill down both Mercer's and Richmond's spine.

"Be quiet Vlad. There is no need for that," Alaric scolded.

"Our story is a simple one, but one we don't wish others to know. Alaric is Lord Richmond's cousin and now my apprentice. The hooded man is a monk." Eldred offered a flimsy excuse.

"But…"

"I would advise you to except that explanation and move on," Richmond was stern.

"Yes, my lord." Mercer quickly finished his second ale.

"Is there anything else you can tell us?" Alaric asked, trying to deflect the conversation.

"The only thing left to say is to avoid central Remidia, unless you have a death wish."

They had no plans to travel though central Remidia. Alaric had wanted to go to the mountain via Arsiliac, but Eldred had talked him out of it. Time was of the essence and his hometown was out of the way. The quickest route would bring them to the west of Remidel, but Alaric wasn't so sure if that was the best idea. If Remidia was overrun by Nyrra's forces then he had to do something about it. There was no point in trying to save Arsiliac if it was already destroyed.

"Thank you for the information Mercer. I think it is time to be running along," Eldred suggested.

Mercer had just received another ale and looked like he was settling in for the night. When he heard Eldred's words he shot Richmond a look. He was under the assumption that the lord was going to pay for all his drinks all night. Richmond simply shrugged his shoulders.

"Do you think he will keep his mouth shut?" Alaric asked after Mercer had left the common room.

"He will if he knows what's good for him." Eldred's threat was empty.

"I could always take care of him," Viper added.

"Enough Viper." Eldred didn't know if he was serious or joking.

"How can we leave Remidia to burn?" Alaric hadn't been listening to the conversation. He couldn't think of anything else.

"I didn't want to go to the mountain in the first place," Eldred argued. "Now I don't think we have any other choice."

"You need to see what Adder is up too," Viper added. "There is something wrong with this whole situation."

Alaric knew they were right. He could feel the tug of the prophecy trying to pull him to the north. Something important was going to happen at Mount Scorpio and he couldn't be late. He just wished for once he could do something that he wanted to do, but again that would have to wait.

"I guess it is sorted then. We leave in the morning." Alaric didn't sound happy.

"You are making the right decision." Viper agreed.

"If I want to hear from you, you can be sure that I will ask," Alaric snapped.

"Be calm Alaric. He was just trying to help."To everyone's surprise Richmond defended the creature.

Alaric simply shook his head. "I think it's time to get some rest." He looked at Alena who had been happy to listen to the conversation and remain quiet. "I suggest you all do the same."

Eldred didn't argue, but he other two didn't seem so happy. They had only just finished their midday meal and were not at all tired.

"I have been stuck in that room every since you left. Surely we can stay here a little longer," Viper complained

"There is still a lot of daylight left and we haven't been quite as busy as you have," Richmond returned.

Alaric had to admit they had a point. Although he wasn't tired himself he didn't know when he would have another time to spend with Alena in a soft bed under a roof and he didn't want to miss out on the opportunity.

"Very well, but don't go getting into trouble," Alaric said before they left the common room.

"What do you suppose that is all about?" Richmond asked absentmindedly.

He knew that there was a spark between the two, but he had yet to notice them being intimate with each other. It came as a surprise to see them walking away, hand-in-hand. For a moment he forgot who he was sharing a table with.

"It seems as though the prophecy is coming true. I am sure that Nyrra will be upset with this turn of events." Viper also spoke without thinking.

"What does that mean?" Richmond suddenly realised what he'd said.

Viper cursed himself for speaking out of turn. As much as he was there to help there were still things that he didn't want to reveal. He had formed a kinship with the lord during his confinement and if he tried to deflect then he would lose Richmond's trust and that was something he couldn't afford to do.

"It is something one of the Dark Knights told me many years ago. I can't remember which one, so don't bother asking." It wasn't a Dark Knight who had told him, but Richmond didn't need to know that. "It is written in the *Crenallous*, Nyrra's version of the prophecy, that one of the conditions for Nyrra's victory is that he needs to seduce the Chosen One's lover. I was to kidnap Alena before she and Alaric became close. Nyrra figured it was his best chance of succeeding."

"And you thought that it wasn't worth telling us earlier?" Richmond did his best to keep his voice low, but he did nothing to hide his anger.

"As I said, it *was* my mission, but it isn't anymore, nor was I ever going to do it. I had to pretend to do as the Dark Lord commanded to keep his knights off my back. Now that I am free of that yoke I have no intention of putting it back on."

The excuse seemed to be solid enough, but that still didn't excuse the omission. Richmond signalled that he wanted a drink. Although it was still early there was little else he could do. It would take a number of ales to calm his nerves.

"And what else is it that you have decided not to tell us?" Richmond asked.

"Nothing of any consequence." Viper wasn't going to dig his hole any deeper.

Richmond knew that it wasn't the truth, but he wasn't going to push any further. He would need to tell the others what he had discovered, they would need to know his motives. It was a disturbing thought and it would take a lot more ale to get it out of his head.

"I am here to help," Viper added when Richmond didn't speak.

"I know you keep saying that, but your actions make it hard to believe."

Richmond wished that Viper would leave him alone. He had grown accustomed to the serpentant and that had made him complacent. He couldn't shake the feeling that in the end Viper would betray him. That made sitting and drinking with the creature very uncomfortable. In the end he decided that it would be just as pertinent to go to bed.

***

"Your shout Mercer, for turning up so late," a call came from the bar at the Drowning Duck.

"It wasn't my fault Cutler. I was called away and you still owe me from last night."

Cutler was a large man who looked as though he had already drunk his fair share, even though it was only mid-afternoon. His belly hung underneath his dirty shirt. His face was covered by a dark, bushy beard and it looked like it had been a number of days since he had bathed or even changed his clothes. Sitting next to him was a portly woman with scruffy hair. She smiled as she saw Mercer, revealing that she was missing a number of teeth. As with Cutler it looked as though it had been a few days since she had bathed.

"Come on, darl, surely yer could buy us a drink," Darla's drawl was clearly affected.

Mercer cringed at the sight of the unkempt woman. For some reason she had taken a shine to him. Perhaps it was because he was clean, he thought. He didn't really want to give the thought any further time, he was happy to be pleasant to her, but that was all.

"Of course I will buy you an ale Darla, since you asked so nicely." Neither recognised the sarcasm.

After buying a round he sat at the bar with them. He kept a reasonable distance as the smell was not pleasant. He was still rattled by what Eldred had told him before he left. It would take more than one drink to settle his nerves. The experience had not been what he was expecting.

"So yer been wit' that lord of yers?" Cutler jibed

"Yes as a matter-of-fact I have." Mercer was not in the mood for any further attacks.

"Oh, and what did yer lord say to you?" Darla added.

"In fact he is leaving in the morning, if you must know. His friends have returned and they have business to the north," Mercer didn't even realise he was divulging too much information. "He wanted me to go with him, but I told him I have business to the south."

"I'm sure he did. I'm sure your business to the south is much more important." Cutler sounded as though he was deliberately being offensive.

The truth of that matter was that Mercer would soon have to make up his mind what he was going to do. His gold was starting to run thin which meant he had to move on. He had managed to sell some of his wool in town, but not at a great price. Since he couldn't take a ship towards Castalia he would have to go by land and that wasn't a promising thought. With the major trade routes shut down he would have to take an alternative path and that was not a great idea. It was the only way he could be sure not to run into Remidian customs guards. The road, at best, was poorly constructed and filled with bandits and other rogues. Without a strong mercenary guard it would be a suicide mission. The only way he could afford more guards was if he paid them at the end of the journey and it would be almost impossible to find mercenaries who would accept those terms. Standard payment was half at the start of the job and half at the end. That left him with few choices. Even if the ships were sailing, he had spent the money for ship hire on ale and rum.

"What? What were you saying?"

"Hah, yer losin' yer mind." Cutler burst out laughing. "Hanin' around nobility too long."

"He is a lord and he is leaving on an important mission in the morning," Mercer slammed his empty mug on the table. "As will I. I can't sit here any longer. I'll end up like you lot."

He had made his decision. For better or worse, he was going south. It might be a death wish, but it was better than sitting around drinking himself to death. He would have to make do with the guards he already had. They wouldn't like the change of plans, but they had no choice. The bartender came around to offer another drink, but Mercer shook his head. Instead he stood and promptly left the tavern.

No one noticed the hooded man sitting in the corner. The light from the many candles seemed to pull away from him. He sat with a bottle of wine and a metal goblet. The wine looked as though it hadn't been touched. The conversation from the bar had caught his attention and he had listened intently. When Mercer left in a huff he lifted the goblet and drained the remaining liquid. He carefully placed the goblet back on the table before leaving. No one in the tavern noticed that his hand was green and scaled.

Chapter 31: Tracking Terror

Eldred was up early. There was something he wanted to do before he left.

The morning air was brisk with a sea breeze blowing a salty smell through the streets. It wasn't as fresh as the smells from the Island, but it still reminded Eldred of home. As much as he enjoyed being on the move he also missed his little house. When the Seven Kingdoms were finally safe he would spend a decade or two reacquainting himself with his home.

It didn't take long for Eldred to find the house he was looking for. The mayor's house was the nicest in town and with Vance's directions it was easy to find. He didn't know why the Council had put a halt on the ships leaving port, but he was going to put an end to it.

"What do you want?" the mayor's wife answered the door after Eldred knocked a number of times. It was obvious that she had been woken by his knocking.

"I am here to see Mayor Peers." Eldred made his tone formal.

"Go away, it's too early. Come back when it is closer to midday." She tried to close the door, but Eldred had already placed his foot in the doorway.

The sun had only just bridged the horizon, but Eldred would have thought the mayor would have been ready to go to work. There was no excuse for him to still be in bed and Eldred really didn't have time to waste.

"Get your foot out of the door. I will have the night watch come and arrest you, whoever you are."

"Go and get the mayor. You can tell him that Eldred Zauber is here to see him." The command in his voice spoke for itself.

Everyone in Shoretown knew the names of the seven wizards. As much as Eldred didn't want to use his position, he didn't have time waste. He would have to reveal his identity to the mayor anyway.

"Ye… yes my lord. I will get him straight way." She nearly fell over herself as she rushed away.

Eldred let himself into the house. There was something unsettling about being out in the street. For a while he had been sensing that someone was watching him. The feeling was growing stronger with every minute and it was enough to make his skin crawl. There was something very disturbing about the fact, but for the moment he didn't have the time to investigate further.

The house was a shambles. There were dirty dishes scattered throughout the kitchen. Clothes were tossed around the house in no particular order. It didn't look like anyone had done any housework in a week, if not longer. Eldred didn't think the situation looked right at all.

"What do you want Bertrade? I don't feel like getting up yet," Mayor Peers snapped at his wife.

There was a moment of silence followed by some hushed voices. Eldred didn't need to hear the conversation to know what was being discussed. He had to smile and chuckle to himself. The mayor wouldn't know what hit him.

"Er, um, hello there Lord Eldred." Peers was frantically brushing his wispy white hair as he rushed out of the bedroom. He was a little surprised to see Eldred standing in the hallway. "Shall we go to the study?"

"No, that's fine. I won't be staying long. I came here with one purpose in mind, but now I am a little perplexed with the condition of your house."

"Yes, I... Um, Bertrade, get to cleaning woman," he barked at his wife and instantly wished he hadn't.

"Who do you think you are speaking to, Mayor Peers?" Bertrade stormed out of the bedroom and instantly went red in the face when she saw Eldred standing before her. For a moment she had forgotten the wizard was there. "Sorry, my lord, I will get to cleaning, straight away."

"Relax, my dear, there are more important matters to deal with. Please, tell me how the house of the Mayor has come to be in such a state?" Eldred spoke in a calming voice.

The redness in Bertrade's face only deepended at Eldred's words. It seemed as though Peers would have to speak for her.

"We used to have a serving maid to help with the day-to-day chores, but soon after the docks were shut she left with her husband." The statement was followed by a confused expression on Eldred's face. "He was a sailor by profession. He waited for a few months to see if the docks would be reopened, but when they didn't he moved on. A few of the sailors left at the same time."

"But I thought the Council was paying for all the sailors to remain in port?"

"That was the reasoning behind the Council's decision, but that was not how it was administered. The various ships' captains were paid a monthly fee from the Council and then they were to pass on the payments to their crew. The payments they did pass on were nowhere near what they would earm if they were working on a ship. Some decided to stay, some decided to leave and look for work at another port."

"This doesn't sound right. Surely the Council would not have let things get into such disarray."

"All the Council cared about was getting the gold to the Captains. Once that was done they did nothing to make sure that the coins reached their rightful destination. It was lucky that any gold reached the sailors as it was."

"And what did you do to right the situation?" Eldred accused.

"I tried my best," Peers sounded shocked at the accusation, "but there was nothing I could do. At first I ordered the Captains to pay the rightful fee, but there are many more Captains then there are Mayors. With the extra money they were able to pay off the town's guards. For the last few months I have stayed inside as much as possible. We only venture out to get the essentials. As it stands the Captains run the town and not too well if you ask me."

Eldred shook his head. He couldn't believe that his brothers and sisters could have made such a mess. He should really stay to fix things, but time and anonymity didn't allow for it. Instead he could just do what he came to do and hope that it would fix the problem.

"This should start to repair the damage that the Council has created." Eldred handed the Mayor a folded piece of parchment.

Mayor Peers took the parchment and studied it carefully. He wasn't sure if he should be reading it in front of Eldred, but it seemed as though the wizard wasn't going to leave until he did. As the Mayor came to the end, he raised an eyebrow in anticipation. He had to admit to himself that it wasn't at all what he was expecting.

"Are you sure this is right?" Peers questioned the parchment. "It's not that I don't trust you Lord Eldred, but the Council said they would let everyone know when the ports were to be opened again."

"Just be grateful that things have changed. You need to try and recover the economy, not that it will do you much good now anyway."

"What do you mean?"

"There is a rumour that King Faxon has closed Remidia, so I doubt any of the ports will be taking goods at the moment. You might have to wait it out a little longer, but at least this is a start."

"I will do what I can, but I fear that we shall have the same problem with the Captains as we did before. There is no way to make sure the money will go to the right people."

"You can let the Captains know that I will be back and if I find out things are not as I have left them then there will be trouble." There was no need to elaborate.

Eldred really wanted to do more, but there was no time. The sun was well and truly above the horizon and they needed to be leaving. There were many more miles to travel and little time to do it in. He quickly took his leave and left the Mayor and his wife to discuss what they were going to do.

"This is very generous," Bertrade said after she had read the parchment. "What shall we do with all the gold they are offering?" Her face lit up when she finished reading.

"We shall do exactly what Lord Eldred has told us to do. We will get the ships running and we shall compensate those who have missed out." Peers shook his head at what his wife was suggesting.

"But we have suffered as much as anyone else." she wasn't going to let it go. "Surely we deserve compensation for our troubles." There was a whine to her voice that annoyed Peers.

He had never struck his wife, but her complaining was really starting to push him. The pressure was on for him to help his town recover and he didn't need his wife making life any harder for him. If he was going to succeed in such an auspicious task then he would need to plan it right through to the end.

As he was deep in thought there was a sudden knock on the door. It startled him and his heart skipped a beat. His initial reaction was that Eldred had returned.

"Well, don't just sit there. Answer the door," Peers barked, harsher than he planned.

Bertrade thought about berating him, but another knock on the door changed her mind. There was plenty of time for her to teach her husband some proper respect. For the moment she fulfilled her role with a pleasant attitude.

As soon as she opened the door a gust of icy wind entered the house. She shivered before looking at the man standing before her. The figure wore a dark robe with the hood covering its head. She tried to look into the hood to see who it was, but she couldn't see through the darkness. There was something very peculiar about him.

"Can I help you with something?" she said the first thing that came to her when she realised she hadn't spoken.

The figure reached out and a green scaly hand poked out of the robe. Bertrade looked at it, confused and took a step backwards. When she realised what was coming towards her she opened her mouth to scream, but no sound came out. Her throat had already started to tighten even though the scaled hand was still a foot away.

The creature took a step forward into the house and shut the door behind him. Although there was no one on the street he didn't want anyone to know he was there. He needed secrecy if he was going to succeed. When the woman's body went limp he let it drop to the floor. She was insignificant. It was the man he needed answers from.

"Who is it love?" Peers called out.

"I am here for answers." The voice hissed.

"Who are you?" Peers retreated a couple of steps when the robed figure entered the sitting room.

"That is insignificant." The serpentant wasn't interested in small talk. "You will tell me what you were discussing with the man who just left."

"That is none of your business." Peers quickly stashed the parchment under a number of papers he had scattered on his desk. "I think that you should be leaving now. There is nothing I can help you with."

"I am going nowhere," the voice hissed.

"Bertrade!" Peers called out to his wife. "Bertrade!"

"There is nothing she can do for you now."

"What are you talking about?" Peers was suddenly deeply concerned and took a cautious step backwards.

"You will be seeing her soon." The serpentant took a mirrored step forward.

"Bertrade!" he called out again.

"Tell me what I need to know."

Slowly the scaled hands reached up and pulled back the hood. Peers retreated as far as he could, until he bumped into the wall. The look on his face was pure horror. He couldn't believe what he was seeing. The creature's head was shaped like a serpent with large flaps on either side. They flared out when he revealed his head. A forked tongue flicked from its mouth and yellow eyes stared at him.

"What... what... what are you?" Peers stammered.

"I am Cobra and this is your last chance to tell me what I need to know."

"Nothing happened. Lord Eldred just told me that the Council was opening the ports again. That's all I swear." Peers was close to tears. He wanted to run, he wanted to see if his wife was alright, but he couldn't move. He was too scared.

"Where is he going?" Cobra asked.

"I don't know. I swear to the Gods, I don't know."

Cobra wasn't sure if the mayor was telling the truth, he had been away from the wretched creatures for too long and had forgotten all about their little idiosyncrasies. There was another way to find out if it was telling the truth and that was much more pleasurable.

Taking a step forward Cobra reached out toward Peers. Instantly Peers felt something compress around his throat. Although he could still breathe he couldn't suck in a full lungful or air. If the pressure remained he would die a slow and painful death.

"Tell me where are they going?"

"I don't know," the words were only just audible.

Cobra felt that the man was telling the truth, but he still couldn't be completely sure. There was only one way he could certain. Suddenly Peers felt a shooting pain in his chest. It felt as though his heart was going to explode. He tried to gasp for breath, but nothing came. A heat filled his heat and he felt as though he was going to lose consciousness. That would have been compassionate, but Cobra wasn't going to let him slip out of reality.

"This is your last chance worm. Answer my question or die."

Peers looked as though he wanted to say something, but he couldn't. His face has gone a bright red and no air was reaching his lungs anymore. As much as Cobra didn't want to release him he needed answers. Slowly he let the grip on his neck slip away. When his throat opened Peers sucked in as much air as he could. The sudden movement in his throat caused him to cough making it even harder to breathe. He didn't mind, he knew it gave him extra time to live. His next words were going to sign his death sentence.

When he was able to catch his breath he finally spoke. "You can go to hell, Snake." He spat blood on the floor, which had risen from his chest. There was a half smile, half grimace on his face. He knew what was coming and was prepared for it.

Peers wanted to scream out in pain when Cobra started his grip again, but no sound left his mouth. He knew that this time the snake wouldn't let him go. Cobra revelled in the impending death. The only regret he had was that he didn't get the information he needed. His brothers were planning something and he wanted to know what it was.

***

Alaric looked at the sky and wondered where Eldred was. The sun was climbing and he really wanted to get moving. There was a long journey ahead and he couldn't risk being late. He also didn't like Viper being out in the open, the less chance of anyone seeing him the better. On more than one occasion he thought about killing the creature and ending his worries, but he had a bad feeling the serpentant was going to come in handy in the future. Adelanta reflected his rider's anxiety. He was also keen to get moving again and Alaric had to calm the stallion to keep him still.

It wasn't long before Eldred was seen walking towards them. There was a spring to his step that hadn't been there before. This only increased Alaric's curiosity of what he had been doing. The wizard definitely looked pleased with himself.

"What do you have to say for yourself Eldred?" Alaric asked in a playful tone.

The smile left Eldred's face. There had been a subtle change in leadership in the group. When he looked back it had started ever since they had been rescued by Alaric. He wasn't sure if it was a good thing or a bad thing. If Alaric was ready for the trials ahead of them then of course it was good, but if he wasn't, then Eldred didn't want to think of the repercussions. For the moment he would just have to remain subservient and keep an eye on things. It had been a long time since Eldred had not been in control of his life.

"Just taking care of business, now it is time for us to get moving," Eldred returned.

"The time to move was at sunrise, but we can discuss this later. For the moment I think it is best for us to put as much road between us and Shoretown as we can. Ever since I woke this morning a feeling of dread has come over me. I think I will be much happier once we have left."

Eldred simply nodded his head and mounted Tormenta. There was no point in letting Alaric know that he was having the same feelings. All that would do was worry the others and until he knew what they were up against he didn't think there was any point. He felt a little better when he was on the white, Elven horse's back.

There was no further discussion before they moved off. Viper was grateful for small mercies. He had felt the touch of one of his brothers on the morning air and if he was questioned he wasn't sure he could tell the truth. Remaining in the group was tenuous at best and if he was caught lying then he would surely be kicked out, if not killed. He had no preconceptions about his own abilities, if he was able to catch Alaric by surprise he had a chance to kill him, but in a straight up fight he would surely lose.

As they rode through the town, Alaric felt the same evil eyes on him that he had felt when he had woken. The first few times the feeling came he looked around, but even as he did he knew that no one would be there. After that he just did his best to shrug it off.

They had decided to take the highway leading towards Remidel and Alaric felt a little better once they were away from Shoretown. Before they would come close enough to the capital they would take a small road to the west until they reached the duchy of Weston. According to the rumours the city was still safe from Nyrra's army.

The highway led them along the coast for twenty leagues before it turned inland. On their left were the large cliffs and jagged rocks which prevented the ships from being able to dock, this gave Shoretown its main trade. A few tea trees dotted the top of the cliffs and scattered grass covered the rocky terrain. On the other side there were some more sparsely spread tea trees and sloping grassland. There was little chance for anyone to sneak up on them and that relieved Alaric's mind.

"This is amazing," Viper spoke when they stopped for lunch.

"What are you talking about Viper?" Eldred snapped.

"We have travelled a great distance in a small amount of time. I take it wasn't you who created the spell Eldred." He then looked at Alaric.

"How about you keep your mouth shut," Alaric snapped. He wasn't in the mood for speaking with anyone.

"I think you should relax Alaric," to everyone's surprise it was Richmond who spoke in Viper's defence. "It was a positive comment, there was no need to snap."

It was a surprise to Richmond that the words came out of his mouth. The time they had spent together in Shoretown had brought them closer than Richmond would have liked to admit, but nevertheless it was how he felt. The serpentant wasn't bad company, at least when there was no one else to talk to.

"Sorry Viper." Alaric couldn't believe he was apologising. He stood when he finished speaking and the feeling that they were being watched suddenly returned. It had disappeared around mid-morning and Alaric had almost forgotten about it. He looked around wildly, but there was no one there. If they had been travelling so quickly then whatever it was that was following them wasn't far behind.

"What's wrong Alaric?" Alena sounded concerned.

Alaric looked around once more. He thought he saw something in the distance, but when he looked again it had gone. In the end he couldn't decide if there had been anything there in the first place.

"I have a feeling that someone is following us. It is as if we are being tracked and they are able to keep up the pace."

"That would mean..." Alena didn't really know what it meant, although the comment didn't need finishing for everyone else to guess.

"Do you have any ideas?" Alaric asked Eldred.

"I felt the same feeling when I was in Shoretown. It was enough to make my skin crawl," Eldred explained.

"It is one of my brothers," Viper mentioned matter-of-factly as he finished his lunch. He had decided that it would be better if he offered the information. There was no doubt that another serpentant was involved, and he had an idea who it was.

No one knew what to say, so everyone deferred to Alaric. Instead of asking another question Alaric stood and walked to where the horses were grazing. His face held an icy stare and no one could tell what he was thinking. It wasn't until he pulled the sword from its sheath did they realise what he was doing. Before anyone had a chance to move Alaric returned and placed the blade against Viper's throat.

"What is it you aren't telling us?"

It was the question that Viper didn't want to be asked. There was a lot that he wasn't telling them, but he had to read between the lines. He had to be very careful if he wanted to keep his head on his shoulders.

"One of my brothers has been following us since we left Shoretown. I'm not sure who it is so I didn't want to say anything until I was sure." Viper spoke honestly, but Alaric wasn't convinced.

"There is more to this story than what you are telling us. Now if you want to keep your head I think you should continue."

"I don't know what you want from me," Viper's voice remained calm, although he was starting to panic. There were things he didn't want them to know.

"Who is it?" Alaric spoke through clenched teeth.

"I don't know."

"Guess!" Alaric snarled.

"Well, I doubt it would be Adder. It wouldn't make any sense for him to stalk us if he knows where we are going to be. Now that obviously leaves us with a choice of five others and this is where it gets tricky. It has been a long time since I have seen any of them."

"I wouldn't advise taking much longer in getting to the point," Alaric threatened. "I might just decide if it is easier to end your life."

"At a guess I would say it was either Cobra or Python. I couldn't say which one." The more he thought about it the more he was sure it was Cobra, but he didn't want to let them know. He wanted to find out more before he gave away any more information. He didn't know how he was going to leave the group to speak with Cobra, but he would have to make it happen. He really needed to know what his brother was planning. Of all his brothers he had liked Cobra the best, but that didn't mean that things hadn't changed over the years. It didn't make any sense why Cobra should be following them, he hoped that he didn't have any plans to try and rescue him. He needed to let Cobra know that he wasn't a prisoner.

"So how is it that they can keep up with us?" Eldred asked.

"I don't know. If I knew what Alaric was doing I could try and figure it out."

"If I…" Alaric started absentmindedly before he caught himself. "It is not your concern what I am doing," Alaric spoke harshly, more at his own foolishness then anything else. "How he is keeping up with us is irrelevant. What we need to know is what his agenda is. You must have some idea what he is up to?" Alaric moved the blade against his throat.

Viper truly had no idea what his brother was up to. That in itself was disturbing. If it was in fact Cobra, as he suspected, then it was even more disturbing. His brother was supposed to be on the other side of the Seven Kingdoms. He couldn't think of any reason why he was following them. He then realised that he still hadn't answered Alaric's question and they were all watching him.

"I have no idea." Viper shook his head risking severing it against Alaric's blade.

Alaric wasn't happy with the response, but there was little point in pushing him further. There was a much more important matter they had to deal with before they left. Pausing for a moment he thought about it before sheathing his blade. For the moment Viper had kept his life.

"So how can we mask our route from him?" Alaric asked.

Viper again had hoped that wouldn't be a question he was asked. There were things that outsiders really didn't need to know. On the other hand it was the perfect opportunity to gain their trust and that was much more important.

"We track by taste," Viper spoke softly, just in case his brother was within hearing distance.

"What does that mean?" Alaric barked before Viper had a chance to continue.

"I will show you if you like?" when there were no rejections he stood and turned his back to the others. "Now move around and I will tell you exactly where each of you is."

Alaric looked at the others and they all shrugged their shoulders in response. He was the first to stand and change his position, shortly followed by Alena and then Richmond and Eldred. He was unsure how Viper was going to prove anything.

"We're ready!"

With his eyes closed Viper turned around. There was an expression of concentration on his face. Slowly his forked tongue poked out of his mouth and flicked the air in front of him. After almost a minute he pointed to and named everyone in turn. When he opened his eyes a broad smile crossed his face. He had named them all perfectly.

"How did you do that?" Alena gasped.

"That is a secret that I will keep to myself," he knew he was pushing his luck, but he hoped he had revealed enough.

"Fine, keep your little secret." Alaric was sure that it wasn't important. "Just tell us how we can mask it."

"You can leave it to me. I will make sure that he can't follow us anymore."

"I don't think so. You may be gaining my trust, but you still have a long way to go. Now if you would be so kind to explain to me what I have to do we can be on our way."

Viper should have known that would be the response. There was nothing he could do, but give Alaric what he wanted, otherwise he would lose all the good work he had been doing. If he was going to succeed then he needed to gain the man's trust.

"It's quite easy if you understand the process, but I will do my best to explain it to you. I guess the easiest way is to think about it is what you call smell. All you need to do is change your 'scent'. Now what you need to do..."

"I think I can take it from here," Eldred spoke before Alaric had the chance. The spell was quite simple and although Alaric had never cast it before he knew he would be able to.

Eldred closed his eyes and raised his hand above his head. For a moment he stood completely still, almost as if he had been turned to stone. Without warning he cried out one word. "*Aëveni!*" The air shimmered around the group for a second before it returned to normal. Alaric looked around, but it seemed as though nothing had changed. He had felt the tell-tell tickle on the back of his neck and he knew that Eldred had created the spell.

"Now I think it is time for us to keep moving." Eldred didn't wait for a response.

No one noticed that Viper didn't mount with the rest of them. He made a show of moving things around in his pack, which was completely unnecessary. When he was sure no one was paying any attention to him he scribbled in the sand. He had managed to find a relative sheltered spot to leave his message and he could only hope that the wind wouldn't blow it away.

"Ah, the salt brings a freshness to the air." Viper commented as he rode off.

No one heard his words. They were all concentrating on the road ahead.

Chapter 32: Weston

It took them two more days to reach Weston. The weather started to turn against them once they started out again. Dark rain clouds filled the sky, but didn't break until the morning of the following day. At first it was a light rain, which besides dampening their moods did little else. It wasn't until they prepared to set camp for the night did the skies truly open. It was impossible for them to sleep in the open with the rain belting down. Their fire was extinguished almost before it was lit and there was no protection from the downpour. The rain eased during the next morning and then stopped completely when the city came into view, but Alena and Richmond remained drenched.

To everyone's surprise there were people roaming around the surrounding farmlands. They passed them on the road as they transported their goods. All the other small towns and villages they had been through had been completely shut down. The only sign of life had been the occasional eye peeping out through gaps in their curtains. They had not seen a single person on the road between Shoretown and Weston. It seemed as though Weston knew nothing of the terrors that faced the rest of the kingdom. They all agreed that it was a welcome change.

As much as Alaric wanted to keep moving they couldn't pass on the opportunity to gather some information. It seemed as though Weston had yet to feel the yoke of Nyrra's evil, at least that was the way it seemed. They all knew better than to take that for granted.

The city wasn't much more than the duke's castle and a number of cottages and farmhouses dotted around. It wasn't much of a city, but the Duke of Weston insisted that it be called as such. There was no doubt the castle was the focal point. Built from dark stone it was surrounded by a wooden, spiked wall. The wall was more for aesthetic value than any real defence. The castle itself was built in a near perfect square with a tower, one in each corner and a parapet wall connecting them. They were the only real defensive points of the castle, but they definitely made great sniper perches for archers.

No one seemed to take much notice of the new travellers as they rode towards the castle. Viper had covered himself with his robe once the city came into view. He had enjoyed the freedom of riding without the heavy robe and as much as he didn't want to put it back on, he knew it he had to keep his anonymity.

Alaric was surprised to see the people going about their business. It had been the first time he had seen that in a long time. Of course the cities still ran, but not as calmly or apparently carefree as Weston. It was almost like they were deliberately trying not to notice them and that weighed on Alaric's mind. He couldn't shake the feeling that they were walking into a trap, nevertheless he kept his suspicions to himself.

The gates were maned by a pair of guards each holding a long pike. They wore polished breast plates with the Ducal seal stamped in the middle, a fox head encircled with stars. They blocked the gate when they saw the group approach. It seemed as though things weren't as comfortable as they looked.

"Halt!" one of the guards boomed.

"State your business, travellers!" the other followed.

They had decided before they arrived that it would be best if Richmond spoke. He would be the most recognisable and hopefully the guards would have heard of the Darshivallian Lord. If not they were sure the duke would know who he was and there was no way they would leave the lord standing outside in such a state.

"I am Lord Richmond of Bellarome, Darshival. I am here to see the duke.

"Duke Dunn isn't expecting any noble visitors today. You should have sent prior warning of your arrival. As I am sure you know, these are troubled times and we need to be careful who we allow into the castle." The guard sounded quite cocky.

Alaric wasn't at all surprised with the response. It was becoming ever more common and he really couldn't blame them. Although the townsfolk seemed to be going about their day-to-day life the threat was obviously in the back of everyone's mind That thought made Alaric feel a little better.

"We need information," Alaric decided to join the conversation "before we travel any further into Remidia. We really must speak with the duke."

"And who might you be?" the guard sniffed as he spoke, clearly assuming Alaric was a simple servant.

"My name is not important. All you need to know is that we need to gain entry."

No one else knew that whilst Alaric was talking he was also working on a spell. It was something he had been thinking about when he was on the Island. It was a mind spell, different to anything he had tried before. Most mind spells worked on weak minds, but he wanted one that would work on everyone. He wanted to practice on a strong minded person, but he would have to settle for the guard.

"I'm afraid that isn't going to happen." The guard suddenly scratched at the side of his head as Alaric slowly started to release his spell.

The spell had to be released slowly or there was a great risk of exploding the brain. This was something Alaric realised when he tested the spell on some poor melons. It wasn't the same as real test subjects, but it did allow him to gauge the strength of the spell. The guard twitched slightly as he tried to work out where the sudden sensation had come from.

"We really need to see the duke." Alaric continued.

"What... What did you say?" the guard sounded confused. He looked around, as if someone was just outside of his peripheral vision, of course there was no one there.

"We need to see the duke. Now let us pass." Alaric kept his voice calm, yet stern.

As the spell progressed the guard forgot what he was thinking. The words echoed throughout his mind. Something wasn't right, but they seemed to make sense. He wanted to say no, but the words wouldn't pass his mouth.

"Okay, you can go through." His eyes had glazed over and it looked like he was going to lose consciousness.

"But, Morton, we shouldn't let them in."

"Quiet, I have made my decision. Let them through!" he spoke louder than he meant.

"Let's go," Alaric didn't want to wait for the other guard to take control.

"What did you do back there?" Viper asked when they were past the guards.

They rode slowly through the marketplace. It was strangely empty. With all the people moving around outside of the castle they figured it would business as usual inside. It was eerily quiet, besides the sound of the horses' hooves on cobble stones.

"What are you talking about?" Alaric tried to be as innocent as possible. "They just let us in."

Viper knew that wasn't true. He himself had twisted the minds of men before and he knew when someone was being tampered with. What he didn't know was how Alaric had achieved his goal. Viper himself had tested the guard and figured that his mind was too strong to be played with, at least not without the risk of major brain-damage. The second guard was the most logical choice and yet Alaric was able to move the first. He wanted nothing more than to push his curiosity further, but he knew better. For the moment he would have to watch and wait.

Eldred watched the exchange closely. He too noticed that Alaric had done something different. It had taken a while, but Eldred had grown used to the fact that Alaric could create spells that he could neither sense nor feel. It was disturbing that Alaric had surpassed him so soon, but he didn't really know what he had been expecting. The Chosen One was supposed to be more powerful than anyone else.

The large main doors leading into the castle were unguarded. It seemed a little odd, but with the lack of people around there didn't seem to be any point. There were no stable boys waiting to take their horses, which was more annoying than anything else, it meant they would have to take them themselves.

Like the rest of the castle, the stables were empty, not a single horse could be seen, which also seemed odd.

Once their horses had been fed and stabled they made their way back to the main entrance. They saw a side door, but they figured it would be better if they entered from the front. It would be less confronting for those inside.

When they opened the main doors they found the corridors were also empty. Alaric stopped them as they approached the main flight of stairs.

"Something doesn't feel right," Alaric started.

"You're right," Eldred added "but let's just hope that it's due to the eerie silence."

Alaric drew his sword and shrugged his shoulders. They had to continue, but he wanted to be prepared. He would remain armed until he knew what was happening inside the castle.

It wasn't until they reached the second floor that they finally came across someone. A young serving maid let out a squeak when she saw the five of them. She looked at Alaric's sword before dropping the washing that was in her arms and running away. Alaric quickly sheathed his sword when he saw her reaction, but it was already too late.

"I am sure we will get some answers soon," Alaric commented.

They didn't get to move much further before they were met by half a dozen armed men. They marched towards the group but stopped, just outside of striking distance. Alaric's hand went to the hilt of his sword, but a calming hand from Eldred stopped him.

"What are you doing in the castle?" one of the guards barked.

"I am Lord Richmond and we are here to see Duke Dunn."

"The duke isn't seeing any visitors. I thought the guards at the gate would have told you that. In fact how did you manage to get past them?" the guard responded, it was obvious the situation wasn't making a lot of sense to him.

"We are special visitors. He will want to see us," Alaric interrupted before Richmond could respond.

"I don't think so. I think you should spend some time in the dungeons." The guard wasn't going to be dissuaded.

Eldred stepped forward, he'd had enough of the others fumbling. "I am Lord Eldred of the Council of Wizards!" He boomed. "I demand a sitting with your duke."

The spell he used caused the words to echo down the hall. He also seemed to loom above the guards, creating a long shadow. Those who had never seen the trick before found it quite intimidating, it was the exact effect Eldred was after.

"Yes, Lord Eldred, of course you can see the duke. I'm sure he will be pleased to hear of your arrival. Come this way!"

"You see, there are easier and safer ways to get people to do what you want," Eldred spoke to Alaric.

"Yes, but it is safer if people don't know who I am. The enemy has many spies."

"But at least this way you don't risk frying someone's brain. That is why such spells have been outlawed. If the rest of the Council found out what you were doing then they would be less than impressed," Eldred warned.

Alaric shook his head. "For starters there was no risk to frying the city gate guard's brain. He might have a slight headache for a while, but that is all."

In truth the guard would have a severe headache for the rest of the afternoon. It was a side-effect of the spell, that Alaric had no idea existed. With his experiments there was no way of finding out any after effect on real people. He knew couldn't explain that to Eldred, so it was easier if he just lied. When everything was over the Council would need to re-evaluate the way they thought. Alaric had plans, but they hinged on him surviving and that was something he wasn't sure of.

"You might what to keep your voices down," Alena whispered as she noticed the guards trying their best to eavesdrop.

Eldred nodded although he really didn't think it mattered. They knew who his was and he was sure they would have a fair idea of what he was capable of.

They walked the rest of the way to the throne room in silence. As much as the guards had some idea who they were they really didn't need or want to know any more. Eldred had hoped to keep his identity a secret, at least until they reached the duke. The more people who knew who they were the better chance the enemy had of finding out.

"It's a pleasure to welcome you to Weston," Dunn greeted them when they arrived.

Sitting on the throne next to Dunn was his wife, Duchess Norina. His son Odunn stood on one side and his daughter Nora stood on the other. The duke had a broad smile on his face, which was in complete contrast with the other three. The Duchess, Odunn and Nora all looked somewhat frightened. Alaric thought the expression had been on their faces since before they had entered the room, but he quickly shook off the feeling.

"What brings you to my little old city?"

"We have come for some information and shelter from the weather," Eldred thought it best if he spoke first.

"I see." Duke Dunn stroked his short, brown goatee. "I think you should dry yourselves before we speak. You don't want to catch a cold." He didn't seem to notice that Eldred, Alaric and the robed and hooded Viper were perfectly dry.

Alaric hadn't even thought of the others. Richmond and Alena stood shivering, but they would not say anything to draw attention to themselves.

"Thank you for the offer, but our business is too important," Eldred responded.

"Don't be silly. I will not have you standing here in those wet clothes," Dunn clapped his hands when he finished speaking.

Alaric still couldn't shake the feeling that something wasn't right. He looked at the fear on the faces of the duke's family. He couldn't understand what they could be frightened of. The city was untouched by the Evil One and surely they weren't scared by the new arrivals.

"Thank you, duke, you are too kind." As Eldred spoke a door behind the throne's opened and six staff entered.

"See that our new guests are given rooms. They will need baths and fresh clothes. I am sure you will be able to find something suitable for them," Dunn ordered.

The six serving staff bowed and curtsied quickly in response. They all kept their heads down and their eyes lowered. Normally Alaric would have thought it was a sign of deference, but there was something different in their attitude. It was almost as if they were scared of the duke.

"Very good, off you go then." Dunn spoke to them. "Please come back here when you have dried off and changed clothes. I will certainly give you all the information you need."

Alaric had to admit he was looking forward to a long bath. The servants took them straight to the bath house where the baths were all in individual rooms. Alaric thought it was strange as he had expected the baths to be in one room, or at least one for men and one for women.

"I think I will go to my room," Viper said. He didn't need to bathe and he didn't think it would be a good idea for him to remove his robe.

"I'll take your things to be cleaned," the softly spoken servant said when Alaric was about to step into the bath.

Alaric jumped slightly with surprise. He had thought he was alone and didn't hear anyone enter. He realised the stones were all sitting next to his bags and he silently scolded himself for being so lax.

"That's alright. I can bring it when I'm done," Alaric replied as the servant picked up his pack.

"The duke said we should take all of your things and make sure they are all cleaned and returned." The servant replied as he continued collecting Alaric's possessions.

Before the servant could pick up one of the stones Alaric suddenly reached out with his right hand. The movement was so sudden it sent the servant flying backwards. He dropped Alaric's pack as he crashed into the wall. He slumped to the ground, not unconscious, but very confused at what had happened.

"I'm sorry," Alaric wasn't sure if he should be apologising, but he did anyway. "You can take my pack, but please, leave the rest."

The servant shook his head as he picked himself up from the floor. The man still had no idea what had happened. He looked at Alaric, but there was no response. Alaric had sunk into the bath and was trying his best to pretend that nothing had happened.

"Just take the pack. Don't touch the rest." Alaric repeated, a little more casually this time. His clothes didn't need cleaning and he didn't want to wear something from the castle when he was finished. For some reason he only felt comfortable in the leathers he made for himself.

"The duke told me to take all your possessions." The servant sounded nervous. "I must do as he commands."

Alaric was too concerned with the stones to worry about what was causing the servant's agitation. He didn't realise that there was something more sinister at work.

"Be that as it may, you can leave everything else." Alaric tried to remain calm.

"I am sorry, my lord, but I really need to take everything," the servant reached for the small pile of velvet covered items, not knowing exactly what they were.

Alaric sensed what was happening before he saw it. Without thinking he reached out again, this time wrapping the servant in a bond of air. The look of fear increased on the servant's face as he suddenly realised what was happening.

"Now I appreciate your situation, but you must really understand... you can't take those," Alaric's voice was icy cold.

The servant tried to nod his head, but he couldn't move. The bond kept him all, but motionless. He wanted to speak, but he couldn't out of fear. There was nothing he could do to agree with Alaric. He wanted nothing more than to leave the room, although he wasn't sure that what was waiting for him on the other side was any better.

"Now, off you go and don't make me say it again," Alaric released the servant when he finished speaking.

The pack, which had remained in his hands, dropped to the ground. He quickly scooped it back up and then left the room. The duke was not going to be happy. They had all been told to take every possession from the visitors, but he had been specifically told to get all of Alaric's. On the other hand he couldn't take him on. The wizard's apprentice, at least that's what he assumed he was, was too strong for him. There was nothing he could do.

Alaric relaxed into the water, but not before locking the door. The spell was simple enough and he was starting to grow used to doing menial tasks with magic. It wasn't worth the effort to lift himself out of the water and walk across the room, the last thing he wanted to do was to let the servant come back and make another attempt at taking the stones.

The toll of increasing the speed of their journey was starting to weigh on him. Closing his eyes he let the water soak in around him. He felt as though he could fall asleep right where he was and before he knew what had happened he had drifted off.

***

"What do you mean?" Dunn barked.

"I'm sorry, your Grace, there was nothing I could do. The apprentice was too strong from me." The servant was close to tears.

"What about the sleeping powder in the bath salts?"

"When I went back the door was locked. There was nothing I could do to open it." The servant pleaded. "Please, I did everything I could."

"Everything you could? If you had done everything you could then you would have brought me what I asked for. No, you didn't do everything you could. Now you will pay the price for failing me."

"Please father," Odunn objected. "This is not justice. At least let's see if his claim is true."

"Be quiet," Dunn boomed "lest you will share the gibbet with him. This has nothing to do with you."

"Please, my love," the Duchess pleaded. "This is not like you."

"Take him to see the hangman. I want his head on a pike by morning." Dunn would not be dissuaded.

The soldiers walked to where the servant was cowering in front of the duke. As much as they didn't agree with his judgement they were still faithful to the crown. The duke was in power and until he died or was disposed they would do as he commanded. The servant sobbed out loudly as he was dragged away.

"I think that I will retire now." Duchess Norina sounded faint. She steeled herself to watch the poor servant being taken, but that took all her remaining strength. "Nora, Odunn, please help me to my chambers." She made a point not to ask her husband for permission to leave. It was a risk, but she had to draw the line somewhere.

"Very well, Norina, I will be along shortly," she cringed at the thought.

They quickly left the throne room. None of them wanted to stay with the duke. It was only a matter of time before his temper got the better of him again and they didn't want to be around when that happened. They all remembered when the duke was a kind and loving ruler. That had all changed almost a month ago. Now he was a cruel and ruthless leader. It was no wonder the townsfolk stayed away from castle.

The duke remained seated on his throne. He stared out at the empty hall before him, that was how he liked it. There was no one there to betray him, that was his greatest fear. He was sure there was someone who was planning on assassinating him and those closest to him were top of his list. With his new visitors there were just more people who wanted to usurp his power.

As if on cue the door opened and Lord Eldred and Lord Richmond entered the room. The woman and the mysteriously hooded man were nowhere to be seen. He knew Alaric would still be in his bath, but that was something he would keep to himself.

"Thank you for seeing us!" Eldred looked around and was surprised that there was no one else in the room.

"Of course, please, have a seat and tell me what you need to know." Dunn offered.

"Thank you, but if you don't mind I would like to wait for my apprentice to arrive." Eldred thought it was best to keep up the pretence. The duke didn't really need to know who he was.

"I am sure that he will be along shortly. I know sometimes I can get lost in the baths. Surely we can talk candidly without him?"

Eldred thought that Dunn's statement sounded fair enough. He knew that Alaric would like to take part in the meeting, but he was sure he could catch up later. It wouldn't be long before he joined them, Eldred was confident about that. There was no reason why Alaric would stay longer than necessary in the baths.

"I trust that your lady friend and the other man travelling with you are comfortable," the duke's voice sounded pleasant.

They had decided that it was best that Viper remained in his room. Alena, on the other hand, was given the job of trying to get some information out of the duke's family. There had been something strange about their original meeting. When they passed the three leaving the throne room it was a simple decision. Alena slipped in behind and followed them back to their quarters.

"I am sure they are fine," Eldred replied. He looked around nervously hoping to see Alaric enter the room.

"Now, what is it that you wish to know?" There was a wry smile on the duke's face.

Chapter 33: Deception from Within

Alena followed the three, being careful not to be noticed. She had hoped to gain some insight before she revealed herself, but it seemed as though they weren't going to speak. They moved quickly through the corridors as if the paintings were watching them. There was something very nervous about their movements. This piqued her curiosity to the point where she tripped on a rug and gave away her position. They turned around quickly when they heard her stumble.

"Lady Alena, you startled us," Duchess Norina tried not to sound scared, but failed. "What are you doing following us?"

"I'm sorry if I scared you. I was simply hoping to have a discussion with you."

Norina looked at her son and daughter. They looked like they didn't know what to do. She had hoped for some reassurance, but received none. The decision was completely up to her, but she didn't think the elf was in league with her husband and that was a promising sign. She didn't know how far she could trust Alena and the others, one wrong move and she would end up hanging from the gallows.

"Of course, but not here, sometimes I think that the walls have ears. It will be safer in my chambers," Norina offered.

Alena followed the three of them to Norina's private chambers. The Duchess locked the door behind them, but not before checking the hallway to see if anyone was following them. Once inside she moved to a table where a pot of tea was waiting for her. She poured four cups before taking a seat. Alena didn't really feel like a hot drink, but she thought it would be rude not to accept it. She took a little sip before putting the cup down. There was a floral aroma to the tea that Alena had never smelt before. The flavour was better than she expected.

"I'm sorry if I seemed rude before, but we must be careful where we speak." Norina started.

"That's perfectly fine," Alena paused to take another sip of tea, it was very refreshing. "I can understand perfectly. The enemy has spies in the most unusual of places."

"That isn't the half of it," Odunn spoke and then quickly silenced himself.

"Please, Odunn, let me explain," Norina's voice was soft, yet firm.

"I noticed that things were a little tense in the throne room before. Are you able to elaborate?" Alena asked.

"About a month ago my husband suddenly changed. He was once a loving, caring man, the man I married all those years ago. Now he is hard, harder than stone. At the drop of a hat he will send people to their deaths. Once he nearly sent his own son to the hangman's noose. I can't tell you what I had to do to stop him. Let's just say his appetites have changed and not for the better." Norina took a large sip of tea and gulped it down, as if she was trying to get a nasty taste out of her mouth. "It's like he's possessed."

Alena thought for a moment. It did sound very much like he was possessed, but what she didn't know was whether he was a willing host or not. She would have to be very careful with her line of questioning.

"Before this sudden change, did the Duke have a habit of disappearing during the night?" it was a little more direct than she had wanted, but it got to the point.

"What are you getting at?" Odunn snapped.

"Be calm Odunn, or leave my chambers. Lady Alena is our friend and she shall be treated so." Norina paused as she thought. "I don't know about disappear, but for a year now on every full and new moon he would come to be late."

That in itself could be explained, the new and full moon were a little strange, but it could be explained. She needed more information if she was to confirm if Dunn was indeed an agent of the Dark One. It seemed as though Norina knew what she was asking, but she would still have to tread lightly. Odunn, however, was clearly not pleased with her line of questioning.

"Was there anything else strange about those nights?" Alena pushed slowly.

"Now that you mention it, he did always come to be smelling of rose water. It seemed that he always had a bath before he came to bed. At the time it didn't really seem strange, but now that I think about it he never bathed any other night just before bed. What do you think it means?"

Alena had a fair idea why the Duke would bath before returning to his wife. Many of the Dark One's rituals involved sacrifices, both animal and human. His followers would paint themselves in the blood of those they had killed. She knew it would be too much to explain to his family, instead she would just have to make her accusation.

"I don't really know how to say this, but I believe your husband is a follower of the Dark One." She paused to let the information sink in.

Odunn instantly stood when Alena stopped speaking. "This is an outrage. I can't believe you are going to just sit there and take this insolence."

"Sit down Odunn, I won't tell you again," this time Norina sounded annoyed with her son. "You would have to be a complete dolt not to have suspicions. We all hoped that it wasn't true, but you can't say it comes as a big surprise."

Odunn had to admit that his mother was right, but he still didn't want to accept it. He looked at his sister who looked as though she was going to cry at any moment. Her green eyes were watery and her bottom lip was starting to tremble.

"Don't just sit there Nora. You were closer to father than me, surely you can't believe what this elf is accusing him of?" Odunn couldn't contain his rage.

That was all that was needed for Nora to start weeping. "It's true," she sniffed. "He is pure evil."

"What are you talking about?" Norina didn't like what she was hearing.

"Please don't be angry with him. I didn't know who I could trust." Nora sobbed even louder.

"It's alright child," even though Nora was adult by human standards Alena thought it would be a comforting moniker. "No one is here to judge you."

"Don't you say a word Odunn," Norina warned as he opened his mouth.

"Just tell us what happened." Alena soothed.

"One night I couldn't sleep. I saw father leaving the castle from my window. He was dressed in a dark robe, but I knew who it was. I don't know why I followed him, I guess I just wanted to see where he was going at such a time of the night." She took a moment to blow her nose. The confession had stopped her tears, at least for the moment.

"What happened next?" Alena asked.

"He walked through the forest to the south of the city. I followed as close as I dared. I don't know why I didn't want him to see me, but I didn't nevertheless. I don't know how long we walked, it seemed like hours, but I really couldn't tell you. He stopped at a clearing and I remained hidden in the forest. A fire was burning in the centre of the clearing and six men were waiting for my father." Nora shuddered as the memories came back to her. "I moved as close as I could dare without being seen. I could see a stone altar in front of a smaller fire. At first I didn't think there was anything there, but when I blinked I saw a young woman, about my age. She was naked and unconscious. I couldn't see any bruising on her body so I assumed that she had been drugged. When father arrived they stood in a circle around the altar and the fire. When they were in position they started chanting, in a language that I couldn't understand. Slowly the woman started to wake up and I realised she had been bound to the altar. When she realised where she was she started to panic. She struggled against he bonds, but there was nothing she could do to escape. She screamed out in fear and frustration." Nora started sobbing again.

"It's alright. Nothing can hurt you," Alena soothed again.

"Father had an evil looking dagger and he raised it over the naked woman. She cried out again, but the men just continued to chant louder and more vigorously. I wanted to do something, I wanted to help her, but I couldn't move. Then he brought the knife down, stabbing into her chest. Blood spurted out and the men continued to chant. Father pulled the blade from her chest and then dragged it across her neck. The last sound that came from her was a gurgled scream before her body went limp. It was at that point that I screamed out in horror. I could hardly believe the sound that had come from my own voice. When I realised what I had done I turned and ran. I didn't get far before he caught me. He grabbed me by the arms and spun me around to face him, blood was smeared across his face and he had a rage in his eyes that I had never seen before. I thought for a moment he was going to kill me. Then he told me I couldn't tell anyone what I had seen. He told me if a said anything he would kill you and Odunn. I didn't know what to do." Nora broke down in tears.

Alena thought on what she had been told. There was no doubt that Dunn had been a willing participant in the evil ritual. That was much more dangerous than if it been the other way around. She looked at his wife and son. The Duchess seemed disappointed, but not overly surprised. Odunn, on the other hand, looked enraged. It was that feeling that would be the most dangerous. For the moment it was best that the Duke didn't know what they knew. She needed to speak with the others to work out the best course of action.

"Thank you for your candour, Nora," Alena started. "You must now keep this secret amongst yourselves."

"You have got to be kidding. He has betrayed his family and has betrayed his people. I can't sit idly by and let him continue to rule," Odunn had started pacing backwards and forwards.

"Calm yourself," Alena spoke before Norina had a chance to scold her son further. "You father is a dangerous man. I don't know exactly what ritual they were performing or what they achieved, but I do know that you shouldn't confront him. There is no telling how much power he has gained. You really need to leave it to us."

Odunn didn't look like he really cared for what Alena was telling him. If he wore his sword it would already be in his hand.

"Please, sit and listen to Lady Alena. Remember the loving man who was your father." She tried to calm her son. "Is there a chance he can be rescued?" She asked Alena.

"I don't know. I will know more once I have spoken to the others. If anyone will know what to do it will be them." She didn't want to reveal Alaric's true identity. Eldred had kept it a secret and there had to be reason behind that. Alena wasn't going to be the one to disclose it. "You must continue on like nothing has happened."

"You heard Lady Alena. You must return to your own quarters and stay there for the night. I will have your meals brought to you so you don't have to see your father."

"Won't that be suspicious?" Nora asked between sniffles.

"It is not the first time you two haven't turned up for the evening meal." Norina tried to reassure them. "I will go to and simply explain that you are fighting again and I have sent you to your rooms."

The explanation was weak, but it would hold. It had not been the first time that she had scolded her children. It had become less since they had both reach adulthood, but it still happened. Alena could only hope that it would work. She could see problems with both Nora and Odunn. Odunn was angry and wanted to confront his father. Given the chance he would challenge the Duke to a duel, there was no doubt about that. On the other hand it seemed as though Nora wanted to clear her conscience. Now that she had revealed her father's secret she would also want to confront him. She still yearned for her father's approval.

"What about you Norina?" Alena asked, concerned for the Duchess' safety.

"I will continue as I always have. It is not a great shock. When you share a bed with someone you know when they have changed. It just confirmed what I already thought was true, I will do nothing to change the way I react around him." She reassured Alena.

"Very well. I will do what I can. We should meet here in the morning, by then I am sure I'll have an answer for you," Alena sounded hopeful, although she wasn't sure how it was going to end. For the moment she would just have to trust that the Duke's family would do the right thing.

***

Alaric woke with a start. The bath water had turned cold and the candles had almost burnt out, leaving little light in the room. He had not remembered falling asleep. His mind was still hazy from the drugs in the water, but he put it down to the fact he had just woken. There was no real way for him to realise he had been drugged and there was nothing he could about it anyway. At first he struggled to remember where he was, but when he did he suddenly jumped up out of the water. His first thought was of the stones. He had remembered casting the spell to lock the door, but that had been over... over an... he rubbed his head. There was no way he could tell how long he had been asleep and the spell had only been a temporary one. It was designed to dissipate after half an hour. If he had kept it going then he would have struggled to relax in his bath. Now he wished he had.

Suddenly Alaric remembered what he had been concerned about. He looked to the small table where the stones had been. They were missing along with his sword and bow and arrow. All that remained was a simple white robe.

Without wasting any more time he jumped from the bath. The cool air struck his body making him shiver as his skin started to pimple. The cold water had done nothing to help his cause. All he could think about was the stones. Someone had clearly stolen them. He had specifically instructed the servant not to take anything and he had been ignored. It was the Duke who had made the command and it was he who he suspected the most. There was no reason that Alaric could think of that would make Dunn want to steal them, at least not one that bared thinking about.

His clothes suddenly appeared on his body and he was completely dry as he made his way to the door. Alaric tried open it, but found it had been locked shut. Things were starting to get more suspicious by the second and Alaric had a bad feeling that he had missed something important. On the plus side he couldn't hear any voices in his head, which he assumed meant the stones were still covered by their velvet prisons. There was still a chance that whoever had taken them didn't really know what they were, but he wasn't overly confident.

Unlocking the door was an easy spell. It was simple enough to slide the bolt across from the outside.

Slowly he poked his head through the doorway and looked left and right. There was no one guarding the door and it seemed as though the ruse of being Eldred's apprentice was working. He surmised that the Duke didn't believe he was strong enough to warrant a guard. On the other hand if the Duke did indeed know that he carried the stones then he would know his true identity. If that was the case then Alaric could very well be walking into a trap. Either way he had to keep going. There was no way he could let Dunn keep the stones, or pass them on to someone more powerful.

His head was still hazy from the drugs and he didn't know which way he had to go. If he was in fact a prisoner he couldn't ask for help, although he wasn't sure if things had gone that far. He was sure that the Duke couldn't be that simpleminded. Even if he didn't know who he was he did know Eldred, and his reputation would have preceded them.

Unless the Duke was a strong magician or was in league with one there was nothing he could do to stop them.

For no real reason he decided to go left. He had not taken more than half a dozen steps before he heard the clinking of armour approaching. In a moment of panic Alaric opened the nearest door and entered the room without checking to see if anyone was inside.

When he was sure the door was safely closed behind him he looked into the room. He had come across the ducal laundry. There was only one young woman working the large washing drums. She had a large pole in her hands which she was using to stir the dirty clothes. It took her a moment to look over at him, but when she did she let out a little scream. Alaric reached out with his hands, indicating for her to be quiet. When he did she put her hand over her mouth to suppress the noise.

"Please, I'm not here to hurt you." Alaric tried to reassure her.

"Why would I think you'd hurt me," she spoke in a much more confident tone. "I though you were here for…" she blushed.

Alaric looked confused for a moment before he suddenly realised what she was hinting at and blushed slightly himself. "What? I would never…" he didn't know what to say.

"You're not from around here are you?" it was a rhetorical question. "I like the look of you." She smiled a wicked looking smile. Alaric wasn't sure he liked the look of it. She had stopped stirring the laundry and had taken a step forward. "I'm sure we can come to some kind of arrangement. It has been a long time since I've had someone who looks like you."

Alaric had to admit she was an attractive looking woman, if she cleaned the day's grime from her skin at least. Her blonde hair fell around her face and her clothes were tattered, but nevertheless there was something about her that interested him. Another time and place and he might have considered her suggestion, but it was neither the time nor the place. As she took a tentative step forward he heard the soldiers passing the door on the other side.

"I thank you, but I'm afraid I'm not here for that."

Alaric returned his attention to the noise and he didn't notice the washerwoman slowly approaching him. Having already dismissed her he had concentrated on listening. It wasn't until she was three paces away did he realise that she had continued towards him. Just as she leaned in to kiss him, Alaric reached out to grab her shoulders to stop her. She pulled her arm from behind her back and revealed a small dagger. If Alaric had not already been moving to restrain her then she might have been able to stab him, but instead he gripped her wrist and quickly twisted the blade out of her hand. When he was done, as gently as he could, he dropped her to the ground. He kept a knee on her chest so she couldn't move as he prepared to interrogate her.

"I'm sorry," she sobbed, underneath Alaric's full weight, her voice hoarse. Tears started to roll down the side of her face and she started gasping for breath. Alaric relieved some of the pressure, not wanting to seriously injure her and she coughed as she gasped for breath.

"I think you should tell me why you did that," Alaric ordered.

"We were all ordered to by the Duke. He gave us all your description and said if we saw you wandering through the castle we should kill you. He then gave us all those daggers to do the job." Alaric instantly assumed that the blade would be poisoned. "I promise that I really didn't want to, but there was nothing I could do. I am just a washerwoman."

Alaric thought for a moment. There was definitely something strange happening. Why would the Duke want him dead? There had to be a simpler explanation.

"Tell me why the Duke would want me dead?"

"I don't know, he didn't tell us." The woman spoke between sobs.

"This doesn't make any sense," Dunn had to be a worshipper of Nyrra. That was the only reason Alaric could come up with. If he was, it meant the Duke would know who he was. Things were just getting more complicated. "He must have given you some reason."

"He doesn't have to give us a reason. He is the Duke. We have to do what he says no matter how crazy it is. Please don't kill me. I really didn't want to follow his orders," she pleaded.

Alaric wasn't completely sure he trusted her remorse, but on the other hand he couldn't stand there all day. For that matter he had no idea what time of day it was. He figured that it couldn't be too late since she was still working, although he really didn't know how late she should be.

"What time is it?" He changed the subject so abruptly that she became confused and stopped crying.

"It is nearly dusk, I think. As you can see there isn't much light in here." She suddenly didn't sound so scared.

Alaric had to admit she was right. There were no windows in the room and therefore no way to exactly tell what time it was. In any case she would have a better idea than he did.

The next thing Alaric had to do was to decide whether he should let her go or not. He had picked up the dagger and slid it between his trouser and his belt. If nothing else she wasn't going to be able to stab him, but he wasn't sure if that was the extent of the danger. She seemed to be more scared of the Duke than she was of him. That in itself wasn't a good sign.

"What is happening with the Duke?" he asked, giving her one last chance to give him some information.

"I don't know." She started sobbing again. "He has changed. Everything has changed." Alaric almost felt sorry for her, but there was something about her attitude that he didn't quite trust. He didn't believe her tears were completely genuine. "No one is safe anymore. If we don't do what we are told we risk ending up on the gibbet or worse. Please, I'm too young to die."

Alaric sighed, there was still something about the washerwoman that didn't seem right. There was only one thing he could do and that was to make sure she couldn't go after him. He looked around the room and saw a number of bed sheets hanging to one side. He quickly wrapped her in a blanket of air. She tried to get up, seeing a chance to escape, but she couldn't move.

It would have been much easier for Alaric just to leave her tied up in magic, but he needed to make sure he had all his strength for what lay in front of him. He had no idea what he was up against and he couldn't risk weakening himself. Grabbing a number of sheets from the line he quickly had the washerwoman tied up tight.

"Now if you know what is good for you I would keep quiet. I am sure someone will come by soon to let you out, but until then you will remain here quietly. If you truly do fear for your life then you will fear me." Alaric really didn't want to make the threat, but he had to get his point across. He couldn't let anyone know he was wandering the halls, especially since they were all instructed to kill him. Alaric felt much better when she was contained. "Now remember what I said to you."

"Please don't leave me here. There won't be anyone here until morning." She whimpered.

"Just you remember." Alaric didn't feel sorry for her anymore. The woman would have killed him given half a chance.

When he was sure there was no one outside the laundry he left. At least he had a weapon, not that it would be much use to him against an armed soldier. He would have to use his magical abilities if he came up against one or more of them. He wished he had his sword.

The further he continued, the more he realised he had no idea where he was going. There was only one thing he could do and that was to ask for directions. The only problem was there was no one he could trust. They were all out to put a knife in his back. It was a lose-lose situation.

It didn't take long for Alaric to run into another group of servants. This time it was an older man and a middle aged man. Neither of them seemed to recognise him at first, so he figured it was a good opportunity to ask for directions. The two men didn't take much notice until Alaric stopped them to speak.

"Wait a moment," the younger of the two said. "Isn't that the man…?"

"Please wait." Alaric put his hands up in the air. "There has been a misunderstanding."

The two men drew their daggers, exactly the same as the one Alaric had taken from the washerwoman. It didn't seem like he was going to be given a chance to explain his situation. Before they had a chance to advance Alaric drew his own dagger. He really didn't want to kill the two men, but it didn't seem as though he was going to have a choice.

The battle didn't last long at all. The Duke had instructed them to kill Alaric and had armed them, but he had not given any instruction on using the weapon. Alaric dodged the two attackers and waited for his opportunity to strike. It only took a simple scratch with the blade to cause the two men to drop to the ground. This confirmed his suspicions that the blades had been dipped in poison. It became more apparent that Dunn was a worshipper of Nyrra. Without knowing how strong the poison was Alaric thought it was best if he replaced the dagger he had with the two from his opponents. It was clear in his mind that they would still be potent.

There was no joy in killing the two men. They didn't deserve to die. Alaric was sure they were good men just following orders. It still meant that he had no idea where he was going. The thought of wandering aimlessly through the halls was even less appealing. He wondered how many innocent people he would have to kill before he made it to the throne room, if that was even where the Duke was hiding.

"What is happening?" the voice was like a whisper inside his head.

Alaric stopped suddenly. At first he was confused, but it didn't take him long to realise what it was. The Duke had started to unwrap the stones. The voice in his head was distant, which meant he had gone the wrong way.

"Who are you?" he asked, not that it was overly important, but he wanted to know which stone it was.

"Emerald!" the voice sounded annoyed. "What is happening?"

"You have been stolen, by an agent of evil." The words came inside Alaric's head. He knew they were his own, yet they sounded different. "I need to know where you are if I am going to rescue you." He wasn't sure if 'rescue' was the right word.

"Follow my lead and be careful. There are many traps waiting for you."

Alaric felt a warm feeling inside. He wasn't sure if it was real or fabricated, but he liked it nevertheless. It seemed as though he was becoming akin with the stones and that could only be a good thing.

Chapter 34: Treachery

"So Lord Eldred," Dunn spoke as they ate dinner. "What is it that brings you to my little old city?"

Eldred, Alena and Richmond sat at the opposite end of the table to Dunn and his wife. They had already started their meals even though Alaric was yet to join them. Viper had been instructed to remain in his room, they simply told Dunn he was exhausted from the day's travelling. It was a legitimate enough excuse.

They were all concerned about Alaric's whereabouts. He should have joined them over an hour ago.

"I was just asking where my apprentice was." Eldred kept the pretence, although the longer things continued the more he believed the ruse hadn't worked.

"Ah yes, I believe that, like your other companion, he has retired for the evening."

The lie was flimsy and everyone knew it, just as they knew there was more to the reason why Odunn and Nora weren't joining them for dinner. Eldred was not at all happy with the situation, but for the meantime he would have to play along.

Alena sat nervously in her chair. She had not been able to speak with Eldred and Richmond before they met for dinner. There was so much information that they needed to know, but there was no opportunity to tell them. She was also worried for Alaric now that she knew Dunn was a follower of Nyrra.

"Of course," Eldred took a nervous drink. There was something different to the wine, but Eldred couldn't figure it out. He was too concerned with the situation in front of him to worry about inconsequential things. "I am sure he is alright," he spoke to himself.

"Now what is it that I can do for you?" the duke signalled for Eldred's goblet to be filled again, although it had not been completely drained. "I am here to help."

"We have heard some rumours of the Evil One's agents roaming freely around Remidia. We were just wondering if this was true?" Eldred asked.

Alena had to bite her tongue. She looked at the Duchess who wouldn't return her stare. Norina was worried that Alena was going to give away her secret. She hated to think what would happen if her husband knew she had been untrustworthy.

"I haven't heard any rumours I'm afraid to say, I guess I can't help you on that matter," Dunn replied.

Eldred took another drink as he watched Dunn closely. The tension in the room was growing. There was definitely something happening between Alena and Norina, he knew that. Richmond was the only one who didn't seem to realise the situation.

"What about you, Duchess?" Eldred decided to push for information. It was clear she knew something.

"I am sure that she doesn't know anything." Alena was quick to jump in.

Dunn was quick to pick up on the comment. He looked at his wife and then back towards Alena. Both were trying to look nonchalant, but the duke knew something had happened between them. He needed to get to the bottom of it, if his wife had betrayed him then she would need to be punished. It was at that point that Eldred finished his wine. When Dunn realised what he had done a smile crossed his face and he forgot all about the betrayal.

"Well Lord Eldred, it seems as though you aren't as smart as I gave you credit for," a broad smile crossed the duke's face.

"What are you talking about?" Eldred had to admit that the wine had left a bad taste in his mouth, but he really didn't think it was worth the smug behaviour.

"That wine you've been drinking has been tainted with a certain herb."

Eldred's heart suddenly skipped a beat. He didn't need to listen to the rest of the duke's words to know what had happened. He tried to reach for the power around him, but there was nothing. It was not the first time he had felt such a sinking feeling. He should have been more careful when he suspected the duke of being an agent of Nyrra. He looked around the room and saw all the exits were guarded by soldiers. If they had their weapons then there was a chance they could fight their way out, but as it was they were trapped.

"What is this all about?" Eldred slammed his fists on the table. He wanted to rise, but thought it might be seen as aggressive. "How can you hold us hostage?" Eldred looked around at the soldiers.

"Don't look at them Eldred. They are loyal to me. They know who I am and where I sit at the Great Lord's table. You will get no help from them."

"Please Dunn, don't do this," Norina pleaded.

Without looking at his wife Dunn struck her across the side of her face.

"Don't you think that I don't know you have been plotting behind my back? Are you that stupid?" He waited for a response, but knew none would come. "You have no idea how pleased I will be to see your body hanging in the courtyard. Yours will be the first death in the morning."

"You can't execute me. I am the Duchess and cousin to King Faxon. He will have your head if you do anything to me." Norina held the side of her face, but her voice was still resolute.

"The king supports me. I am the ruler of this land and I make the decisions. I am sure he will be sad to hear of your passing, but he will understand my decision."

It was clear to Eldred that the duke had gone insane. There was no way he could believe what he was saying if he was in his right mind. Hopefully he would be able to use it to his advantage. If the soldiers guessed the same then there was a chance they would turn good again.

"You know you can't get away with this." Eldred was desperately trying to come up with a plan.

"I am not trying to get away with anything. You are an enemy of the state. Have you not heard? Faxon has placed a bounty on your heads. You are wanted men in Remidia." There was a wry smile on the duke's face.

Eldred didn't know what to say. If what Dunn was saying was true then it meant that the Evil One had indeed infiltrated the capital. Things were starting to get away from him. It was not the way things were supposed happen, but then again when had anything gone to plan? He still had an ace up his sleeve.

"You know that Alaric is not my apprentice, he is in fact the Chosen One. You have made a fatal error by not capturing him like the rest of us." Eldred tried his best to be smug.

The words were met with boisterous laughter form Dunn. Eldred didn't think it was a good sign. He wished he hadn't drunk the wine, he'd had his suspicions about the duke and he should have been more careful. Not be able to touch the power surrounding him made him completely vulnerable.

"Your Chosen One is safely trapped in the baths and I have all of his toys." The duke snapped his fingers.

A servant brought over a bundle wrapped in a small rug. Eldred didn't need to see it to know what was inside. Something was very wrong. Alaric would never give up the stones, not without extreme duress and even then he wasn't sure it would happen.

"You see. I have all the stones now. Your Chosen One was no match for me." Eldred wanted to wipe the smile from the duke's face.

"Hah!" Eldred laughed when the servant revealed what was wrapped in the cloth. "You don't have anything. Just some trinkets that he likes to carry with him."

Dunn looked worried for a moment, but then figured that Eldred was lying to him. There was only one way find out if he was telling the truth. Carefully he opened one of the velvet pouches and dropped a gold band onto the table. Inset in the bracelet was an emerald stone. Dunn smiled when he saw it.

"There, the Emerald S*tone of Power.*"

"That isn't the Emerald *Stone of Power.* That is just a simple emerald bracelet. You are indeed a fool. I can't wait until you present such a foolish gift to your *Great Lord.*"

There was no doubt in Eldred's mind that it was in fact the Emerald stone. He could feel the power emanating from it. Although he could feel it he would not touch it, he knew better than to try and tap into the power of the stone. Everything was starting to work out. All he needed to do was get the duke to pick it up.

Duke Dunn smiled as he looked at the Emerald stone. A small light glowed in its centre and transfixed his gaze. There was no doubt in his mind that it was the right stone. He reached out slowly to pick it up, but stopped only inches away. Something inside his head was telling him it was the wrong thing to do and he pulled his hand back.

"Nice try, wizard, but you won't ensnare me that easily. I know better than that. I know that I am not powerful enough to pick up one of the *Stones of Power.* That honour is kept for the Great Lord himself." The next problem Dunn had was getting the stone back in its pouch, but that was something he could work out later. For the moment he was having too much fun toying with the great wizard.

It seemed as though Eldred had failed on his first attempt to trick the duke. "So it seems as though I have underestimated you Dunn, but it also seems as you have underestimated us as well."

Dunn waited for Eldred to elaborate, but it soon became clear that he wasn't going to. "What are you talking about? I have covered all my bases. The Chosen One is trapped, you are powerless and weaponless and I am sure that your hooded friend isn't going to bother us." Eldred had to admit that he was right about Viper. He wished he'd brought him to dinner, his power would be an asset.

"There is one thing that you haven't factored in…"

Suddenly one of the doors burst open and the soldiers were sent flying across the room. The entrance took everyone except Eldred by surprise. He didn't know what had happened to Alaric, but he was sure the Chosen One was not finished.

"Duke Dunn, you have betrayed your people." Alaric had been preparing his grand speech while he'd been traversing the corridors. That was all he managed to get out before the soldiers started to close in on him. This was also something he had been prepared for. Before he entered the throne room he had drawn in a great amount of energy. As he entered, he ended the spell which sent the soldiers flying into the walls, knocking them out. When they were all unconscious he was able to concentrate on the duke.

"This is an outrage. How dare you come crashing into my private dining room unannounced?" It seemed as though Dunn hadn't noticed his soldiers were all lying, unconscious on the floor. "I will have your head for this outrage."

"You will have nothing," Alaric boomed back, ignoring the ridiculousness of Dunn's outburst. "You have sold your soul to the Evil One and for that you have to pay."

"Kill them, kill them all," the voice in his head roared.

"You will be quiet," Alaric spoke with his mind's voice. "I will kill no one that I don't have to."

His words were met with a whimper. Alaric was getting a lot stronger and he was no longer putting up with the demands of the voices.

Duke Dunn stood up and grabbed his sword. It didn't even occur to him that he had no chance against Alaric. The move perplexed Alaric and he stood there confused before he quickly released the spell. Dunn was instantly disarmed and was forced back into his chair. The confused expression on Dunn's face made Alaric laugh, the irony was hilarious.

"What are you doing to me? I am the duke of this land. The Great Lord will protect me. He will burn you for this insolence." Dunn continued to rant although he couldn't move.

"Are you quite finished?" Alaric sat at the table. There seemed no reason to stand back anymore. When there was no response he continued. "We need information and that might be the only thing that keeps you alive."

"Please, he is still my husband and the father of my children." The Duchess was close to tears.

Alaric steeled himself and ignored Norina's pleas. The months of travelling had hardened him. Not that long ago Alaric would have felt some sympathy, but he could no longer afford such feelings. The duke had made his own bed and it was time for him to lie in it. Alaric hadn't made his final decision on the duke's fate, but he would find it hard to keep the man alive.

"We need information," he repeated himself, "and I think it is time for you to speak."

Dunn looked even more confused as he suddenly realised that all of his soldiers were unconscious. He tried to look around, but he could only move his neck and head. He couldn't believe the sight before him. It was as if he was seeing Alaric for the first time and suddenly realised the severity of the situation.

"The Great Lord will protect me. There is nothing you can do to me. I will live to see you bow down before the Great Lord and beg for forgiveness." Dunn was starting to foam at the mouth.

"Kill him. He will betray you," the voice came again. Alena was the only one who noticed the Emerald stone start to glow a little brighter. "Kill him and then kill them all. They will all betray you."

Alaric felt a sharp pain pass through his head. His eyes closed for a moment and his eyelids flickered. Although the pain was only there for a second it was quite intense. He had never felt anything like it before.

"What was that?" Alaric almost said the words out loud, but his question was met by silence. It was at that point he realised that everyone at the table was waiting for him to speak.

"You will tell me what we need to know," he said, grasping at straws.

His words were met with laughter from Dunn. There was no doubt that for the moment it was a hollow threat. Alaric had not expected such opposition. He had underestimated the hold Nyrra had on the man. It would take more than just simple words to break him.

"I can help!"

Sometimes Alaric wished the voices would stay out of his head, but it seemed as though this time it might come in handy.

"How can you help?" Alaric asked the voice.

"It isn't my specialty, but I do have a few tricks up my sleeves, if I had sleeves." Alaric thought the comment was followed by laughter, but he wasn't sure.

"Not that I don't like these little conversations, but can we get to the point. Everyone is waiting for me and they may start to think that I'm the crazy one." Alaric tried to make a sign of thinking.

"His mind has been tainted by all the rituals he has been participating in. No matter what you say there is nothing you can do to get through to him. I can attempt to bring his mind back to a state of reality, but there is a chance I will fry his brain. It is the only way to make him see sense." The voice sounded sincere.

Alaric wasn't convinced it was the right course of action. He didn't know if he could trust the voice in his head. They had helped him, tried to hinder him and tried to take over his mind and body. It was a risk, but as he looked from the duke to the duchess he knew it was one he had to take.

"What is it you need me to do?" He knew it wouldn't be simple.

"Take the stone. You need to have contact if you want me to help."

The words were followed by silence. It was up to Alaric to make his own decision. The stone sat in its bracelet on the table in front of

Dunn. It was now glowing a lot softer, not that the duke noticed. There was no doubt the duke wouldn't just hand it over, but Alaric didn't think there would be any problem. His powers far surpassed anything Dunn cold muster and so far the duke had shown no magical abilities.

"This is your last chance Dunn. Surrender and tell me what I what to know." Alaric knew what the response would be, he just wanted to distract Dunn as he worked out how to get the stone. If Dunn did have some power he didn't want to get caught off guard.

"You don't scare me. The Great Lord will protect me. He will destroy you and all who follow you. This is your last chance to surrender. If you don't then you will burn in the fires of the Cauldron Mountain."

Whilst Dunn was distracted with his rant Alaric was preparing his spell. It wasn't that he thought the duke would be able to counter him, but he didn't want to take any chances. He was an agent of Nyrra and there was no telling what evil powers he had been given. For the moment he just looked like a fanatic, but Alaric knew that looks could be deceiving. He had one chance to regain the stone and he didn't want to blow it.

After Dunn's rant the room went silent. Everyone was waiting for Alaric's response. Instead of speaking he simply raised his hand. At first nothing happened, but then suddenly the Emerald bracelet flew from the table and into his hand. Dunn tried to reach out for it, but it was too late. With the stone in his hand Alaric felt a surge of power pass through his body. For a second his eyelids fluttered as his eyes rolled up into his head before he returned to normal. No one noticed there was a slight green tinge to his eyes.

"Now open yourself to me," the voice sounded a lot harsher now.

It was what Alaric feared. The last time he opened himself to one of the stones he struggled to return. It would be a lot easier if just killed the duke and moved on, but something was telling him it wasn't the right plan. He could only assume it was the prophecy leading him around again. Sometimes he wished the prophecy would just leave him alone, but in the end he knew that wouldn't make things better.

"Fine, but don't try anything. I am a lot stronger than I used to be." He needed to reassure himself more than anything else.

The warm, powerful sensation increased within his body. He felt the heat rise as was about to lose consciousness. The room started to darken as he fought to remain awake.

"Let yourself go. I need complete control if I am going to succeed," there was a slight strain to the voice.

As much as Alaric didn't want to let go he had no choice. He had gone this far so there was no reason to hold back.

"Remember. If you betray me then you will suffer," Alaric wasn't sure how he would follow through on his threat, but he needed to make it nevertheless.

Alaric let himself relax and the room went completely dark. The power filling his body was exhilarating. He revelled in the ecstasy. There was no better feeling in the world. He wanted nothing more than to remain in his current state, but he knew that's what the stone wanted. He needed to control himself if he was going to keep his sanity.

Concentrating, Alaric blended his mind with the Emerald stone. Slowly the room came back into view, except everything now had a green tinge. He heard his voice speaking, but he wasn't controlling what was being said.

"You have been tainted by Ruby's ward. Now I will remove the hold he has over you," he spoke in a monotone voice.

"I don't need your pity." Dunn was a little unsure of himself. "The Great Lord will protect me. He is no one's ward. He is the ruler of the…" suddenly he was cut short.

Alaric felt a sudden surge of power pass through his body that made his stomach churn. It wasn't the same exhilarating feeling he had felt before, this time it was sickly. He was sure if he had control of his own body he would have lost consciousness. Dunn's body suddenly went dead stiff.

Suddenly Alaric could feel himself searching through Dunn's mind, although there wasn't really much to find. He had no control over his movements, he was just a willing participant. He floated in the nothingness for what seemed like an age before everything suddenly changed. The nothingness turned into swirling colours. If he could vomit he would, but his body remained motionless.

"What's happening?"

"Quiet! I'm looking for something," the voice sounded annoyed.

Alaric tried to understand what was happening, but there was nothing he could do. He had no control over anything and the sight before him was blurred. In future he knew that knowledge of what was happening would be useful.

"There it is!"

Suddenly the swirling colours coalesced in a sweeping meadow. The change was such a shock that Alaric felt as though he would fall over. He could see a figure standing on the other side of the meadow, cloaked in darkness. Evil radiated from it and Alaric wanted nothing more than to back away. He wanted to turn and run, but he couldn't. There was still nothing he could do to move. He was completely vulnerable.

"What is it?" Alaric finally found the words he was looking for.

"That's what's keeping Dunn from realising his mistake." Surprisingly, a soft feminine voice came from next him and not from inside his mind.

Looking to his right, Alaric saw a green figure standing next to him glowing softly. He thought he could see a woman in the centre, but he couldn't be sure. There was an urge to move forward, but he didn't know how or if he even could. He would have to wait for the green figure to lead him.

"Let's go see what we can do to rectify this situation," the voice was almost playful.

Alaric slowly felt himself being led towards the darkness. With every inch he took something screamed out inside him to run away. The darkness radiated an evil presence, one that he wanted nothing to do with. No matter what he tried there was nothing he could do. The movement forward was completely involuntary. He followed the green figure, step for step.

"What are you doing here? This is not a place for visitors." The voice rasped from inside the miasma of darkness.

"This isn't a place for you either," the female voice cooed.

Alaric wanted to join in the conversation, but no words came out. He wished he could remember how to move and talk. It was not the first time he had been in such a place, although normally it was within his own mind, but he knew it was the same theory. The difference was that he had given control to the Emerald stone. That was why he couldn't control anything himself, although he didn't realise it.

"It is time for you to leave now. The duke is not yours to keep," Alaric thought the voice was very pleasant. It reminded him of someone, but he couldn't remember who.

"No, it is time for you to leave," the voice snarled.

The scene before them started to reverberate. Alaric could feel the vibrations. It was like there was an earthquake. If he had actually been standing he was sure that he would have fallen over. The entire situation was starting to make Alaric feel extremely nauseated. The green glowing started to intensify and slowly the scenery returned to its calm state.

"Impossible. You can't do this to me. This is my man, I control him now. You can't do this." The rough voice sounded confused.

"You have already spent too long here. It is now time for you to leave." The woman's voice was stern. It was almost like a mother scolding her child.

Again all Alaric could do was watch. He wanted to help, but he was completely useless. In fact, by opening himself to the Emerald stone, he was doing more to help than he realised. If he resisted then it would make things almost impossible.

"Who do you think you are? I am the Great Lord of Darkness. You are no match for me."

"You are not the Great Lord," she said. "You are but a mere residual trace of him. You are a disease, a sickness of the mind."

There was a moment of silence as the enemy had to think. It wasn't at all what it was expecting. It had been in control of the duke for so long it wasn't prepared for an interrogation.

"You don't belong here. This is mine. You will leave now." It suddenly didn't sound so confident.

Suddenly the scenery started to glow a soft green. It was as though the Emerald stone had only been buying time. It was time for action and the enemy wasn't prepared. The darkness surrounding the figure started to fade by the encroaching green, but only for a moment before it intensified again.

"You will not have him. I have worked too long and too hard to let him get away so easily." There was something fierce in the voice.

Alaric felt nauseated again as the scenery suddenly changed. He was now surrounded by light. On one side of him was a strong green and the other was deathly black, with a few swirls of purple. In the centre of both colours were two silhouettes. Alaric wasn't even sure he was still there. There was nothing physical to represent him, just his consciousness. The colours swirled around and he wanted nothing more than to shut them out, but he had no eyes to shut.

"Stay strong Alaric, I need your help," the woman's voice sounded strained for the first time.

"That's right. I'm too strong for you. There is nothing you can do."

The colours swirled and fought each other, back and forth, for what seemed like a lifetime. Each time the darkness crept forward Alaric felt as though he was going to vomit. Each time he steeled himself and prepared for the next attack. With Alaric's renewed strength the green light fought back.

Slowly the emerald light started to inch forward. Only a small section at a time, but it was definitely winning. Alaric knew if he was in his body he would be sweating profusely and wondered if his body was indeed suffering from the effects. The slight lack of concentration gave the darkness a chance to fight back.

"Focus Alaric," the woman's voice was weak.

"It's too late. I have the advantage. It's all over." The darkness pushed forward.

"No!" Alaric finally found his voice. "You have lost."

With all the strength Alaric could muster he focused his energy on the green light. Suddenly green flashed over the entire scene, it was like the entire universe went completely green. Then he flashed back to reality.

Alaric took a deep breath, not because he was short exhausted, but because of the shock of the change of scenery. When he realised he was back he looked at the others. There wasn't the look of surprise on their faces that he was expecting. That made him wonder at how long he had actually been inside Dunn's mind. He nodded towards Eldred, too exhausted to speak himself.

"We need information Dunn," Eldred kept his voice calm. Although he didn't know what had happen he knew that something had. Alaric had suddenly become very weak.

"What do you want to know?" Dunn sounded resigned, the madness slowly creeping out of his voice.

Chapter 35: A Breath of Fresh Air

The news from Remidia was much the same as the rumours they had heard. A Dark Knight was indeed in the palace at Remidel. Dunn wasn't sure of the extent of his control over Faxon, but it was clear that the king was no longer in control of his own kingdom. The news, although not unexpected, was still disturbing. Alaric had hoped that his homeland would remain unmolested, but deep down he always knew that wouldn't be the case, he could see that before he left.

It seemed the condition of the rest of the kingdom was just as dire. When Dunn finished speaking about Faxon and Remidel, Alaric returned the Emerald bracelet to its velvet pouch. To his surprise there was no voice inside his head. He had to admit that things had worked out better than he had expected. As always he had expected a battle within his head, but thankfully that hadn't happened.

"What about the rest of the kingdom?" Alaric asked.

"I believe the Evil One has agents roaming throughout, but I don't know for sure. He has been happy to leave us alone I guess the worshipping has held for something." It was a poor joke. "I suppose now I will need to hunt those who supported me in my foolishness."

The last comment was met by silence. Alaric's energy had disappeared as soon as he returned the Emerald stone to its pouch. He instantly wished he hadn't. It would have been so much easier just to reveal it again, but he knew that wasn't an option. No matter how bad he felt he couldn't rely on the stones for energy. That would be the best way to lose control. The only way he was going to feel better was to get a good night's sleep, but for the moment he had to assume the mantle of strength.

"I wouldn't be so quick to reveal the other traitors," Alaric didn't choose his words too carefully. Being diplomatic was the last thing on his mind. "Whilst the Evil One thinks you are a loyal subject he won't send anyone to attack you. It will be better for everyone if you continue playing the evil tyrant."

"I wouldn't risk performing anymore rituals though. You don't want to give Nyrra a chance to infiltrate your mind again." Alena warned.

"I have done some terrible things." He shook his head as his mind returned. He couldn't believe some of things he had done. "I have a lot to make up for. The last thing I want to do is make my people suffer anymore."

"I think they might be right," Norina soothed. "I know it's hard, but the alternative is worse. We need you to be strong now." Everyone could tell by the tone in her voice that she was close to tears. "I'm just glad to have my husband back."

Dunn didn't look happy, but he had to accept the advice he was given. He had a lot to make up for and the last thing he wanted to do was make things worse. The thought of posing as a traitor didn't sit well with him, especially since he had been one for so long. The duke wanted nothing more than to restore the faith of his people, but that would have to wait.

"I think it's time to call it a night," Alaric suddenly saw his opportunity. "We can meet again in the morning before we leave." His voice suddenly weakened.

"I think that's a good idea. It has been a stressful day for all." Alena was the first to stand. She recognised that Alaric was starting to falter and she wanted to be able to support him. Rumours would start flying around the castle if he collapsed in the hallways, that was something they couldn't afford. Although the duke was back on their side there were still plenty of traitors within the castle.

The two walked towards their apartment with their arms wrapped around each other. To those not paying attention it would look as though they were just happily in love. Alena was doing her best to keep Alaric upright. The strain of fighting with the disease inside Dunn's brain had taken more out of him than he had expected. It was tempting to use the Topaz stone to refresh himself, but he didn't. He counted himself lucky that there was no fight with the Emerald stone for his consciousness and he didn't want to take a risk with the Topaz stone. He would just have to rely on some old fashioned bed rest to cure his fatigue.

"How are you feeling?" Alena asked when they reached their apartment.

"Tired," was all Alaric could bring himself to say.

"Are you sure?"

There was something saucy in Alena's voice that made him turn around. To his surprise he saw her wearing a silk slip. He had no idea how she had put it on so quickly. It didn't take long for all thoughts of sleep to leave his body. Since they had left the Wizard's Isle there had been little chance for intimacy and Alaric wasn't about to pass up the opportunity. Despite his fatigue he walked towards her.

A smile crossed her face as she realised her plan had worked. She waited for him to cross the room before taking him in her arms. He felt weak, but that wasn't going to stop her, or him.

***

Alaric woke late the next morning. As much as he wanted to be on the road early there was little chance of that happening. The strain of the previous day had prevented him rising early and no one was going to wake him. Although he felt better for the extra rest he knew he needed a lot more.

"What time is it?" he asked when he realised Alena was sitting vigil.

"Mid-morning," she replied softly. "How are you feeling?"

"Like death warmed up," he smiled as he spoke. "All the better for seeing you though." The memory of the night before came rushing back. He thought for a moment and wondered if there was enough time, but then decided that his extra sleep had eaten up all he spare time he had. They needed to be on the road again.

"That's good. I'm sure the duke will be waiting to see you before we leave," Alena stood and opened the curtains. Alaric had to shield his eyes from the sunlight.

Alaric had forgotten about the duke and his worries, if only for a moment. He wanted nothing more than to sneak out of the castle, but that wouldn't happen. Once again he would have to solve an impossible situation. He had no idea what he was going to say.

"Our bags have been packed and sent down to the horses. Come on, let's have something to eat before we leave."

Alaric had to admit it was a good idea and his stomach rumbled in agreement. Although the duke couldn't reveal to anyone that Alaric wasn't to be killed anymore, he knew the food wouldn't be poisoned.

With the way things were going in Remidia he didn't think there would be another chance for a nice hot meal until he returned from Mount Scorpio, if he did. That was enough motivation to get him out of bed.

"Welcome Alaric!" Dunn greeted them when they entered the food hall. "I am so glad you could join us this morning." Just to be on the safe side, the duke would be eating with them.

There was clearly something different about Dunn and his family. They had a renewed sense of comfort whereas before there was just fear. Alaric wasn't sure if it was a good thing. It wouldn't take long for the staff to realise that something had changed.

"Please sit!" Norina offered.

Alaric looked around the room before he sat as the table. There were six serving women standing around the outside of the room. There was no chance for privacy. There was a chance Alaric would be able to eat and leave, avoiding an uncomfortable conversation.

"Don't worry. These servants are trusted to me." Dunn smiled.

"I don't think it is a good idea to speak in front of them," Eldred said. "A secret shared is a secret lost."

Dunn didn't look happy with Eldred's comments. Alaric had to admit the old wizard was right. If the servants found out what was happening then it would only be a matter of time before the entire castle knew. When the duke looked at him Alaric nodded. It was only then did he command the servants to leave.

"Is that more to your liking?" Dunn's snide remark wasn't lost on anyone.

"Please father, let them speak!" Norina chided.

Alaric had taken the opportunity to start eating. There was little time to waste and it seemed as though the duke was happy doing his own thing. He was halfway through a mouthful when he realised that everyone was looking at him. It was clear that they were waiting for him to speak, as he had yet to do so since entering the hall. He had even managed to skip the pleasantries of the morning greeting.

"The Alliance will be coming this way soon," he wasn't sure where the words came from, they just poured out of his mouth. He had known the prophecy too long to fight it. If it wanted to use his body then he was more than happy to let it. "You must have your soldiers ready to join when they pass by."

"I don't understand," Dunn sounded confused. "We only have a small army to defend our lands. We can't give up our soldiers, we will be left defenceless. I thought you wanted me to continue the ruse that I am worshipping the Evil One?"

Alaric was sick of hearing the same story over and over again. No one wanted to help the Alliance. Everyone just wanted to protect their own borders. Little did they know their only hope was with the Alliance. If Nyrra was left unchecked then eventually he would overrun all of the kingdoms. He wished more than anything else that he didn't have to keep repeating himself.

"They will help you round up the traitors before they leave. Then they will move on to the Capital. General Bern will need all the help he can get and that includes you. You have a lot to make up for Duke Dunn. Some might say that your betrayal is unforgivable, but I don't. This is the only way you can make up for your crimes." Alaric was stern.

"He will make up for what he has done, we are just happy to have our father back. I am sure the city will be happy just to have their duke back," Odunn defended his father.

"With all due respect there are more lives at stake than just you and your family." Alaric was trying to remain calm, but his blood was starting to rise.

"Excuse me!" Dunn spoke in support of his son.

"I'm sorry, but there is no time for tact. This is the harsh reality of the things." Alaric was taken aback. "The entire Seven Kingdoms is at stake, not just your little piece of it. If you don't assist the Alliance then you put everyone at risk."

Alaric quickly returned to his food when he finished his tirade. He wanted to be on the road again and he wouldn't do that until he had a full stomach.

"I don't have to put up wit..." duke started.

"I'm afraid you do," Eldred interrupted. "If you don't do what Alaric is saying then soon enough there will be no city for you to run. As you know the Dark One has agents in the Capital. How long do you truly believe you will be able to keep up the ruse of being a faithful servant? Once he knows you have turned he will send his army here to subjugate you. Without the aid of the Alliance how do you propose to survive such a battle?"

Eldred's words, although heated, seemed a lot calmer than Alaric's. Dunn knew they were true. It wasn't just the fact that he had no other choice, but he now realised it was the right thing to do. He had to do his bit, no matter how small it seemed, to help the Alliance.

"You're right. I will do as you have instructed." Dunn sounded resigned. "Tonight we will celebrate. A feast to make our union official," Dunn bounced back.

Alaric shook his head, but didn't speak. There were so many things wrong with that statement. He hoped that Eldred would explain the fact as he finished his breakfast.

"You must keep this to yourself until the Alliance gets here," Eldred started when he realised Alaric wasn't going to speak. "We don't know how far away they are, but I would imagine that the Dark One's forces are much closer."

"Plus we have to be on the move again." Alaric added as he wiped his mouth with the soft lace napkin. "There is little time and much to be done." Alaric stood. "I hope when we meet again it will be under more fortuitous conditions although I fear it won't be." Alaric was trying to be as diplomatic as possible without letting Dunn start another conversation.

When he finished speaking Alaric stood from the table and indicated for the others to do the same. He could see the opportunity to leave and he wasn't going to waste it.

"What do I do now?" Dunn asked before they had a chance to leave.

"Enjoy the rest of your breakfast with your family. When you leave this room you have to resume the guise of being an agent of the Evil One. You must keep this up until the Alliance passes this way. It's the only way you can keep your people safe," Alaric kept his voice level. It seemed like a fitting way to leave.

Alaric turned his back on the table and walked out of the room. He didn't want to give the duke another chance to speak. They found

Viper waiting for them in the courtyard with the horses. Alaric was happy to see that they were ready to leave. All in all the morning had gone off without a hitch.

"What's the plan?" Viper asked.

"We ride for Mount Scorpio. We have wasted enough time." Alaric looked straight ahead as he mounted Adelanta.

"I figured that much," Viper sounded annoyed. He didn't like being left out of the plan. He was getting accustomed to not being trusted, but being left out was something different altogether. "Do you have any idea how we are going to get there?"

"Yes!" was all Alaric said.

As much as he didn't want to speak with Viper he also hadn't made up his mind how they were going to get to there. All he knew was that they had to avoid any major cities. For that matter they would have to avoid any towns and villages as well. There was no telling what they would come across and they didn't have the time to fix anymore problems. He wished he had taken the time to look at some maps before they left. It seemed like an age since he had seen a map of Remidia. Due to his trade he knew all the major highways and some of the back roads, but that wasn't going to help their current predicament. For the moment they would just follow the road to Remidel. He hoped he would just know when to divert their path.

"We need to talk," Eldred spoke to Alaric once they had left the city. He kept his voice low so no one else would hear him.

"What is it?" Alaric spoke a little louder than Eldred would have liked.

Eldred looked back at the others. They didn't seem to notice the sudden question. To be on the safe side he created a small spell to prevent the others from hearing what they were saying. The spell was so subtle Viper wouldn't even realise it had been created.

"I was reading through the prophecy last night and came across a disturbing passage," Eldred kept his face straight ahead as he rode.

Alaric had felt the spell that Eldred had cast and knew he wanted to keep the conversation private. Sometimes he wished that he wasn't so in tune to the magic around him. With each contact with the stones his sensitivity seemed to increase. There was no way he should have been able to sense the spell, even if Eldred didn't mask it.

He was also starting to be able to feel the plant life around him, or at least the larger life forms. He couldn't sense the grass or the flowers, but he was starting to feel the trees. It was almost as if they were trying to talk to him only they couldn't find the words. Whenever they passed a tree he could feel a flutter in the back of his mind. If he was expecting it he was able to block them out. When they took him by surprise there was nothing he could do. The feeling that someone was watching him was unbearable and he had to keep looking around. Each time all he saw was a tree swaying gently in the breeze. It was quite discerning.

"I wouldn't take much notice of the prophecy," Alaric spoke, somewhat distracted. "It changes constantly and makes no sense."

"Be careful what you say!" Eldred couldn't help himself. He had to turn his head to face Alaric as he spoke.

"I wouldn't do that unless you want the others to know we are having a private conversation," Alaric kept his head straight and ignored the annoying feeling that someone was watching him. The more it happened the easier it became to ignore.

Eldred quietly scolded himself, but that didn't change the disturbing fact of what Alaric had said. Everything was based on the prophecy. *The Prophecy of the Stone* was the one true prophecy. Alaric couldn't deny that fact and to do so would be folly. He had to admit that sometimes, well most of the time, the prophecy was hard to read, but that was just the way it was. It didn't change the importance of the words it held.

"What are you talking about Alaric? The prophecy is our guide. We have to trust its advice. If it wasn't for the prophecy then none of us would be here and Nyrra would have control of the lands." Eldred strained to keep his head straight. It wasn't how he envisaged the conversation going.

"The prophecy pulls us as the prophecy wills. If we stray from the path the prophecy will tell us, in its own little way. I really don't think there is any point in pouring over the book. I have done so, many times, and not once has it been the same. I guarantee that you will struggle to find that passage again." Alaric started twitching as they passed another lone tree. He didn't have to look to know it was a cypress, that realisation was starting to concern him. He didn't know what it meant, but he knew it wasn't natural.

"Be that as it may, there are insights in the book that we need to know and that brings me to my point." He paused, giving Alaric a chance to rebuke him. When none came he continued. "The passage reads:

In the middle of the night
When the moon has changed
On top of the Scorpion
A meeting shall take place
The snake shall rise
And strike again
Brother and brother

Shall fight to the death
Who shall win?
None could tell
But one will fall

I think that should be clear enough for you. Viper's brother will betray us. He will fight with Viper and one of them will die."

Alaric thought on Eldred's words. He understood why Eldred wanted privacy. One thing he wasn't sure of was the validity of his theory. The prophecy was not renowned for telling things straight and the passage in question seemed a little too straight forward. On the other hand it wasn't totally unexpected. The serpentant's couldn't be trusted, but Alaric was a little dubious on whether they would attack each other. He doubted if that would happen, but there didn't seem to be any other explanation.

"That is interesting," Alaric finally spoke after a long pause. "Was there anything else to prove your hypothesis?"

"No, nothing else made any sense. This is a sign. A sign that we are walking into a trap."

That was never the question. They were always walking into a trap. Alaric knew that when he was given the message from Bern and the fact that Viper suddenly showed up only strengthened the idea. Nothing was ever that easy though and Alaric needed to ponder the riddle.

"I don't think we should jump to conclusions. The prophecy is never so obvious." Alaric hoped that would be the end of the conversation.

"We shouldn't pass on this opportunity to see into the future. What we do now will affect that result."

"What are you suggesting?" the approaching woods had Alaric distracted. He could slowly feel the trees calling out to him. The closer he came the louder they were becoming. He had managed to block out the sound of individual trees, but a large group was entirely different. He was glad it was just a small wood and not an entire forest.

"I think we should stop and eat." It wasn't long past midday and Alaric was still full from breakfast, but he needed time to think.

Eldred noticed the others rein in beside him without question. It took him a moment to realise that Alaric had broken his spell. He shook his head in disbelief. The spell was only a weak one, but he still should have been able to feel it being broken. It was just another disturbing sign. There seemed to be more and more strange things happening. It was a fair sign that the final battle was coming.

Alaric stared at the trees while they ate their midday meal. There was little conversation. They could all see that Alaric was preoccupied with something and that wasn't a good sign. His current state didn't ease anyone's nerves. Other than the fact that they were headed for Scorpion Mountain they had no idea how they were going to get there. There was a lot of danger ahead.

"What is it Alaric?" Alena finally asked.

"What... sorry, what were you saying?" Alaric stumbled over his words.

"There is something on your mind. You have been quiet ever since we stopped. What's bothering you?"

"Nothing really, it's just..." Alaric was searching for the right words. There was something very disturbing about the woods in front of them. He couldn't put it into words, but he knew they shouldn't enter. "I think we need to give those trees a wide berth."

"But the road leads through there. We are still far enough away from Remidel that we can keep to the road," Richmond complained.

"Is it the prophecy?" Eldred asked, still a little suspicious of Alaric's motives. There had been something off with their conversation and Eldred wanted to know what it was.

"It could be." Alaric knew for a fact that it wasn't. "It's hard to tell. All I know is that we need to go around."

"Are you sure we have time for a detour? The moon has almost half disappeared. By my reckoning we have no more than seven days before the moon has completely waned." Viper added.

Seven days left. Alaric had to admit that he hadn't been paying attention to the cycle of the moon. He thought there was more time. They had at least a month's worth of travel to do in seven days. He wondered if he had lost days somewhere, he could have sworn there was more time left.

"In short, no we don't have time for a detour. On the other hand we definitely can't enter the woods." Alaric had made his decision. He had no idea whether to go around the woods to the east or the west, but they had to avoid the trees at all cost. "Now I think we should get moving."

"Left or right?" Viper pushed.

It was the question he hoped wouldn't be asked. He had hoped he would be able to make the decision when it needed to be made. In truth he was hoping the prophecy would pull him in the right direction.

"We'll head west. We'll need to give Remidel a wide berth."

"At the same time that will take us further away from Mount Scorpio," Richmond explained as he mounted his horse.

"I know, but better to arrive late than not at all." Alaric wasn't sure if they were the right words, but it was all he had.

Alaric wasn't in the mood for more conversation. He had made his decision and that was final. If they arrived late then he was the one who would have to live with the repercussions. He would do everything within his power, however, to arrive on time, if not earlier.

They came within a mile of the trees before Alaric couldn't stand the sound in his head. It was like the roaring of the wind blowing through the leaves. He knew the sound could be translated into words, but he didn't know how. If he did then he would know if what he was trying to avoid was a true threat, There would be time for understanding later, much later. It was something he could quite happily ignore, except for the fact that Mount Scorpio was in the Great Northern Forest. There were more trees there than in any other forest in the Seven Kingdoms. One way or another he was going to have to come to terms with his new gift.

Chapter 36: Thirty Days in Seven

Alaric didn't feel better until they were further away from the trees. He didn't know what evil was waiting for them on the inside, if there even was any. Whatever it was they had survived and moved on. The path Alaric had taken them took them round to the west. He felt much better when they had diverted from the road. The roaring in his head subsided even though they had moved no further away from the woods. He wasn't sure what had happened, but he knew it was a sign. What that sign indicated was another question altogether.

Once they had left the road they made the decision not to follow it any further. There were a number of small towns and villages between the woods and Remidel and as much as Alaric didn't want to leave people suffering, there were more important matters at stake. He had come to terms with the fact that Viper's brother, had something important to tell him. The fate of Arsiliac was now inconsequential. That was how he justified his decision to leave to other towns to their fates.

If something was written in the prophecy then it had to be true? That was another thought that kept running through his mind. He definitely needed to be at Mount Scorpio just before the new moon. If it was written in the prophecy then there was nothing he could do to change it. He also knew that wasn't true. It was the most likely outcome, but that could change. The prophecy could change at any time, without any real reason.

The next problem Alaric had was the time left for them to reach the mountain. Something didn't sit right with him. He was sure they should have more time. It was as if they had missed days if not weeks. It was like the days had just disappeared. In a different time and place Alaric wouldn't have thought it was possible. If the Dark One was shifting time then that was definitely a trick Alaric needed to learn. It seemed as though he could slow time, but not on purpose, so it would make sense that he would also be able to speed it up. All he needed to know was how to do it and that was not as easy at it sounded.

On the afternoon of the fifth day from leaving Weston they topped a small hill and saw the grand city of Remidel on the horizon. Alaric stopped the group to look at the marvel below them. He had never seen the capital before and he couldn't believe the pure immensity of it. Although Remidel wasn't as big as Castalia there was something awe inspiring about it that had him transfixed.

"What is it Alaric?" Alena asked after they had been stationary for almost ten minutes.

"Something is wrong," the words came unbidden.

"Of course something is wrong," Richmond responded. "There is a Dark Knight in command of that city. That isn't right by a long shot."

"That's not what I'm saying." Alaric wasn't sure what he was talking about, but he knew that wasn't the problem.

"What are you talking about?" Alena asked.

"It's taken too long to get here," Viper hissed.

"What do you mean?" Richmond sounded confused.

"It should have only taken us three days to get here and that's at a gentle pace. We have been pushing hard and it has almost taken five," Viper answered.

"He's right," it suddenly hit Alaric. "We now only have two days to reach Mount Scorpio before our time is up. We avoided helping those in need to make up time and we have done nothing. We are now even further behind." Alaric couldn't believe what he was saying.

His words floated away on the breeze and as if to accentuate their mood, dark storm clouds started to appear over the city. A bolt of lightning struck one of the turrets above the castle; no thunder followed.

"I guess we only have a few hours before we start getting wet," Viper didn't sound happy.

"That is the least of our concerns," Alaric sounded even more morose. "We are never going to make it to Scorpio in time."

"Can't you jump or travel or whatever it is you do?" Richmond asked.

Alaric suddenly felt a chill down the back of his spine. Jumping through the fabric of reality was something he had wanted to keep from the serpentant. It was bad enough the Dark Knights had the ability to do it and he didn't need another enemy to know.

"What is this about?" Viper couldn't help himself.

Without really thinking Alaric created a cone of silence spell. Everyone except for Viper could hear what they were saying. He tied off the weave so the serpentant wouldn't be able to break it. He didn't care that Viper knew he was being left out, it was easier than sending him away.

"I can't. I would be too weak for whatever trial I am about to face. I can't trust Viper or his brother. If they see I am weakened then they will destroy me."

"What about Eldred?" Alena asked.

"With all due respect Eldred isn't strong enough to make a jump that far and without having line of sight to the mountain it would be nearly impossible to hit the right destination, even for me."

Eldred didn't like Alaric speaking for him, but he was right, at least about the distance. He knew that trying to make a jump that far would drain of all his energy. If he was able to survive the ordeal he would be bedridden for at least a day. That wouldn't help anyone. Whatever was waiting for them at Mount Scorpio he would need his strength for it.

"I have been to Mount Scorpio before." Eldred hated to admit that, but it wasn't the time for his ego to get the better of him. "You said we could jump to a location we have been to before. That was one of the things you said when you were training us on the island."

That was true and for a moment Alaric saw a glimmer of hope, but it still didn't change the fact that the distance was too great. Eldred wouldn't be able to make the jump.

"What about the Topaz stone?" Alena suggested. "Couldn't you use the stone to heal you when we arrive?"

It was another good idea, but again one that wouldn't work.

"I can't. I don't trust the stone," Alaric wasn't sure how else to explain it and he hoped she didn't question him any further.

Alena noticed Alaric was uncomfortable with the question and didn't push any further, although she really didn't understand his response.

"I wouldn't try that again," Alaric spoke through his spell at Viper. He noticed that the serpentant was trying to break his spell and listen to their conversation. It was never going to happen, but he needed to let Viper know he was onto him.

Viper turned away from the group. He didn't like being left out of the conversation. Whatever they were talking about he wanted to know about it. It was just another sign that they didn't trust him. He really didn't know what else he had to do to be part of them. A time would come when they would need his help and he wasn't so sure he would want to anymore.

"There has to be something we can do?" Richmond was starting to feel useless.

Alaric had to think. There had to be a way to get them to the mountain on time, a way that didn't involve using the aid of the Topaz stone. Of all the stones he trusted Topaz the least. It was the stone he needed the most when he was at his weakest and the one he would be most vulnerable to losing himself to.

"What about Viper?" Richmond suggested at a whisper, almost too scared to mention the words.

The first response was another bolt of lightning. This time the thunder shook the ground, indicating how close the storm was becoming. It seemed to be moving a lot quicker than it should be. Even though Alaric had been staring directly at it he didn't seem to notice until the lightning struck.

"Does that storm seem to be moving faster than normal?" Richmond asked, suddenly changing the subject.

"I have no idea what is normal anymore," Alaric returned absentmindedly. "There is nothing that can come as a surprise anymore." That wasn't exactly true.

"What about Viper?" Alena returned to the subject.

"What about him?" Alaric snapped and then instantly wished he hadn't.

"Should we think about using him to transport us to Mount Scorpio?" She ignored the snipe as the rain started to fall.

"We can't give him the power to travel wherever he wants in the Seven Kingdoms. There is no telling what he would do with it." Alaric dismissed the idea. "I don't even know if he is powerful enough to get us there."

"Maybe not by himself, but if I help him I am sure the two of us could get us all there," Eldred sounded hopeful.

Alaric could see no other option. There was a reason why he had brought Viper with them and this seemed to be it. There was no telling how long it would take to ride there. Thirty days was the estimate, but with their delayed travel time it could take them up to three times as long. There was no way Viper's brother was going to wait, Arsiliac would be burnt to the ground. Suddenly he felt the tug of the prophecy. It was as if it was telling him it was the right course of action and that was both promising and frightening at the same time. He couldn't work out why the prophecy would want a serpentant to have access to the power of travelling.

"We don't have a choice." Alaric sounded defeated and could hardly be heard over the increasing storm blowing around them.

"So we're going to do this?" Eldred asked, not sure if he had heard correctly.

"There is no other…" Alaric started yelling and then he had a thought. A quick spell and the noise would be blocked out. He would have to drop the first spell, but there seemed no reason to keep Viper out of the loop any longer. "There is no other way." Everyone was surprised to hear Alaric so clearly and the storm reduced to a subtle background noise.

"What are we doing?" Viper asked when he realised he was part of the conversation again.

Alaric slowly shook his head. He couldn't believe he was going to teach the serpentant the spell. One thing he had promised himself when he agreed to let Viper join them was that he wouldn't let him know any secrets. He was going to have to break that promise. He wondered to himself if it was at all a coincidence or whether the prophecy had planned it all along. It was the reason why he refused to read the great tome anymore.

"We are going to jump to the base of the mountain. It's the only way we are going to make it on time," Alaric explained as he wiped the rain off his face.

Viper couldn't control himself when he heard the words come out of Alaric's mouth. If it wasn't for the hooded robe his excitement would have been more apparent. What they did see was his forked tongue dart out and flick the air. He quickly retracted it when he realised what he was doing. The others didn't realise what it signified and Viper was grateful for that.

"How are we going to do that?" Viper hid his excitement.

"I will teach you," Alaric couldn't believe the words came out of his mouth. "Not here though. This is not the place to be learning spells."

It was more the storm raging around them that made it a bad idea. There was a need for privacy and Viper would have to concentrate. Although they couldn't see anyone around it didn't necessarily mean they were alone. The last thing Alaric needed was for someone to learn the spell he was going to teach Viper. He would also need to end the spell that was keeping the sound of the storm at bay. It would be very difficult teaching and learning with such a commotion happening around them.

Alaric scanned the scenery, looking for a suitable place to take cover. Eyesight alone wasn't enough to find anywhere and he had to reach out with his senses. The landscape around the city was fairly bare, but eventually he found an empty farmhouse that seemed perfect

"I've found somewhere close. I would suggest you close your eyes as this can be quite disturbing."

That was all the warning he gave them before they suddenly blinked out of existence. Alena and Richmond took his advice. Eldred, who had travelled before, didn't bother and Viper didn't react quickly enough. Alaric was able to land them in the farmhouse and leave the horses outside.

They returned to existence almost as quickly as they left. Viper was the only one who stumbled forward when they arrived. The others landed and simply remained standing. There was much to be said for keeping one's eyes shut.

"What a rush!" Viper exclaimed breathlessly.

"I warned you," Alaric looked around as he spoke.

It was clear the farmhouse had been vacant for some time. Cobwebs filled the corners of the room and a thick layer of dust covered the furniture. They had arrived in the dining room, not that it really mattered where they were. They weren't going to stay long.

"Please light the room Eldred." The dark storm clouds were preventing much light from entering the room.

Eldred created a small spell to light the many half burnt candles around the room. Suddenly the room was filled with a warm glow which made Alaric feel much better. There had been something disturbing about being in the dark.

"Now let's get started. I hope you're a quick learner. You have to become extremely proficient in an extremely short amount of time if we are going to succeed," Alaric explained.

"Let's just get onto it. You will see the power I possess," Viper hissed.

Alaric started slowly. He taught Viper how to jump from room to room. The serpentant wasn't as proficient as Alaric had hoped when they started. His first jump sent him crashing into a bedside table. There was no control to his movements and that was dangerous. Alaric couldn't risk the jump to Scorpio until Viper was more disciplined. Even with Eldred helping it would still be up to Viper to control the destination.

When Viper understood what he was trying to do he started learning very quickly. Soon enough he could jump away from the farmhouse and then back again. Alaric was impressed. He wished the council had have been able to learn as fast. If they had then he would have been able to leave the Island sooner.

"Do you think you're ready to take us to Mount Scorpio?" Alaric asked after an hour of training. He hoped he hadn't pushed Viper too hard. The jump would only work if he still had enough strength to get them there.

"I was ready a long time ago." that wasn't strictly true. "Let's get moving if we want to reach Scorpio in time."

Alaric ignored what he was insinuating. There would be time for reprisals later. All that mattered was reaching their destination on time. There would be plenty of time to reprimand Viper when he was finished on the mountain.

"Let's go then."

To accentuate the point Viper jumped them to where the horses were waiting outside in the storm. The elven horses were doing their best to stop the mare from bolting. They had been through a lot and the storm did nothing to calm their nerves. The sudden appearance of their riders from thin air did nothing to help.

Viper didn't want to waste any time. Eldred had already started to draw in energy when they were inside the farmhouse. He needed to transfer the power to Viper just before the spell was cast. It would be a while before Viper would be able to cast another spell, but he would remain conscious and that was imperative.

When Viper released his spell they slowly started to disappear. It wasn't like any other time they had jumped. For a moment Alaric thought

Viper had missed the spell before they finally disappeared. A moment later they landed in the Great Northern Forest. As soon as they arrived Alaric started screaming. There was nothing he could do to prepare himself for the assault on his senses. It was like all the trees in the Great Northern Forest were at him. He collapsed to the ground and covered his ears with his hands, not that it did anything to help.

"What did you do to him?" Alena asked accusingly of Viper.

"I did nothing and I need to sit down now," Viper almost collapsed to the ground when he finished speaking.

"Eldred?" She asked.

"I have no idea. He did nothing out of the ordinary."

Alaric rolled on the ground in agony. Nothing he did could ease the pain of the forest screaming out to him. There was only one thing that he thought would help and that was the Emerald stone. The only problem was he couldn't do anything to release the stone from its pouch. When he tried to move his hand the noise was too painful, which didn't really make sense since the sound was inside his head.

"The stone…" his voice was hoarse with pain. "I need the Emerald stone…"

Alena dropped to Alaric's side. She looked through the various pouches and covers until she found the one containing the emerald bracelet. She united the drawstrings and let the bracelet drop to the ground. When she did, Alaric's pain suddenly disappeared. The stone glowed softly bathing them all in green light. It was at that stage they all realised it was night time. When they had left the farmhouse it was still mid-afternoon. What only had seemed to take a moment had in fact taken a few hours.

Alaric sat up and looked at the stone, taking a deep breath as he did. It glowed softly, bathing them all in a gentle green light. For the first time Alaric looked at the stone in awe and wondered at the beauty it held within. He could feel the power of the stone radiating within him. Now he was at peace with the forest a sudden feeling of euphoria passed through his body and for a moment he would have been happy to die. When the feeling was gone so was his feeling of contentment.

"Alaric!" Alena's voice was raised, as if it wasn't the first time she had called out. In fact she had been trying to get his attention ever since she had released the stone.

"What can I do for you Alaric? I take it you didn't free me from my prison for no reason," the voice was calm inside his head. There was something about the tone that seemed very self-satisfied.

Although Alaric was happy the roaring was out of his head he wasn't happy about the voice being back. He wished that he could keep his mind to himself, like before he started his quest. He almost couldn't remember a time when his thoughts where his own. Even when the stones were safely tucked away in their velvet prisons he knew he wasn't truly alone.

"What is the sound that is constantly in my mind? I know it has something to do with the trees around me, but what is it?" Alaric smiled at Alena as he thought the words. He wanted to reassure her that he was alright, but he had more important matters to deal with.

"It looks as though I have given you too much credit. There is a power within you Alaric, but that is not for me to explain, nor is it the question you asked. I will answer your question and then I would appreciate it if you let me sleep."

"You will sleep when I say you can sleep." Alaric didn't really know why he was being combative. "I am sorry," he quickly apologised. "If you could answer my question that would be greatly appreciated." He was so used to the stones fighting him that he wasn't used to one being helpful. That last thing he wanted to do was get the Emerald stone offside. He would need them all before the end.

"You can hear the trees around you. I have unlocked a power inside of you, but it is just in its infancy. Once you have learned to master it you will be able to hear all living things around you, of fauna that is." Alaric didn't like what he was hearing. He had a bad feeling the stone was keeping something very important from him. "If you can tap into that power you will be able to listen to what the trees have to say. You will know if there is any danger nearby. They will tell you if anyone is following you, or if you are on the right track if you are following someone else and that is just for starters."

"What does that mean?"

"That is something you need to learn. It isn't something I can tell you, at least not right now. For now all I can help you try and do is and understand the words from the trees."

"I don't want to understand the words. All I want is the noise to stop." Alaric wasn't interested in learning. There would be time to do that later. For the moment he just wanted the noise out of his head so he could concentrate on the job in front of them.

"They are one and the same. Until you learn to master the power you will constantly hear a confused roar whenever you pass a tree. The more trees the louder the sound. As you can imagine being in the Great Northern Forest is doing nothing to help your cause. You can either put up with it or learn to use it. I know what choice I would make."

No matter which way he looked at it he knew the stone was right. In the end he had no choice. There was no chance of succeeding, with whatever challenge Viper's brother had in store for him, if he didn't get rid of the sound in his head. He doubted he would even make it to the peak of Scorpio. They were a good day's ride away from the base of the mountain and that meant passing many more trees. Alaric cringed at the thought.

"Fine. What is it a need to know?"

"The first thing you have to do, and probably one of the hardest, is to open your mind to the noises you are hearing. There will be great pain at first, but that will only last for a short time," Emerald explained.

"I don't want to trade random noises for methodical ones. I don't want any noises in my head. I don't want to have any more discussions in my head. My head is my own and no one and nothing else should be in here."

"So do you want me to go?" there was a hint of sarcasm in its voice.

"Don't be smart. Just let me know what I need to know and then things can go back to normal." Alaric really wasn't in the mood for such comments.

"Very well. You need to open your mind. You need to stop fighting the sounds and then they will coalesce into something real. Now this isn't the ideal place for this to happen. Ideally you would want to do it around one maybe two trees at most. Being in the middle of a forest means you'll be bombarded by sounds. It will be hard for you to be able to decipher between the voices, which means having a conversation is going be extremely difficult."

"I told you. I don't want to have a conversation. I just want them gone. I want peace and quiet."

"I really wish that you would listen to what I'm telling you," the voice sounded frustrated. "You don't have a choice. The sounds will get worse and worse until you can control them. There is no way for you to just shut them out. First you must understand them before you can ignore them."

Alaric suddenly cut himself away from the voice inside his head. He didn't know how long they had been talking, time in his mind was always so hard to gauge. When he came back to reality he was lying on the ground with his head in Alena's lap. He couldn't continue with his training until he explained he was alright. He knew the others would be worried about him.

"Are you alright Alaric?" Alena spoke softly. "Your breathing slowed down for no reason and I thought you were going to lose consciousness." She sounded concerned.

"I'm fine. I think we should make camp for the night. We will make it to Scorpio tomorrow." Alaric sounded weak, a lot weaker than the voice inside his head.

"Are you sure there is enough time? I'm not exactly sure, but if we leave at first light we are going to struggle to make it to the foot of the mountain by nightfall. That doesn't give you enough time to reach the summit. There is no time to rest. We have to keep moving," Alena replied.

"If we reach the foot by nightfall I will be able to get to the summit in time. There is much to be done, but now we need to make camp for the night." Alaric tried to sound forceful, but it didn't work.

"Come on, I don't have all night," the voice came inside Alaric's mind.

Alaric sighed as he sat up. As much as he would have preferred to remain in Alena's lap he knew she wouldn't move until he did. The Emerald stone was right, they didn't have all night. Alaric had to learn and learn fast.

"Okay, what is it you need me to do?"

"You need to concentrate on the trees around you. Breathe in the clear air and really try and sense the life in them. If you are going to understand the trees then you need to be able to feel them. Now clear your mind and reach out to the life around you."

Alaric closed his eyes and tried to empty his mind. That wasn't as easy as he thought. The thoughts of what lay ahead for him the following night weighed heavily on his mind. Eventually, after taking a deep breath, he was able to set his thoughts free. As his head emptied, his nose was filled with the scent of pine needles. It was the first time that he realised they were surrounded by pine trees. He realised they were in a forest, but he had not been able to take any notice of the type of trees. When he realised his heart started to beat faster, the feeling was exhilarating.

"What is that?" he asked, breathlessly, as if his mind voice drew breath.

"That is the forest. You are finally letting yourself go. This is what you have been missing your entire life. Each time you looked at a tree you could have known so much more about it. The stories they could have told you. You'd be surprised at how helpful they can be."

"You're starting to drift away," Alaric interrupted.

"Yes, sorry, now you need to concentrate on your senses. Feel each breath. Listen to the wind through the trees. Feel everything and you will know your surroundings."

Alaric did as he was instructed. He focused on his breathing, long, slow breaths. Each time he felt more and more in tune with his surrounds. For a moment he felt truly at peace until the voice came again inside his head.

"You can feel it now. That's good. Remember that feeling. It's that feeling that is going to help you survive this."

"Survive this? What are you talking about? You didn't say anything about having to survive. That means there is a chance I will die?"

"Not die as such, but there is a chance your brain won't cope with the change. That is, it wouldn't handle the new sensations that it is about to be bombarded by without my help."

The words didn't really fill Alaric with any confidence. He wasn't sure if he even wanted to continue with the training. There was always the opportunity to get the Emerald stone out while he was in the forest. That would keep the voices out of his head.

"That isn't an option. One way or another you have to learn to control your new skills. You have to step out on your own and not rely on me to hold your hand, metaphorically speaking of course."

That was dangerous. Alaric couldn't keep his thoughts to himself when he was around one of the stones. It definitely didn't make life any easier for him, this was the first time he had cause a stone reading his thought and not just conversing inside his head.

"You need to focus Alaric. There is no time for this. You have to learn and you have to learn fast."

"Okay, let's do this." Alaric steeled himself.

"Focus on that scent. Breathe in the pine smell and rejoice in it. When I release my hold you will be bombarded with sound, just concentrate on that smell. No matter what happens, no matter how much pain you suffer, you have to concentrate on that smell. I have no idea how long it will take or more importantly how long it will feel like it is taking. Regardless you have to be strong and you have to focus."

"How will I know when it is over?"

"Trust me, you'll know."

There was a moment of silence as Alaric prepared himself. Suddenly without warning a rush of pain filled his body. He had planned on keeping the ordeal to himself, but there was nothing he could do to keep the screams inside. The sudden noise brought the attention of the others who were sitting around a makeshift campfire preparing the evening meal. They had left Alaric where he was and had almost forgotten about him. When they heard the screams everyone except for Viper rushed to his side. When they saw his condition, panic filled their bodies. His skin was deathly pale and his body was covered in sweat. Between screams Alaric was writhing on the forest floor in pain and there was nothing they could do to stop it.

"Don't touch him!" Eldred cried out as Alena reached out for him.

"What are you talking about Eldred? We have to do something."

"There is nothing we can do to help. This is something he has to do on his own," Eldred explained.

"That doesn't tell me anything." She wanted to cradle him and try to soothe him.

"I don't know much more than that. All I know is that we shouldn't touch him. Something is happening and we won't know what it is until it's over." Again that didn't explain much, but it was the best he could do.

The pain ripped through Alaric's body and he felt as though he was about to be torn apart. With each breath of air he could smell the pines around him less and less. As he struggled he started gasping through his mouth, making it even harder to smell the pines. Even without the fresh smell it still remained in his mind and he hoped that was all it was going to take to survive as another blast of pain shot through him.

"I can't," Alaric struggled to form the words.

There was no response only wave after wave of pain. His body felt like it was on fire. At any moment he would start to burn like the logs on their campfire... and then it was gone. As if nothing had happened Alaric suddenly returned to normal. The sweat instantly evaporated and all the colour returned to his skin. A new sensation filled his body. He felt... fresh. That was the best way he could explain it. He felt as though he had just bathed in rose water. His skin tingled as he took in a deep breath through his nose. There was a subtle smell of flowers in the air, which he couldn't smell before.

"Who are you and what are you doing here?" the voice was brash and masculine. He knew that it wasn't the stone, but besides that he had no idea why the voice was in his head.

"He is my vessel," Emerald spoke. "He is here to help you. You will do all you can to help him."

"Yes, my mistress."

"What's going on?" Alaric asked.

"You have survived and now you can understand the trees. They will not come to you unbidden, but don't forget them. If you do then they we will lose faith in you and you won't be able to understand them anymore," Emerald explained. "Now I think it's time to get some sleep."

Chapter 37: The Scorpion

When the Emerald stone finished speaking everything went quiet. Alaric knew there was no point in trying to talk to her anymore. Even if he did there would be no response and he wasn't overly upset with that. Although it had been quite an ordeal he felt relatively fresh. With his heightened senses he felt at home amongst the trees. He couldn't remember feeling such a sense of contentment. With that in mind he took another deep breath.

"What just happened?" Alena asked as Alaric sat up again.

"Something wonderful." He said, still basking in the forest around him.

Alena shot Eldred a questioning look who in turn simply shrugged his shoulders. He wished that he had the answers, but he didn't. He had no idea what had just happened or why Alaric was smiling in such a fashion. It seemed every time they turned a corner there were more and more questions Eldred couldn't answer. He remembered a time when he was the one who had all the answers, now it seemed that torch had been passed without his knowledge.

"He is now in tune with the forest around him," Viper spoke from the campfire.

"How do you know?" Eldred snapped. He was still waiting for Alaric to respond.

"It's obvious isn't it? The Emerald stone, the forest, Alaric's strange reaction? Didn't anyone else notice the stone glowed stronger when he was in pain?" Viper shook his head. "It's a wonder how you all survived without me. It doesn't seem as though you notice what is right in front of you face."

"Is he right Alaric?" Eldred was hoping for a different response.

Alaric just wanted to be left alone. It was like he was alive for the first time and he didn't want that feeling to go away. He knew that once he started talking to the others it would simply disappear. It would be too easy to remain in his happy little haze, but he still had a long journey ahead. He couldn't let himself slip away until he'd accomplished what he'd set out to do.

"What? Yes, well, somewhat anyway." Alaric stumbled over his words as his feeling of euphoria left him.

"What do you mean by that Alaric? I think it's time you started explaining yourself." Eldred didn't sound happy.

"It's a long story. All you need to know is that everything is alright. Now I think it is time we had something to eat and then get some sleep. We are going to need to push hard in the morning if we are going to reach the mountain by nightfall," Alaric snapped.

Eldred wasn't pleased with the response. It told him nothing. The fact that Viper seemed to know what had happened and he didn't annoyed him. If Alaric didn't trust him anymore then there was little he could do. Not only that, but he was starting to doubt if he was able to help at all.

"Alaric you really need to confide in me." Eldred wasn't going to let it go.

"I will, but not now." He looked towards Viper, although it was an excuse and not the real reason. "For now we should just prepare for tomorrow."

Eldred didn't like the response, but he wasn't prepared to push it any further. He knew the next day would be hard on Alaric and it wasn't worth making life harder for him. Even though he didn't know what betrayal was waiting for them he knew that it was coming. He would have another look through the prophecy once he had eaten and the others were asleep. If the answers were in there then there was only one way he was going to find them.

Alaric kept to himself until it was time to sleep. Alena tried to get close, but his cold shoulder was enough to send her away. She told herself he was still recovering from whatever had tormented him. It was a weak lie, but it was enough to reassure her.

"I don't think you will find any answers in that book of yours," Viper spoke to Eldred when the others had gone to sleep.

Alaric was only pretending to be asleep, he was trying to regain the sensation he felt from the trees around him. The scent of the forest wasn't enough to regain the feeling of euphoria and the sound of Viper's words diverted his attention.

"What do you know, Snake?" Eldred asked as he put the prophecy down, it seemed as though Viper was going to stay awake for longer than he anticipated.

"I don't think my brother has called this meeting to betray Alaric."

"And what makes you say that?" Eldred pushed.

"It doesn't make any sense. There is no reason why he would lead Alaric into a trap. We have no reason to back Nyrra in this war, a war that has nothing to do with serpentants." Eldred wasn't sure if he entirely trusted Viper's words.

"What does this have to do with the prophecy?"

"I just don't think you will find anything of use in there," Viper tried to sound innocent.

Eldred didn't like what he was hearing. If anything it only made him think there was something more pertinent to find. Viper's attitude did nothing to calm his nerves.

Alaric was silently agreeing with Viper. He couldn't see how the serpentant could win by betraying him. When it was said and done they too would prefer to see Nyrra fall. That was the only way they could truly rescue their Goddess-Queen. It was with those thoughts in his mind that Alaric drifted off to sleep.

There was no point in pushing Viper any further and Eldred knew it. The only way he was going to find answers was in the prophecy. He simply ignored Viper, leaned back against a nearby tree and opened to a random passage. It was in that position that they found him in the morning after he had finally fallen asleep.

"Did you find anything pertinent to our situation?" Alaric doubted it, but he had to ask. He ignored the fact that prophecy was lying out in the open for all to see. If Viper was going to try and steal the great tome there would have been no better opportunity.

"I'm afraid not. It seems like we have all the information that we are going to receive." Alaric wasn't surprised with the answer. He wanted nothing more than to throw the damn book in the dying campfire.

"Should we jump to the mountain?" Viper asked, somewhat excited. He was keen to practice what he had learnt.

"No," Alaric responded quickly. "You aren't skilled enough to get us there safely. There is a good chance you will land us somewhere in the middle of the mountain. We will travel there by horse."

"Surely if we land in the mountain then we can just jump out again? I'm pretty sure that I can make it from here. Remember that last time was a much larger jump."

There was a chance Viper would land them in the mountain, not a big one, but that wasn't the reason why Alaric didn't want to travel that way. Ever since he had woken that morning he'd had a bad feeling of impending doom. He knew it was related to the mountain and the meeting with the serpentant. In fact it wasn't just the mountain that was causing his angst, but he didn't want to believe it. Either way he knew they had to arrive at the foot of the mountain at the allotted time. The prophecy wouldn't allow for anything else. Alaric silently cursed when he came to the realisation.

"Then you should send us there," Viper suggested, although he really wanted the practice. Now that he had learnt and art thought long forgotten he didn't want to risk forgetting it. "I am sure it is not too far away for you. You should be able to sit us on the head of a needle."

He knew what Viper was trying to do and he wasn't going to fall for it. The jump to the mountain would be an easy one for Alaric and he wouldn't need to break a sweat, but that was beside the point. They still needed to ride to the mountain and there was no other way around it.

"I said we are riding to the mountain and that is exactly how we are going to get there. If you wish to travel there by other means you are certainly welcome to go on alone, but don't be expecting a warm reunion when we arrive." There was something very evil in Alaric's tone.

"No, I will ride with you." Viper sneered under the hood of his robe. He was grateful that Alaric wasn't able to see it.

Alaric was grateful for the response and didn't care about any underlying issues. He had actually grown used to Viper's presence and wasn't ready to see him go. As much as he still didn't trust the serpentant he was getting close to it. That thought in itself should have made him send Viper packing.

"Now it's time to get moving. We have a lot of ground to cover and little time to do it. We need to be at the foot of Mount Scorpio by nightfall."

It wasn't until he was on the back of Adelanta and he took a deep breath in, did he take in the glory of the forest. It had been something he had wanted to do since he had woken that morning, but he had restrained. He was unsure what the reaction would be and he wanted to make sure they were moving first. The scent of pine was intoxicating. It was like he could feel the trees growing around him. All he wanted to do was take another breath, but he wasn't sure what it would do to him. There was only so much bliss he could take at once. He could quite happily just lie down and breathe for the rest of his life, but that wouldn't get the job done.

"There is something wrong ahead." Alaric nearly fell from Adelanta's back when he heard the soft voice inside his head. He turned around to see who had spoken, but there was no one there.

"This one isn't too bright, is he?" There was another voice

"No. His whole life will pass him by if he doesn't stop to smell the flowers, so to speak."

"Yes. I don't even know how he got the ability to hear us."

"I don't want it!" Alaric spoke aloud by mistake. The others instantly looked at him.

"What don't you want?" Eldred asked.

"Ah, nothing. Sorry, I think I was drifting off in the saddle. I didn't get much sleep last night." It was a plausible lie.

The response seemed to make sense so no one questioned him. They all thought the lie was a little weak, but they all let it go. Alaric tried his best not to blush with embarrassment.

"What do you want?" Alaric used his mind voice.

"Oh, so you can talk to us?" It was the first voice again, although there was a subtle difference to it.

"He might not be as bad as he looks."

"He might be the one we have been looking for?"

Although the voices all sounded alike it was almost as if they were different, but still the same. The more he thought about it the more it started to make his head hurt.

"I don't know. He doesn't look like much. I have my doubts."

"Doubts? You always have doubts. Let's have some faith. I like him. He has a friendly aura about him."

"You know I can hear what you're saying," Alaric focused so he didn't speak out loud. With all the voices in his head it was a lot harder than when he was speaking with one of the stones.

"Ooooh, he can hear us."

"Well isn't that amazing." The voices were also very sarcastic.

It didn't seem as though they wanted to talk to him, just about him. As much as he really wanted to be left in silence he thought it best to use the opportunity to try and gather some information.

"Who are you?' he instantly regretted asking the question.

"Who are we?" "Who are we?" "Who are we?" the voices resonated in his head. He thought his head was going to explode.

"Quiet! The lot of you, keep quiet!" it was all Alaric could do to keep the screaming inside his head. He wanted to call out, but he knew that wouldn't do him any good.

Suddenly his head went quiet. For a moment even his own thoughts went blank. When he settled himself he remembered the acrimonious tone and cringed. He needed answers, but he couldn't stand the voices in his head. He wished that they would return, but there was only silence. He let out a sigh, of both relief and frustration.

"Are you alright?" Alena asked, as she rode next to him.

"Yes, I'm fine, thank you. Why do you ask?" he tried to hide his discomfort at the question.

"You just seem preoccupied. I know that you have a lot on your mind. It's just... well... there is something else. Something seems to have changed. I don't know what it is, but it has me worried," Alena spoke softly so the others couldn't hear.

"No, I'm fine. There's just a lot on my mind at the moment." If only she knew the truth of it. "I think we should pick up the pace or else we won't make it in time."

It was an easy way for Alaric to divert the subject. He didn't want to discuss it further until he knew what was happening. On the other hand they did need to push on and it would also give him time to himself. He could only hope the voices didn't return whilst they were galloping ahead.

As much as Alaric didn't want to stop for the midday meal the others forced him to. Not only were they hungry, the animals were as well. They had been ridden hard and needed time to rest if they were going to make the rest of their journey, especially the two mares who weren't of elven breeding. Alaric had been enjoying the ride and the fact there were no voices inside his head made it all the better.

When they sat to eat Alaric took a deep breath. He couldn't help himself. He wanted to breathe in the scent of the forest around him.

"So you have decided to listen to us again." The voice was so sudden that it made Alaric jump. It was the only move he made and everyone else was too busy to notice.

"Are you ready to talk to me or just at me?" Alaric kept his inner voice level, trying to hide his surprise.

"Well I never. I seems like there is fire in this one after all."

"Yes, who would have thought it?"

"Fire indeed."

"Enough! If you can't be civil then I will silence you again." Alaric's headache started to return.

There was silence and for a moment Alaric thought the voices had disappeared again, but there was still something there. It was a like a whimpering in the corner of his mind. A smile crossed his face as he realised he was starting to win and quickly removed it before anyone else saw him. It was getting more difficult to hide what was happening from the others. Until he knew exactly what it was he didn't want to speak to anyone else about it.

"Now that's better. This is my head and I make the rules. Do you understand?"

"What do you want?" the voice sounded much more subservient. It wasn't a direct response to Alaric's question, but it was close enough.

"I want you to tell me who you are. I think I already know, but I want to hear it from you."

Again there was silence. He thought he could hear whispering somewhere in the back of his mind, but he might have just been imagining it. He hoped that wasn't a sign that he was going insane. The last thing he needed was to lose control of his mind completely. There were plenty of people and things that would be happy to move in and take control of it.

"We are the Great Northern Forest, at least that is how you know us."

"We are the voice of the forest."

"The voice of the trees to be more precise"

"The voice of the pine trees to be exact."

"What do you mean? I don't understand?" asked Alaric

"He doesn't understand?"

"Maybe he's not the one, maybe he's not what we thought his was."

"Shhh, there is time. Let's listen to what he has to say."

"I have my suspicions, as I said, but I need to hear it from you." Alaric cut in.

"You're not ready to hear it from us."

"There is a secret you need to know. There is something you need to know before we can tell you."

"What's the secret? What do I need to know?" Alaric asked.

"When you know."

"Come back to us."

"Come back when you have the answer." The last comment drifted away in his mind, like it was floating on a summer's breeze.

"I don't even have the question. What is it you want me to know?"

"A name."

"A name."

"Our name."

Alaric wanted to ask another question, but he knew it would be no good. They wouldn't give him any more clues, not that they had given him any. There was only one way he could get help and that was from the Emerald stone. He looked at the others to see if they were watching him, but they were all too busy eating to pay any attention to him. If he was going to speak to the Emerald stone it was the perfect opportunity. Carefully he pulled the bracelet from its pouch and held it behind his back. If he had been able to look at the stone he would have seen that it wasn't glowing, not at all.

"I need your help again," Alaric tried to concentrate his words on the stone.

He was met by silence.

"Come on. I just need to ask you a quick question."

Again there was silence and it finally dawned on him that he was going to have to figure out the secret by himself. He had no idea how he was supposed to work out the name the trees wanted and then it suddenly dawned on him. The trees had said that the Northern Forest was the term he used. There must be another name. A name the trees call themselves.

"Does the forest have another name?" Alaric blurted out.

His sudden words took everyone be surprise. They had all been concentrating so much on eating that there had been no conversation.

"What do you mean Alaric?" Eldred was the first to recover.

"I know we call it the Great Northern Forest, but was there ever another name for it?"

"Why so you ask?" Eldred was trying to understand Alaric's sudden questioning.

"Just curious." Alaric tried to act casual.

"The Northern Wood Elves have a different name for the forest. They call it *Nordliga Akastiere*. Is that what you're after?" Alena added.

"*Nordliga Akastiere?*" Alaric thought on the name. He hoped that he pronounced it correctly. "That is an interesting name," he spoke aloud. "*Nordliga Akastiere!*" Alaric thought again.

There was no response to his answer. It could only mean that it wasn't the answer they were looking for.

"Is there any other name? Maybe one older than that?" Alaric asked again.

"Not that I know about?" Alena replied. "You should eat something. We need to be going soon and you haven't touched your food."

Only then did Alaric realise he had been so preoccupied that he had forgotten to eat. He quickly started stuffing food into his mouth. He shot Eldred a questioning look, hoping for an answer to his question.

"I don't know of any other name. I am sure there was one along time ago, but it has been lost to the ages."

Alaric then turned to Viper.

"*Nordliga Akastiere* is the oldest name I know of."

They started riding again as soon as Alaric had finished his meal. He knew they had already stayed too long, but he didn't want to leave until he had the answer. He believed that he needed to know what the trees were trying to tell him before he met the serpentant and he only had half a day to figure it out.

The name *Nordliga Akastiere* ran through his head throughout the afternoon. Each time he thought he heard a response, but there was nothing further. Another name kept popping into his head, but it was at the back of his mind. Each time he thought he knew what it was it disappeared. Although he didn't know what it was he did know it was the answer he was looking for. It was close to the elvish word, that was something he did know.

"Give me a clue!" Alaric called out in his mind as the sun started to set. He knew they weren't too far away from the foot of the mountain.

There was no answer to his plea for help. It seemed as though the forest was true to its word. It wouldn't speak until he knew the right name.

Alaric created a small disc of light when the sun had completely set. Dark storm clouds completely covered the small sliver of moon remaining in the sky and they still had a league to travel before they reached the foot of the mountain. The feeling of dread that Alaric had felt that morning had intensified as they neared their destination. Panic filled his chest as he desperately tried to remember the original name of the forest.

"Here we are, thanks goodness!" Eldred announced when they reached their destination.

"What do we do now?" Viper asked, anticipation dripping from his words.

"You make camp for the night. I'm going to the pinnacle." Alaric sounded distracted as he dismounted.

"What are you talking about Alaric?" to everyone's surprise it was Richmond who spoke. "We didn't come all this way to be left behind. We're coming with you."

"He's right Alaric. We can't just wait here. There is no telling what's waiting for you at the summit." Alena added.

"Thank you, but I must do this alone." Suddenly a word popped into his head. 'Nordligträ.' That was the word he was looking for. That was the name of the forest before there was anyone to name it.

"Well it's about time."

"I didn't think he was ever going to get the answer."

"I suppose we know that this is who we are looking for."

"Now we can trust him."

"Yes we can trust him."

"I have to go." Alaric wanted to stay and get answers, but time was running out.

"There are things you need to know."

"Yes there are things you need to know."

Suddenly Alaric blinked out of existence. It came as a shock to everyone, even those inside his head.

Chapter 38: Treachery from Above

Alaric suddenly appeared on the top of the mountain. Snow was falling around him and he shivered once before creating the spell to cut out the cold. The snow flakes gave him a wide berth and those that didn't melt before they touched him. Alaric didn't have time to notice the phenomenon; he was too busy looking for the serpentant. A shot of fear passed through his body when he couldn't see the creature, not that he could see much in the darkness.

As he looked around he suddenly saw a dim light not too far in the distance. His heart started pounding when he realised what it was. There could be no other explanation for a light on top of the mountain. Taking a deep breath Alaric prepared himself for the confrontation.

"I was wondering when you were going to get here. One more day and I would have made good on my threat," the serpentant was clad in the same fashion as Viper. A soft light encompassed his body and, like Alaric the snowflakes seemed to dance away from him. "I must admit I was looking forward to destroying your home town. It has been a long since I have been able to unleash such chaos."

"I can assure you, if you had done anything to Arsiliac it would be the very last thing you did. You may be strong, but you are not that strong." Alaric wasn't going to take any threats lightly. He needed to be dominant from the start. "Now I'm sure you didn't get me up here to make silly comments. For starters I would like to know who I am speaking with."

"Very well Alaric, I was just trying to make some small talk. I thought it might make things a little more comfortable." It seemed as though he was stalling on his identity. "I am Adder, although I am sure my brother would have told you."

"And what is it you want from me?" Alaric wasn't in the mood for small talk. He regretted leaving the others so abruptly. There was something in the back of his mind telling him that there was vital information he needed from the trees. "I'm sure you didn't get me all the way up here for small talk. Now let's get down to business."

Adder took a step closer and Alaric took a step back. Seeing Alaric's reaction made him stop his advance. Although there seemed to be no need for secrecy he didn't want to yell what he had to say. It seemed as though Alaric was uncomfortable getting any closer. Adder thought that might come in handy.

"Straight down to business? I suppose that isn't a bad way of doing things." Adder paused as if he was waiting for a response. "There is a stone somewhere in the mountain."

"There are many stones in the mountain." Alaric completely missed the point. "This is no great revelation."

"There is a *Stone of Power* in the depth of the Scorpion." Adder continued when he realised Alaric wasn't just being facetious.

"What stone?" Alaric suddenly realised what they were talking about. "Where is it?"

"Calm down, calm down," Adder started laughing. "I don't know which stone or exactly where it is. I have just been told to pass on the message."

Alaric didn't like what he was hearing. It sounded very much like a set up. He looked around quickly, but there was no one else there. Whatever it was must be waiting within the mountain.

"Who sent you here? Who gave you the message?" As much as Alaric thought he already knew the answer he wanted to confirm it anyway.

Adder shook his head. As much as he was expecting the questions he had hoped they wouldn't be asked. He had been expecting so much more from the so called Chosen One.

"Who sent me here is irrelevant and so is who gave me the message. All you need to know is that there is a stone waiting for you somewhere inside the mountain."

Alaric knew that wasn't the entire truth. He knew, at least, that Adder believed there was a stone in the mountain, he had known that as soon as he arrived. There was something about the place that made him feel akin to the area. That could only mean there was a stone nearby. All the warnings played on his mind and he needed answers.

"What else do you know?" Alaric pushed. "You wouldn't have come all this way just to tell me about a stone. You could have told me this message anywhere."

"That is true, but the reason why I am here is a mystery even to me." That was a lie, although Alaric wasn't sure how he was going to prove it. "I had a debt to pay and now it's repaid. That is all I know and all that you need to know."

"I know that's not true. I'm sure you know what I am capable of. Now don't make me force the truth from you." Alaric threatened.

"Well there was one more thing…" There was a pause as Adder thought for a moment. "I was tempted not to follow through on this part, but I guess I can fulfil my debt now."

When he finished speaking Adder outstretched his arms, through the sleeves of his cloak. Alaric quickly prepared himself for a challenge, but none came. Suddenly there was a rumble deep within the mountain.

"What was that?" Alaric asked, expecting the earth to move, but it didn't.

"My debt has been fulfilled. You will find out soon enough."

Before Alaric had a chance to respond Adder blinked out of existence. The first thought that came to Alaric's mind was the fact that he could travel. That narrowed down the side the serpentant was playing for. Only the seven on the Council of Wizards knew the spell and none of them would teach it to a serpentant. That only left a Dark Knight. But why would a Dark Knight want to tell him the location of a *Stone of Power?*

For a second Alaric thought about going after him, he was sure he could follow the subtle trail the serpentant left behind, but in the end he decided against it. There were more important matters for him to deal with.

With the disappearance of Adder so too went the light and Alaric was left in complete darkness. There was no chance of the sliver of moonlight being able to cut through the dark clouds. Almost as an afterthought Alaric created his own small ball of light. It bounced and bobbled over his head creating a gentle glow around him. There was something very disturbing about the whole situation and he wanted time to think before he continued.

Nothing made sense. There were more questions than answers floating around in his head. Why had Adder chosen the mountain top for their meeting? Which one of the Dark Knights would have taught Adder the spell to travel? Why would a Dark Knight tell him the location of another stone? That was the most disturbing question of them all, but only just. There had to be something terrible waiting for him in the bowels of the mountain, but it still didn't make any sense. As much as he wanted to figure out the riddles himself he knew he wasn't going to find the answers he was looking for.

Suddenly he blinked out of existence.

***

"Now I think it is time you talk to us!" Alena turned to Viper not long after Alaric disappeared. "What in the God Kings' names are we doing here?"

"I don't know what you're talking about. I have nothing to do with this." Viper was struggling to find an answer.

"You have to know something." Alena was becoming angry.

"There is nothing I know that you don't. I haven't spoken to one of my brothers in almost a century. What he does is his business and not mine."

"You all work towards the release of the Serpent Queen," Alena snapped back.

"Our Goddess is not to be taken lightly." Viper took a menacing step forward, but refrained from approaching her further. "Her capture is an abomination and shall be rectified."

"And all you creatures do is work towards that end, so don't tell me you don't know what is happening on the mountain top." Alena wasn't going to back down.

"Calm down Alena." Eldred stepped forward until he was almost standing between the two. "Alaric will be alright, I'm sure of that. There is nothing more we can do here.'

"I'm sick of not being able to do anything. Viper knows something and I can tell. I want to know what it is."

Viper took a step backwards. He had thought he had hidden his secret deep down inside, but it seemed that wasn't the case. He silently cursed his brother, whichever one was on the mountain top. There was a good chance he had ruined all of his plans. He just hoped whoever it was, and he was pretty sure it was Adder, knew what he was doing, their Goddess's freedom was at stake.

"I don't know what you're talking about." Viper replied defensively. "I am not keeping anything from you. As I have told you in the past, I am here to help you. I have no allegiance to anyone, just that of the Goddess, and it is your side that will help me to free her." Viper bit his forked tongue as he realised he had already revealed too much. "We really should be concentrating on our next move. Alaric will return shortly." Viper looked around their campsite for something to do.

The small fire burned happily in the middle of their camp. Their bedrolls had been laid out, although no one really thought they would be doing any sleeping that night. No one felt like eating, so no one had unpacked any of the food. It was just the distraction Viper needed.

"Now come on, let's have something to eat. I have a feeling we're going to need all our strength for our next challenge."

His ruse did the job and his words did make sense. Although no one could guess what they would be up against, they knew Viper was right. They would all need their strength and there was no telling if they would have time to eat once Alaric returned. Alena hoped that he would return soon.

They ate in silence and as they finished Alaric suddenly appeared. Alena jumped to her feet and rushed to embrace him. She didn't care what information he had for them, all she cared about was knowing he had returned safely.

"What happened?" Eldred asked.

"There is a stone in the mountain, somewhere," Alaric replied slowly, watching to see if there was a response from Viper.

"I don't understand," Alena replied. "Why would he bring you here to tell you where a stone was? That doesn't make any sense."

"I know," Alaric replied. "I have yet to work out the riddle. I know that it was either a Dark Knight or Nyrra himself who sent Adder to the mountain. That I am sure of."

"So do we trust his word and enter the mountain in search of another stone or do we leave?" Richmond asked the question that was in everyone's thoughts and the one Alaric didn't want to answer.

Ever since he had arrived at the foot of Mount Scorpio he knew he would be entering the great mountain, even before he knew what reward was waiting for him. The only problem was not knowing the danger that was also waiting. There was something, there was no doubt about that, he only wished that Adder had told him. He would have to question Viper, although he was sure the serpentant wouldn't have the answer.

"What is waiting for us in the mountain?" Alaric asked him.

"I don't know." That wasn't a complete lie. He had felt some sort of kinship with the area. He wasn't going to take any guesses, so his response would be the same. "Whatever it is it can't be good if your guess is right on who sent Adder here."

That was what worried Alaric. There was something more to Viper's words, but he really didn't want to push him any further. The tug that was pulling him towards the mountain was becoming unbearable. Whatever was waiting for him couldn't wait until morning. He doubted it could wait until he had something to eat, not that he was all that hungry anyway.

"I will go alone." Alaric decided.

"I don't think so," Alena was the first to respond.

"We are not waiting here for you," Richmond seconded.

"You know we are coming with you," Eldred finished.

Alaric had to admit he was glad for their response. He really didn't want to enter the mountain by himself. Regardless of the danger they were all in he felt better for the company.

"What about you?" Alaric asked Viper.

"I wouldn't miss this for all the Seven Kingdoms," Viper sounded excited, which concerned Alaric.

There was no time for idle chatter. Once Alaric was sure the horses were secure he started for the base of the mountain. He then realised he had no idea how he was going to find the entrance. He didn't really think it would be much of an issue, he was sure the tug of the prophecy would lead him in the right direction. It was increasing with every step he took.

"Does anyone know how we get in?" Alaric asked when they reached the foot of the mountain.

"It has been a long time since I have been here. Unfortunately my memory isn't that good," Eldred explained.

Alaric hadn't waited for a response. He had already started climbing the mountain, leading them around to the left. The prophecy was definitely leading him somewhere. It was more curiosity than anything else that had made him ask the question. Viper knew a way in, but felt it pertinent to remain silent. It seemed as though Alaric was leading them in the direction he would have suggested. Whatever that meant he wasn't sure it was a good sign.

Alaric's light, which had followed him from the mountain peak, was enough to light their path. Although the snow had not fallen any further than half way down the mountain the night air was still cold. It was getting close to snow season in the forest. The snow generally only fell for a couple of weeks and didn't continue for long, but it would be enough to hinder their travel. Alaric hoped to be gone before it started.

"Do you know where you're going?" Richmond asked after they had been trekking for nearly half an hour.

"No idea at all, but I know we are going in the right direction," Alaric's responded.

The terrain was starting to get more difficult to traverse. The trees had thinned out and the slope had become steeper. At some stages they had to climb over a number of large rocks to reach the path on the other side, but it wasn't long before they rounded a corner and found a small tunnel leading into the mountain. Alaric paused and listened before he entered. For a second he though he heard a great rumble from deep within, but he figured he was just imagining it.

When Alaric entered the mountain his little ball of light remained outside. It gave him a small amount of light inside the tunnel, but not much. When Alaric realised what was happening he turned around, as if to scold the ball. He stopped before he did and thought about it. It seemed odd that the light wouldn't continue to follow him.

"Do you know why it is doing that?" he asked Eldred.

"It doesn't seem to want to enter the mountain," he replied.

"I can see that." Alaric tried to avoid his frustration. "Is there a reason why?"

"I can't say I have even seen a light ball act in such a manner. Just create another one and let this one die." Eldred remained in the mouth of the tunnel. Until Alaric moved on there wasn't room for him to move any further.

As much as it didn't really answer his question it did make sense. One ball of light was just as good as another. Alaric created the small spell, but nothing appeared. After a moment of contemplation Alaric tried the spell again and again nothing happened. He was sure he was getting the spell right. It was one of the simplest and the first taught to most novices by their masters.

"What's the hold up?" Eldred asked.

"I don't know. The spell doesn't seem to be working." Alaric's response was absentminded as he tried to figure out what was happening.

"Exponenä!" Alaric boomed the voice command to create light. From the limited study he had done it was one spell he could remember. He waited in hope, but again nothing happened. Slowly he walked out of the tunnel feeling slightly defeated.

"Nothing seems to be working," Alaric sighed.

"Let me have a go!" Eldred puffed up his chest as he entered the tunnel.

They waited outside the entrance until Eldred returned. There was no light following him indicating that he had also failed.

"There is some kind of magical block in the mountain. I don't know how far it goes, but it seems as though we can't use magic for the meantime," Eldred explained.

"How are we going to move forward? It's pitch black in there. There is no way we will be able to find our way through." Alaric sounded resigned.

"Maybe we could find another entrance. This block might only be here," Eldred suggested.

Alaric knew that wasn't an option. If nothing else he knew they had to enter where they were.

"You know not everyone relies on magic. Us regular people have managed before," Richmond sounded smug as he stepped forward.

As he unslung a pack from his shoulders he revealed a number of torches. As much has he expected the magic users to create light, he wanted a back up just in case he got separated. Before anyone could light them for him Richmond produced a small tinder box. He lit one of the torches and then the other two before passing one to Alaric and one to Alena.

"Now this should keep us going and there are a couple spare if these run out," Richmond explained.

Alaric took a torch as did Alena and Richmond kept one for himself. Eldred would walk between them to receive enough light from their torches. As far as Viper was concerned Richmond didn't really care. If the serpentant banged his shins every now and then it would be no great loss. As much as they had grown close with their time in Shoretown, Richmond couldn't risk treating him as a friend.

When he had the torch in his hand Alaric didn't wait to go back into the mountain. The irritating urge at the back of his neck had been growing. Whatever was inside the mountain it obviously didn't like being kept waiting. The tunnel was narrow and only just allowed Alaric to walk without bending over. By the look of the dust on the walls and the occasional spider web it had been a long time since the tunnel had been used.

At first the tunnel was icy cold, but it didn't take long before it started to get warmer. The heat reminded Alaric of the Cauldron Mountain.

"Is this mountain volcanic?" Alaric asked, hoping someone was within earshot. It had been fifteen minutes since he had heard Eldred's footsteps. He had been looking for a place to stop and talk, but there was nothing but narrow tunnel.

"I think it was, many years ago, but not anymore." Eldred called back.

"Are you sure? It's getting awfully hot and we are sloping down. The last thing I want to do is walk into a pool of lava." Alaric was starting to sweat. He attempted to regulate his temperature with a spell, but remembered he couldn't. It seemed as though no magic would work inside the mountain. Alaric hoped that it didn't cause many problems. For the moment he would have to suffer like the others.

The tunnel had been sloping gently downward ever since they had entered. It made Alaric more concerned about the heat. If there was fire in the mountain then it would be close to the base. He wasn't at all happy with Eldred's response. When they had a chance to rest he would question him further, hopefully before they walked into their death.

Before too long the tunnel ended in a large cavern with a giant pit in the centre. The torch light wasn't bright enough to shine across the hole to the other side. It also wasn't strong enough to see the roof or the bottom of the pit. At least Alaric couldn't see any fire at the bottom and that reassured him.

"Be careful!" Alaric called back as softly as he could. "There is a long drop ahead."

Alaric moved along the wall, allowing room for the rest of the group. He took a moment to listen to the noises around him as he waited for the others. There was an eerie silence. Every now and again he though he could hear the sound of something breathing, a subtle breath that echoed around the cavern walls. Just when he thought he could hear it clearly Eldred entered the cavern and it was gone. Alaric hid his disappointment and continued trying to survey his surroundings.

"Do you know where we are?" Alaric asked Eldred when the others arrived.

"No idea. I have never been in here before." Eldred looked around in wonder. He had been inside the Scorpion before, but he had never seen the cavern. Although it had been such a long time ago there was a chance it didn't exist back then. There was something about it that gave Eldred a very bad feeling. "Something doesn't feel right. Are you sure this is where we are supposed to be?"

Alaric almost started doubting himself when Eldred asked the question. The bad feeling that Eldred had was washing over him as well. There was something waiting for them in the cavern, he knew that. Whether it was the stone they were looking for or something else he couldn't be sure. All he knew was they were in the right and wrong place at the same time.

"Up or down?" Alaric replied.

"What?" Eldred didn't understand.

"Do we go up or down? There is nothing telling me one way or the other," Alaric asked.

There was a moment of silence as everyone looked up and down. It was Viper who was the first to speak.

"We go down!"

That didn't fill anyone with confidence, but Alaric knew he was right. There was something waiting for him below and if it was the Ruby stone then it was worth the risk. The bad feeling didn't leave him when they started making their way down. If anything the feeling got worse. Every so often Alaric thought he could hear the sound of breathing again. When he did he signalled for everyone to stop, but each time the sound didn't come again they continued. After the fifth time, Eldred finally had to ask the question.

"Why do we keep stopping?"

"Keep your voice down," Alaric spun around and spoke as harshly as he could without raising his voice.

"What is it?" Eldred whispered.

"There's something at the bottom of this cavern. I can hear it breathing or at least I think I can. Every time I try and listen, it disappears. It is one of the most frustrating feelings." Alaric explained.

Eldred tried to sense what it was that Alaric was feeling, but he couldn't. No magic would work inside the mountain, so it seemed odd to Eldred, but there was other explanation. There was more to Scorpio than what he had expected. They would have to be extremely careful if they were going to survive.

"If it's dangerous then maybe we should turn back," Eldred suggested.

"There's no turning back now. There is only one way to find out what is waiting for us." Alaric didn't sound overly confident, but he wasn't about to turn back.

The further they travelled the hotter the cavern became. Sweat was pouring from Alaric's brow. There was much to be said for the simple spell that regulated his body heat.

Before they reached the base of the cavern the path they were following suddenly cut into the wall. As soon as they entered the tunnel their torches went out. The change was so sudden that Alaric stumbled on the uneven surface and went crashing to the ground, closely followed by the others.

"What happened?" Richmond cried out from behind.

"Keep your voice down," Alaric returned.

"These torches should have lasted for at least another hour and in these conditions I would have put my money on two," Richmond did his best to keep his voice low.

"Well you brought reserves, light them up!" Alaric did his best to remain calm as he picked himself up.

Richmond wanted to make a snide comment, but decided against it. He could tell that Alaric was under a great deal of stress and he didn't want to add to it. Instead he produced the tinderbox from his belt pouch and tried to strike a spark. After a dozen attempts he threw it down on the ground in frustration.

"What was that?" Alena asked when she heard the noise.

"I can't get a spark. It seems as though we aren't meant to have light," Richmond wanted to curse himself, but refrained. By throwing down the tinderbox there was little chance to recover it. In the pitch black that was the only chance for some light and now it was gone. "Looks like we will have to go on in darkness."

"What is going on here Eldred?" Alaric asked as he steadied himself. It was hard to keep balance without any light.

"I was going to ask you the same question," Eldred was at a loss. He had neither read nor heard about anything like this before. He only wished he had more time to investigate the situation further. Once everything was over, if he was still alive, he planned on coming back to Scorpio and giving it the research it deserved.

"I guess we just try our best to make our way in the dark," Alaric resigned.

"Are you sure that's a good idea?" Alena responded. "If there is indeed something waiting for us we don't want to stumble right into it."

"I know, but there is no other option. This is what we have to do."

Alaric placed his hand on the wall and slowly started to walk forward. It was a slow journey in the dark. The last thing he wanted to do was rush forward into a danger he couldn't see. Even being as methodical as he was there was nothing he could do when the roof of the tunnel suddenly dipped and he banged his head. It was all he could do to stop from yelling out in pain and frustration. All he could do was warn the others.

After what seemed like an eternity the wall disappeared from Alaric's side. He stumbled forward, but was able to recover before he fell. He tried to find the wall again, but he couldn't. He was now standing in the middle of nowhere and had no idea where he needed to go. He knew he was facing away from the tunnel, but that was as far as it went.

Suddenly a deep breath followed by a low rumble could be heard somewhere in front of them. The sound made Alaric's heart race. There was no doubt that something large and alive was waiting for them ahead. By the sounds of the breathing it was asleep, at least that's what Alaric was hoping for. He nearly cursed when he felt Eldred bump into him from behind. It was enough to make him fall over.

"Please be careful," Alaric kept his voice as low as he could.

"Where are we?" although Richmond whispered the question it felt as though he was yelling. Alaric just wanted them all to be quiet until he knew what they were up against.

"We are in the belly of the beast," there was something sinister about Viper's words.

Alaric chose not to take the conversation any further. Whatever it was, was very large and, by the evil feeling that penetrated his bones, not friendly. He was positive there was a *Stone of Power* nearby, he could sense the magical presence. It was almost like it was calling out to him, but the noise was just out of reach.

"No one move," Alaric whispered the order "And no one speak." He didn't want to be bombarded with questions.

Alaric took a tentative step forward and then another. It was almost impossible to walk in the darkness without something to hold onto. He looked around and noticed a gentle blue light in distance. The soft blue light had swirls of red, yellow and green. A glimmer of hope entered Alaric's heart. All he had to do was grab the stone and then they could leave. Slowly he took another step forward.

As soon as his foot touched the ground there was a great rumble around the cavern. Suddenly what looked like a number of balls of fire shot from the side, lighting the entire area. Alaric's heart stopped when he saw what was in front of him. He had only seen such a creature once in his life, but there was no doubt what it was. The sound of muffled screams could be heard from behind him as the others saw the great dragon.

"What is that?" Richmond asked, aghast.

There was no response. No one wanted to say anything. It was Viper who was the first to speak.

"That is one of the last great dragons. I didn't think any where alive still. This is the greatest day of my life," Viper started walking forward.

"Not another step Viper," Alaric had drawn his sword and levelled it at him. "We get the stone and we leave. No one needs to know we were here."

There was a rumble from somewhere deep within the dragon and slowly its body started to shift. No one knew what to do. All they could do was stand and watch.

"Well," a deep voice came from the dragon. "I never thought I would see the day." Slowly it turned around until it was facing the group.

Like Cain, the dragon before them was a scaled reptilian creature. It had large wings folded across its back and a tail with a spiked barb at the end. Unlike Cain, who was a green dragon the one before them was a sickly black colour. Its eyes were red and looked as though they were about to ignite. There was nothing pleasant about the dragon before them.

"Raheem!" Eldred gasped. "How long has it been?"

The dragon looked at Eldred for the first time. At first he didn't recognise the wizard, but soon recognition passed over his face.

"Eldred, I never thought I would see you again." Raheem lifted his belly from the ground and threatened to take a step forward, but he lay back down before he did. "It has been over a hundred years since you imprisoned me here."

Everyone suddenly looked at Eldred. He had said he didn't know what was waiting for them and claimed he had never been in the cavern before. The lie ripped through Alaric like a sharp blade.

"What is he talking about?" Alaric spoke through clenched teeth, trying to hide his chagrin.

"Now isn't the time or the place, Alaric." Eldred kept his gaze on the great beast.

"Oh, great wizard, I think now is just the time to explain how you betrayed me." Raheem almost growled as he spoke.

"I didn't betray you Raheem. You betrayed all of your kind by turning to the Evil One. I helped capture you, but I wasn't the one who imprisoned you here. I had no idea where you were. You betrayed your king, Raheem. You were once green and then you turned black. Now you are just somewhere in-between. You can hardly blame me for that."

Raheem turned his attention back to Alaric. There was something about the man that commanded attention. He could only assume this was the man he was waiting for, the reason he had been woken from his slumber.

"Who are you?" he asked.

"I am no one of consequence. I've just come for the stone and then I will be on my way." Alaric tried to be as calm as possible, even though his heart was racing.

"So you've come for my treasure?" He looked around as he spoke. "Not my normal stash, but then again this isn't my home." His eyes turned to the Opal stone, sitting on a small pedestal, when he realised there was no other treasure. "In fact you want to take my only treasure. It seems as though I am here to guard the stone. So I best be doing my job." With that Raheem reached out and grabbed the stone.

When it was safely secured within his talon he beat his wings and lifted himself from the ground. The force of air almost knocked everyone from their feet. Viper was the first to recover and realise what was happening.

"Run!" he cried out before turning back towards the small tunnel.

The other four looked at each other before Alaric bolted towards the pedestal and grabbed the small velvet pouch.

Chapter 39: Raheem

"Why are we running?" Eldred called after Viper, who was moving as if Nyrra was on his tail.

"Raheem wouldn't dare breathe fire in such an enclosed space, but with a little height he'd have no problem torching us alive." Viper called back with fear in his voice.

Once they were through the short tunnel they were able to see the dragon slowly making its way up through the cavern. Its massive wing span spread the full width making the climb painfully slow. That was the only thing that kept them alive.

Viper led the way at a blistering pace. He didn't want to be left on the pathway when the inevitable attack came. Alaric brought up the rear but as he continued to run upwards his legs started to feel the strain. Suddenly he felt as though he was running in wet sand whereas the others were nearing the safety of the top tunnel.

"Come on Alaric, there's no time to rest," Alena called from the mouth of the tunnel as Alaric slowed to a walk.

No matter what Alaric did there was nothing he could do to make his legs move any faster. As he looked up he could see Raheem had almost reach the roof of the cavern.

"Keep moving," Alaric called back. "I'll make it."

When Alaric was no more than a few steps from the tunnel he looked up and saw the dragon breathing out a giant ball of fire. The shock suddenly sent a wave of heat through his body and magically his legs started moving again. Taking two more steps Alaric ran into the mouth of the tunnel just as the fire ball engulfed the cavern.

"What happened?" Alena, who was standing just in front of him pulled him in as he fell onto the ground.

"I don't know. For some reason my legs didn't want to move, but they're fine now, let's get out of here." Even as Alaric spoke he could hear Raheem moving around the cavern. "Run!" Alaric called as he jumped to his feet.

Alaric was glad his legs were working again. It would take next to no time for Raheem to reach the height to breathe fire into the tunnel. Alaric wanted to push past Alena, but there was no room to overtake. He could hear the dragon breathing and it would only be a matter of moments before he was ready to fire.

The first sign that Raheem was firing again was a great rumble from behind. Alaric could feel the heat as the fireball approached them and he knew they hadn't travelled far enough into the tunnel. Without really thinking he stopped and turned to face the fire. If nothing else he was going to try and absorb most of the flames so the others could escape. He didn't know if it was going to work, but it was worth a try.

The heat started to intensify at the fire ball approached.

"Alaric!" Alena cried out when she realised he was no longer behind her.

Alaric didn't have the heart to return her call. He had to concentrate if he was going to survive, not that he had any idea how he could. He still couldn't create any spells, so he needed to rely on a miracle. As the flame approached, Alaric felt a sudden freeness inside. It was like his journey was finally over and he could now rest. All he could do was close his eyes and wait for the fire to envelope him. In a vain effort to protect himself he raised his forearms above his face.

Before the flame could reach Alaric it was stopped by an invisible force-field. It took him a moment to realise that he wasn't dead and opened his eyes to see what had happened. The flames were pushed up against the invisible barrier, but couldn't get through. Eventually the fire hit the wall and then disappeared. Next came a scream of frustration from the dragon when it realised its attack had failed.

"Come on Alaric." Alena had waited for him, whilst the others had continued towards the exit. "It's only a matter of time before Raheem finds the entrance to this tunnel and when he does we don't want to be inside."

Alaric was still in shock. He should have been fried alive . Ever since they had entered the mountain he had bee unable to create any spells. To test his theory Alaric tried to create a small orb of light, but nothing happened.

"Move Alaric!" Alena grabbed his arm and tried to pull him forward.

The sudden touch of Alena brought him back to reality. Her words finally reached him and he knew she was right. If they didn't beat Raheem out of the mountain then there was a good chance they would all die. With that in his mind he forced his legs into action. Alena was almost bowled over in surprise when he moved, but she was able to recover in time to keep herself moving.

This time there nothing that was going to slow Alaric's run. The adrenaline pumping through his body was enough to keep him moving. Once he was outside the mountain he would feel a lot better. Not being able use magic was very unsettling, he had grown so used to the power and it was disturbing not having it around. In another time he thought he could find peace in such a place.

Once they were out into the night air Alaric remembered how cold it was. It was like being hit by a sheet of ice. At that point he realised that he could access the power of the life force around him. The first thing he did was regulate his body temperature. That was something he had definitely missed since entering the mountain. There was no need to create a light orb as Eldred had already done so.

"Easy on the light?" Richmond spoke softly as he looked up.

Alaric's eyes followed Richmond's and realised what he was talking about. With another loud screech the dragon exited the mountain. The light would be a beacon for Raheem to target and Eldred quickly realised his mistake and dimmed the light. He would have liked to have been able to extinguish it all together, but they needed to see where they were going.

"What do we do now?" Richmond asked.

"We get off the mountain!" Viper replied, pointing to where Raheem was circling above them, a certain amount of awe in his voice. "It won't be long before Raheem is finished stretching his wings. When he's done he'll come for us."

Alaric wasn't sure if Viper believed that to be a bad thing. Either way he knew that the serpentant was right. The longer they stayed on the mountain the greater the danger they were in. He waited a moment as he watched the great creature in the sky. He thought he could see the Opal stone sparkle in its talon. Whatever happened he had to get the stone. It was with that thought in his mind that he ordered the group to move.

Once they were in the relative safety of the trees Alaric stopped them. They had been heading towards the horses, but then he didn't think that was such a great idea. Until the threat of the dragon was behind then, he didn't want to take any unnecessary risks.

"How are we going to stop that?" Alena asked as Raheem made a low pass over the trees.

"I don't think there is anyway we can stop a dragon," Viper started. "They are somewhat immune to magic, so that isn't going help us. You can try shooting arrows at him, but his hide is thick and as hard as armour. Needless to say sword fighting is out of the question, unless anyone here can fly."

It was a very negative approach, but it was one they all shared. There didn't seem to be any solution to their problem. It would have been nice if they could speak with Raheem and find out what he wanted, but for the moment he just seemed content to hunt them. Alaric doubted that the great creature wanted to discuss matters any further. It was kill or be killed, there was no other solution. The only problem was how.

"You must have some idea how to kill a dragon," Eldred almost accused Viper. "You are somewhat related."

"Even if I did know I wouldn't tell you. Dragons are the Goddess's most precious creation, notwithstanding me and mine that is. I wouldn't let you destroy such a wondrous creature. Only another dragon can kill another dragon."

There was no way to tell if Viper's words were true to what he actually meant. Alaric thought Viper had meant to say 'only another dragon has the right to kill another dragon.' When Alaric heard Viper's words he felt a sudden weight on the index finger of his right hand. Over his travels Alaric had completely forgotten about the ring that Cain had given him. If only a dragon could kill another dragon then he would have to call in on a debt to be repaid. He fingered the ring slowly as he weighed up the moral dilemma. A sudden screech from above made up his mind. There was no other option. Slowly he twisted the ring. As he did the wind suddenly stopped blowing, just for a moment, but Alaric knew what had happened.

"What was that?" Alena asked, also noticing the effect.

"We are about to get some reinforcements. Come, let's find some open ground." Alaric remained mysterious.

"Are you insane Alaric?" Richmond gasped, hardly believing what he just heard. "If we move out onto open ground then we'll be a sitting target for Raheem."

Alaric didn't respond. He wanted the arrival of Cain to be a surprise, just in case the dragon didn't show. He was sure that he would, but he wanted to be sure before he revealed his plan.

Raheem made another circle over the top of them when they started to move, their movement had been enough to catch his eye. On his next pass he breathed a mighty ball of flame towards their general location, but luckily they had moved quickly through the forest. The trees directly in the blast zone were burnt to the ground creating the open space Alaric wanted to be able to meet Cain. The fire slowly starting to spread around the clearing would act as a beacon.

"We have to keep moving. He will be back any second!" Eldred urged when Alaric called for them to stop.

"We need to go to the clearing Raheem has created for us." That was all Alaric said as he started back towards the flaming trees.

Once they were all inside the clearing he looked towards the sky.

"What are we doing here?" Eldred asked.

"Besides waiting to be fried?" Richmond added.

"Watch the skies and be quiet."

It was clear Alaric was trying to concentrate. In the black of night it was hard to see anything in the sky.

Suddenly the storm clouds parted and instead of a slight, sliver of light there was a bright full moon. In a second the sky was dimly lit and they now could see not only one dragon but a second in the distance.

"What's happening?" Alena asked, breathlessly.

"Something that hasn't happened in a long time," Alaric replied, not taking his eyes from the sky as Raheem prepared for another attack.

"This isn't right. You shouldn't have done this Alaric," there was horror in Viper's voice.

The tone of Viper's voice brought Alaric's attention from the sky. There was something venomous about his words that concerned him. Raheem was in a position to attack one more time before Cain would reach them, so he needed to prepare his own attack and defence at the same time.

"Keep an eye on him Eldred," Alaric warned.

"You can trust me!" Viper defended himself. "As much as I don't agree with what you are doing I will myself do nothing to stop you." He still didn't sound happy.

Alaric prepared the barrier that would prevent any of the fire from reaching them. His attack was going to be more of a distraction than anything else. The plan was to wait for Raheem to attack before he retaliated. His focus was purely on the dragon approaching them.

Raheem let out an ear piercing screech as he prepared for his next attack. With his prey out in the open it would be all he that needed to finish things. This time he ignited his breath before blowing it out. A stream of fire blew from the dragon's mouth instead of the ball of flame. Alaric was prepared for such an attack and released his spell as the flame neared the clearing. The fire engulfed the trees as it went, but as it reached the clearing it was blocked by an invisible barrier. Alaric had created a dome over the clearing which became apparent as Raheem flew over.

Once the fire had disappeared it was time for Alaric to attack. He knew that it wouldn't have much effect, but hopefully it would distract Raheem for long enough for Cain to make his first attack. Raising his arms Alaric released two bolts of ice from his hands. He figured a cold attack was his best chance to annoy Raheem. The first bolt narrowly missed his head and as the dragon turned around for another attack the second bolt struck him on the back between his two massive wings.

It seemed as though Alaric's plan had worked. Instead of taking an arched turn, which would have put Cain in sight, Raheem stopped in midair, flipped around and prepared for his next attack. Alaric braced himself. It didn't look as though Cain was going to reach them before Raheem attacked again.

Alaric released the same spell that created the shield as before. As the flame hit the barrier small chunks of fire penetrated the dome and hit the ground below. Luckily there was no one in the firing line and Eldred was quick to extinguish the small spot fires.

That was the last chance Raheem had to attack before Cain arrived. He entered the battle with a large screech as he landed on top of the black dragon. He sunk his sharp talons into the armoured scales of Raheem's back, just below his wings.

In retaliation to the sudden attack Raheem struck out with his wings. He slapped Cain across the face, giving up the ability to fly. That worked in his favour as Cain didn't have the strength the keep them both in the air. He had to release his grip or else go crashing to the ground.

Once they were free from each other both dragons ascended into the sky. Both wanted the advantage of height before attacking each other again. Cain had started above Raheem, but the black dragon had much more powerful wings. Realising that it wouldn't be long before Raheem was above him, Cain knew it was time to attack. He stopped his ascent and flew in for the kill.

The two dragons met in a fierce battle. Talons scratched at each other and powerful jaws with razor sharp teeth snapped, trying to find a soft spot in the underbelly of their opponent. Flames puffed from their nostrils and mouths, due to the strain. The fires would be completely useless against another dragon. Raheem held onto the Opal stone only allowing him to attack with three talons. This gave Cain a distinct advantage, but Raheem would hold onto the stone until the death. It was his most prized possession.

All they could do was watch from below and hope that Cain was victorious. Alaric couldn't help but focus on the Opal stone. Every now and then it sparkled in the false moonlight drawing his attention away from the fight. He was sure if he could work out a way to pry the stone free he would be able to help. The others simply watched the battle in awe. There was no doubt it was a once in a lifetime event, one that they would never see again.

The dragons wrestled in mid-air, each trying to gain the advantage of height. Raheem had more strength in his wings, but without the use of one talon it evened the battle. He could only defend with his free talons and attack with his powerful jaws. Each time he stretched out with his neck he risked being slashed. It had been a long time since either of them had fought, but the knowledge quickly returned.

Raheem beat his wings and broke free of Cain's grasp. With the stone in his possession he knew he was never going to win a grappling fight. Once he was free he sent a fire ball at his opponent, purely as a distraction. The ball struck Cain on the chest and exploded in a yellow brilliance before disappearing completely. In the end Cain only looked mildly annoyed.

"What is that all about?" Cain asked as he snorted away a puff of smoke.

"I could ask you the same question Cain. Since when have you done the bidding of those pesky little worms?" Raheem retorted, happy to keep his distance and not look for the advantage.

Both dragons had to raise their voices to be heard over the beating of their wings. Their voices carried to those below.

"We made a pact with men after the last war." Cain blew out two small fireballs from his nostrils showing his disgust. "You have betrayed everything we work for."

"That was over a millenium ago and us from the Black Dragon Clan never agreed to that pact. I am surprised you still hold to it, especially after what they did to your clan."

Alaric didn't like what he was hearing. There was an edge to Raheem's voice, like he knew something that Cain didn't. Alaric needed to do something to get them fighting again. He had a bad feeling that the longer the discussion continued the worse it was going to get.

"What are you talking about?" Cain asked.

"About five hundred years ago the kings and queens of the Kingdoms of Men hunted all remaining dragons they could find, even the Green Dragon Clan, the one clan that always protected them." Raheem snarled.

Cain didn't know what to say for a moment. The information came as a shock and he looked down at the group below. If what Raheem said was true then that changed everything. On the other hand he still had a debt to pay Alaric for rescuing him.

"Who told you this?" Cain responded finally.

"Kahn told me. He told me that the race of men was coming to kill us. That is why I have slept for so many years in the heart of the scorpion. Only here have I remained safe whilst my brothers and sisters have been slain. I am surprised to see you are still alive. What started off as imprisonment ended up being my saviour."

"Nyrra held me prisoner in the City of Night for longer than I can remember." Cain was trying to work out what was happening. If what Raheem said was true then his imprisonment might have also saved him. His last memory from the world was that the Black Dragon Clan was his enemy and men were to be respected. Now he didn't know what to think. It had been a man who had saved him from his prison, but on the other hand he had not been able to find a single green dragon since he had left. That in itself was a disturbing sign, but whether he could trust the word of a black dragon was another question altogether. "I have been away from the world of man and their kingdoms. It was a man who set me free and a man who I owe my allegiance."

There was a sound that was similar to laughter coming from Raheem. The noise didn't sound right coming from the great creature.

"You would trust a man? I guess there is no accounting for green dragons. You never were the smartest of clans. I guess you must now make your decision. Protect those who betrayed your clan to their death or join me and seek your vengeance and the vengeance of all dragons." The offer was very tempting.

"Don't listen to him," Eldred called from the ground, magic carrying his voice. "You know the Black Dragon Clan can't be trusted, especially their leader."

Cain had to admit Eldred made a point. Kahn had never been one to be trusted. For that matter none of the Black Clan were trustworthy. Alaric had been the one who saved him, not another dragon. The voice had to be right.

"I will not be tricked by you Raheem."

"Very well, but don't say I didn't warn you!"

Both dragons screeched again as they raced towards each other. They met with speed and crashed into each other, both scratching and biting, trying for the fatal blow. There was no longer time for talking. Both dragons would make sure the other would die.

"Is it true?" Alaric asked, keeping his eyes on the sky.

"Now is not the time,' Eldred replied.

"It is true!" Viper snarled, the sound was strange coming from him. "The dragons were betrayed and all but slaughtered."

"There is more to it than that Viper," Eldred snapped. "Now is not the time to discuss it."

A rage was starting to brew inside Alaric. He couldn't believe what he was hearing. The history books were always so vague, to the point of legend, regarding dragons. He had never believed they were true, but now he knew better. Now he tried to remember what he had read when he was younger. There had been something about the Great Knights of Darshival slaying the dragons. It was written in such a way that the knights were heroes, but Alaric doubted that was true. He needed to get to bottom of things, but Eldred was right, it wasn't the time for such conversations.

The dragons continued their battle in the sky above the clearing. Occasionally small balls of fire dropped to the ground causing the group to move quickly out of the way. The earth was scarred each time and was almost completely blackened. Cain still had the advantage with the use of an extra talon. Scratches and wounds appeared on both dragons' underbellies, but more on Raheem. The black dragon would have to make a decision to either drop the Opal stone or die. It seemed as though it was a relatively simple decision.

Alaric had been preparing a spell to attack Raheem, but at that distance and the closeness of the fight he didn't want to risk hitting Cain.

He felt useless on the ground watching the battle, but he couldn't risk making things worse. If Cain didn't win Alaric didn't know what he was going to do. He needed the Opal stone and that seemed to be the only way he could obtain it.

The longer the battle continued the closer to the ground they came. They weren't able to keep their altitude with the ferocity of their battle. The closer they came the more those below could see the nature of the wounds appearing on their underbellies. This gave Alena an idea. Without anyone noticing she left the clearing in search of their campsite. Her bow and arrows were resting with her pack. She could sense the horses nearby.

When she returned the two combatants were even closer. This gave Alena a greater chance of hitting her target. She figured with the already gashed wounds her arrows had a greater chance of hitting their mark. She fired the first arrow before anyone had even realised she had left the clearing. The arrow hit its mark and sunk into one of Raheem's open wounds. The great dragon screeched out in pain, but didn't release its grip on Cain. Alena had already nocked another arrow before anyone could react.

"What are you doing?" Alaric asked before she had a chance to fire.

"Helping!" She didn't like Alaric's tone, but she didn't let that distract her.

The arrow was in the air before Alaric could continue. Again Alena hit her target. This time the pain forced Raheem to release his grip giving Cain the advantage. Raheem pulled back whilst Cain pressed forward. The green dragon slashed out with all four talons, the moment Alaric had been waiting for. The only way Raheem could defend himself was to release the stone. Slowly at first the Opal stone started to drop before plummeting towards the ground. The two dragons didn't even notice it land as they resumed their battle. The stone fell outside the clearing and Alaric quickly left to find it.

Now that the stone was free Alaric's attention had shifted from the battle above. He wouldn't leave Cain to fend for himself, but he did need to retrieve the Opal stone before he could help. It didn't take him long to see the gentle blue glow of the stone with subtle green, red and yellow swirls. He stopped as he stood over it. For some reason he wanted to wait to touch it. It was a feeling he had not felt with the other stones. It was almost like he was afraid of the power it held within. For a moment nothing else mattered and the world stopped. Alaric picked up the stone and only then did he realise it was inlaid in a golden crown.

When he touched the stone Alaric's eyes suddenly rolled back into his head and his eyelids started to flicker. He felt as though an electric current had been passed through his body. There was nothing he could do to move and then suddenly it was like a veil had been lifted from his mind. Years of information returned to him as if he had known it all his life. He felt as though he had just woken up from a lifelong dream. For the first time he could see the world for what it truly was. He knew what he needed to do to end the battle.

Alaric had no idea how long he had been, but when he returned the battle had progressed further than he had expected. A pool of blood had formed in the middle of the clearing with plenty of blotches around. The two dragons had resumed their climb to get further away from both the ground and Alena's arrows. She had managed to plunge one more arrow into Raheem's soft underside before giving up. She didn't want to risk hitting Cain. He had already received many serious blows and since Raheem was no longer hindered by holding the Opal stone he didn't need any further opposition.

"Did you get the stone?" Alena asked as she side-stepped another large drop of blood.

Alaric didn't answer the question, he was too busy concentrating on the battle happening above him. There was a look in his eyes that no one else noticed. If they had they would have been concerned with what was about to happen. Alaric watched the two combatants waiting for his opportunity to strike. He wanted to avoid striking Cain, but as the battle continued he knew that was no longer a luxury he could afford.

Without warning a ball of ice shot from Alaric's outstretched arms towards the two dragons. The ball stopped before it hit either of the two and promptly exploded. Most of the shards of ice struck Raheem, but Cain was also hit. The ice rendered both dragon's motionless and they dropped to the ground. Cain landed in the clearing while Raheem crashed into the trees nearby.

There was no time to see if Cain was alright. Both dragons would only remain paralysed for a short time. If Alaric was going to kill Raheem then he would have to do it quickly. Without waiting he ran into the forest in the direction Raheem had fallen. He found the great dragon trying his best to move.

"Have mercy," Alaric had not expected the words from the dragon. "I have wronged you, but I don't deserve to die."

Alaric paused as he approached Raheem's chest. His sword was drawn as he had prepared himself for the final blow. He heard the pleas, but they didn't register. He had a job to do and that was all he was interested in.

"Please, don't do this," there was panic in Raheem's voice as he sensed his own mortality. "I can help you. There are things I know that can be useful to you."

The words fell on deaf ears. Alaric moved into place before Raheem was able to move again. He strained to regain control of his legs and talons. If he was able to move then he would be able to defend himself, but there was nothing he could do. All he could do was watch as Alaric trust his sword into his chest and pierced his heart. Suddenly a flame started inside his chest as Alaric pulled out his sword. There was a look of pure shock on Raheem's face as he breathed his last breath. Alaric moved back as the corpse suddenly burst into flame. It was something he hadn't been expecting, but then again he had never killed a dragon before.

He didn't stay long at the burning corpse. He said a few words under his breath, he thought it only fitting that such a great creature should have some kind of send off. It would be a shame for a dragon to leave the Seven Kingdoms alone, even if it was his slayer who stood by his side. When he was happy with his little service he returned to the clearing where he found everyone standing around Cain. The green dragon hadn't moved since he had crashed into the ground

Chapter 40: End of an Era

"Are you alright Cain?" Alaric asked softly when he reached the dragon's head.

"I'm dying Alaric. Is Raheem dead?" Cain coughed a small amount of blood.

"He is dead and gone. His body burst into flame after I killed him," Alaric's voice was soft.

"Then that is it. I am the last of my kind," there was a wry tone to his voice. "It's a sad day and yet I feel at peace."

Alaric wasn't sure he should speak, but he couldn't let Cain die without knowing the truth. "You are not the last of your kind. Kahn still lives."

"Then you must kill him Alaric." It wasn't the response they had been expecting.

"You can defeat him," Alaric responded. "I can heal you." He started to draw in the energy around him. For what he had to do it would take a lot of power. He had already searched for the injuries and although the body structure of a dragon was different to anything he had felt before, he knew exactly what he had to do.

"Save your energy Alaric, it is my time to die. You can't steal my destiny, not matter what the excuse." Cain coughed as he spoke.

"There is no need to be brave. I can save you, it's no problem at all." Alaric continued.

"Let him die Alaric, it is his time," Eldred spoke calmly.

Suddenly Alaric let the energy flow from his body. He silently cursed himself that healing wasn't an option.

"Is there anything I can do for you?" he asked, realising that comfort was the only thing he could offer.

"No, thank you. I have lived a long life and I have achieved much. Now it is time for me to die in peace."

"Do you want us to stay?" even as he asked the question he knew the answer.

"It is my want to die alone. Now my time is drawing near and you still have many miles to travel. It is now your job to see Kahn dead, if not he will join with Nyrra and cause death and destruction to the world."

If Alaric's heart hadn't already steeled itself he thought he would cry. Even though there was still one dragon left alive, Cain was the last of the Green Dragons and that was a sad occasion. As much as he wanted to stay he knew it was time to go.

"Soar high and far!" Alaric said his goodbye.

"Soar high and far Alaric!" a wry smile appeared on Cain's face as he lowered his head and let it drop to the ground. His breathing was laboured, he didn't have long left to live.

"Let's find the horses. There is much to be discussed before you rest for the night." Alaric's words were somewhat mysterious, but they followed nevertheless.

"What was that all about?" Richmond asked, confused at the exchange with Cain.

"Dragon's know at an early age when they are going to die," Viper thought it was best he explained. "It is both a curse and a blessing."

"So Raheem would have known he was going to die?" that didn't seem right to him. What was the point of the battle if they already knew the result?

"Black Dragon's are a little different. They gave up their birthright for more power. Raheem would have had no idea what was coming."

"What about Cain? He would have known he was doomed to fail?"

"Yes he would have, but he would also have known that he would kill Raheem."

"So would Raheem have not fought if he had known about his death?" Richmond was struggling to get his head around it.

"There is nothing they can do to stop the inevitable and they wouldn't try. It is the way of things and they had accepted that fact."

"So it wasn't a great loss for the Black Dragons to lose that ability?"

"To know one's death is to truly know peace. It is possible for a dragon to prolong his death, but when they do they are guaranteeing a more painful demise. There is more to it than that, but it is a little hard to explain to someone who doesn't know the will of the queen. All I'll say is that Raheem will now be paying for his choices." Viper wasn't prepared to reveal anymore.

Richmond still didn't understand what he had just been told. He would be more than happy to give up that right, although he didn't truly know the implications. It had been a very interesting night and he would be just as happy to forget most of it. Suddenly he felt very tried as they walked back to their campsite.

The horses were waiting patiently for them. The elven horses were doing their best to reassure the other two mares. Both looked scared from the sudden appearance of the dragon in the night sky. It was all Adelanta could do to keep them from bolting and he was glad to see the group return. Their presence did wonders to calm the nervous animals.

Alena was the only one to really notice the horses condition, the others didn't seem to care.

"So what do we do now?" Richmond asked as he sat around the small fire Eldred had created.

The night air was bitterly cold. Once the adrenaline rush had worn off, Richmond noticed the freezing night air. It was only a matter of time before it started to snow. One thing Richmond wanted to do was be out of the forest before that happened. It never snowed in Darshival, but he had felt the snow once before when he was travelling in Hondin Lel and that experience had been enough to last him a lifetime. He didn't leave the inn for a week, until the snow had melted, and he didn't enjoy it. He really hated the intense cold.

"You need to leave for Lel Dinion in the morning." Alaric spoke to the fire and no one in particular.

"What do you mean?" Alena didn't like what she was hearing.

"We need to rescue Marina from the Dark Knight Argoz and in doing so free the Sapphire stone."

"We can certainly do that," Eldred added.

"That's not all, is it?" Alena asked.

"You must travel via Harskar Peak to the north along the Cloumid Mountains." Alaric explained.

"That is far out of the way!" Richmond cried out, not only that, but the further north they travelled the greater the chance of snow, especially if they had to go trekking through the mountains.

"I know, but that doesn't change the fact that that is the way you must travel."

"Why do you keep saying 'you' and not 'us'." Alena sounded concerned.

"I won't be going with you. There are other things that I have to do."

"I don't understand Alaric," Eldred added. "There was nothing about this in the prophecy."

"And that is exactly the problem. That tome of yours is too unreliable. I am going to look for some answers and for that I must go alone," Alaric explained.

"We will go with you, you know that." It sounded as if Alena was almost about to start crying.

"Where I'm going you can't come with me and nor would you want to if you knew. I must go now. I'm leaving Adelanta in you care. Please look after him. I am also leaving the stones with you." That brought a round of arguments from the others, except for Viper. "It is safer if you take them with you. It will all become apparent in due course, but for now you'll just have to trust me." When he finished speaking Alaric stood and promptly disappeared.

The suddenness of his disappearance left them all speechless. Something had happened to Alaric since they had left the mountain. They couldn't explain what it was, but they all knew it. There was a new purpose to him that hadn't been there before. He seemed a lot more confident in himself and there was a coldness that disturbed Alena. She couldn't believe that they had been separated again. The last time that had happened she had spent months in the prison in Jarrat. That memory sent a shiver down her spine. It was a memory that she wished she could never remember again.

"Did anyone else find that exchange to be a little strange?" Viper was the first to speak and although he had not known Alaric all that long he knew something wasn't right.

"What do you mean?" Eldred asked, keen on the Serpentant's insights before he revealed his own.

"Well, he left the stones for starters. In all the time I have been travelling with you I have never seen him without those pouches. Now he just ups and leaves them with us? There was also something strange about the tone to his voice, it was almost like he wasn't really here. I felt as though he was somewhere else. I don't know, it's hard to explain."

Eldred knew exactly what he was talking about, but he wasn't going to let anyone else know. Something strange had happened and until he was sure of what it was there was no point in theorising. All they could do was focus on the task Alaric had left them. In the meantime Eldred would continue to read the prophecy and hope to find some answers. As much as Alaric no longer believed in it Eldred was sure there were still clues to be found.

"I think for now we should eat something and then get some sleep. We have a long road to walk and by the feeling of the cold in the air I wouldn't be surprised if we get some snow soon. We want to be out of the forest before that happens."

With that, the conversation was over. No one complained with the suggestion of food. They all knew there would be no easy answers and there was no reason to think about it on an empty stomach. They all went to sleep without discussing Alaric's new persona. There would be plenty of time to ponder the enigma when they hit the road again.

Epilogue: Hard Decisions

"We need your army," Bern didn't sound happy.

"I can't. The city is still in turmoil. Za'aroz's reach was further than what we thought. He still has supporters in the Grand Cathedral." Augustus defended his decision.

"I thought you were able to get a list of all his followers from Tybalt," Bern replied.

"We tortured him to the point of death, but it seems as though he was still keeping some names to himself."

"Then keep going until you get all the names." Bern didn't agree with the tactics, but he had used them himself in the past so he couldn't judge.

"Someone sneaked into his prison cell last night and killed him. That's why I believe there are still traitors in the Grand Cathedral, not to mention those instilled in the city. If I give you my army then I leave the city vulnerable." It seemed reasonable enough, but Bern knew he didn't need the entire army.

"I don't want to leave you short, but you have the largest army in all of the Seven Kingdoms. We need your support if we are going to succeed."

"I am sorry, but I cannot give you what you want."

Bern had procrastinated in making his decision on who would be the High Chancellor. He had let Augustus resume his old role, but he wanted to see what decision he would make and whether he would atone for his past mistakes. It had almost been a week and it seemed as though he was digressing to his old ways.

"And what of the mines Augustus?" Bern made a point of not calling him the High Chancellor. "You said you would release the slaves and open the mines to the dwarves and other mining guilds."

"I will, I will, but now is not the time. My kingdom is in turmoil. I have more important matters to deal with. When I have time I will make sure all the slaves are set free and properly compensated."

Bern was amazed at how quickly Augustus had forgotten about his imprisonment. He was so grateful when Bern had rescued him, but now he was back to his normal self. It was very doubtful that Augustus would ever free the slaves. Once he counted the profits of the diamond mine he would soon forget his promise. His greed would overcome him in the end and that would be his downfall. Bern could not allow him to make the same mistakes.

"You are relieved of your position as High Chancellor." There was no point in keeping up the pretence. Bern had made his decision two days prior, but had been avoiding the conversation.

"Wait…. What… what are you talking about?" Bern's words struck him as if he was hit with a fist. "You can't do this. I am the High Chancellor. I decide what happens here."

"Your first mistake was not making sure the man you deposed was dead. I have had Linus study up on Castalial law and it seems that until his death Julius was still the High Chancellor. Therefore his last edict still stands."

"What are you talking about general? Guards!" Augustus called out. There was more fear than command in his voice.

"The last thing Julius said to me was that you were not to sit on the Golden Throne anymore. At first I wasn't sure if that was the right thing to do, but how easy it is for us to forget the mistakes of our past? You have failed to stand up and change and I can't believe you."

"You don't have the authority. Now you will see what it is like to spend your life in my mines." There was an evil sneer on Augustus' face as the door to his chambers opened.

The look on his face quickly changed from confusion, to fear. Instead of the head of his personal guard leading the way into the room it was Linus. Behind him was a mixture of the High Chancellor's guard and Bern's soldiers. His heart sank as he realised that his rule was coming to an end.

"What is this treachery Linus?" there was venom in his voice.

"The treachery is your own Augustus. Did you really think you could get away with all your crimes? Now it is time for you to pay," Linus almost sounded happy. "Lieutenant, shackle this impostor and take him to cells."

Linus waited until they were alone before he spoke again. "I think that went rather well." He then moved to a side table and poured himself a glass of wine. He offered Bern a glass, but he shook his head.

"Then why do I feel as though I have made a big mistake?"

"It isn't easy holding a position of power. It takes time to get used to making tough decision, but I think this is the right one." Linus smiled.

"So how do you think you will handle it?"

"That is something that I don't have to think about tonight. My inauguration is in the morning. I will worry about it then."

Bern was happy with that statement. It would be nice to have a night not having to worry about anything. He couldn't remember the last time he could have a relaxing night, although he still couldn't truly relax. He didn't know if he was ever going to be able to relax again, at least not until he was dead.

***

"Well as I live and breathe," the voice was deep and brash and Hulkan recognised it instantly.

"Hello father. It has been too long," Hulkan greeted.

"I didn't think I would see your face again, not after your betrayal." Hulkan's father, Ilar, put down what he was doing and took a step forward. He didn't seem too happy with the reunion.

"You should know by now that the betrayal was not mine, but my brothers. I only left to avoid any bloodshed." That wasn't the entire truth, but it was somewhat true. As much as he didn't want to spill Gilgi's blood Hulkan had also felt the tug of the prophecy urging him to leave. He wasn't sure when Gilgi had been possessed by the Dark Knight, but he wanted to believe it was before he had usurped Hulkan's command of the guild. It was clear in his absence that Gilgi had been telling lies.

"Your brother knew that you were weak. He saw his opportunity and he took it. There is no shame in what he did. The shame is yours for allowing him to take your power so easily. I can't believe you have shown up like this. With your brother gone, defending his own, you have decided now is the time to reclaim what was once yours. You continue to bring shame on your family."

Hulkan knew it wasn't going to be easy speaking with his father again. Ilar had taken it personally when his son had left. He hadn't agreed with what Gilgi had done, but Hulkan had simply left and not tried to defend his status. Hulkan had to steel himself for his next comment. It wouldn't be easy for Ilar to hear the news.

"Your second son is dead." Hulkan didn't know if it was exactly true, but he assumed that was the case. It was either Gilgi's body with the Dark Knight inside or the Dark Knight had murdered his brother and assumed the façade. He hoped that the latter was the case. "He was killed by a Dark Knight who has assumed his body." He thought that was the best way to explain it. "It was he who stole power from me and if I had known that then I would have stayed and fought, but the past is the past and there is nothing I can do about it now."

Hulkan paused to let the information sink in. His father was a consummate dwarf and very rarely showed his true feelings, but even he couldn't hide the horror brewing inside him. Suddenly his world came crashing down around him. His son was dead, the son he had thought was his favoured son, but even that wasn't true.

"I fight with the Alliance father and I fight for everyone," he continued. "But I cannot do it alone. I know the Dark Knight has taken the bulk of our army, but I need the rest."

"What do you want me to do? As far as anyone is concerned Gilgi is still the leader of the guild. They will only do what he says," Ilar sounded resigned. "There is nothing we can do."

"Who runs the guild in Gilgi's absence?" Hulkan wasn't going to be dissuaded.

"That would be Brac." Ilar paused for thought. He was still struggling to get his head around things.

"He is a good dwarf. I am sure he will support our cause."

"But that still doesn't change the fact that there is nothing he can do without the approval of Gilgi," Ilar retorted.

"That will be for the council to decide. I am sure they will understand when they hear what has happened to their leader and with the added help from the High Chancellor I'm sure they'll come around."

"Well it looks like you have everything sewn up nicely. What is it you need from me?" Ilar didn't sound at all remorseful, not that Hulkan was expecting anything more.

"Well I would like to have dinner with you and mother, at least once before I have to leave again. More to the point I need you to gather the council so I can speak with them."

"Let's start with dinner son and see what happens after that," Ilar suddenly sounded very cheerful and slapped his son on the back of his shoulder.

That was one small battle done. He would spend the night with his parents and then in the morning he would meet with the council and gain more soldiers.

***

Suddenly Alaric appeared in the main hall of the castle in Jarrat, he appeared to the side of the thrones. His sudden appearance caused the entire room to go quiet. At first Duke Xarles didn't realise what had happened, but then he was relieved when he saw Alaric standing next to him. He had thought he was never going to return. The queen had not improved at all since he had left and Xarles was starting to give up hope that she would ever return to normal. A glimmer of hope appeared in his eyes.

"Clear the room!" Alaric boomed at the top of his voice. If he was feeling any after effects from the spell it didn't carry to his voice.

At first no one moved, but once his words sunk in they rushed into action. Everyone in the room could see his strength and no one wanted get on his bad side. It wasn't long before the only people left in the room were Xarles and Alaric.

"It's good to see you again Alaric. I was afraid that you weren't going to return."

"How's the queen?" Alaric cut him short. He wasn't in the mood for small talk. He looked as though his mind was elsewhere.

"Her condition hasn't changed."

"Is she still in her apartments?" Alaric asked before the duke had a chance to elaborate.

"Yes, but…"

"Close your eyes!"

Alaric only waited a split second before they promptly disappeared from the room. When they reappeared in the queen's chambers, Xarles stumbled and fell to the ground. He felt like retching, but everything remained in his stomach. It was the most unsettling experience and he wished he had closed his eyes like Alaric had suggested. When he was able to regain himself he noticed that Alaric was already standing over the bed where the queen lay. Normally one of her servants would have bathed and dressed her by now, but for some reason that had not happened.

The queen looked pale and drawn and for a moment Alaric felt sorry for her. The emotion was one that he'd not felt in a long time and one he wasn't sure he was going to feel again. He had to steel his heart if he was going to complete his tasks, that he knew that for sure. He could no longer risk the luxuries of soft emotions. He shook the thought from his mind and concentrated on the job at hand. It was not going to be an easy task removing the disease from her mind. He knew it would have been so much easier with the stones, but where he needed to go he couldn't take them with him.

Slowly Alaric let his eyes close. He focused on the room around him without drawing in any of the power. He needed to use it without drawing it, a skill that had been long lost to the world. The problem was deep within Queen Oriana and that's where he needed to find the power. Only by using the queen would he be able to save her. Drawing power from another living person was a dangerous act. Taking too much and the donor would die, completely defeating the purpose.

The process was slow, but Alaric didn't have the time to waste. It was a risk he had to take, there was no other way to save her. The power he needed to enter her mind was a lot less than before. The Opal stone had unlocked something inside of him and it was time to put it to the test.

Suddenly everything went dark and Alaric felt as though he was floating. The spell he used needed even less power than he had thought. Even though he had been in the void before it was still unnerving. He didn't think he would ever grow used to being in someone else's mind, it was hard enough being inside his own.

Even though he couldn't see anything he felt the evil, somewhere in the distance. He knew it was the residual mark of the Dark Knight Ra'naroz and it wouldn't leave without a fight. As if to confirm his theory he thought he heard a growl somewhere ahead. That in itself was promising. It seemed as though he was on the right track.

"What are you doing?" Xarles' voice came as if in a dream.

As much as he had learnt to control both his physical self and who he was inside the queen's mind it was still distracting.

"I'm busy, be quiet!" Alaric spoke aloud.

The residual evil wasn't anywhere near as strong as its source, but it would still put up a decent fight. Alaric still needed to concentrate or else risk being trapped inside Oriana's mind.

Suddenly the world coalesced and he was standing in an open meadow. The wind rustled the lush green grass which grew up to his knees. If it was anywhere else he would have thought it peaceful, but he knew it was trap to make him complacent. He had one job to do and he wasn't going to deviate from his path. Although he couldn't see the disease he knew it was somewhere in front of him.

"What are you doing here? She is mine, not yours. Find yourself another receptacle." The voice was harsh and rasped.

"I am not here for the body, I am here for you," Alaric's voice echoed in the space before him.

Suddenly a black cloud appeared in front of him. He assumed it was about a dozen feet away, but distance had no meaning in this place. The miasma swirled and flared in a dark rage. There was no doubt the diseased remnant of Ra'naroz was angry. Alaric was using the time to prepare himself. Now that he knew what he was up against it would be a lot easier for him.

"Then you will remain here as my prisoner," the cloud loomed as it spoke.

"I highly doubt that."

It was time for Alaric to attack. He tried to close his eyes, but then remembered he had no eyes. Once he recovered he sent out the spell that would destroy the residual evil, but it was ready for him. It seemed that it wasn't going to disappear quietly. Alaric strained to force it out of Oriana's mind, but its will was strong. It had been bunkered down inside her head for a long time and had a few tricks of its own. Suddenly the cloud disappeared, but Alaric knew he had not defeated it and cursed silently to himself. He had underestimated the disease and now he was going to have to hunt it.

The scenery suddenly changed around him and he was standing at the foot of a large mountain pass. Dark grey rocks loomed up on either side. This was not what Alaric wanted. If he was going to succeed he needed to take control. The rocks started to shimmer and then disappear. In their place was the clam meadow again. That was a much better place to fight. Slowly the cloud started to return as Alaric sought it out. He wasn't going to let it run and hide.

"What are you doing? This is impossible. This is my place, not for you to command."

"This is not your place. You shouldn't be here and now it is time for you to leave."

There was a scream of anguish in the distance as the cloud started to swirl wildly. Now Alaric had done what he set out to do. The disease was trapped with nowhere to run and nowhere to hide. It sizzled and popped as it slowly started to dissipate. Sparks could be seen on the inside, if Alaric had been looking. No matter how hard it struggled there was nothing it could do against Alaric's will. With a soft pop the cloud disappeared.

As soon as the disease was out of Oriana's mind, Alaric felt something different. It was as if someone was waking him from a long sleep and that wasn't too far from the truth. For a moment he felt like staying, but knew that wouldn't be good for the queen. He had freed her from Ra'naroz's evil and now it was time for him to leave. Suddenly he disappeared and the queen's bedroom coalesced around him.

The queen was already sitting up in her bed when Alaric returned to full consciousness. Xarles had a look of pure surprise and joy on his face. As much as he had faith in Alaric he didn't think Oriana would ever return to her normal state. She looked around slowly, trying to gauge the situation around her.

"Where am I?" she asked slowly, although that wasn't the real question she wanted answered.

Xarles looked questioningly towards Alaric.

"She has been… well let's say not herself for a long time now. It will take time for her to regain her full memory." Alaric explained.

"Will she remember everything that happened while the Dark Knight was here?" Xarles almost didn't want to ask the question.

"In time, yes, she will remember everything." Alaric's voice was cold. "Now it is time for me to go." Alaric promptly disappeared from the room without another word.

Xarles had already turned his attention to his queen and neither heard nor noticed Alaric leaving. It was going to be hard when Oriana started to remember her time with the Dark Knight. The thought almost made Xarles vomit. All he could do was comfort her as much as he could.

"You are home now, my queen," there was a tear brewing in his eye.

***

Marina sat in her apartment in the palace at Lel Dinion. She had no idea how long she had been there or why she had come. The last few weeks were hazy. The last thing she could truly remember was leaving Alaric just outside of Jarrat, although she had no idea why. She had been happy with him, or at least that's how she remembered it. She stared out of her window at the waning moon.

The door opened, breaking her reverie, and Prince Rives entered. He was a slender young man with fair hair. Recently he had been promoted to heir apparent when his brother Lisle died in a tragic riding accident. Although he was the youngest of the three children he had convinced his father that he should be king opposed to his sister who had the rightful claim to the throne. The only person who was with Lisle when he died was his brother, but no one thought that circumstances were suspicious. That in itself worried Marina, but she didn't know why.

The prince had tried on more than one occasion to share her bed, but she had rejected all his advances. Each time he came to her it was getting harder and harder to say no. He was an attractive man, but she was in love with Alaric, or at least she thought she was. He had left her when she needed him, not that she knew what she needed him for or why she had left him in the first place. There had been something important that had brought her to Lel Dinion. She was still a Princess of Darshival, so it would make sense for her to make a stately visit to a neighbouring capital, but it just didn't seem right to her.

"What are you doing this fine evening my dear Princess Marina?" Rives asked in his softest of voices.

"Just staring at the moon, or at least what's left of it. I don't know. For some reason it seems to soothe me."

"And what do you need soothing from?" Rives glided across the room to where she was seated.

The question seemed logical enough, but she couldn't find the answer. Her mind had been getting hazier and hazier of late. It was like there were cobwebs in her mind and she just couldn't shake them out. The effect seemed worse whenever she was around Rives.

"We missed you at the evening meal tonight," he placed a comforting hand on her shoulder.

At first his touch made her skin crawl and she wanted nothing more than to brush it aside, but as it remained there it became more comfortable. Slowly he moved his hand to the back of her neck and started stroking it.

"I'm not feeling well tonight." It was the only excuse to avoid contact with the prince. For some reason the king had decided that

Marina would make the perfect queen for Rives. He was drafting a letter to King Unwin requesting his permission for the union. Marina had respectfully declined, but she knew if her father agreed there would be little she could do. She figured if she could avoid the king then he might lose interest in the letter and leave it up to her to make the decision.

"Then you should be in bed if you are not feeling well. You shouldn't be sitting by an open window," Rives cooed.

"Yes, you're right. I do need to lie down." She didn't want to get into bed. That was the last place she wanted to be whilst Rives was in the room, but she couldn't resist his soft, sweet voice. Slowly she stood and let him lead her.

"Now I think it would be better if I stay with you tonight. Just to make sure you're alright." Rives suggested.

"No thank you. I think I would just like to sleep," although she wasn't tired she yawned to try and accentuate the lie. "I'm sure I'll be fine in the morning. You don't need to worry about me."

Rives smiled to himself as Marina crawled into bed. He could push his agenda, but he had little time. It was more fun this way. If he broke her over time then his control over her would be absolute and that was want he wanted. He knew that Alaric had feelings for her and that made it even sweeter.

"Good night my princess. I'll see you in the morning," Rives blew her a kiss before leaving the room.